CW01263280

LUCIA

A Roman Slave's Tale

by

Steven A. McKay

Copyright ©2019 Steven A. McKay

All rights reserved. No part of this book may be reproduced, in whole or in part, without prior written permission from the copyright holder.

ALSO BY STEVEN A. MCKAY

The Forest Lord Series

Wolf's Head
The Wolf and the Raven
Rise of the Wolf
Blood of the Wolf

Knight of the Cross
Friar Tuck and the Christmas Devil
The Rescue and Other Tales
The Abbey of Death
Faces of Darkness

The Warrior Druid of Britain Chronicles

The Druid
Song of the Centurion
The Northern Throne

Over The Wall (Kindle only novelette)

Acknowledgements

Thanks to Mirella Banfi for her help in naming Villa Tempestatis and to Bernadette McDade and Bill Moore for their suggestions on how to improve the first draft. Huge gratitude to David Baird and David N. Humphrey for listening to, and reviewing, the Audible edition of *Lucia*.

Thanks to the fantastic people at Audible – Andrew, Alys and Victoria – and of course Imogen Church, who brought the audio version of this book to life. Please give it a listen if you haven't already.

Books that were really useful in my research and plotting include *How To Manage Your Slaves* by Jerry Toner, *Life In The Villa In Roman Britain* by John Burke, and *Roman Villas* by David E. Johnston.

Final thanks to fellow author Matthew Harffy, who mentioned he might write a standalone novel and that's what set the wheels spinning in my own head, resulting in *Lucia*!

*Dedicated to all the men, women and children
forced into slavery
and forgotten by history.*

PROLOGUE

It was the terrible smell that woke her. The acrid stench of burning penetrated her sleeping mind and she awoke with a start, gasping for breath. Confusion, panic, fear – all threatened to overcome her as she realised her bedchamber was filled with smoke and the village outside clamoured with raised voices. They echoed her own terror, but they were also filled with desperation and anger, and hearing them the girl finally came to full wakefulness, noting the clang and clatter of weapons meeting in battle.

She coughed and fell onto her knees to escape the smoke, dragging the thick woollen cloak from the floor beside her bed and pulling it on, wondering where her parents were. The sounds of fighting were closer now, but a loud crack came from the room adjoining her bedchamber, suggesting the roof there had collapsed, and she knew there was no option but to get out, into the night where the battle raged.

Who was fighting?

She pulled back the shutters on her window and looked outside, smoke billowing past her into the cold night air. There appeared to be no one at the back of the house, the fighting apparently all taking place at the front, so she put a foot on the ledge and clambered over, falling onto the grass on the other side, coughing and retching, tears streaming down her cheeks as she prayed to Freyja, goddess of love and war, to protect her and her family.

Where were her mother and father? Should she look for them? Or hide until the fighting stopped?

The questions assailed her young mind – she was only eight years old after all – but she forced herself to calm now that the debilitating coughing fit had passed.

Another roof beam collapsed with a crash and a shower of sparks that illuminated the night behind her and she crept away from the dangerous building – her home! – towards a neighbour's house which seemed, in the darkness, to have been spared from the fires so far. From the orange glow that encompassed the horizon all around, she knew most of the settlement must be ablaze.

A scream pierced the air, cut off by a thump and the girl knew a man had just died out there in the night, not very far from where she crouched, shivering, wide-eyed, wondering what to do next.

It was clear the village was under attack, possibly from one of the neighbouring tribes, more likely by the Romans who had been trying to subjugate Germania for generations now. Whoever was killing her people though, it didn't really make much difference to her current predicament. She had no weapon, and no knowledge of how to use one anyway.

A lump came to her throat as she admitted then what she'd been trying to ignore since waking: her parents had gone to fight off the invaders and left in such haste that they'd not had time to say goodbye or advise her what she should do.

Panic rose up in her again, the terrible sounds of men – and women – dying coming ever louder, carried on the breeze which also brought the sickly smell of flesh burning. Animals perhaps, trapped in their pen, unable to escape the conflagration, burning to death in agony. Yes, she could hear the tortured screams of pigs to the north and guessed they were the ones old Jonas kept; she fed them herself sometimes, watching with fascination as their fat, hairy snouts rooted in the hay for the handfuls of corn that she would toss into their pen.

She forced herself to breathe slowly, gritting her teeth against the mounting dread that could lead to a mistake and prove fatal.

The pigs couldn't be helped now, and she doubted there was any way to find her parents without showing herself to the warriors battling her kinsfolk. The only thing to do was to run, hide in the nearby woods until the conflict was settled, the danger passed, and she could return to search for her family.

Her father was one of the tallest, fiercest fighters in the village, she thought proudly, picturing him with his long hair and moustache, wielding his axe like Thunor himself. Her mother was no stranger to violence either, having fought in more than one battle against the Romans beside many other tribeswomen. Not like the soft, weak Roman ladies – the women of Germania were shieldmaidens who often took up arms beside the menfolk.

The young girl almost smiled as she thought of how strong her parents were. They were able to look after themselves, and she must do the same. Then they would all meet again in the morning when the dust settled and the task of putting the village to rights was begun.

Standing, she looked warily to the southwest, seeing the grove of trees there silhouetted in the light – not from any fires, but from a crescent moon. She would be safe there until dawn.

As she started moving towards the woods, she noticed the sounds of fighting had faded, as if the battle was over. Only angry shouts and pained cries of the defeated or injured could be heard now. The girl thought about turning back, still confident that her people would have repelled the invaders, but caution won out and she kept heading for the trees. The earlier panic had subsided as she forced her mind to calm and the fresh air cleared her lungs of smoke.

The house she was crouching beside came to an end and the open ground between the settlement and the woods opened up before her, so she glanced back, saw no-one, and put her head around the corner of the building to make sure that side was clear too.

A hand shot out, grasping her roughly by the hair and she screamed in shock, attempting instinctively to break free of the shadowy figure's grasp. But her captor was much too strong.

The house beside them had also been set on fire she noticed now, and the light from the blaze allowed her to take in the features of this tall warrior who eyed her coolly, as if she was an animal he was buying from the market.

Her heart almost leapt from her mouth when she recognised the armour the man wore: Roman.

He grunted something in his own tongue, nodding to himself in satisfaction, then dragged her by the hair back towards the centre of the village. The girl had seen the barely-restrained violence in his eyes and the crimson blood that coated his arms and armour and so she walked with him instead of struggling, whimpering however, at the pain his merciless hold was causing.

As they drew nearer to their destination she saw the bodies of her compatriots, dead and dying, strewn all around the place. The Romans had been victorious and now the soldiers were stripping the slaughtered villagers of any valuables – weapons, brooches, rings, and torcs of silver, gold or bronze which were worn around the necks of the highest status members of the tribe. She began to cry but her captor took no notice. They reached the village centre and he handed her over to a fat man who grinned and pulled her into a workshop which she knew well: the blacksmith's.

Before she understood what was happening iron chains were fastened around her wrists and ankles and she was led back out to sit on the ground with a dozen other survivors, mostly women but also two or three boys of a similar age to her.

Her eyes scanned the ground, dimly lit by the fires that were rapidly consuming the buildings that had been her home for all her eight years, searching for any sign of her parents, but she couldn't see them anywhere.

"Where are they taking us?" one of the sooty-faced young boys asked, hysteria making his voice much shriller than the girl had ever heard it before.

The fat man who'd commandeered the blacksmith's forge looked down at the boy as if he understood what was said and the captured girl noticed the jailer looked more like one of them, German, than a Roman. He answered the question, confirming her guess, and his words froze her to the bone. If she hadn't already been sitting on the ground she would surely have collapsed at his reply.

"Slave market. Now shut up the lot of you, and don't make a fuss or you'll not get there alive. The Romans don't take very good care of captured slaves."

BOOK ONE

CHAPTER ONE

Southeast Britannia, AD 168, Summer

"Master's coming home today. We need to get everything ready for his arrival."

Lucia, concentration rudely broken, winced as the darning needle pricked the tip of her finger and she let out a gasp of pain, sucking away the drop of blood that oozed from the wound as she looked up at the manageress, a stern, middle-aged woman with broad shoulders and breasts that hung almost down to her waist. Lucia hid her irritation, knowing it would only earn a hard slap about the head.

"What time will he be arriving, Paltucca?" one of the other slaves asked.

"Late afternoon," the woman replied brusquely, lifting Lucia's pile of mended stockings from the table, inspecting them with a critical eye and shaking her head as if the girl's work was poor. "So we have just enough time to get the place looking fine for him. You all know your business, so be about it, or you'll have me to answer to." She dropped two pairs of the stockings onto the table and glared at Lucia as the rest of the slaves hurried out of the room, glad they weren't the ones about to be told off. "Your stitching on those isn't good enough, girl, but we have other things that need doing before master gets home so you'll have to fix them later. Get on with you, and help that dullard Sennianus clean out the furnace that heats the bath-house. Master is sure to bring guests with him and they'll all want to freshen up before their evening meal."

Lucia kept her eyes fixed on the floor to avoid irritating the manageress further and nodded assent as she jumped up and hastened from the room. She made her way along the covered walkway that ran the length of the southern wing of the villa, enjoying the warm summer air on her bare arms and drinking in the sight of the colourful blooms that the gardeners had planted in long pots all along the way. The scent of those flowers – roses, lilies, acanthus and violets amongst others – filled the air and Lucia breathed deeply, a small smile on her lips as she approached the bath-house which as a fire precaution was set slightly apart from the main buildings of the farm.

The villa was a wonderful sight on a July day like this, with its white plastered walls and red-tiled roofs seeming to glow in the sunshine, while its position on the hill afforded superb views of the land around: well-tended fields of corn and grain; groves of trees once sacred to the native Britons; and the sparkling waters of the narrow river that flowed past the western wing, providing their water for drinking, cleaning, cooking and, of course, bathing.

Sometimes, on particularly beautiful days, Lucia forgot about her previous life, as the daughter of a warlord in Germania. Forgot about her previous existence before she was captured by the Romans who had destroyed her village, slaughtered her people and sold her at the market to her master.

It had been a year already since Publius Licinius Castus, a young Roman officer himself, had bought her from that terrible slave-market and shipped her here, to his lavish country villa in this damp land.

Villa Tempestatis.

A lump came to her throat as an image of her parents – happy, smiling down with pride on their beloved daughter – came to her, and she angrily brushed away the tears forming in her eyes before they had a chance to streak her grimy cheeks.

Yes, sometimes she was able to forget her previous, free life in Germania, but it was never long before reality returned and she felt her spirit crushed so hard that it almost stopped her heart from beating.

The beauty of the villa and its surroundings hid the pain of dozens of slaves who had lived here over generations, young and old. Some of them, like Paltucca, were able to adapt and even thrive in such conditions, while others wilted and eventually, under the weight of what they'd lost, rendered themselves useless to the master. Those unfortunates soon disappeared, never to be heard of again.

Lucia wondered if she would end up like that one day, sold to be worked to death in a mine perhaps, when the stolen memory of the joy of her childhood became too much to bear.

But she was strong – a warrior's daughter – and she always, as she did now, gritted her teeth and forced the pain beneath the surface, telling herself the gods had let her live for a reason.

She went into the bathhouse via the rear slaves' entrance, and down the stairs to the furnace, which was cool at this time, the fires having lain dormant for most of the time the master was away from home. It would be lit occasionally, if neighbouring noblemen came to use the facilities – paying for the privilege of course – but this day it was to undergo a thorough clean before being relit in time for the master to enjoy a relaxing bath on his homecoming.

Bath-houses could be dangerous places if not maintained properly, as leaks in the walls or floors might allow lethal fumes to escape into the building, not to mention the ever-present danger of fire spreading beyond its containment area.

"Hello, Regalis," she said as she saw the muscular furnace-keeper brushing bits of bark and other detritus into a pile. She stepped onto the cool stone floor, adding, "I've been sent to help clear up."

The man straightened, piercing blue eyes softening as he looked at her, and he nodded towards the narrow stoke-hole which led into the main hypocaust.

"Sennianus is already in there," he said. "Grab a brush, lass, and join him. You'll find a damp rag for your face over there, a cloak to cover your clothes, and a light on the shelf up there. No tarrying, you hear? This should have been done yesterday but no one told us master would return so soon. Typical. They expect us to have the whole place sorted and ready to go in the blink of an eye. Bastards."

Lucia smiled as Regalis continued grumbling away to himself and she took a hand brush, blackened after years of hard use, from its place on the rack. She went to the sink next and lifted a rag from where it hung, wet it in the rather grubby-looking water, and wrapped it around her face so she didn't breathe in all the loose soot and ash she'd be cleaning. She chose a long cloak, utterly black from accumulated soot, and threw it over her head. The candle she took from the shelf was made from tallow, which would give off almost as much greasy smoke as it did light.

Finally, not relishing the allotted task at all and taking a deep breath, she got down on her knees in front of the low stone archway that framed the entrance to the stoke-hole.

The hypocaust was a clever, if simple system, long since perfected by Roman engineers. Heat from the furnace, which slaves like Regalis kept fed, would travel beneath the floors in the adjoining rooms, heating the walls and the water in the baths. Those floors sat on raised stone piers, but they were too low for an adult to manoeuvre around underneath them, so the smaller slaves, such as Lucia and Sennianus, had to clean those subterranean areas. It was dark, even with the tallow-light which Regalis lit for her with a taper, and horribly claustrophobic. The thought of all that water over her head always made Lucia nervous when she had to perform this job, but there was no alternative – until she grew too big to fit, she simply had to steel her nerves and get on with it.

"Are you in there Senni?" she called, lowering herself onto her belly and wriggling through the stoke-hole, candle before her, eyes already beginning to water. A muffled reply came from the left side of the low chamber, so she moved to the right, in order to clean the side that the boy hadn't started yet.

Although she was able to rise up onto her knees now, the ceiling wasn't far from her head and she had to be careful not to bump it. She had more than one scar under her brown hair to remind her how hard that stone was. To add to her discomfort, as well as being cramped the dim illumination from her candle showed the air was filled with dust and ash from Sennianus's brushing. The damp rag would protect her from some of it, but she knew when she spat or blew her nose later the sputum would be thick and black. Her eyes had no protection at all, other than tears.

Pushing aside her discomfort, and the ever-present hatred of her masters, she began brushing the piers, walls and ceiling, loosening the build-up of burnt deposits and sweeping it back towards the stoke-hole where it could be collected and thrown outside.

"Do you think the master will be alone?" Sennianus asked from somewhere in the dark. Lucia looked around but he was out of sight, apart from the pitiful glow of his own candle. "I overheard Paltucca saying something about extra guests with him."

Like her, Sennianus came originally from Germania, like quite a few of the slaves in the villa who shared a similar mother tongue.

Others, the two tall Nubians for example, couldn't speak their language, which made things difficult for everyone; this was a deliberate tactic employed by many Roman masters, to try and ensure their slaves couldn't conspire together. Romans had a great fear of being murdered by unhappy slaves.

In truth, the language barrier simply made life a little harder for everyone.

"More damn work for us then," Lucia grunted, using the back of the brush to scrape away a particularly stubborn piece of ash. It thumped onto the floor, releasing a cloud of dust, and she closed her eyes, shaking her head and trying to waft it away with her hand. "No doubt he's bringing his soldier friends and they'll want the bath hot, with fresh meat, fruit and wine to eat and drink, and the slave women lined up for them to use however they please." She lifted the rag from her mouth and spat, coughing, although it came out more like a dog's bark.

"At least you don't have to worry about that," Sennianus replied. "Not for a year or two at least, I think."

A shiver ran down Lucia's back at his words, and the matter-of-fact tone in which he delivered them, and she returned to her task with a renewed vigour born of anger bordering on despair.

She tried never to think about her eventual womanhood, but it was impossible to ignore, especially on nights when groups of the master's acquaintances visited and had their way with the female slaves. Of course, some of those women made the most of their feminine wiles, earning rewards and favour with the Romans and Briton noblemen, but many of them hated to be used in such a way. Lucia knew of three such, who had either killed themselves or run away, never to be heard from again – and this was just in the year that she'd lived in Villa Tempestatis.

"Keep it to yourself," Sennianus said, so close to her she jumped, not noticing his approach, "but I overheard Paltucca – fat cow that she is – saying the master has been married since he was away. He might bring his new wife here to live."

"You have big ears for such a small boy, Senni," Lucia smiled, sweeping a pile of gathered ash towards the stoke-hole, adding it to the collection already there. "But if he's married maybe he'll leave the women alone."

The lad shook his head sagely. "Nah, a wife won't do the things for a man that a slave does."

"Oh really?" Lucia asked. Like her, Sennianus was nine years old although he often acted as if he were some wise old philosopher. It amused and irritated the other slaves in equal measure. "Like what?"

"You know," the boy shrugged, clearly not knowing himself, and Lucia found herself glad for their joint naivety, silently thanking the gods for that small blessing. Many noblemen preferred young boys or girls rather than women – both Sennianus and Lucia were truly lucky that they hadn't been violated by the master or his wealthy companions.

"It might be good to have a woman in charge around the place," she said, returning to their task. "I mean, other than Paltucca. She's practically a man anyway."

"Keep your voice down," Sennianus hissed, eyeing the stoke-hole fearfully, as if the manageress might somehow force her great body through it any moment and beat them for their appraisal. Lucia just laughed. "We're nearly half finished," the boy went on, changing the subject and glancing around at their handiwork.

"Are we?"

"Aye," he nodded, and the corners of a smile could just be made out at the edges of his grimy face-rag. "Regalis only needs this chamber cleaned. The others haven't seen much use yet this year and Paltucca wants the fire lit as soon as possible, since it takes so long to get the water heated up."

"Well then," Lucia said, wiping her eyes with the back of her hand which did little to relieve the burning tears in them, "I'm away out to have a drink of water and a crust of bread. I've not eaten yet today."

"That's not fair," Sennianus replied in a whining tone that made him seem even younger than he was. "I've been in here longer than you. If anyone deserves a rest, it's me."

"I'm oldest," the girl laughed, falling to her belly and wriggling back into the smoke-hole, happy to feel the fresh, clean air on her face again. "So that makes me in charge. Don't worry, Senni, I promise I won't be long."

She took off the filthy cloak and walked quickly up the stairs, waving to Regalis who smiled in return. Then she went into the kitchen where she found some bread and poured herself a cup of water from a stone jug. The liquid was cool and tasted delicious in her dry mouth, which felt, as it always did after cleaning the hypocaust, like it was filled with ash.

She'd only taken a few bites of her small meal when Martina, one of the other slave women, stuck her head around the door and gestured vigorously.

"Wash that soot off, and come with me, girl, hurry. I'm hanging some fresh drop curtains in the entrance hall and I need someone to help me. I'd prefer someone bigger, but you'll have to do."

Lucia knew better than to argue with one of the older slaves, so without a word she placed the half-eaten bread down onto the plate, rinsed her hands and face, and hurried out of the room after the woman, who was already far along the corridor on the way to the main, northern wing of the villa.

The job was a relatively easy one, simply taking the weight of the drape in her hands as the woman hooked it around the pole over the tall archway that visitors passed through when they first entered the house. It meant standing halfway up a ladder, but Lucia was a good climber and, despite the good-natured huffing and swearing of the older woman – who had the harder task by far – they eventually completed the task just before midday.

The girl ran back to the kitchen, hoping to finish her bread before going back down into the dreaded hypocaust with Senni, but when she got there she could hear Regalis piling the wood, ready to light the fires.

Chewing her remaining food quickly she went down to the stairs. Another man had joined Regalis now and they had a good load of fuel piled inside the furnace, almost ready to light.

"Paltucca came and ordered me to get the fires going," the tall man said, spotting her watching them and rolling his eyes at the manageress's haste. "What's the rush?" he demanded, rhetorically, turning back to throw more logs onto the pile. "It's a sunny day, the master will want to make the most of it outdoors, surely, not lounging around in a steaming hot bath."

Lucia grinned, pleased to know she wasn't the only one that didn't like bossy Paltucca very much, and began to head back upstairs, either to continue her sewing from earlier, or, more likely, to be given some other pressing task in order to make the villa presentable for the exalted one's return.

She gritted her teeth at the thought: all these people working like, well, slaves! Just to please one man who was no better than any of them except by an accident of birth and the wealth and power that had brought to him.

In truth, Lucia knew very little about the man everyone called 'the master'. Paltucca didn't encourage gossip about him and punished anyone she caught at it.

The man's name was Castus, Lucia knew, and he was some kind of high-ranking soldier in the army – a prefect or tribune or something like that. He was young too, as far as Roman officers went, maybe only in his late twenties. His position meant he was away from the villa for most of the year, off fighting for the glory of Rome – the slave-girl spat mentally at the very idea – and when he wasn't on active duty he spent a lot of time in Rome itself.

She thought he must have been part of the army that destroyed her village back in Germania, which was presumably where he saw her and had her brought to serve here in his villa in damp, cold Britannia. She couldn't be sure of that, and to ask Paltucca to confirm it would only lead to a beating, but that was what she had believed for the past year.

On the few occasions Castus came here Lucia would look at his face surreptitiously and wonder if he had killed her parents with the sword hanging at his waist.

Just then Paltucca came storming down the stairs, her great bulk almost filling the small passageway.

"Where's that little bastard Sennianus?" she demanded, stopping to glare at Lucia who shrank back a step involuntarily.

"I-I don't know," the girl stammered, trying not to meet the manageress's eyes. "I left him cleaning the hypocaust so I could get something to…I mean, to help Martina put up the clean drapes. I haven't seen him since."

"Well he's supposed to be outside helping the men pluck chickens for the master's feast and he's not there." She shoved past the girl and went on down to the furnace. Lucia waited on the stairs, listening to the conversation. It seemed Regalis hadn't seen the boy coming out of the hypocaust, he'd just assumed the boy had left when Lucia did.

An icy shiver ran own the girl's back and, heedless of the manageress's legendary temper, threw herself down the stairs two at a time.

"When I find the little shit I'll flay the skin from his back," Paltucca was telling Regalis and his companion who both stared back at her, stony-faced. "Now get this fire lit. I want the water nice and warm for the master so he can wash off the dust from the road as soon as he gets here, should that be his wish."

"Wait!" Lucia cried, running across and grasping Regalis's muscular forearm as he reached for his tinderbox. "What if Senni is still in there?"

They all looked in the direction of the stoke-hole, now completely hidden by the fully loaded cast-iron furnace.

"How dare you come in here questioning my orders?" Paltucca shouted, eyes wide in surprise and fury.

"Wait, she's got a point," Regalis said, holding his hands up. "No-one knows where the lad is and the last place anyone saw him was in there." He walked across to the stoke-hole and shouted, "Sennianus! Are you in there boy? Senni!" but there was no answer.

"Of course he's not there," the manageress retorted. "Why would he have stayed in there while you two fools set the logs up ready to light? The lad might be touched, but he's not stupid enough to get himself trapped in a furnace. You!" she pointed at Lucia. "Get up those stairs and be about your work you little bitch. If you ever question me like that again I'll make you sorry you were born. And you two: light the fire."

She strode across to the stairs, muttering about what she'd do to Sennianus when he eventually turned up, but Lucia was certain that the boy was, for some reason, still inside the hypocaust.

"Please, Regalis," she said, tears filling her eyes as she grabbed his arm again, trying to stop him lighting the fire. "He's in there. I know he is. You can't burn him!"

Paltucca turned around at the continuing discussion and Lucia knew fear like she hadn't felt since the night the soldier captured her in Germania. The manageress stamped back across the room and grabbed her by the hair, twisting it expertly and forcing the girl to her knees on the blackened stone floor.

"If the boy *is* in there, that's his problem. I *will* have that fire lit now. The master shall come home to find this villa perfect and exactly how he likes it. And that means with the bath-house warm and ready to use. Now for the last time, Regalis – light that damn fire or you'll be part of the kindling!"

She turned away, pulling Lucia along behind her and the big man shrugged. Even the powerfully built furnace-master knew better than to cross Paltucca, and he walked over to lift a taper, lighting it from the small blaze which he kept almost-perpetually lit, for times just like this, in a brazier in the corner.

CHAPTER TWO

The pain in Lucia's scalp was terrible but the thought of her little friend being set alight in that hideous, claustrophobic chamber gave her strength.

"What will the master say when he comes home and the entire bath-house reeks of burning flesh?" she cried out. "The whole place will stink for days, until we can clean it all out again! And then Castus will know you killed one of his slaves."

The manageress stopped in mid-step and glared at her. The thought of Sennianus being immolated hadn't touched her, but the idea of the master being displeased was anathema to Paltucca.

She turned back and, releasing Lucia's hair, threw her down the stairs, to sprawl on the floor again.

"Get the wood cleared and send that little wretch in to see if the boy is there, Regalis. And be as quick as you can, this delay is unacceptable." She turned her gaze back on the slave-girl and sneered. "You'd better hope, for both your sakes, that the boy *is* in there, because if he turns up somewhere in the grounds I'll have you both whipped and thrown in the prison for a while." Once again she looked at Regalis. "If she isn't back out of there by the time the bell rings to announce the master's arrival on the road, light that fire. I'll have those baths heated for him whether there's a stink of roasting meat or not."

The sound of her feet slapping furiously on the steps receded until there was only silence from above and Regalis blew out a long breath.

"Come on then," he grunted, blowing out the burning taper and addressing the other male slave, Sosthenes, who'd remained silent during the entire confrontation with Paltucca. "We better get this lot shifted as fast as we can. Hurry up Lucia, you can help too, lass, but get that cloak back around you before you go in – can't have your clean clothes getting dirty or we'll be in trouble for that too."

The three of them soon cleared away enough wood for the girl to slither through into the hypocaust, although she received a few scratches and bruises on the way, and she was petrified the furnace-master might drop the tallow candle which he handed through to her. If it landed on the kindling the remaining wood would ignite and she'd be dead.

"Senni? Senni are you still in here?"

Her voice seemed terribly loud in the oppressive atmosphere of the hypocaust and she held her breath, listening intently for a reply. There was no light visible from the candle Senni had been using, and no other sounds apart from the vague, muffled noises of the villa going about its business overhead. She cursed her luck; she'd have to go in deeper and search for the boy.

With a final nervous glance back at the stoke-hole she crawled in further, heading to the right, where she'd left Senni what seemed like an age ago. She squinted into the gloom which the smoking candle barely illuminated, her eyes watering from the tallow's stinking fumes, and then, praise Freyja, the shadows seemed to recede and there he was!

The boy lay before her on the soot-blackened floor, unmoving, eyes closed. A nerveless hand had knocked his candle on its side, extinguishing it when he collapsed. She crawled hurriedly towards him, tears streaming down her filthy cheeks, praying to Freyja that he might still be alive, but she knew in her heart it wasn't to be.

"Senni," she said, voice cracking as she knelt beside him and shoved him tentatively. Nothing. "Senni," she repeated, louder, pushing harder, then, again, "Senni!" but this time her eyes widened and relief flooded through her.

His mouth had moved.

He was alive!

Then came the sound she'd been dreading: the bell to announce the appearance of their master's entourage on the road outside.

"Lucia," Regalis shouted into the stoke-hole. "Is he there? He is?" The relief in the big man's voice was obvious and the girl loved him at that moment. Not all the slaves were uncaring monsters like Paltucca. "Hurry then and get him out before she comes back and forces me to start the fire."

"Senni, wake up," Lucia commanded, slapping the unconscious boy on the face. When he didn't stir she grabbed his arms and tried dragging him bodily towards the stoke-hole.

She was a little bigger than Sennianus but not strong enough to move him and she cried in despair, exhorting him to wake up before they were both burned to death, fuel to heat Castus's bath water. Again, she pulled on the boy's arms and this time, praise the gods, the pain of the rough floor on his back got through to him and he made a noise that reminded Lucia strangely of a cat.

"Come on lass," Regalis shouted again. "Where are you?"

At last, Sennianus began to realise what was happening and, guided by Lucia, he started to crawl slowly towards the furnace-master's voice. The sight of daylight coming in through the stoke-hole, and the fresh air that accompanied it, was the most beautiful thing the girl could ever remember experiencing and she grinned at Regalis when he spotted them coming.

"Come on, hurry," he repeated, reaching a powerful arm in to help them out.

Lucia, petrified as she was that Paltucca would reappear and order them to be entombed in the furnace, supported the groggy boy as he manoeuvred his way past the logs and kindling with the aid of Regalis.

Just as Lucia slithered breathlessly back out of the hypocaust herself the manageress flew down the stairs, great breasts bouncing in her tunic in a way that always made Lucia feel slightly nauseated.

The woman glared at them, using her tongue to poke at one of her remaining upper teeth, then she nodded, apparently satisfied, for now.

"Light it," she growled. "And you two get back to your duties. Once the master is settled and everything is sorted, I will deal with you properly."

The threat in the manageress's voice was unmistakable, and everyone in the furnace knew it would be carried out with painful efficiency, but as she went back up the stairs to greet the master Lucia couldn't help laughing in relief.

They would suffer a beating later, but at least they were alive.

As her euphoria left her though, she looked at the pitiful figure of Senni who still didn't seem to know where he was. Regalis muttered something about him passing out from lack of air and this not being the first time it had happened, but she didn't fully understand what he was talking about, for right now all she could think about was Paltucca. The manageress had been prepared to burn them to death simply to make the baths warm for the master.

Paltucca was a slave herself, yet cared so little for her peers that she would murder them without a thought. Lucia already loathed the woman, but this added a new edge to her hatred.

The Romans might have captured her, and it was the master who had bought her and shipped her here to damp Britannia, but Paltucca was as bad as any of them. Worse!

Aye, the gods had saved Lucia for a reason while her parents and the rest of her settlement were being butchered by the Romans, and now she knew what that reason was: revenge.

One day it would be hers.

CHAPTER THREE

When the master arrived at the villa he wasn't alone. He had indeed been married since his previous visit to the villa and he brought his new wife, along with her personal slave-girl, a young woman who looked down her nose at Lucia and the rest of the household slaves. Also in the master's retinue were six men wearing togas. These were friends of Castus, and word had been sent in advance that they'd be staying for a few days. So Paltucca, efficient as ever, had ordered guest bedrooms to be swept and aired, with freshly cut flowers placed in vases to remove any damp or fusty smells.

Lucia, along with those of the other slaves who didn't have pressing tasks to attend to, was called out by Paltucca to the courtyard in the centre of the villa and lined up to form a welcoming party for the master and his guests. When they rode through the gate, Castus himself at their head, the girl couldn't help but be impressed. She hadn't seen him very much in her time in Britannia, but it always struck her how self-assured and confident he looked. He sat astride his great horse, sun shining on his face as if he was the ruler of the world. Which, in the environs of this sprawling villa, he was, she thought grimly, watching him dismount expertly and gaze around at his property.

Tall and powerfully built, he looked every inch the soldier; the scar running along his jaw only added to the air of martial power which he wore around him like a purple toga. The man reminded Lucia of her father, although increasingly she struggled to remember what her parents had actually looked like.

A male slave hurried forward and knelt, face down, on the ground beside the master's wife's horse, allowing her to use his back as a step. She smiled at Castus as she placed her dainty feet onto the ground, and he took her by the hand, returning her happy look.

If Lucia hadn't hated the master with every fibre of her being she'd have smiled herself at the happy scene.

"Ah, Paltucca," Castus said, gesturing to the manageress who, eyes on the ground, shuffled forward. "This is my new wife,

Dianna. She will be staying here with us for a while, although, of course, you will continue to run the household."

The manageress bowed but remained silent. The new lady of the house, beautiful, and younger than her husband by a good seven or eight years perhaps, looked at Paltucca with a bored expression, then she glanced at the rest of the slaves, eyeing them one by one before nodding approvingly.

"I'm tired, my love," she said, in a soft, almost childlike voice that even Lucia could tell was put on for his benefit. "Do we really need to meet all these slaves one by one? I need a bath."

Castus laughed and shook his head. "Of course." He waved a hand towards Lucia and the others. "Paltucca, get them back to work, and have the baths heated."

"They are already warm, master," the manageress said softly. "I had the furnace fuelled and lit earlier."

"You see?" Castus grinned, turning to address the rest of his now-dismounted guests. "I told you my manageress was a wonder." He looked again to the slave-woman. "Good work, Paltucca. A wagon is following with all our luggage on it, make sure it's unloaded without anything being damaged. I assume the guest bedrooms are ready? Yes, of course they are, and no doubt filled with lavender and whatever other flowers are in bloom just now. This is my wife's handmaiden, Elaine." He gestured to a pretty young woman with flowing brown hair who met Paltucca's gaze proudly and perhaps a little haughtily. "She will arrange the *domina's* things in her wardrobe. Come all, let's get settled."

As the nobles entered the main living quarters, beneath the grand entrance hall with the drapes Lucia had helped hang earlier that morning, Paltucca turned to the still lined-up slaves and, scowling, waved them away with an exhortation to be on their best behaviour or suffer her wrath.

From that point on, the day was a blur of activity for Lucia.

Usually, her work consisted of chores such as weaving, sewing, cleaning, weeding and other tasks related to the running of the villa, which was essentially a large farm. But now, with the master's return, the focus of her work changed to that of a serving girl, concerned with making sure Castus and his guests wanted for nothing.

Dianna, the mistress or *domina*, took a bath with just her husband, and Lucia was there, along with Sennianus and two older slaves: to bring wine in exquisite goblets; to make sure oil and clean strigils – the curved blades used to scrape dirt and sweat from the bathers' bodies – were at hand; to provide towels and robes; and to help dry the clean, water-wrinkled, dark skin of the master and mistress as they moved from the warm to hot and cold rooms.

First they started in the dry heat of the tepidarium, with its wonderful mosaic depicting a hunt, where they were massaged by slaves and the grime and sweat cleaned from their bodies by slaves using oil and strigils.

In the second room, the caldarium with its hot plunge bath, Lucia couldn't help watching from the corner of her eye as the bathers came together and, with grunts and moans of pleasure, copulated unashamedly in the water, as if the slaves weren't even there. It was another reminder to the girl, that her master – her owner – didn't see her as a real person. She was simply a tool in human form, there to be used however he, or his noble guests, saw fit.

Lucia thought it just as well Castus and his new wife didn't notice the bulge in Sennianus's tunic as they made love in the steaming water. Perhaps they would have laughed at the confused young boy's arousal, or maybe they'd have taken offence to it and had him beaten. Lucia was glad her emotions couldn't be read so easily as her friend's.

Oh, how she longed to jump into that inviting water! Back at home in Germania she'd washed infrequently, and then only in a barrel with cold or, at best, tepid water that was barely cleaner than her own grimy little body. Here, in the villa, Paltucca insisted on the slaves being clean and presentable for the master at all times – even when he was away on campaign with the army or back at his other, main house in Rome – but they had to wash in a separate bath-house, located in the west wing. That was grimy, gloomy and chilly even in summer, and equipped with only one pool.

The luxurious baths the master and his wife were rutting in right now were so close, yet they might as well have been in Germania – she would never feel that warm water around her skin. Although, as the new mistress climbed out, dripping wet, her lithe figure glistening in the sunlight that came through the glass bricks in the walls, perhaps it wouldn't be so pleasant after all.

"You'll need to have that water cleaned," Dianna said, smiling wickedly at her husband, and pointing at the small patch of grey-white fluid that had risen to the surface of the water. "Your friends won't want to bathe with all that floating about in there."

The master winked and sniggered like a naughty child. "Why not? I hear it's good for the complexion."

Dianna shared his laugh but shook her head as a robe was placed around her shoulders by one of the older slaves. "No, you can't leave that there. They'll think you a barbarian."

"Maybe I am," Castus said, leering at her and smacking her firm behind as they wandered out of the room, into the caldarium with its hotter water. "Oh alright," he finally relented. "You! Scoop out that mess we've left."

"You mean that *you've* left!" the mistress giggled, sliding into the water and crying out at its heat. "Oh, in the name of Sulis, that's burning!"

The slave Castus had addressed nodded and headed back into the tepidarium to carry out his unpleasant task as Lucia walked in with the wine, followed by Sennianus who held two clean towels. She stood in the corner, in the shadows, and looked at her new mistress, trying to see what kind of woman this Dianna might be.

Tall and slim, the mistress was toned, almost athletic, with a lovely face that was accentuated by her stunningly white teeth. She spoke in a soft voice, fluttering her long eyelashes, and touched the master's arm often. Lucia, although very young, was a good judge of character, and she could tell Dianna was playing up to the master.

This new mistress was smarter than she appeared.

Lucia wondered if Castus knew it or if he believed her to be as dim as—

Suddenly the slave-girl's reverie was broken and her face flushed hot as she realised the master was gesturing towards her.

"Are you deaf, girl? Gods, did I buy a deaf slave? Yes, you – bring the wine now, girl, or Paltucca will hear about this."

Lucia hurried forward, but her foot slipped on the wet floor and she almost dropped the amphorae. It was a miracle she retained her footing and somehow caught the hideously expensive wine from smashing onto the ground.

"Clumsy little brat too," the master growled, shaking his head, and Lucia's blood ran cold at the thought of the beating she would receive later from the sadistic manageress.

She was surprised to see Dianna shaking her head and slapping Castus on the bicep.

"Don't be unkind," said the new mistress. "She's just a girl, and probably petrified of you. Are you usually horrible to the slaves? No? Well, good. Thank you very much, my dear. What's your name? Lucia? Very pretty, it suits you. You'll be a beauty when you're older I think. I'll need to keep an eye on my husband then, eh?"

Lucia, wide-eyed, backed away, glad that the mistress had finished talking to her. She stood again in the shadows, mind whirling, and finally decided that she hated the master, but liked Dianna. Castus's new wife would be a good mistress and life would be better with her in the house. Hopefully the lady would visit often.

She caught Sennianus looking at her and smiled.

Dinner was another new experience for Lucia. When the master visited the villa before, Paltucca had not used Lucia to serve drinks or food, instead keeping her out of the way, presumably because she was too small to be of much use in the social setting. After the nobles had all bathed, though, Lucia was ordered into the dining room to carry plates of food from the kitchen to the table.

The dining room was very big, with couches for the diners to relax upon set on three sides around the low table. Light from the lamps was reflected by the silver tableware, and the gold pendant worn by the new mistress, Dianna. At the diners' feet was an intricate mosaic in shades of red, yellow, black and white, depicting Cupid riding a dolphin and other scenes from Roman legends. Lucia saw Castus proudly describing the various scenes to the guests, who were much taken by the workmanship.

Appetisers, olives, various breads, nuts and goat's cheese had already been placed on the tables, and the first course was soon also ready, and Lucia helped the other slaves carry each dish to the table. The slave-girl didn't even know what was on the plates she brought, but it smelled wonderful and she had to surreptitiously swallow the saliva that filled her mouth.

The mistress smiled at her, as did the master himself as they began their meal, and Lucia tried to return their friendly expressions, but she was very nervous. She knew Paltucca would be watching everything that the slaves did, and any mistake or transgression would be punished with a night in the basement, which often served as a prison for those who drew the manageress's ire.

"There's no need to be so nervous," Popillia, one of the other serving girls, had told Lucia before the dinner party started. "The master doesn't punish us harshly if we make a mistake. In Rome, if a slave so much as coughs when serving food, he'll be beaten with rods! In Rome, slaves serving at table are usually supposed to be completely silent. Our master is happy to talk with us though, you'll see, and if you need to cough or even sneeze softly, you may." Her smile had turned to a warning frown then. "Still, though, try to be as quiet as possible and only speak if one of the diners speaks to you first."

When it was time for the main course, Livinia, the cook, came out herself from the kitchen to cut the meat for the guests. There were suckling pigs with pastry and dates, roast chickens, and hare in a wine sauce, and everyone ate with gusto, declaring it the best meal they'd eaten in months, which brought a small, appreciative smile to the master's lips.

Lucia stood against the wall, watching as the sumptuous feast was devoured. She wondered if Popillia was making it up about slaves being beaten with rods for coughing. Surely no-one, even a slave, would take such punishment without becoming sullen and unproductive? Why would a master treat his servants so harshly when he had to live under the same roof? If Castus beat Lucia with a rod she would stab him with a knife and run away into the woods, even if it meant she would die herself.

She shuddered, knowing her fantasy was nothing more than that, imagining how terrible life must be for slaves who had a sadistic master.

"I'm full," the mistress announced, once the final course, some milky pudding Lucia didn't really like the look of, had been served and devoured. "I'd like to go to bed if you don't need me, Castus?"

The master kissed his new wife's hand and assured her he didn't mind if she wanted to retire.

"Popillia," he said, gesturing to the slender slave-girl. "Show the mistress to our bedchamber please; just in case she gets lost in her new surroundings."

Dianna's handmaiden threw Popillia a look of disdain but kept her mouth shut – Elaine was a slave just like the rest of them, as Lucia knew, even if she did appear to think herself above the rest of them.

When the women had left the atmosphere seemed to change. Perhaps it was simply down to the wine which had been consumed but Lucia noticed the diner's voices grew louder, their conversation bawdier, and their language more profane.

The talk up until then had mainly been about the emperor, the cost of living, the political situation in Rome and similar topics which had been discussed quietly and respectfully. Now, the men spoke of chariot races, or their favourite gladiators, or battles they'd fought in themselves. Then, when Popillia returned from escorting the mistress to her room, their conversation turned to sex.

"She's a nice piece," one of Castus's guests noted, eyeing Popillia up and down appreciatively. "I bet you've spent a bit of time on top of her, eh?"

The man leered but Lucia saw the master frown and guessed he didn't appreciate such talk.

"I would, if she was one of my slaves," another guest grunted, and he stared at Popillia hungrily, sending another shiver down Lucia's spine. There was no jocularity in this one's tone.

"I like to surround myself with beautiful things," Castus said. "And that includes my slaves. I don't make a habit of bedding them very often though, Camulorix."

Lucia recognised the man's name – he owned a villa not far to the south and he was a native Briton, despite his speech and manner of dress. As such, she wondered if Castus, a high-born Roman, looked down on Camulorix and had invited him here simply to maintain cordial relations with his neighbours.

"You can have her for the night if you like," the master said, shrugging as if what he said meant little.

Camulorix grinned and nodded lasciviously at Popillia.

"That's not fair," another man cried out, laughing. "What about the rest of us? Your wife's handmaiden, Elaine is it? She's a beauty, can I have her?"

Castus smiled and shook his head in mock exasperation. "You can all take your pick later on," he promised. "I have other slaves just as pretty as Popillia, and just as willing. Leave Elaine alone though; my wife would never let me hear the end of it if her maid was roughly used."

"That cook of yours then," one of the men leered. "Can I have a go on that? She wasn't much of a looker, but, by Mithras, what a set of tits!"

Camulorix, quite inebriated, rocked with laughter, knocking over his goblet of wine and spilling the dark liquid all over the floor. Lucia was the slave nearest and she hurried forward without thinking, placing the goblet back on the table and wiping the mess with a cloth that had been tucked into a pocket of her tunic for just this purpose.

As she got back to her feet a hand grasped her wrist and she found herself face to face with one of the diners, a nobleman of at least fifty, with grey hair and bloodshot eyes. He gazed at her for a long, uncomfortable moment, then spoke to the master.

"I'd like this one, Castus."

CHAPTER FOUR

Lucia stared at the man, confused, and then she understood what he meant. It was all she could do to remain standing there.

She tore her eyes away from the old diner and looked pleadingly at the master. The thought of the grey-haired drunk forcing himself upon her frightened her more than anything. Her mind raced as she imagined him touching her.

"You can choose another, Vibidius," Castus replied softly, waving the man's request away. "No one touches her. Lucia is off limits."

"Oh, what a shame, she's so sweet!" the grey-haired guest cried, laughing as if he'd made a great joke. But he released the slave-girl's arm and she scurried away, back to her place against the wall, heart pounding and breathless with shock.

She wanted desperately to lie down on her mattress and cry but that was impossible. She had to retain her composure while the dinner party went on. Yet her fear didn't abate as more and more alcohol was consumed by the revellers and they became ever louder and more obnoxious. Popillia found herself being pawed at every time she approached the table with the amphorae of Falernian wine and Lucia was petrified at the thought of Castus changing his mind about letting the old man bed her. And what if the master passed out, drunk, and the guests decided to rape her anyway?

All these thoughts and more tormented her as the party dragged on, and on, for what seemed like hours.

Once or twice the grey-haired guest commented again on Lucia but each time the master firmly refused the request and changed the subject.

By the time the men staggered off to bed with adult partners from her fellow slaves, both male and female, Lucia was utterly exhausted. She didn't think about what the drunken guests were doing to the slaves in the privacy of their bed-chambers, she was so relieved to take her bed in the rafters over the kitchen that their suffering meant nothing to her.

When she realised that, she felt guilty, but only until the grey-haired old lech's face filled her mind once more and she lay there, terrified, knees against her chest, sobbing.

Despite her fatigue she found it impossible to sleep. Fear of Castus's drunken guests kept her awake, despite the door which Paltucca had locked before retiring for the night herself. That door was there to prevent the male and female slaves from enjoying their own nocturnal liaisons, but even its sturdy lock didn't make Lucia feel safe.

At last, though, sheer exhaustion began to take over and her eyelids became too leaden to hold open any more. As she drifted off a thought struck her, and happiness flooded through her. The master had protected her! He would never let anyone abuse her, he'd said as much himself: 'Lucia is off limits.'

For the first time since she'd been brought here to Britannia the slave-girl felt some affection for the master. He wasn't like the sadists she'd heard lived in Rome – he was a good man. He would protect her and, one day, she would earn her freedom and return home to Germania.

* * *

It wasn't all work and drudgery for the slaves. Castus knew, like any good master, that the servants needed some relaxation and fun just like any free man of Rome. Summer offered the chance to mix work with pleasure for Lucia, and she jumped at the chance to collect fruit one fine, sunny afternoon.

Sennianus went with her, the lad carrying two empty baskets for the fruit they could find growing near to the sprawling villa. Strawberries were cultivated in the main gardens, protected by nets from the hungry birds, but raspberries, gooseberries and cherries were all also ripe and soon filled the large baskets.

"Let's go for a swim," Sennianus suggested, pointing to the river which flowed nearby. It wasn't a very wide, or deep river—more of a stream at this time of year—but there was a pool the slaves knew of where the water was deep enough to bathe.

Lucia grinned. "Good idea, they won't be expecting us back at the house for a while anyway."

"If they need us we'll hear Paltucca's booming voice calling anyway," Sennianus said.

"They'll probably hear her all the way in Rome," Lucia replied nastily and both of them laughed.

The pool didn't take long to reach, and they set down the baskets in a shaded spot, with stones on top of the woven lids to make sure no squirrels tried to steal the berries. Then, stripping unashamedly, they walked towards the water.

Lucia dipped a tentative foot in and jumped back, squealing.

"It's cold!" she said.

"What do you expect?" the boy replied. "It's fed by the waterfall, so doesn't have time to heat up in the sun."

Lucia nodded at the explanation and shaded her eyes as she looked where Sennianus pointed. The 'waterfall' was only small, about the same height as her, but it was very pretty, the clear fresh water rushing down in a torrent. The gentle sound it made, and the summer flowers that grew on either bank, almost let her forget where she was; who she was.

With a whoop, Sennianus jumped into the water, cold spray splashing onto Lucia. She shrieked again but the boy resurfaced, grinning in delight.

"Come on," he shouted. "It's wonderful!"

The girl hesitated, thought about walking in slowly to allow her skin to acclimatise gradually to the coolness of the water, then followed her friend's lead and jumped, eyes screwed tight shut, in beside him.

The shock was intense but passed quickly and she resurfaced, wiping her face, gasping and laughing.

"Oh, you were right," she murmured, stretching back and glorying in the sunshine on her face. "It really is wonderful."

"And the master will be pleased," Sennianus said. "He likes all the members of his household to be clean, and this is much better than using an old sponge with a bucket of grimy water, eh?"

"This is even better than the bath-house," Lucia replied, ducking her head under again and rubbing her limbs to dislodge any ground-in grime. When she came back up she inspected one of her arms and laughed. "Look," she said, nodding. "Look how white my arm is where the dirt's come off. I never realised I was so filthy!"

"Make the most of it," the boy grinned. "If we need to help in the furnace later we'll end up as dark as one of the Nubians again."

For a while the two slaves swam and relaxed in the water, which no longer felt cold to Lucia. She might have spent all day there if they hadn't needed to get back soon with the berries, which, despite being in shade, would get warm and sticky before too long.

"Do you like the master?"

Lucia was lying on her back in a shallow part of the pool, the water only half covering her body, and she used her hand as a shade to look at Sennianus who was swimming leisurely around back and forward.

"I don't know," she replied, eyes moving away from her friend to make sure no-one was nearby. A wrong word could mean a beating or worse from Paltucca. "We don't see him very much, do we? It's humiliating to live as another person's property but he doesn't treat us badly, does he?"

"I heard a story about a nobleman in Rome," Sennianus said, "who got annoyed at one of his slaves for doing something silly – spilling ink on his work or that – and threw him out of the window!"

Lucia's stomach lurched at the thought. "Were they high up? Did the slave die?"

"Yes, his head was all smashed in," Sennianus replied. "But d'you know what the master did? He made the slave's partner clean up the blood once the body had been taken away."

"No!" Lucia sat up, clutching her arms about herself as the water washed delightfully across her. "I don't believe you. There's laws to stop slaves being treated like that nowadays."

Sennianus stood up, water dripping off him in rivulets, and shrugged. "Maybe it happened a long time ago," he admitted. "I don't know, it was just something I overheard a couple of the others talking about one night. Anyway, I'm just saying: at least our master doesn't do things like that."

They stepped out of the water and lay on the bank, side by side, lost in thought, the hot sun drying them quickly without any need for towels.

"We'd better head back before this heat spoils the berries and we get into trouble," Lucia said at last, reaching across to gather her clothes. As she pulled the tunic over her head there was a cry of alarm, a loud splash, and, as the garment came down, allowing her to see again, there was no sign of Sennianus on the bank.

CHAPTER FIVE

"Senni! What are you doing?" she shouted, irritated more than anything else. The boy didn't resurface though, and she called his name again, a touch of fear creeping into her voice. She stepped back into the water, allowing it to come up to her knees as she peered into the pool, trying to see her friend. There was no sign of him, and the ripples the splash had stirred up were gone.

"Senni!" What had happened to him in the name of Freyja? Why had he gone back into the water? She looked around, fearfully, wondering if someone had sneaked up on them and pushed the boy in but she seemed to be alone. Whatever had happened to him, she had to get him out of the water before he drowned.

Without taking her tunic back off she dived into the deep part of the pool and swam down, looking all around the murky depths for some sign of Sennianus. All she could see was gently swaying foliage Her eyes began to hurt, forcing her to return to the surface, where she drew in lungfuls of air, gasping, terrified by the strange disappearance of the slave-boy.

The sound of laughter made her look sharply towards the bank. There, bent double with mirth, was Sennianus.

"You little bastard!" Lucia shouted, half-swimming, half-running as fast as she could manage across to him, charging out of the water, fists clenched, teeth bared in anger, but he dodged away and hid behind the great old oak that had provided the shade for their fruit baskets.

"I'm sorry," Sennianus gasped, still laughing so hard he could hardly talk. "I'm sorry, I didn't think you'd jump in to rescue me."

"What *did* you think I'd do?" Lucia demanded, trying to catch hold of the boy's arm, but he was too fast and dodged from one side of the massive trunk to the other, keeping out of her reach despite his mirth. "Look at me – I'm soaked now," she shouted, gathering the hem of her tunic and squeezing a small stream of water from it.

"You'll dry out by the time we reach home again," the boy said, finally allowing himself to be caught and suffering the punches

Lucia rained on his arm with only a yelp or two. "Sorry, sorry, ow, sorry!"

Her fury left her quickly and she was soon laughing along with Sennianus. They collected the baskets and began the short journey back to the villa, Lucia shaking her head ruefully, the boy still giggling. As he'd suggested, the hot sun quickly dried her tunic and, by the time they walked into the cool kitchen she felt clean, refreshed and happy.

"Thank you for jumping in to save me," Sennianus said quietly as they placed their baskets in the sink and set to cleaning the berries with a jug of clean water. "I mean it."

Lucia shrugged and punched him on the arm again. "I couldn't just let you drown, could I? You're my best friend, even if you are a little shit."

They finished rinsing the fruit in companionable silence, separated the different kinds of berry into individual bowls, covered them and placed them in the larder, which was surprisingly cool despite the sun beating down outside.

"What should we do now?" Sennianus asked, but before Lucia could reply, a familiar voice filled the room.

"What are you two doing standing about here looking into one another's eyes? The entrance needs cleaning; there's horse crap all over the road. Move!"

Even Paltucca's sour face, or the thought of shovelling and mopping horse dung, couldn't ruin the young slaves' mood. They hurried off, heads bowed respectfully, to find buckets of water and lye soap, but their eyes were sparkling as if they'd been told to take the rest of the day off.

Sometimes it wasn't a bad life, even for a slave, thought Lucia.

* * *

Regalis was a good friend to Lucia at that point in her young life, making sure the older slaves didn't take advantage of her by stealing her food or wine rations or the blanket that was given to every slave by the estate. He also made sure the younger slaves weren't forced to do tasks previously allocated to others. In fairness, Paltucca also tried to make sure everyone did their fair share, but it was the burly furnace-master who took Lucia and Sennianus under his wing.

Regalis was one of the few slaves Castus allowed to marry, as a reward for five years of loyal and valuable service. Some of the other men and women were jealous of the marriage, but it showed one reward the slaves could expect if they worked hard and didn't cause trouble.

Regalis's wife, Antonia, was almost as tall as he was, and attractive too, with dark hair and skin. Lucia suspected the master had allowed them to marry so they would produce more slaves for him – the offspring of two strong, handsome slaves like Regalis and Antonia were bound to make good workers in the household. As it was, the marriage had been blessed already with two children, who were three and four years old and, this summer, a third was due to be born.

"My wife has taken a shine to you."

The slaves not working out in the fields or tending the livestock were sharing their afternoon meal in the kitchen. It was mostly just bread and watered wine but Lucia had been allocated a little extra salt that month in recognition of her hard work recently. The girl shared the valuable condiment with Sennianus, who promised to return the favour whenever he was similarly rewarded by Paltucca, although Lucia doubted that would ever happen. The boy was too much of a dreamer and that irritated the manageress. Poor Senni was more likely to be given the lash than an extra portion of salt.

"I like her too," she replied, smiling at Regalis. The furnace-master had a larger plate of food than most of the slaves, simply because his work was so physical and he needed more energy to keep up his prodigious strength. "She's always smiling; it's nice to see a happy face, especially when it's as pretty as Antonia's."

The furnace-master beamed at the girl's compliment as if the emperor himself had delivered it and finished chewing the last of his bread.

"Well, lass, Antonia would like you to help with the birth of the babe. Paltucca thinks it'd be a good idea too – you'll have to give birth yourself one day, so it'll let you know what's involved. I'm guessing you haven't seen a baby being born before?"

Lucia shook her head. "Maybe back home in Germania but if I did I was too little to remember it. I've heard some of the other slaves having their babies here in the villa though – it sounds very painful."

"Aye," Regalis agreed. "It can be. I don't envy women having to go through that. But," his face brightened, perhaps realising Lucia might become frightened at his words, "it can't be that bad, since they all keep having babies, eh?"

Lucia nodded thoughtfully, his point seeming a good one. A few of the slave-women had sported swollen bellies in the year that she'd been there, although thinking about it now, she wasn't sure where those babies went, since there were never any about the place. The furnace-master was waiting for her response, and she looked back at him with a smile. "What would I have to do?"

Regalis got to his feet as Paltucca rang the bell signalling the end of the meal. "Just make sure there's clean water and towels and…well, I'm not really sure myself, I always keep well out of the way, but there will be other women there to make sure everything is all right, don't worry."

Lucia returned to work, rinsing laundered clothes with a couple of the other slave-women down at the river, her mind filled with thoughts of babies. Of course, Regalis and Antonia were envied by those slaves who weren't allowed to 'marry' or have families of their own, but the memory of those screams and cries of pain from far-off rooms played on the girl's mind. The furnace-master might have played it down, but giving birth was obviously not an easy, or pleasurable experience.

Yet Regalis himself wouldn't need to suffer the pain, so…Lucia pictured his face and wondered why he'd looked so saddened by the thought of bringing another child into the world. Maybe just the fact the babe would be a slave too was enough to dampen his mood.

She went about her work diligently, as usual, until one afternoon Paltucca sent for her.

"Antonia has gone into labour. Make your way to her chamber and do whatever the women there tell you to do."

There was no smile or kind word of encouragement, but Lucia had expected neither. She wasn't sure if she'd ever seen Paltucca smile.

Antonia and Regalis had a chamber of their own which they shared with their two small children, Blandinus and Arethusa.

When Lucia entered the room, which had one window, unshuttered to let in the light, Antonia was on the birthing chair, her face pale and sweaty. She didn't even look at the girl as the door opened but let out a small gasp and then a moan.

"Is she alright?" Lucia asked the women, who were sitting around on normal chairs, knitting jumpers from lamb's wool. That seemed odd to the girl – shouldn't they be helping with the birth?

"She's doing fine, lass," Balbina, an older slave with silvery-grey hair replied. "Antonia's an old hand at this, she knows what to do after half-a-dozen births. This could be a long night though, so you can make yourself useful by fetching her a jug of wine." She saw Lucia's look of surprise and shook her head in exasperation. "We're not going to get her drunk! That wouldn't help at all. But a mug of wine will help her relax and that's the best thing for a woman trying to bring a little one into the world."

On the chair, Antonia let out another groan and, wide-eyed, Lucia ran back out of the room to fetch the drink. By the time she returned the labouring slave was gripping the arms of the birthing chair, gasping for breath. She took the mug Balbina filled from Lucia's amphorae and drank it down in two quick swallows. It seemed to have the desired effect, for within a short time colour returned to her face and the gasps became somehow less pained.

Balbina's words proved prophetic though, and the labour went on long into the night. It was pitch black outside and not much lighter within the chamber thanks to the smoke from the dim tallow candles. Lucia felt utterly drained by the time Balbina – who'd even gone away for a nap and returned – squatted down before the birthing chair between Antonia's spread legs, and drew forth the baby.

It looked nothing like Lucia expected, being covered in blood and other mess she couldn't even begin to wonder at. But Balbina and the other women knew their business and the umbilical cord was quickly cut and tied off and the little red and crying bundle was wrapped in a towel and carried from the room.

Lucia watched, her happiness at their successful operation turning into a confused frown. She had always thought new babies would be handed to their mother to nurse, or just to let the exhausted woman see the wonderful reward for all her hard work.

Yet the babe had been carried away by one of the other slaves and there was no sense of triumphant joy in the room now.

The girl looked at the women moving about the chamber, tidying the rumpled sheets Antonia lay upon, collecting soiled towels and cloths and basins of blood-reddened water and she felt naïve and embarrassed.

These women had probably presided at dozens of births over the years. Some of them might even have had children of their own. No wonder there was no great outpouring of happiness at the babe's arrival – it was just another event in the life-cycle of the slaves.

The thought made Lucia sad. The child had been a noisy, red mess, but she thought it the most incredible little person she had ever seen in all her nine years. She wished she could run out of the room after the slave who'd taken it and ask to hold the tiny bundle in her own arms, even just for a few moments.

Where had it been taken anyway?

To be cleaned, Lucia guessed. And they would do it in another room so the tired mother could rest, obviously.

"Here, take these to the kitchen and then get yourself to bed." Balbina handed a basket of stained towels to Lucia, placed a lit candle in her other hand, and waved her towards the door. "You were a good help tonight, girl, well done." The older woman managed a small smile, but Lucia was shooed away before she could make any reply, and so she went, finding herself in the corridor as the door was opened and closed behind her by a pale-faced Popillia.

It was cool in the quiet corridor, deliciously so after the hot, oppressive atmosphere of the birthing chamber and suddenly Lucia felt ravenously hungry, and thirsty too. She hurried to the kitchen and set down the candle on the table before depositing the dirty towels in the washing pile, rinsing the blood from her hands in a basin, and finding a loaf of bread. She tore off a thick chunk, slathered it with butter, and bit into it with gusto, pouring a small cup of wine for herself as she chewed.

On the platform in the rafters overhead, she knew half-a-dozen of her companions were sleeping – she would join them up there soon enough, and sleep like the dead until Paltucca woke them with that bellowing voice of hers in just a few short hours – but the room was peaceful just now.

She took her time finishing the simple meal, savouring the taste of the bread which had been freshly baked just the day before, and the wine which, although watered, made her feel slightly dizzy, almost euphoric, in her exhausted state.

So that was how a baby was born, she thought, staring into the darkness in a half-stupor.

What an incredible experience. How amazing it was to see a new life coming into the world. Lucia remembered the midwife telling her Antonia had given birth half-a-dozen times before, and she wondered where all those other children were. They must have taken ill and died in their early years or been sold to other 'owners' by the wicked *dominus*, as Lucia had only ever seen Blandinus and Arethusa around the villa.

Her head dropped down onto her chest and she jerked fully awake again, startled by how exhausted she felt.

It was past time to sleep.

She slipped off her shoes and climbed the long ladder up to her pallet. This was one of the best places in the villa for slaves to sleep in winter, as the kitchen was warm all day from the cooking fires, although in summer it wasn't quite so pleasant for the same reason.

Still, although it was somewhat stifling that night, Lucia soon found herself drifting off with a contented, proud smile on her lips.

In the silence she almost fancied she could hear the cries of Antonia's newborn baby, somewhere outside in the night.

* * *

The next morning was fine and sunny again although there had been some rain during the night. It lent the air a fresh, new smell and Lucia was smiling as she and Sennianus collected fishing poles and hand nets to take to the river, which was full of roach and perch at this time of the year. Sennianus came from a village in Germania near Besontio and he'd learned from his father how to fish there.

Lucia had never tried in her life to catch a fish until Senni noticed the tackle in a store-room one day and, after asking Paltucca for permission, taken the girl down to the river to show her how it was done.

She was far from expert even now, despite the boy's tutelage, and found it fairly tedious, but she enjoyed being in the fresh air, especially on a beautiful day like this, so she was more than happy to go with the lad when they were sent to catch dinner. Besides, the last time they'd fished, Senni managed to catch a large bream and the other slaves were very impressed with the fine meal it provided, earning Lucia almost as much praise as the boy who'd done all the hard work.

"I delivered Regalis's new daughter last night," the girl said airily as they walked on the soft grass towards the tree-lined river less than a quarter of a mile from the villa buildings.

"Really?" Sennianus replied, eyes wide with interest.

"Well, I helped," Lucia amended, somewhat lamely before rallying, her smile widening again. "It was amazing. I mean, it seemed quite painful for Antonia, but it was…I'll never forget it!"

Senni's brows knitted together and he swung the fishing net in the air, trying without luck to catch a fly that had been plaguing him ever since they left the house.

"Regalis and Antonia already have children," he said. "Some other slaves would like to start a family too and they might not be happy with the master allowing Regalis to be a father again."

"You sound as if you want a baby," Lucia laughed and the boy reddened, his ears turning almost purple at her teasing.

"I do not! All they do is eat and shit themselves," he retorted, as if an expert on the subject. "I'm just saying; Castus is usually good at keeping the slaves – us – content. I've heard at least a couple of the older men complaining amongst themselves at night, saying Regalis gets treated better than everyone else." He shrugged. "Doesn't matter to me anyway, I'm just telling you what I've heard."

They walked on in silence for the rest of the way, but his words seemed to stir something in Lucia's mind. Senni was right: the master did treat them fairly, by and large. Castus seemed to believe that letting his slaves live with respect and dignity was better than brutalising them continuously until they dropped, or went mad from the horror of their empty lives, or tried to kill themselves or him. Paltucca, on the other hand, acting as his agent when he was away on campaign or in Rome, could be vicious in her punishments as Lucia knew from bitter experience.

Certainly, thinking about it now, Lucia would have already attempted to run away if her life in the villa was unbearably harsh. Of course, she missed her parents and her home in Germania terribly, but she wasn't beaten or starved or...touched, by the master and his friends.

Presumably Senni and the other, older slaves, were similarly content with their lot. Regalis, for example, with his size and strength, could easily have drowned the master in the baths one night if the notion had taken him. Lucia knew there had been slaves in the past who had murdered their masters, or even, like the fabled Spartacus, led an entire army of slaves against their despised Roman overlords.

So, with all that in mind—why had Castus allowed Regalis and Antonia to add another child to the two they already had in their family, when so many of the other men and women – particularly women – would like even just one baby of their own?

The slave-girl found the answer to her question on the riverbank.

Castus hadn't allowed the furnace-master and his wife to add another child to their family.

The newborn Lucia had helped bring into the world just a few hours before lay there in the grass before them, dead.

CHAPTER SIX

Despite the discovery of the baby's abandoned body, and her own resultant loss of innocence, that summer was to be one of Lucia's happiest ever. Years later, she would look back on the time with fondness, as memory did its usual protective trick of hiding the bad and revealing mainly the good. But the season passed soon into autumn, then winter, and the hot days collecting fruit amongst the flowers or enjoying cooling baths in the river – although at a new pool, away from the hateful place where they had discovered Antonia's exposed babe – turned to a harder time.

The grain had been gathered and stored in the large shed; the older animals had been slaughtered, flesh salted to last the winter months; fruit preserved in wine, vinegar or salt-water; much wood – fuel for the hypocaust and other fires – was collected and covered with animal hides to keep it dry; and the villa buildings painted and repaired where they needed it, to stop draughts or rain coming in.

Such daytime work, hard as it was, Lucia found enjoyable to an extent. At least it kept her warm when the icy wind was blowing in from the distant sea, unlike evening chores. Mending and remaking clothes or blankets was hellish at this time of year, as the slaves only had a dim light to work by and, although the kitchen where the women sewed wasn't as cold as other areas of the house, their fingers were still numb, making the intricate tasks that much more unpleasant and difficult. If they wanted the room warmer, it meant closing the windows, and that meant working amidst the cooking smells and steam and smoke. There was always an argument between those who hated the cold more than the smoky air, and those lucky few who seemed to be perpetually warm, even in winter.

Lucia was clever enough to avoid taking sides; she simply kept her head down and completed her work as best she could, without complaint. Well, she would complain long and loud to Sennianus whenever they were alone, but the girl liked to just watch and listen to her elders, mentally noting their traits, for entertainment as much as for future reference.

Publius Licinius Castus and his wife departed with the close of summer, even before the leaves had started to turn brown on the beech trees that grew along the road. Lucia overheard Paltucca telling Antonia he wasn't returning to his legion who were now stationed in northern Gaul; instead the tribune was to spend winter in the warmer climes of Rome. Castus's absence meant even his living quarters – one of the only parts of the house to have underfloor heating – were often as chilly as the rest of the villa. In fact, Lucia suspected the cosiest part of the entire grounds was the grain store, which had a miniature hypocaust system of its own, with a small furnace fed by Regalis to make sure the precious seeds didn't grow damp and begin to germinate or spoil.

What a world they lived in, where people froze and grain was kept cosy and warm!

The days were short and bleak, their routine only – broken when one of the neighbouring noblemen visited to take advantage of Castus's bath-house. The master was happy allowing others to use his facilities, as they paid for the privilege, and the regular heat from the hypocaust fires kept the damp from setting into the stone walls. On such days, Paltucca would select a handful of slaves to prepare the baths, wait on the visitors, and finally to clean up after them. It was a task most frowned upon in the summer, but, in the chill of December, Lucia was happy to spend a day in the lovely warm environment if given the chance.

Most of the time, though, life in the villa during winter was dreary and boring.

Until the festival of Saturnalia.

Around the middle of December, when the days were at their shortest and the balmy days of summer were a distant memory, Saturnalia was celebrated all across the Roman empire, bringing fun and laughter and more than a little madness to the lives of everyone, from the lowest slave to the emperor, Marcus Aurelius himself.

Traditionally, roles were reversed, as master became slave for a short period, and Lucia wished Castus had been home during this period, just to see if he would join in with the spirit of the festival. She had a feeling he would; the master had a sense of fun. The manageress, on the other hand, was a different matter.

"Where's Paltucca? I haven't seen her since this afternoon, before the feast started."

Regalis looked around at Lucia and grinned. "She *hates* Saturnalia," the furnace-master said, a gleeful expression on his face that wasn't simply from the extra wine the slaves had been given that night. "Every year it's the same, do you not remember last time? No? I suppose not, you're just a lass, your memory won't stretch to things like that, will it?" He chewed another morsel of meat and handed some of it to his wife to try before turning back to Lucia. "Paltucca locks herself away in her chamber throughout the festival, going over the finances and such. It's just an excuse to avoid having to serve the rest of us. At least old Tiro gets into the spirit."

Regalis raised his cup as if he were a nobleman, and Castus's secretary here in the villa, the freedman Tiro, hurried across from the corner of the room with an amphora from which he tipped wine, refilling the outstretched empty cup. Tiro, the highest-ranked member of the household in the master's absence, acted every year as the king of Saturnalia.

"Begone now, you old goat!" Regalis shouted as his cup overflowed, laughing and adding an even coarser epithet to his description of the secretary as the man bustled away.

"This is what Saturnalia is all about," the furnace-master said happily. "Abusing your betters and getting drunk and fat on the nicest food we taste all year."

Lucia nodded, returning his grin and watching Tiro move around the room at the slaves' beck and call, refilling cups or fetching platters of food as directed. The secretary seemed happy enough to do it, although the slaves didn't abuse him too badly – they all rather liked the man who was quite polite to everyone.

Unlike Paltucca, Lucia mused grimly.

The slaves would take advantage of the manageress if she were here tonight at this meal. Not just advantage – revenge. The more drink was consumed, the more any simmering dislike people held for her would bubble to the surface and who knew what might happen then? The girl burst out laughing at the mental image of Regalis riding Paltucca's back as if she was a horse.

That could well happen – indeed, she was quite sure poor Tiro would be subjected to something similar later on – but Paltucca would suffer surreptitious kicks and slaps in such a situation whereas the well-liked secretary would be patted gently and thanked for the ride.

Arguments would inevitably break out, for Paltucca would find it impossible to allow her minions to abuse her like that and, well, Lucia knew drunk folk didn't behave rationally in an argument.

It was best for everyone if the cruel manageress stayed out of the way for the next few evenings.

The slave-girl felt a pat on her arm and she turned to look at Sennianus who had the seat on her right.

"I got this for you," the boy said, somewhat shyly, holding out a small bundle wrapped untidily in paper.

"Oh, thank you Senni," she said, taking the parcel and unwrapping it. She beamed as the paper fell away to reveal a plain brooch, much the same as the one she already used to fasten her tunic across her shoulder. "I love it! Where did you get such a beautiful piece of jewellery?"

The boy's face split in a relieved grin at her words and he shrugged as if he always handed out expensive gifts to people. "I was sent with Felix to Durobrivae last month for supplies – nails and things, remember? Well, I saw that on one of the market stalls there. I knew the clasp on your old brooch was starting to come loose so…" He shrugged. "I hope you like it."

She threw her arms around him and hugged him tightly. "I do," she said, and meant it. The plain pewter piece was nothing compared to the gold, gem-encrusted items Dianna wore every day, never mind the exquisite jewellery the *domina* kept locked away for special occasions, but, to Lucia, Sennianus's gift was beyond compare. She wasn't sure if anyone had ever given her a present before.

"You must have saved up for a long time to be able to afford it," she said, taking off her broken old brooch and pinning the new one in place.

The boy shrugged again. "Not really," he replied but Lucia knew how much a brooch like this cost, and she knew how much Sennianus was paid, as it was the same as her. The piece, simple as it was, represented a month's pay to the boy.

Knowing that made her feel rather guilty as she brought forth her gift for him: a box of fishing hooks which she'd got from, coincidentally, Felix, the native handyman who performed many jobs about the villa. It wasn't wrapped, and Lucia flushed in embarrassment at how poor it looked in comparison to what Sennianus had given her, but his face broke into a smile as he took the box and peered inside.

"Just what I've been needing," he laughed. "Thank you very much. The bream will be quaking with fear in the Nene when they hear I've got new hooks for my fishing pole."

They looked at one another, a little drunk from the wine they'd been given, oblivious to everything around them, neither one noticing Regalis nudging his wife and nodding in their direction with a knowing smile.

Something hit Lucia on the side of the face, breaking the spell, and she cried out, putting a hand to her cheek and feeling the wetness on her fingertips.

Pickled fruit.

"You!" she jumped to her feet, outraged, but then laughed just like everyone else as she saw pretty, blonde-haired Popillia, grinning back from the other side of the table.

Another handful of berries flew through the air then, this time hitting Antonia in the forehead and suddenly the whole room descended into chaos as the inebriated slaves launched whatever came to hand about the place. Pickled eggs, chunks of bread, slices of cheese and fish, even a half-eaten leg of chicken whipped past Lucia who threw her own food as enthusiastically as any of the gathering.

"Enough!" a powerful voice filled the air although food continued to be thrown about until, again the voice thundered in the room like a ballista on a battlefield. Lucia looked to her left and saw Regalis with his hands raised, a frown on his face. "That's enough now. We'll need to clean all this mess up ourselves in the morning you know."

Lucia let out a sigh, knowing he spoke the truth, but then she spotted the freedman, Tiro, walking up behind Regalis with a bucket.

"Come on now," the furnace-master growled, sitting back down. "We've had our fun, let's just—"

His words were cut off as old Tiro, apparently fed-up with being the butt of everyone else's joke, raised the pail and upended it over

Regalis's head. It wasn't clean drinking water in there either, Lucia could tell from the stench.

Tiro stretched back, roaring with mirth, as did everyone else in the room, even Antonia.

Lucia, almost unable to breathe she was laughing so hard, looked at Sennianus. The boy was even more intoxicated than her from the wine and the fun, and she saw him lift the first thing that came to hand and throw it, grinning the whole time, at the freedman.

This was no piece of pickled blackberry though – it was a hard-boiled hen's egg, a rare delicacy at this time of year, and it hit Tiro in the face, bouncing off to land on the hard floor where it split apart in a damp white mess.

Sennianus's laughter trailed off as the secretary bent over, clutching his eye, and Lucia stared in horror, wondering if the boy's too-well-aimed missile had seriously injured the freedman.

Whether he had or not seemed of little account to the drunken revellers though, who broke into another fit of laughter at what had just happened. Regalis with his face and shoulders dripping and stinking, food plastered all over the walls and floor, and unlucky Tiro, still holding his eye and shouting, "Ow, you little bastard, you could have blinded me!"

To Lucia's great relief, Tiro was smiling again. She knew the freedman had drunk as much as any of the other slaves and the wine no doubt dulled the pain from the egg striking him. She gasped in relief and realised she'd been holding her breath.

Imagine if it had been Paltucca struck in the face by a slave's rogue missile! It didn't bear thinking about.

Still, Sennianus was clearly mortified and he ran around the table, face a mask of anguish, and grasped Tiro's hand, apologising profusely for what he'd done. The secretary smiled benevolently and ruffled the boy's hair, reassuring him it was alright, no real harm done, and Lucia bent her head to the table, feeling the effects of the unaccustomed wine she'd drank that night. She didn't enjoy this feeling, the loss of self-control that everyone about her seemed to revel in.

It was time to go to bed.

Sennianus returned to his seat beside her, an expression of relief plain on his handsome young face.

"You're lucky Tiro didn't thrash you for that," Lucia said reproachfully.

The boy nodded, a sheepish smile on his lips.

"I know. I told him I'd make it up to him," he replied. "It really was an accident you know? I like Tiro more than most of the people in the villa. I didn't mean to actually hit him, I was just playing like everyone else." His voice trailed off and Lucia noticed a change in his expression.

"Are you alright?"

"No," he shook his head, staring wide-eyed at the table as if it was moving around before him.

Suddenly he pushed himself back and vomited all down himself. It was over in an instant, but, when he finished, he fell to his knees beneath the table, retching and choking as the final remnants of his stomach tried to come up.

The boy's sickness didn't bring a rush of people to his aid – instead it brought more laughter and many of the other slaves crowded around the kneeling boy in a half-circle, jeering at him. Lucia rolled her eyes in exasperation, knowing their humour would be short lived – most of them would join the lad soon enough in spewing out their guts.

She looked up, noticing movement from the corner of her eye, and jumped back instinctively as Tiro, another bucket of stinking, soiled water from who-knew-where in his hands, walked across somewhat unsteadily and emptied it across Sennianus's back.

The laughter was almost deafening.

It was all too much for Lucia. She filled a cup with clean water, drank it down, and ascended the rickety wooden steps to the sleeping quarters in the eaves over the kitchen. She lay there listening to the fun below for a long time, half expecting some drunken idiot – Sennianus probably – to come up and drop one of those putrid buckets all over her, but no-one did and, at last, despite the noise, she began to drift off into sleep.

It had been a good night, and a fitting end to Saturnalia. She looked forward now to the first snowdrops appearing in the hard soil, heralding the return of spring.

* * *

When Lucia awoke the next morning, even before Paltucca rang the bell, she recalled the previous night's events. The snoring of her few companions in the beds amongst the eaves was impossible to ignore and she knew hangovers would lead to a marked drop in the villa's work rate that day.

Throwing off her blanket, she stood up and pulled on her clothes and shoes, the small fire that still smouldered in the hearth below providing just enough light to see around the room.

She shared these quarters with five other women and their faces now were an amusing sight for Lucia, who crept from one sleeping figure to the next, grinning at the slack-jawed, gaping mouths and bare limbs lying at strange angles, their owners too drunk to feel the cold. Two of the women lay enfolded in one another's arms, like lovers, and Lucia wondered if that's what they were.

She shivered, a draught bringing goose-pimples to her arms, and decided to go downstairs and begin the day's chores. Before she went, she covered up her companions' bare arms and legs with their blankets, feeling like a mother tending to her children, and vowing never to let wine addle her brain the way it had the revellers last night.

She brought the dormant fire back to life with the poker then took a dish of butter and one of yesterday's loaves from the larder which adjoined the kitchen and carried them back. The butter was cold and rock hard and impossible to spread, so she set it next to the hearth to allow it to melt a little and began cutting the loaf into slices. The women would feel sickly when they awoke, the girl knew, but they'd need something to soak up the wine in their bellies before tackling the day's chores. They might not thank her for a slice of bread and butter at the time, but would be grateful later on.

"Who's that down there?" someone groaned from above.

"Me," Lucia replied, continuing to prepare the simple breakfast.

"Oh, good," the voice said, and Lucia recognised it as belonging to Popillia. "Could you bring me a drink of water? I don't feel very well."

"Anything else, *domina*?" the young girl retorted.

"No, just water would be good," Popillia muttered, apparently unaware of the girl's sarcastic use of the title reserved for their Roman mistress.

Before Lucia even had a chance to fill the cup, the kitchen door was thrown open and Paltucca, looking as fresh as always thanks to her nights of sobriety while everyone else revelled, strode into the room, ever-present frown on her long face as she climbed just far enough up the wooden steps to see the resting women amongst the rafters.

"All of you useless drunkards get up and come to the vegetable garden. And don't keep me waiting."

"What's happening?" someone whispered, but no-one had any idea. Lucia had a strange sense of foreboding though – whatever this was about, it was surely nothing pleasant.

Paltucca's words meant there would be no breakfast for anyone after all, and the women hastily rinsed their faces in the basin by the fire before filing out into the corridor, grumbling amongst themselves in low voices and brushing their hair with small hand-combs as they walked to the garden.

Lucia listened surreptitiously to the hushed conversations and was shocked to hear one of the women talking about her liaison with a male slave the previous night. Somehow the pair had circumvented the locked doors that separated the women from the men and, apparently, made love somewhere in the grounds.

The woman, who was only in her twenties despite a heavily lined face and sagging breasts, noticed Lucia listening and lowered her voice even further, while also throwing the girl a dirty look.

The woman was sturdily built, almost a younger version of Paltucca in frame, and would probably be able to absorb a beating well enough, unless it was administered by one of the bigger men. Lucia expected Regalis, biggest of all the slaves, would refuse to dole out such a punishment, but there were other men who were almost as big as the furnace-master and quite willing to take rod in hand and deliver Paltucca's justice with it. Some of the slaves could be sickeningly sadistic when it came to their fellows' punishment and Lucia began to feel sorry for the woman who'd enjoyed her late-night tryst. A beating was no small thing, always ending in tears and cries of agony; a lesson to be learned by all not to break the master's rules.

The vegetable garden was the traditional place for slaves to be punished and it didn't take the party of women long to reach it. Apparently, the blood from any wounds inflicted by rods or wands helped the plants grow and so, like the stinking urine they collected in great barrels to wash clothes, it was a liquid too valuable to be wasted.

And nothing was wasted at Villa Tempestatis.

Of course, at this time of year not much was growing in the garden – only some leeks, cabbages and onions – and as they walked slowly out into the cold morning air, the plants' leaves shimmered with white frost, the sun not yet high enough to burn the mist away. The male slaves of the household were already gathered, Regalis towering grimly above them all, his lips compressed in a thin line.

Lucia noticed Paltucca by the facing wall, and then her mouth opened in a silent gasp of shock.

Sennianus stood beside the towering manageress, dwarfed by her broad frame, his youthful face drawn into a mask of sheer terror.

CHAPTER SEVEN

Lucia was, at first, surprised to see her friend standing there like a frightened dog. That feeling soon passed though, and she was shocked to realise she was not only furious, but jealous too.

Sennianus had made love to that older slave-girl? How could he? She'd thought…

What had Lucia thought? She had no real idea, but she knew the thought of Senni lying with that old slut made her blood boil. Well, he deserved everything that was coming to him, and so did his saggy-chested partner!

The boy's eyes fixed on her for a moment, silently pleading for help, but her lip curled and she shook her head in disgust. Sennianus looked down at the frosty ground in confusion as the women gathered next to the male slaves who already faced the manageress and her young prisoner.

Paltucca glared at them all, from left to right along the line, disdain evident on her round face as she used her tongue to clean a piece of trapped meat from her teeth.

"At long last, you ladies decided to join us," the manageress growled, and there were low, angry murmurs from the women who'd hurried there as fast as could be reasonably expected. "Good."

Lucia looked along the line at the slave-woman who'd boasted of meeting her lover the night before and was surprised to see relief plainly written all over her seamed face. In fact, as Lucia watched, she saw the woman lean forward and share a surreptitious smile with one of the men.

Of course, Senni hadn't slept with that old hag, the very idea was ludicrous. And, now that she could look on the other female slave impartially Lucia saw she was in fact both young and pretty. Lucia's shame was almost unbearable – she liked to think she was a clever girl, who knew how the world worked and didn't allow her emotions to drive her, but jealousy – a new emotion to her – had clouded her reading of this whole incident.

Paltucca's hard voice brought her back to the present with a jolt.

"You lot have been enjoying Saturnalia, haven't you? Drinking and fornicating and acting like bloody idiots for days on end." There was, predictably, no reply to her tirade and she went on inexorably. "But you took it too far last night, up until all hours, drunk and making the freedman, Tiro, serve you as if he was lowborn scum!"

Lucia eyed Sennianus who stood, downcast and silent, and a thrill of fear ran down her back.

This was about Tiro.

"The freedman enjoys himself as much as any of us—" Regalis growled, but Paltucca angrily waved him to silence.

"The freedman can do as he pleases," she said in a low voice. "But that does not mean you can mistreat him." She turned on Sennianus who shrank away, screwing his face up as if expecting a blow. *"How dare you assault a freedman you little shit?"*

Again, Regalis tried to speak up, to defend the boy, saying the egg striking Tiro had been an accident but Paltucca rounded on him, face red with fury.

"Shut your mouth, furnace-master," the manageress shouted, eyes bulging and Lucia felt her legs grow weak. She couldn't remember ever seeing the woman as angry as this, and she dreaded what was coming. "One more word from you and you'll share the brat's punishment. I am in charge here, not you, despite what you seem to think."

Regalis's wife, Antonia, laid a hand on the big man's arm and hissed a warning at him. It worked – he kept his mouth shut, but the rage in his eyes flared just as brightly as that in Paltucca's and Lucia could see him clenching his fists.

"The secretary has a black eye, you will be pleased to hear."

Sennianus cowered as the woman rounded on him again, poking a finger into his chest.

"I served a master in Rome when I was younger," Paltucca went on, staring fixedly at the terrified boy. "If we so much as coughed when we were serving his dinner he would have us savagely beaten with rods. He once beat one of my friends so badly he shattered the girl's spine."

Lucia was shocked. Not so much at the brutality of the Roman master, but the fact Paltucca had once had friends. What had the manageress been like back then, and what had turned her into the unfeeling mistress she was now?

"The Emperor Hadrian gouged out his own slave's eye as punishment for some minor offence," the woman went on grimly, spreading her hands as if to encompass everyone gathered in the frost coated vegetable garden. "You, me, all of us, are here merely to work and obey our master's rules. If we break those rules we must expect to be punished severely."

Sennianus's skin had turned deathly white and Lucia could see him shivering. Everyone knew what this was leading up to – some of the gathered slaves must have heard this speech, or something very like it, before, and perhaps been on the receiving end of it themselves.

"If the *dominus* was here, I believe he would want to show you how unacceptable it is to strike a freedman. Indeed, I don't think there would be any legal repercussions should he order you maimed or even killed for your impertinence."

Antonia had to pull Regalis back into the line at that threat and Lucia knew from his reaction that this was *not* like any speech Paltucca had delivered before.

The crime of striking Tiro was a severe one, even if the secretary himself had taken it well enough at the time. It would have been quite a different matter had Senni merely hit one of the other slaves – they were nothing compared to a wealthy freedman.

"However," Paltucca continued. "It is my job not only to see the villa runs as it should, but also to protect its assets. Our master would think it wasteful to kill you or punish you so severely you would never be able to carry out your duties properly again."

At this the boy burst into tears, sagging with relief, and Lucia felt a lump in her own throat. She wanted to run to her friend, to hug him and tell him everything was alright. Despite Paltucca's threatening talk, he wasn't going to be maimed after all.

Lucia noticed a figure on the very edge of the crowd. Elaine. The *domina's* handmaiden was watching proceedings with great interest and, when she noticed Lucia staring at her, Elaine's lips curled in a cruel, knowing smile.

"Sosthenes."

The manageress's hard voice brought Lucia's gaze back again, to stare in confusion at the line of male slaves, watching as one of them moved forward and walked to Paltucca's side. Of average height and build, he was unmistakeable thanks to the brand on his face. Sosthenes, like the manageress, had been owned by a different master in the past. He had run away but been recaptured and had the mark of a slave burned into his face to make sure he could never pass as a free man again. Castus must have then bought him although Lucia couldn't think why, as the man was a lazy, unpleasant waster who wasn't well liked by the others in Villa Tempestatis.

He was handed a leather strap.

"Oh, please Sulis, no."

The girl began to sob as Paltucca pulled the tunic roughly from Sennianus's back, leaving him completely naked in the freezing garden. He too started to cry again, as did some of the slave women, but this was life for them. They had all seen worse than this in the past.

As Sosthenes landed the first, stinging lash across the ten-year-old boy's freezing back Lucia dropped her head and cried like she'd not done since her earliest days as a slave here in Britannia.

Lucia didn't see Sennianus all the rest of that day. She carried out her chores in a daze, praying the gods would give her the means one day to take revenge on Paltucca, Sosthenes, Castus and the entire twisted population of Rome who thought treating people like possessions was normal. Even the thought of kindly Tiro angered her, as she suspected he must have complained to the manageress about what Senni had done.

She fed the chickens and pigs in the morning, the task brightening her somewhat, as she derived pleasure from providing sustenance to the animals who couldn't help themselves, caged and penned as they were. Their life wasn't much different to hers, she thought, and it felt good to see their excitement at the meagre food she threw to them. After that she sewed together the toe-ends of a dozen pairs of stockings which Antonia and another woman had made, happy in the knowledge the garments would keep her fellows cosy in the harsh winter.

Finally, in the afternoon, she helped Balbina, the midwife, prepare a meal from some smoked meat and a few of the leeks she collected from the vegetable garden, then sat at the table with the others to eat. They were all there – everyone who'd been present at the beating that morning – except Paltucca who never ate with the other slaves, and poor Sennianus.

Night had drawn in early, as it always did in Britannia, Lucia thought, and it was even colder than usual. The kitchen was a refuge for them all though, with its bright hearth, which always seemed to have a perpetually cooking stew or clear boiling water in the cauldron suspended over it. On this night it offered a welcome heat to the bitterly cold workers.

Sosthenes ate hungrily as Lucia, who had no appetite herself, watched him from beneath lowered brows. He talked animatedly to those next to him, meat juices running down his branded face, and seemed to care nothing for his vicious earlier task.

It seemed insane to Lucia, that a man could beat a child so badly, then eat dinner just a few hours later as if nothing had happened. How could a person behave like that unless they were moon-touched? She would like to take his leather strap and beat *him* with it, until her arm ached and the crimson blood streaked his pale white back as it had Senni's.

Even Regalis appeared to have forgotten the morning's events. He sat with Antonia, laughing and enjoying his food as much as ever. As she watched the slaves around the table act like nothing had changed, something changed inside Lucia.

These people were the closest thing she had to a family now that her parents were dead. Her life was here in this villa, as the possession of a Roman soldier, and yet none of them cared – really *cared* – about one another. It wasn't their fault, nor their choice – circumstances had made them like this.

If everyone felt a murderous rage any time one of their peers was punished there would be another slave revolt and Lucia knew very well how that would end.

There was no point in Regalis, or Popillia, or any of the others dwelling on Sennianus's fate. It was all simply a part of the world they were forced to endure. Something of their humanity – the friendship and love that Lucia had known back home in her village in Germania – had been stripped away from them so they could survive.

The only thing any of them could do was to accept things and move on, like Antonia – who was greedily chewing a piece of meat – must have done when her baby was left to die by the riverside.

The girl felt as if something was shrivelling inside her. Something that would never grow back again. But, watching the slaves eat and drink, she accepted it.

So be it.

If this was the only way to survive then what choice did she have? The only other way out was to kill herself, and she would never do that; not when the desire for revenge burned in her like the flames that fed the hypocaust.

She would accept her life of bondage, and all the things that brought with it, and she would not grieve for miseries suffered or the life that should have been hers.

But not yet. First she had a question, and the sight of these people eating and laughing was irritating her.

"Where is Sennianus?"

Silence fell around the table at the question and all eyes turned towards her. Some of the slaves looked downcast; some, irritated at their meal being disturbed; and, bizarrely to the girl, a few looked as if they were trying not to laugh.

Antonia answered the question and she, at least, looked somewhat upset.

"Paltucca ordered him taken to the basement after his…" and her eyes flashed to Sosthenes as her lip curled, "beating."

Lucia turned her own gaze, cold and blank, on Sosthenes, and nodded slowly. The basement was used for various things, from storing wine and food to acting as a prison for wayward slaves. Sosthenes stared back at her and Regalis spoke up, meaning well no doubt, but his voice was gruff and jarred in the silence.

"He'll be fine, lass, don't worry about him. The basement's the best place for him – it'll keep him out of Paltucca's sight for a while and let him rest and recover. He'll be right as rain in a while and we'll move on, same as we always do."

Lucia turned to him and gritted her teeth.

"'Move on'? That bitch had him—" she jerked her head at Sosthenes, "beat Senni bloody and then lock him away in the pitch-black basement, and we will all just 'move on'? Is there a warm fire down there to chase away the rats and keep Sennianus from freezing to death? Move on you say!"

The furnace-master's expression grew dark and his voice grew harsher, but he kept it level as he replied. "Aye, we do move on, Lucia, because that's the only thing for it, and complaining will just lead to worse trouble for all of us." There were nods of agreement around the table at those words of wisdom. "Besides, the idiot boy *did* give the freedman a black eye. By Jupiter, Paltucca spoke the truth when she said other masters would have seen him maimed or killed for that. He was lucky to get off with just a beating."

Lucia's eyes blazed and she jumped up.

"Lucky? Lucky to get off with being lashed to bloody strips by that animal? What Senni did was an *accident*!"

Regalis glared back at her and shrugged. "The boy was drunk—"

"On wine you all gave him!"

She noticed Sosthenes grinning and rounded on him, ready to curse him in the name of Freyja and Sulis and Jupiter and Minerva and whatever other gods or goddesses she could think of, but Regalis, tired of the argument, threw back his chair and rose to his full, imposing, height.

"This is the way of it, girl!" he roared, his great voice absolutely deafening in the kitchen, and everyone in the room cowered at its ferocious power, including Lucia, who felt tears filling her eyes. "Besides," he went on in a quieter voice, "I didn't notice you standing up for the boy when he was being lashed. Where was your tongue then? Or do you expect the rest of us to do all your talking for you; and suffer the punishment too?"

Antonia pulled her husband back into his seat and ordered him to hold his peace, but it was too late.

Lucia stared at Regalis, the one man she had thought a kind, gentle friend in this hellish place, her top lip trembling, and then she turned and ran up the creaking wooden stairs to her bed in the rafters overhead. She lay there, smoke and steam from the evening meal swirling around her, even its wonderful smells not enough to cheer her, sobbing again as if her heart would break.

She knew, in fact, that it already had.

She pictured Sennianus in the basement, with no windows and no candle or rushlight to chase away the darkness, his back a bloody, agonised mess, frightened and hungry and lonely, and she sobbed until there were no more tears left to shed. Below, the rest of the slaves continued their meal, surely glad that her brooding influence was gone.

One day she vowed to make Sosthenes, and, especially, Paltucca regret this day.

By the gods, that evil bitch would *pay, and so would the 'master' for bringing them here!*

CHAPTER EIGHT

Sennianus wasn't allowed out of the basement prison the next day either and Lucia wondered how he would be when he reappeared. Would he be changed forever as a result of the experience? Would she, if she were left in that damp, dark hellhole with its scurrying rats and insects?

Undoubtedly – she was a changed person already after this whole nightmare, and she hadn't even been the one to suffer punishment.

Balbina sat next to her at the morning meal, before they started their chores, and smiled.

"Cheer up, girl. Senni is alright."

Lucia's eyes flashed up from the bowl of porridge she was stirring rather than eating.

"You've seen him?"

"Aye," the midwife nodded, spooning food into her mouth with relish. "Paltucca gave me the task of tending his wounds and making sure he wouldn't die after his beating. I'm just back from taking him some bread and water."

Porridge forgotten now, Lucia grasped Balbina's arm, halting the laden spoon on its way to the older woman's open mouth.

"How is he?"

The midwife shrugged sadly and turned her kindly gaze on the girl. "He's in a lot of pain, even with the salve I applied to the welts on his back. But he seemed well enough, and he finished off the food I took him so there's nothing wrong with his appetite."

Lucia sighed and let go of Balbina's arm, allowing the woman to resume eating, which she did with gusto, but when she finished the porridge the midwife took hold of Lucia's hands and stared into her eyes.

"You're a good girl," she said with a half-smile. "A good worker too, as is Sennianus, so this has come as a shock to you. But you'll need to get used to Paltucca's beatings, because you'll see a lot more of them before you – gods willing – can buy your freedom and, perhaps, head back to Germania before your…twentieth birthday."

Lucia's head dropped and she looked at the table without really seeing it. Ten more years of this? If she was lucky, and Castus actually allowed her to go home. Tiro had never left the villa even when he'd been freed – part of the conditions of his freedom was that he must remain in Castus's service for another few years although Lucia didn't know exactly how long.

The secretary was, legally, a free man, not a slave any longer, but he still couldn't go where he liked. Admittedly, that didn't seem to bother Tiro, who was quite happy living in the villa, going about his daily work and, undoubtedly, saving his wages. Lucia had heard the other slaves talking about Tiro's gathered wealth which was, apparently, considerable.

Lucia's idea of being free was quite different to the bald secretary's, although, as she thought about the reality of it, how could she return to Germania? Her whole tribe, not just her parents, had been wiped out by the imperial army. She was sure of that; it was how the Romans worked.

"He isn't fit for work today," Balbina was saying, breaking Lucia's maudlin reverie. "So it's probably a blessing he's to spend another day and night in the basement. Someone, maybe me – although I don't know for sure – will take him more food later and make sure his wounds are cleaned and tended to. By this time tomorrow he'll be better able to resume his usual tasks, and he'll be stronger for it too, you'll see."

"I saw that cow Elaine smiling as Senni was being lashed bloody," Lucia muttered. "She's got a vicious streak in her that one, it's not the first time I've noticed it. I'm glad the *domina* keeps her out of our way most of the time."

Balbina nodded pragmatically. "Aye, not everyone is as nice as you or me, but we all have to live together as best we can. Forget about Elaine. And forget what happened yesterday too, you'll be happier for it."

Lucia eyed the midwife cynically but Balbina didn't seem to notice, instead shoving the girl's uneaten and now-cold porridge back in front of her and exhorting her to eat.

"You'll need your strength, lass. Don't want to be too weak to do your duties and get on the wrong side of Paltucca yourself, do you?"

Lucia couldn't help a bitter sneer twisting her mouth but she relented, taking the proffered bowl and forcing the thick, almost paste-like porridge down. It wasn't the nicest meal the slaves were given but it was nourishing and filled their bellies, which was more than many in the empire got.

"Good girl," Balbina smiled, pushing her stool back and getting to her feet. "Don't worry about your friend – he'll be fine. And," she leaned back down, a serious expression on her face now, "don't judge Paltucca too harshly. We're all moulded by the things that happen to us in life. She just wants to see the villa run as well as it can and, sometimes, punishments are required to keep everyone in line."

The jovial midwife strode from the kitchen, leaving Lucia frowning in surprise.

* * *

"Senni!"

Balbina's prophecy proved correct, and, the next morning, Sennianus was back at work. Lucia saw him when she was making her way to the well for water and she almost dropped the bucket she was carrying in her relief at seeing the boy on his feet again.

She ran to him and threw her arms around his shoulders, grinning wildly, bucket clattering off her left arm as she embraced him.

"Ow!" The strangled cry of pain suddenly reminded her of Sennianus's injured back and she pushed herself away, mortified.

"I'm sorry, I forgot…"

The boy lowered himself down onto his haunches, eyes closed, teeth gritted, hugging himself as tears streamed down his cheeks.

"I'm so sorry," Lucia repeated, her own eyes filling up as she looked on, horrified at the agony she'd caused by her thoughtlessness.

"It's fine," Sennianus replied in a cracked voice, but he glanced up at her and managed a half-smile. "I'm still a little tender, but I'm happy to see you too."

He looked at the ground again for a long moment before wiping his face and getting back to his feet with a determined grimace.

"Was it very bad down there?" she asked softly, pointing at the hard, frosty ground of the courtyard. "Were you frightened? I would have been. I prayed Sulis would keep you safe."

The boy nodded, a haunted look in his eyes and he seemed lost in a daydream, staring into the middle-distance before shuddering and answering her questions in a near-whisper.

"Yes, it was horrible. My back was agony even after Balbina came and put her salve – which stank by the way – on the wounds the whip had made. But the worst was the cold. That was even worse than the dark." He looked at her then, and she could tell he wasn't exaggerating the horror of his ordeal. "I thought I'd die from the cold, even with the blankets Balbina had brought me. It was freezing down there, like I've never felt before in my whole life."

They stood for a time, lost in their thoughts, breaths misting in the winter air, before a shout from the door in the east wing brought Lucia back to her senses. It was the cook, Livinia, and she wasn't pleased.

"Where's that damn water? I can't start the evening meal without it, girl. Hurry up in the name of Dis!"

"I have to go," Lucia said, wide-eyed, and she hurried towards the well.

"I'll help you," Sennianus volunteered, following her like a puppy. "Hauling a bit of water up the well shouldn't be too hard, even with a sore back."

They found the empty bucket and Lucia lowered it down as fast as she could without dropping it. The slaves knew better than to simply throw the thing down as it could hit the walls and break or snap the rope. A damaged bucket meant trouble from Paltucca and a delay as it was mended, so she was always mindful to lower it carefully.

"What's that?" she said, surprised as there was a thump that echoed back up the stone walls of the well and the rope she was feeding out went instantly slack.

Sennianus peered down into the blackness and Lucia followed suit but, in the gloomy morning it was too dark to make out what had happened.

"Bring it up and swing it around to the other side," the boy said. "Maybe it's got stuck on a rough piece of cement in the wall."

Lucia did as he suggested, even walking around to the other side of the well before lowering the bucket again. It made no difference; they could hear the thump as before and, again, the rope she held went slack. It was as if the bucket was hitting some barrier before the water.

"It must be frozen," the girl said in wonder. "I've never known the well to freeze over before. It must be colder than I thought!" The idea made her shiver and she pulled her thick winter tunic about her shoulders, still looking down, trying to see what was happening at the bottom of the well.

"What should we do?" Sennianus asked, looking around for one of the older slaves to help them.

Lucia shrugged. "The ice can't be that thick surely." She pulled on the rope, drawing the bucket back up the well a few feet, and then dropped it quickly, hoping the momentum would be enough to break a hole in the ice.

The result was the same as before; the bucket landed with a thud that echoed back up to them and Lucia cursed. She'd hoped for an easy day now that her playmate was restored to her but apparently it wasn't to be.

"Hey, Dentatus," the girl called, noticing one of the older slaves at work nearby, planting seeds for the spring crop. The man looked up, a dull look on his face that betrayed his lack of intelligence, and she gestured him across.

"What is it?" he demanded suspiciously, glaring at the two youngsters by the well, perhaps fearing they wanted to laugh at him. His teeth were terrible, hence the rather ironic name of Dentatus that he'd been saddled with.

"The water is frozen in the well," Lucia said, smiling at the older slave disarmingly. "I've never seen it like that before – what should we do?"

The man peered over, into the depths, just as the two children had done and with as much insight.

"Dunno," he grunted, clearly not interested. He had his own chores to take care of without worrying about someone else's. "Call Paltucca. She'll deal with it."

"Idiot," Sennianus growled, shaking his head dismissively and Lucia had to stifle a giggle.

"Who are you calling an idiot you little bastard?" Dentatus shouted, arm snaking out faster than Lucia would have thought possible, his dirty hand catching Sennianus on the back of the head.

The boy bent over, grimacing as the movement tightened the welts on his back, and Dentatus sneered before turning away and heading back to his own work.

"Tell Paltucca about the well," he repeated over his shoulder and Lucia sighed.

There was nothing else for it. Or was there...?

"This is silly," she muttered, walking away towards the road just outside the walls. "It's just a bit of ice, it can't be that thick." She stared at the frosty ground, eyes scanning from side to side as Sennianus watched curiously, and then she gave a small cry of triumph.

"This will do it." Her hand closed around a large rock and she headed back towards the well, an expectant grin on her face. "Ready?"

Sennianus's face split in a smile almost as wide as Lucia's and she dropped the rock. They looked down into the inky blackness, waiting for the splash as the stone broke through the ice, freeing the water to be collected, as usual, by the bucket.

There was no splash, though, just a thump reminiscent of the sound the bucket had made when it hit the bottom.

The ice was obviously much thicker than Lucia had suspected.

She cursed, knowing there was nothing left to do but call Paltucca for help. To further dampen Lucia's mood, Livinia's angry, flushed face appeared at the door behind them and, again, the woman demanded to know where her cooking water was, why it was taking so long, and how Lucia would suffer a thrashing if she didn't hurry up.

Just then Paltucca herself appeared and Lucia breathed out slowly, bracing herself.

"What's happening out here?" the manageress demanded, powerful legs eating up the ground between them until she stood, glaring down at them, hands on hips. "Why are you two idiots standing around? Have you no work to do, 'cause if you don't, I'll find—"

"The well has frozen over," Lucia broke in, shivering with more than just the bitter cold. It took an effort not to shrink away as she half-expected a similar blow to the back of the head as Dentatus had given Sennianus.

Paltucca shook her head irritably but, to the slave-girl's surprise, didn't appear overly surprised.

"So get a couple of buckets and collect some water from the river. You pair really are idiots, aren't you? Can you not think for yourself? Were you just going to stand around here, gaping all day? Hoping the sun would come up and melt the ice?"

Lucia knew it was best just to do as they were told and go to find the buckets, but she was curious.

"Has this happened before?" she asked, and instantly regretted it as the manageress gave her such a look of disbelief, as if Lucia was the stupidest person in the world.

"Of course it has," Paltucca shouted. "It happens every year at least once or twice, when the weather changes. Do you not understand how winter works? Get on with you, fool, and, gather that water from the river."

From somewhere in the shadows, Dentatus hooted with laughter at their telling-off and Lucia's face flushed red. To add to her humiliation Livinia appeared once again in the doorway, shouting yet more threats.

Sennianus led the way towards one of the nearby sheds to fetch buckets and Lucia followed his shambling form, head bowed, muttering curses under her breath, wishing she could kill every one of her – their – tormentors.

They found the wooden buckets easily enough and, lifting a pair each, headed back out of the shed towards the river, Lucia leading the way, making sure they wouldn't arrive at the spot she'd found the dead baby what seemed like a lifetime ago.

It had been summer then, and they'd worn short-sleeved tunics with bare legs. Now, they had breeches, thick woollen socks and heavy cloaks – a necessary evil for Sennianus who obviously found the weight of the winter garments painful against the injured skin of his back.

It started to snow as they walked and Lucia began to wish she'd come alone.

"Hurry up, Senni," she grumbled, glancing back over her shoulder as the lad struggled to keep pace.

"I can't go any faster," he said, face twisting with every step. "It hurts too much."

"I'll go on then, and fill these," the girl said, walking back towards him and taking his two buckets from him. Then she hastened her pace and turned to shout back to the boy, guilty at leaving him. "We don't want to be out in this too long in case it gets really heavy. When you catch up I'll have these ready to carry home!"

The snow had indeed come on heavier by now, and it swallowed any reply Sennianus might have made as Lucia strode on, widening the gap between them. She glanced around again and smiled at his determination as he continued to plod steadily after her.

Even after a whipping he was one of the hardest workers in the whole estate. She wondered what he would be like as a man. Tall for sure, and muscular as well, with all the physical labour he would be forced to do. Handsome? Lucia tried to picture him in ten years and giggled as, bizarrely, her mind conjured an image of adult-Sennianus with a perplexed frown on his face.

She looked back, still grinning, and was surprised to see the boy not that far behind. His wounded back must have been agony, yet he pushed on through the steadily falling snow, slipping every so often but ignoring the pain as much as he could. Lucia wasn't sure whether his refusal to give in, to bend at all, was a good trait, or if he was just too insensitive to let things get him down.

It didn't take too long before she reached the river and, finally spotting the well-worn little path, carefully made her way down the frost-hardened bank. The running water wasn't frozen like the well, in fact it was higher and flowed faster than she could ever remember seeing it.

She stepped carefully, knowing a slip could prove fatal. If she fell into the river and soaked herself, the freezing temperature and biting wind would overcome her quickly, and Sennianus would be little use since there was no way he'd be able to carry her back to the warmth of the kitchen, or even run for help.

An image of herself lying on the snowy riverbank – hair and clothes soaking wet, face almost as white as the snow as she stared lifelessly up at the sky – filled her mind, and she pushed it away with effort. Did such thoughts assail everyone at some time, or was it only her?

Leaning down, she placed the first bucket into the rushing, clear torrent, allowing it to fill. Then she pulled it out and did the same with the second. She stood then, grasping the handles of both the wooden receptacles and tried to climb back up the short incline but, laden as she was, she found it impossible. Her feet slipped and, with no free hands to steady herself or look for purchase amongst the clods of frozen grass that flanked the path, she had to put down one of the buckets.

Despite the incredible cold she lifted her hood and wiped sweat from her brow, peering through the snowstorm, trying to see Sennianus. Staring hard, the entire landscape now appearing to be white, she at last picked his limping figure out in the near-distance and nodded with satisfaction. He was still coming.

By the time the boy caught up she had filled all four buckets but, as they took one in each numb hand Lucia had to wonder at Paltucca calling *them* 'idiots'. Why had the manageress sent a ten-year-old skinny girl, and a boy who could hardly walk from the whipping he'd recently suffered, to carry heavy buckets of water all the way from the river?

Regalis could have completed the task in half the time. In the name of Sulis Minerva, even that ugly, toothless whoreson Dentatus would have been better suited to the job than children!

As they struggled, painfully slowly, back towards the villa with their precious cargo, Lucia realised Paltucca was no idiot: she had done this on purpose.

The giant manageress was undoubtedly sitting in a warm room at that moment, probably with a cup of warm wine in one hand and a roast chicken leg in the other, laughing at Lucia's plight.

It was so unfair!

And yet, the girl knew that if she and Sennianus didn't return with all four buckets of water soon they would be punished for their failure.

Even with that knowledge spinning in her angry mind Lucia had to stop – again – to rest. Her biceps burned from the weight of their load, as did her thighs from walking in the ever-deepening snow.

She glanced across at Sennianus, ashamed that her thoughts had only been for her own suffering when she saw the tears of pain and frustration streaking his face.

"Stop," she grunted, setting down her buckets in the snow and arching her back, trying to stretch out a little of the pain there. "This is no use."

Sennianus dropped his own load, regardless of the drops that spilt out onto the frozen ground, and hunched over with a whimper that infuriated Lucia.

Why was that old bitch Paltucca punishing them like this? Hadn't Senni suffered enough? And for what? He was a good slave, he didn't deserve this!

"We're taking too long," she said, nodding towards the great, spreading branches of a nearby tree. "You go and shelter there. I'll run as fast as I can back to the villa with the buckets."

Sennianus stared as if she'd gone mad.

"I'm fit and strong," she said, shooing him away towards the big tree which, although leafless at this time of year, was the only real shelter anywhere nearby. "I'll run back with the buckets one at a time, and I'll get you an extra cloak too."

"You can't do that," the boy sobbed, looking at her in disbelief, the snow whipping into his face so he had to shake his head and wipe the damp flakes away. "You're not strong, or big, enough."

"Even if it takes me all day," she shouted, "it'll be faster than this!"

He opened his mouth to reply but no sound came and Lucia, brows furrowed in surprise, turned her head, following his gaze to see what had silenced him.

Almost hidden by one of the very few bushes that remained green all year round, the slave-girl could see a lean, grey figure, with dark eyes that stared hungrily at them, and, somehow, her spine tingled with a chill that made the whirling snow all around them seem like a warm July day.

A wolf was stalking them.

The girl had never seen a wolf this close before. They could be heard at times, howling in the night, the eerie sound making even the toughest of the men look out into the darkness warily. But she only ever saw them from a distance, as the cattle herders kept them well at bay with hunting bows and spears.

It was huge.

Lucia stared at it, motionless, her mind racing, wondering what she should do. Her instinct was to run, then the thought of being taken down from behind by those great paws sent her eyes scanning the area for the closest tree to climb. Wolves were just big dogs, weren't they? Dogs couldn't climb trees.

Then she remembered Senni. There was no way he could climb the tree he'd been heading for. His whipped back would slow him down and the wolf would be upon him before he'd stumbled more than a few steps, never mind made an attempt to get into the branches above.

Her eyes returned to the wolf again, noting how thin it was. Its ribs could be seen through the grey fur and its face looked sunken and leaner than Lucia thought it should be. It was starving.

The girl was no expert on wolves, but she knew they generally hunted in packs—a new thrill of fear ran through her at that idea and she looked about wildly, expecting to see more of the fell beasts, but there were none in sight. This one must have been separated from its pack for some reason.

Desperation had driven it closer to the villa than it would usually venture.

Lucia knew a desperate animal was the most dangerous kind, but she stood rooted to the hard ground, snow continuing to fall on the silent scene as the three beings pondered their next move.

At last, marking Sennianus as the easiest target, the wolf moved towards him, slowly, head lowered, muzzle moving back ever so slightly into a snarl, and Lucia understood then that her friend was going to die and there was nothing she could do to stop it.

Before she could run away to safety though, guilt crushed her relief and she almost vomited at the maelstrom of emotions assailing her. The great wolf began walking faster, working itself up as it gathered pace, until Lucia knew it would eventually take the petrified boy in a killing frenzy that would make his whipping feel like a pleasant morning's relaxation.

The time for thinking was over.

Lucia started to run, but not back to the villa; instead she ran towards the wolf and Sennianus. The beast was much quicker than her though, even in its emaciated condition, and sure enough its powerful jaws clamped around the boy's leg as he rolled over, trying to make himself into a ball, desperately protecting his head and neck.

A scream of pure agony and terror filled the morning air as the beast drew blood, then came another scream, but Lucia finally reached them and, without thinking, threw the water in the bucket over the wolf's back.

The water was freezing cold and, shocked by the unexpected drenching, the wolf let go of the boy's leg, which Lucia could see was bleeding profusely from a terrible wound. The wolf, knowing the screaming boy was no threat, turned its full attention on the girl, but she hadn't stopped her attack yet.

She brought the wooden bucket down on the animal's sodden back and was rewarded with a yelp of pain. It was no weapon though, being too unwieldy for anything other than that first, surprise blow, and, before she could swing it back up for another strike, the enraged and now frightened wolf lunged forward.

Its front paws crashed into her and they both fell onto the snowy grass, but Lucia grasped the bucket by its sides now, instead of the handle, and used it to fend off the wolf's snapping teeth once, twice, before they caught her by the wrist.

Now it was her turn to scream, as teeth dug into her bones, and, despite her absolute fury at dying like this – in the snow, her life short and meaningless – she couldn't fight off the beast which, unlike her, was used to killing prey.

Sennianus had continued to cry and shout for help, mingling with the wolf's enraged snarls and Lucia's wail of pain, but, suddenly, there was a new sound, and it was right beside them.

Something hit the wolf, and this time it wasn't a bucket wielded by a nine-year-old girl – whatever it was, it sent the animal flying sideways. Lucia looked up to see a face she recognised, then the man disappeared from sight and the spear he held must have hammered home in the wolf's body, for everything went silent apart from the slave's ragged breathing.

"In the name of Jupiter," grunted the man, breathlessly. "You two can't keep out of trouble can you?"

He moved to Lucia first, looking at the wound on her wrist and nodding. "Doesn't look too bad, I must have been just in time – you'll live."

The excitement of the fight hadn't left him yet and he grinned at her, a wild, joyful smile that Lucia thought must accompany every man who wins a battle against a deadly foe. It crinkled the brand on the man's face and Lucia slumped back again on the cold grass, staring up at the sky, exhausted.

"You saved us, Sosthenes. Thank you."

The slave didn't reply but went across to Sennianus who had stopped screaming by now but continued to sob pitifully. Lucia looked at him and saw he was half-delirious with the pain and shock of everything that had happened. He was shivering and babbling like a mad thing.

"Oh, gods, that doesn't look good," Sosthenes said, staring at the boy's mauled leg, the red blood that covered it contrasting shockingly with the clean white snow all around them. "Girl!"

Lucia tore her gaze away from the dead wolf which she'd been eyeing, terrified it might get up and try to eat her again.

"Yes?" she replied in an almost inaudible whisper.

"Don't go to pieces just yet, girl," Sosthenes commanded, and his voice bolstered her, jarring her back to the reality of their situation which was still precarious. Sennianus had to get back to the villa for his wounds to be treated and there could well be more wolves around who would be drawn by the smell of blood and battle-sweat.

"What should we do?" she said, pushing herself back to her feet with a deep breath, trying to calm her frayed nerves.

"I'll have to bind that wound on the boy's leg before he bleeds to death. Run back to the villa and raise the alarm. Get some men down here with spears in case any more of those bastards" – he nodded towards the wolf's corpse – "appear. Have them bring the stretcher and blankets. Oh, wine too, unwatered. All right?"

She didn't reply for a moment, trying to take in his words, and he repeated, "All right?" in a harsh tone.

"All right," she nodded, grasping her wrist which had begun to ache terribly.

"Good lass," Sosthenes smiled encouragingly and Lucia found herself utterly bemused by the whole situation. Hadn't this man whipped poor Sennianus bloody just a few days ago? Yet here he was, their saviour, and doing his very best to care for them.

She shook her head, clearing the confusing thoughts, and made ready to run for the villa as fast as possible. Then another thought struck her and she ran towards the three buckets that were still filled with the water they'd collected from the river.

"I'd better take one of these with me or Paltucca will be mad. She'll be mad we've taken so long to fetch it anyway."

She lifted a bucket with her uninjured hand, some of the precious liquid spilling over the side onto the thick snow and Sosthenes reached out to grasp hold of her cloak before she could take a step.

"Don't be ridiculous, girl," he growled, taking the bucket from her and tossing it aside angrily.

"But the water—"

"Why would anyone need to carry water from the river?" Sosthenes demanded, then gestured all around them with his arms. "The whole villa is surrounded by the damn stuff!"

The girl stared at him for another long moment, the implication of his words sinking in, then she began to run through the snow back to the villa, tears of rage blurring her vision.

BOOK TWO

CHAPTER ONE

Villa Tempestatis, AD 177, Spring

Today was a happy day. A celebration.

Lucia refilled her cup from a jug of wine and took a long drink from it, eyes shining, head spinning a little, feeling truly happy because Martina, after many years in Castus's service, was being freed.

It all started one night in the kitchen, when the slaves were about to eat their evening meal. Paltucca had come in, stern as ever, and walked across to Martina who'd just lifted some bread onto a plate for herself and her five-year-old grandson, Gistin. Her son Halius had been allowed to father the child with Popillia so now three generations of the same family served Publius Licinius Castus here in the villa.

Halius wasn't there that night, as he was still out working in the fields with some of the other men, and Martina held Gistin's small hand nervously as she looked up at Paltucca.

"Come with me," the manageress said flatly. "No, not the boy, just you. The master wants to see you alone."

Castus had begun visiting more often in recent years, after he suffered an injury while on campaign and was invalided out of the army. For some reason he seemed to prefer his quiet villa in Britannia to the bustle of Rome these days, although Lucia knew he was some kind of powerful politician so still had to spend much of his time in the great capital.

Martina's face had gone white when the manageress had come for her, and she felt sorry for Martina as she was led away to her fate. The warm summer day they had hung the drop curtains together all those years ago still came often to Lucia's mind – one of those seemingly unimportant, everyday events that sticks in the memory and resurfaces without bidding to remind one of a pleasant day spent in good company.

There was nothing else for it though, and Martina followed Paltucca out of the silent room. Popillia had fed little Gistin, although most of the adult slaves had little appetite left until, a short time later, Martina returned, alone, face still pale, shock written all over it.

Antonia bustled around the table and helped the silent woman back to the seat beside her son, as everyone tried not to burst with questions.

"Are you all right?" Antonia had asked, softly, gently, placing a brimming cup of wine before Martina who took it with a stunned expression, drained half, and then reached out to cuddle Gistin in her arms. He was still happily eating beside his mother, oblivious to the tense atmosphere in the room.

"The master is setting me free."

Now it was Lucia's turn to be stunned, along with everyone else gathered around the table.

Then Martina's face broke into a huge smile, joyful tears filled her eyes and she stood up, Gistin still in her arms, and spun him around, laughing almost hysterically.

Now, a month after that exciting night, Castus had taken Martina to the magistrate in nearby Durobrivae where the ancient rod ceremony had been performed and the woman legally manumitted. Now they were back at the villa, and slaves and invited noble guests of the *dominus* were enjoying wine, food and music, although there was a clear, if unmarked, separation between the two classes.

It wasn't very often that slaves were freed. Why would they be, after all, when their owners would have to pay to replace them? Furthermore, there were laws in place to stop unscrupulous masters from freeing older slaves and kicking them out into the streets with no way to support themselves. A slave who had never learned a trade would often not even want to be freed, which Lucia understood yet still found ridiculous. If it wasn't for her desire for revenge against those who had wronged her, she would rather be free and penniless than live a life of servitude, however comfortable.

Now and again, however, for a variety of reasons Castus allowed some of his charges to be manumitted. It wasn't without costs, though, as the imperial authorities demanded five per cent of the slave's value as a tax, which usually the slaves paid for themselves, from wages saved over many long years of service.

Lucia found herself in front of Martina now, and they grinned at one another, hugging, careless of the wine that spillt from their cups.

"I am so happy for you," Lucia said. "If anyone deserves this, it's you. And you've always been kind to me in the ten years I've lived here in the villa."

Martina waved the words away with her free hand. "You are an easy girl to be kind to, Lucia. You are smarter than any of us, we all know that, and your shackles weigh heavier on you than most, but you've never let it turn you sour. Unlike some others." she said, glancing over her shoulder fearfully, "Paltucca, for example." Then she laughed loudly, drunkenly. "Why am I worrying that old cow might overhear me? She can't do anything to me now – I'm a freedwoman. Dis take her and her fat face!"

"Where will you go?" Lucia asked, almost shouting to be heard over the happy revellers who were all gathered in the courtyard for the celebration. It was a lovely sunny day.

"You know I'm originally from Britannia," Martina said. "So I know the people and the language and I have a trade to support myself. I'm going to set up a shop in Durobrivae where I'll make and mend clothes and other fabrics. It cost me a lot of money for my freedom, but the master was kind and allowed me to keep enough to equip and rent a vacant plot in the town."

It all seemed perfect – a dream come true for the woman, although her son and grandson would remain Castus's slaves which, to Lucia's mind, rather soured the happiness of the occasion. Yes, it was a wonderful day, and it showed every slave in the villa that the master would reward their years of service fairly but…there was still something inhuman and wrong about this whole society the Romans had created to honour themselves over all other peoples.

Martina was drawn away by someone else wanting to wish her well for the future and Lucia wandered off, the cup in her hand forgotten as the well-known feeling of melancholy began to wash over her.

Martina had implied Lucia never let things get her down, but that wasn't true. Everything that had happened to the girl – eighteen-year-old woman now, in fact – had made her hard inside, even if she did manage to conceal it from the other slaves. Most of them anyway.

"Cheer up," a happy voice said in her ear and she forced herself to smile as Sennianus nudged her playfully, sending her stumbling a little, just as he'd intended.

He had grown tall in the nine years since the starving wolf had attacked them by the river. He was tall and strong in the arms and chest, but he would always walk with a terrible limp thanks to the wounds the beast's teeth had made.

The boy had almost died, yet somehow he survived and, instead of blaming Paltucca or Castus for his injuries, he shrugged them off, continuing through life with a perpetual smile on his face, which sometimes persuaded Lucia that there was something missing in his soul, or in his mind. How could he just accept what had happened to him without hating those responsible?

Or perhaps it was *she* who had something wrong with her, for the lad was certainly more content than she was…

"Come on, let's sit," she said, lowering herself onto one of the stone walls that encircled a flower bed full of daffodils bursting with yellow life. "Take the weight off your leg."

Grimacing as pain shot along his damaged hamstring he joined her, sighing when the discomfort passed, and the smile returned to his handsome face, as inescapable as the rising sun in the morning.

"One day we'll be free too," Sennianus said cheerfully. "Although you must admit, life here isn't too bad."

Once, his unshakeable good humour would have angered Lucia – in the name of Sulis, he'd been beaten and maimed for life by a wolf simply because Paltucca wanted to send them on a fool's errand! Yet he continued to see the good in the situation – Lucia remembered her mother, not her face now, but a saying she had; she would have described Senni as a "cup-half-full kind of person".

Lucia was always the opposite, at least as far as she could recall. Maybe she'd been more optimistic before the Romans had captured her and wiped out her kinsfolk, but it didn't seem likely.

She sighed inwardly, angry at herself now for allowing this maudlin view to take over in the midst of Martina's happy day, and vowed to cheer up.

"What's her problem?" Senni whispered, as Dianna passed them, throwing Lucia a dark look, as did the *domina's* handmaiden, but the other slaves were well used to Elaine's sneers. "The mistress was always quite kind to us when she first came here, remember?"

"Yes, I remember," Lucia agreed. But, like most people who resided in the villa for any length of time, they changed, and not in a good way. She knew why Dianna didn't like her, and it was just another of life's unfair blows which the slave-girl had been forced to endure in the past nine years.

"I can't wait to be free," Sennianus went on with a smile, their grim-faced mistress forgotten. "I might become a cattle-herd. I like cows, they're simple and don't cause any trouble."

Lucia shook her head but his smile was infectious and she felt her mood lifting. His dream was nothing more than that, and probably would remain so forever – why would anyone employ a freedman to look after their cows when a slave could do it much cheaper? But she didn't want to smash his plans so, like every time he mentioned them to her, she nodded and murmured polite agreement.

"What do you think you'll do when you're free?" the young man asked, turning away from the chattering revellers to look at her.

For a long moment Lucia didn't reply, her earlier dark mood once again settling over her. Then she muttered in a hard voice, "I will never be free. Even if Castus decides to let me go, I'll refuse."

Senni's brows knitted together and he looked down at the ground in confusion, as if the stone courtyard might reassure him that he'd heard the girl wrong.

Lucia hadn't misspoken though – she would never leave this villa until she repaid those who had ruined her life: Paltucca and the *dominus*, Publius Licinius Castus.

"Master's coming over," Sennianus whispered, voice taut with respectful fear and Lucia felt a chill run down her back as the spring sunshine was blotted out by the tall, powerful figure of Castus.

"What are you two up to?" he smiled and, to anyone looking on they would have seen a man – a good, fair slave-owner – pleased by his good deed in freeing Martina that day. Lucia looked up at him, and seeing his face flushed with wine, shuddered inwardly.

"Just chatting," Senni replied a little nervously. All the slaves were nervous around Castus; it was the natural order of things for a slave to be at least somewhat frightened by the man who held the power of life and death, or at least a vicious beating, over them. The young man returned the master's smile though. "Thank you for the party, *dominus*," he said. "We are enjoying it very much."

Lucia added her own thanks but turned her eyes to the ground again. When she first met Castus here in the villa nine years earlier he'd been aloof, well-mannered and always in control of himself – the model Roman Tribune. An example to all.

In recent years though, since he'd left the army and its disciplined way of life behind, the master had taken more and more to the age-old vice that ruined so many lives: wine. When he was sober he was the calm, pleasant master of old, but increasingly he allowed himself to become drunk to the point where he was no longer master of his own bladder, never mind anything else. And, like most men in their cups, Castus's personality changed dramatically, and his behaviour became erratic.

Vicious.

And wicked.

"I'm glad you're enjoying yourselves, you've been good servants to me and Dianna over the years." He was drunk even at this early stage of the celebration. "You two will be freed just like Martina one day; you have my word on that."

His wife called on him from somewhere amongst the revellers and, with a final grin, Castus left them as quickly as he'd appeared.

Neither slave said anything for a while as they watched his broad back retreating into the throng. Lucia waited for Sennianus to mumble some platitude about how he wasn't the worst master in the world but, for once, even Senni held his peace, picking at the dry skin on his fingertips thoughtfully.

"Come on," she grunted, trying to look happy as she stood up and patted her friend on the arm. "I don't normally like to drink this stuff but..." She looked across at Martina who was dancing now to a tune some of the slaves had struck up on musical instruments and she couldn't help laughing for the older woman wasn't much of a mover. "It is a great celebration after all."

There was a sudden raising of voices and they turned to the centre of the garden to see what the commotion was.

"It's that lawyer from town," Sennianus grunted, eyeing a slim, dark-haired young man who was as drunk as Castus. "Salvius Pettius."

Lucia watched, taking in the scene and understanding what was going on. The lawyer, who looked to be only in his early twenties, had done something to irritate Castus, and now the tribune was making a fool of the younger man.

"You think you're a fighter, eh? Go on then, hit me. Let's see how tough you are, big mouth."

The lawyer looked nervously around, smiling as if it was all a joke, but he flinched as Castus's hand flicked out and slapped him on the cheek. Flushing, Salvius Pettius jerked back, smile gone, and he winced as Castus feinted at him again, and again, toying with him as drunk guests laughed and jeered.

Lucia had no idea what the lawyer had done to deserve such a humiliation, but she felt little pity for him. Chances were he'd done something horrible to one of the slaves, or been bullying someone lower than himself on the social ladder, rather like the *dominus* was now doing to him. She watched straight faced, like all the slaves, as Castus lunged forward, tripping Salvius Pettius and standing over the lawyer triumphantly.

"Smash his face in!" a man shouted drunkenly, and others joined in, thoroughly enjoying the unexpected entertainment. Lucia had seen those same men talking to the fallen lawyer at the start of the celebration, but wine and a sycophantic desire to be liked by Publius Licinius Castus had turned them into this baying mob.

Castus grinned at the men but he saw Dianna staring disapprovingly at him and shook his head.

"He's not worth it. Are you Salvius Pettius? You're no fighter, you're just a damned lawyer. Away you go, back to Durobrivae and count the money you've fleeced out of honest folk."

With that, the master turned and wandered off, swallowed up by his laughing, adoring friends, and everything went back to normal again.

Lucia watched the beaten, scarlet-faced nobleman push himself to his feet and storm off towards the house, undoubtedly to head home where he could lick his wounds. The slave-girl saw fury in his eyes as he passed and knew Castus had made an enemy for life with his drunken antics that day.

With Salvius Pettius gone everyone danced and sang – and drank – for the rest of the afternoon. Those who were allowed to, that is, since some of the household slaves were required to stay sober and on duty or there'd have been no-one to make dinner or take care of the lucky celebrants.

Lucia, Sennianus and the rest of the slaves ate their evening meal as usual in the kitchen but they were all given extra rations of dried fruit and beef, so it was a real feast in comparison to their usual dour fare. Martina, newly freed, was allowed to enjoy dinner with Castus, Dianna and the magistrate from Durobrivae. The balding old official had been invited by Castus to dine at the villa – accompanied by his own wife – after legalising Martina's manumission, and he'd gladly accepted the chance of a sumptuous free feed.

When the sun dipped beneath the horizon and night drew in Paltucca ordered everyone in the kitchen to stop drinking wine and sober up, threatening them with dire punishments should they not be fit for work the next morning. Even in their drunken state not one of them argued with, or even questioned, the manageress who was by now, Lucia guessed, in her mid-forties. Her authority had never wavered in all these years, despite the odd newcomer to the slaves' ranks trying to stand against her.

They learned quickly though, and their rebellious spirit was soon crushed.

Before she left the room, Paltucca had one last direction.

"Merula. You can follow me."

The girl so addressed stared back at the manageress, her mouth open in surprise. "Me?"

"Is anyone else here called Merula?" the older woman demanded, and Lucia felt terribly sorry for the slave who'd been named after the blackbird on account of her glossy dark hair. She had only been at the villa for a month or so and the master had bestowed the new name upon her when she arrived – it was no wonder the poor girl seemed confused.

"Follow me," Paltucca repeated and strode from the room, expecting – knowing – her command would be obeyed without further delay.

The room was silent now and Regalis shook his head sadly. Some of the slaves were probably wondering if Merula, newcomer as she was, might be about to enjoy the same good fortune as Martina and be given her freedom, but Lucia, like the wise furnace-master, knew better.

Her fears were confirmed an hour later when everyone had retired to bed, the men locked away in their own rooms in the opposite, west wing, Lucia and her usual companions on the mezzanine floor beneath the kitchen roof.

The door was unlocked, none-too-quietly, and soft footsteps could be heard ascending the steps to the sleeping quarters. A candle was held by someone below – Paltucca, Lucia surmised – allowing the shadowy, hesitant, figure of Merula to find her way up to the sleeping pallet she'd been assigned.

When the girl was in bed the light disappeared and the bolt could be heard sliding into place once again outside.

Without waiting, Lucia stood up, wrapped her blanket around her shoulders, and walked across the floor to Merula's bed. She climbed into bed next to the girl and put her arms around her just as the weeping began. They lay in one another's arms for a long time, silent apart from Merula's crying which faded at last from heart-wrenching sobs to soft sniffles. Lucia's eyes were damp but she had shed tears enough of her own over the years and had become somewhat desensitized to things like this.

"He raped me," Merula whispered, almost in disbelief.

"It's over now," Lucia said reassuringly. "He won't come here again tonight, I promise."

Lucia had heard this same scenario played out numerous times over the years; sometimes she was the one doing the comforting, sometimes it was another like Popillia or Balbina. Some of Castus's victims wanted to talk about it, others just wanted to be held in silence.

Merula was one of the former.

"Paltucca took me into one of the guest bedrooms. The master was there." The words came out breathlessly at first, until the gusty sobbing subsided a little. "I was surprised – why wasn't he in his own bedroom with the mistress? Paltucca pushed me towards the bed and left the room. There was food, fancy stuff, and wine, and the master told me eat and drink, but I didn't really want to. I was frightened by him – his face was flushed red and he looked ugly. Like one of the old leches he has as guests."

Lucia wasn't sure if the other women in the chamber were all asleep or simply listening silently, but no-one said a word. The night was silent apart from the eerie cry of a female tawny owl somewhere nearby.

"He told me how pretty I was, and how nice my black hair was. Then he told me to take my clothes off."

As Merula began to recount her ordeal, sobbing again as she relived every vivid, brutal sensation, Lucia held her tightly, and a memory of her own, of a night much like this four years ago, flooded her mind.

It was another party where the master and mistress invited their wealthy friends and acquaintances from the neighbouring farms and villas, and others who lived in Durobrivae, to dine with them.

As always, Lucia was one of the servers – the guests tended to like her as she was quiet, respectful and, fourteen now, grown into a very pretty young woman.

Indeed, she'd been party to the conversation Dianna had with Castus about which slaves should serve that evening. The master and mistress often spoke about Lucia and the others as if they weren't there, or nothing more than a piece of furniture, with no more sentience than an empty amphora.

"Popillia should serve," Dianna had said. "She's very attractive and we only want our most attractive slaves on view. It wouldn't do for Paltucca or, Jupiter forgive, that ugly fool Dentatus to be serving our distinguished guests. We wouldn't want anyone to think we're too poor to afford handsome servants would we? Elaine will be around to attend me of course, and we must have Lucia serving too." The mistress nodded thoughtfully. "She's still a bit young but she's better looking than any of them, other than Popillia, don't you think?"

Castus merely grunted and Dianna carried on.

"Shame about that stupid boy, Sennianus, letting a wolf eat his leg. He's grown into a very handsome young man and would've been something nice for our female diners to admire if it wasn't for that horrendous, dragging limp."

Castus, as he generally did when it came to arranging social occasions like this, simply nodded and made marks on a wax tablet listing who Dianna had chosen for each task. The tablet would be handed to Paltucca afterwards to organise everything.

That was something Lucia thought about a lot; how had Paltucca learned to read? And if the fat old cow could do it, could Lucia? She would find out.

The dinner party followed the same basic outline as all the others Castus had given over the years. The guests would arrive, announced by Paltucca in that booming voice of hers, then they would enjoy drinks as they waited for the other guests to arrive. Once everyone was there they would move into the baths and enjoy the warm waters, a thorough massage, and then into the dining room, refreshed and ready to stuff themselves stupid.

Lucia was there to towel the naked dripping guests as they exited the pools but, rather to her relief, she wasn't any good at giving massages – her fingers didn't have the strength for what, as she realised when Paltucca ordered her to learn, was an extremely demanding job, physically. For a slim fourteen-year-old girl at least.

Her main task that day was to wait on the guests as they enjoyed the typically lavish feast Castus provided for them. She refilled cups with drink depending on the guest – some of the native Britons affected to appear more 'Roman' by taking wine, but others preferred the locally-brewed beer – and she brought many small plates of food around.

Publius Licinius Castus, Tribune of Rome, prided himself on throwing the best, most civilised dinners. His were no debauched orgies, Lucia heard him say, like those of Trimalchio, whoever that was. Whatever he meant, the girl was just glad none of the guests tried to fondle her or even make lewd suggestions – at least, not when the female diners were still present.

There had been many parties like this in Lucia's time at the villa, and, increasingly, as she grew into womanhood, male guests would ask the master about bedding her. He would, just as he'd done at the first dinner she'd served at all those years ago, rebuff any such queries. She was truly thankful to Sulis for such a protective master although, deep down, she suspected that, one day, when she was fully-grown, he would allow one of the guests to use her as well.

The thought made her sick, but it was so far off in the future that she didn't think about it too much.

The mistress also frowned on the suggestion, whenever it was made in her presence. Dianna was, like Castus, generally good to the slaves, especially Lucia. Although she and her husband still only spent a few months of each year living at the villa, it was always welcome when they did appear. Paltucca seemed to become less brutal while the master was in residence, and his visits generally coincided with good weather, as if he were some harbinger of summer beauty.

"More beer, lass!" a man called, and Lucia recognised him as Vibidius, the old lech from years ago. The one who'd wanted to bed her when she was only a little girl. She gritted her teeth, selected an amphora and walked across, eyes downcast, taking in every detail of the Cupid in the floor mosaic, rather than meeting his gaze. He wasn't one of the local noblemen, despite his choice of drink; he was, Lucia remembered, and his accent bore out her memory, from Rome.

He'd travelled a long way to be here and she wondered if he and Castus were related in some way. Maybe they had served in the army together – Lucia knew soldiers formed strong bonds of friendship that would make the miles from Rome to Britannia seem inconsequential when it came to visiting one another.

"By Mithras, this one's grown, eh, Castus?"

The old man – he'd been old nine years ago; now he seemed positively ancient – grasped her arm and held her still as he looked her up and down. He might not have been young, but his eyes were bright and alert and drank in every inch of her. It took everything in her not to wince or pull free from his grasp in disgust, but she saw Dianna watching and knew, with great relief, that nothing would come of the decrepit bastard's advances.

Not back then, and not now.

"This is the same girl who served me before? Years back? Yes? Gods, she was a beauty then and she's just wonderful now!"

Castus said nothing and his expression was unreadable as the old man pulled Lucia closer and cupped her breast in his hand.

"That's enough," Dianna said. "You're frightening the girl." Her voice was light, but her eyes were hard and they bored into Vibidius who sensed he'd gone too far and, muttering regretfully, released the slave-girl.

"My apologies, lady," the drunk old lech said, addressing the mistress of the house before turning to Castus. "I forget you take better care of your slaves than most of our compatriots. I meant no harm."

Lucia stood there, humiliated, not only by what he'd done but also by the fact he'd apologised to everyone except her. She was so far beneath him that he might have abused her and even murdered her without its registering in his geriatric mind.

"I told you back then, Vibidius," Castus growled, face flushed from all the rich food and drink he'd consumed over the past few hours, "that Lucia was off-limits. Don't make me tell you a third time."

The old man's face went pale, but it was Dianna's response to the master's words that Lucia noted. The *domina* sat back in her chair, face an angry mask as she glared at Castus.

It was such an unexpected reaction that Lucia wondered what had provoked it. Did Dianna care so much for Vibidius that she resented Castus upbraiding him – humiliating him – in front of the other diners? Maybe Dianna and the old fellow were lovers…?

Lucia almost shook her head at the ridiculous thought. The mistress had Castus to satisfy her every need after all. What could an old man like Vibidius offer the *domina*?

So why had Dianna looked so furious when Castus warned the old man off Lucia?

It was a question the slave-girl had no answer for. These people were an enigma. They lived in an entirely different world to her, a world where they could treat other human beings however they pleased, and the politics of a situation like this depended not on what the slave felt or wanted, but how the owner decided their 'property' should be used.

For the thousandth time in the past six years, Lucia wanted to break down and cry and rage at life's unfairness. For the thousandth time, she held her emotions buried deep inside and stared stoically out at a table of exotic, expensive food she was expected to replenish but never to taste, other than the leftovers the real people didn't want.

When dinner was over, and the master and his guests had retired to their rooms, Lucia, along with the other female slaves, tidied things away, then climbed up to her sleeping pallet in the rafters above the kitchen and lay down, utterly exhausted. The work of serving at table or in the baths wasn't physically taxing, but maintaining a calm, respectful, rigid exterior for hours at a time was more draining, mentally, than a day in the fields sowing corn or wheat.

Despite her tiredness she found it hard to fall asleep. The thought of that old man touching her kept replaying itself in her head, and the master warning him angrily to keep away...

Then Paltucca came in and called for her to come down, and, together they walked through the corridors with only the manageress's flickering candle to light the way to a bedchamber where Castus waited.

"He was so heavy." Merula's harsh whisper brought Lucia back to the present and she shuddered in remembrance. The raven-haired girl was describing an experience almost identical to the one Lucia had been subjected to as a fourteen-year-old: the master's hot, wine-soaked breath on her face; his hands roughly grasping breasts and thighs and anywhere else he pleased; then the incredible, terrifying weight of his powerful body pressing down as he forced himself inside, oblivious to the terror he was causing.

Oblivious? No, he must have heard her cries of pain and fear – he simply didn't give a damn. Lucia and Merula, and all the other slaves he'd violated over the years, were his possessions – not people, just things to be used however he saw fit.

"Shh, it's all right, sweetheart," Lucia heard herself saying, echoing the words Popillia had said to her four years ago. "It's all right, he won't come back tonight."

No. He was satisfied now – he'd be fast asleep, without a care in the world despite the anguish he'd caused to Merula. He wouldn't come back that night, but Lucia knew he would call on the dark-haired girl again in the future.

Just as he had called on her so many times.

Merula's sobbing had quieted by now and at last, mercifully, she fell asleep. Lucia held her tightly, dreading the next time the girl would be taken by Paltucca to be abused by Castus. For whatever reason, the master had moved on from Lucia to a new bedmate; that seemed to be how he always worked. One girl at a time, the previous favourite forgotten in his desire for new flesh.

And Castus's violations weren't the only thing that Lucia resented: Dianna, the mistress who had previously liked and generally been kind to her, turned against Lucia once Castus started raping her. As if Lucia was in some way responsible for, or at least enjoying, the horrific experience.

She closed her eyes in the darkness and held Merula tighter, wishing the girl wouldn't need to suffer this experience again. But Lucia knew she would, many times.

And a part of her was glad, because it wouldn't be her suffering.

CHAPTER TWO

One morning in the spring the master had to go away to Rome on important business for a while. Lucia wasn't even sure what year it was, but she knew Marcus Aurelius was still the emperor as she'd heard Castus talking about it over the previous night's dinner. He seemed excited by the journey and Lucia guessed, from what he said to Dianna, that he hoped for some kind of recognition from the emperor for years of loyal service.

The girl had no idea what his reward might be, as the words used in the conversation made little sense to her, but he drank even more than usual in celebration and called poor Merula to his chamber that night. Thankfully, the girl had become somewhat hardened to Castus's use of her plump body and didn't come back to bed sobbing as she'd done those first few times.

Lucia was glad of that, for it meant a better night's sleep for everyone, and they were all refreshed and ready to see the master off bright and early.

It had been bright too, with the sun high in a cloudless sky, although an hour after Castus had gone – leaving Dianna behind ostensibly to oversee the running of the house (although Paltucca still took care of almost everything) – a man with an ox-drawn wagon appeared on the road leading to the house.

"A peddler!" one of the girls shouted, peering through the window of the kitchen, where she was washing down the morning's breakfast dishes.

Lucia looked up from the hare she was skinning and smiled at the girl's excitement.

"You always love it when a peddler comes, don't you Arethusa?"

"Of course. Don't you?" Arethusa was the thirteen-year-old daughter of Regalis and Antonia and, even at that age, shared her parents' height and sturdy build. "It's always so nice to see what they bring from the outside world."

Lucia nodded. That was true enough, although Arethusa had never known anything of the world outside Villa Tempestatis. She had been born here and, chances were, would die here too, so it was no wonder the girl got excited about seeing new things. Practically anything was exotic to Arethusa.

For Lucia, the peddlers and their wares were simply reminders that life was continuing for all the free people of the world, without her.

"Come on, let's go and see him. Wash that blood off your hands."

Arethusa's innocent excitement was infectious and Lucia allowed the younger girl to take the half-skinned hare and pull her to the sink to rinse the crimson from her. Most of it anyway – they were in too much of a hurry to do the job properly, so Lucia ended up running along, hand-in-hand with Arethusa, dried blood still caked on her wrists.

"Do you think he'll have a nice comb? I would like a new one – my own has many of the teeth missing. Look." Arethusa touched her wavy brown hair and Lucia nodded although, in truth, she thought it would take more than just a comb to tame the girl's unruly locks.

"Maybe he'll have some new clothes for the mistress," the young girl went on, words tumbling from her like a waterfall after a thunderstorm. "I do like to see all the new fashions, don't you? We might never get to wear anything like that, unless it's handed down from the mistress as a reward, but it's still *so* exciting!"

They hurried through the walkway, out into the morning sunshine and joined the crowd of other slaves already gathered, having seen the peddler's approach just as they had. Arethusa went straight to her mother, who appeared just as giddy as her daughter to see what fancy goods were on the approaching cart.

Regalis even came out from the furnace at the rear of the house, squinting and nodding to himself, muttering about needing a replacement for some tool he used to stoke the fire in the hypocaust.

"Are you going to buy anything from him?" Sennianus asked, limping up to stand next to Lucia.

She shook her head. "No, not really. I have everything I need."

"That's not what I asked," Senni replied. "All of us have everything we *need*, but sometimes it's nice to have things just because we want them. You know, a little bit of luxury."

"Move aside." The hated voice of Paltucca boomed across the courtyard and everyone instinctively parted to let her through. She was preceded by Elaine and the mistress, Dianna, whose eyes glittered almost as much as Arethusa's. Even the *domina* looked forward to visits like this, since life in the villa didn't offer much in the way of novelty, one day being very much like the other.

At last, with much creaking of wheels and snorts from the ox, the cart rolled through the entrance archway and lurched to a stop in the middle of the courtyard. Despite their eagerness to look at the items loaded beneath the tarpaulin, the slaves stayed back, awaiting the peddler's introduction and, of course, allowing the mistress to browse his wares first.

"Good morning, lady," the man said, pulling back the hood that protected his bald head from the sun and bowing low to Dianna, who returned his polite greeting with a smile. "My name is Vassinus, and I have treasures the likes of which you've never seen before, on my wagon."

Lucia stared at the peddler, finding him more interesting than any comb or bauble he might have loaded on his cart. The man was maybe in his early forties, but he didn't have the look of the usual travelling salesmen who visited the villa. He seemed more like an old soldier, a veteran with broad shoulders, muscular arms, and a faded scar down his cheek. The slave-girl thought he must be a native Briton, but his time on the road had tanned his skin brown.

He noticed her perusal and flashed a cheeky smile that brought colour to her cheeks. He was rather handsome too, despite being at least double her age.

Sennianus noticed their shared look and grunted, "Baldy old bastard," which brought a surprised laugh from Lucia.

"What? Are you jealous because he winked at me, Senni?"

The lad didn't reply, just said something under his breath which she couldn't make out.

They had remained good friends over all these years, and on some nights, if discipline was relaxed, they even shared a bed, but Lucia didn't see him as a potential 'husband'. Not like Regalis was to Antonia. She knew Senni wanted more than anything to be her mate, but she wasn't sure if she could ever love someone in that way.

She was happy for the furnace-master and his wife, but the thought of having a child with Senni, only for it to be shackled to this damn villa like the rest of them – like poor Arethusa who would likely never know any other life – made Lucia feel sick.

"Oh, look at that silk!" Arethusa exclaimed, clapping her hands and practically dancing in excitement. The peddler undid the rope holding the tarpaulin over his wagon and lifted it clear, revealing a whole host of wonderful wares, including the roll of material that Antonia's daughter had spotted sticking out. She and her mother shared delighted looks, and Lucia wished she could share in their simple pleasure.

"Don't touch it," Elaine snapped. "Your hands are filthy."

Antonia threw the handmaiden a vicious glare, for the accusation wasn't true, but Vassinus continued setting out his goods without comment.

The mistress looked through the goods on the cart first, as was her right, selected a few trinkets and, with a conciliatory smile towards Arethusa, said she'd take the roll of silk as well, which only made her handmaiden's expression sour even further.

"My manageress, Paltucca, will pay you for the items," Dianna said to the peddler, who bowed and flashed his boyish grin at her. "You may rest here awhile once you finish your business with my slaves. Paltucca will also make sure you have food and wine and, if you wish, you may use our baths for a small fee."

The man's smile grew even wider at Dianna's offer of hospitality. "I would kill for a soak," he replied. "It's been a long time since I enjoyed a proper bath rather than the stinking public ones in Durobrivae or the like."

"No need to kill anyone, Vassinus," the mistress laughed. "A few denarii will suffice." She turned away, flicking her hair as she did so, and ordered Paltucca to take care of everything.

Lucia wondered what was so attractive about the middle-aged, bald peddler that had even the *domina* flirting with him. The slave-girl didn't have much experience with people in general, stuck here in the villa as she was, but it seemed to her that some men – and women – had an inherent charisma about them, which drew others effortlessly towards them.

It was a skill she wished she could develop, for it would surely come in handy.

When Dianna and her handmaiden had left, the slaves crowded around the peddler's wagon like vultures finding a fresh corpse in the desert. Even Lucia was drawn in now, curious, just in case the man did have anything that took her fancy.

Ostensibly, slaves weren't allowed to have possessions of their own, including money, but, in reality, they were paid a wage for their work which acted as an incentive. Even the Romans recognised the fact people enjoyed buying things for themselves, and to take that away from the slaves would lead to major unrest throughout the empire.

The masters didn't want a repeat of the Spartacus debacle, or the Servile Wars of a few centuries earlier, and allowing slaves some freedoms – such as money to spend – was one way of keeping the peace. For who didn't like spending money?

"Ah, you *did* find something you liked then?"

Lucia looked up from the simple bracelet she'd bought and saw Sennianus, one eyebrow raised, smile on his face.

"Yes," she admitted, showing him what she'd got for her denarii. It was little more than a leather thong with little beads – rose quartz and jade the peddler had assured her – but it appealed to her and she held out her arm to him now. "Tie it on for me, will you?"

The crowd had begun to disperse back to their chores now, Paltucca exhorting them to work doubly hard to make up for tarrying at the wagon, and, as Senni finished fastening the bracelet to Lucia's slim wrist they saw the manageress gesture to the peddler to follow her inside.

He winked at Lucia again as he disappeared inside, bringing another muttered curse from Sennianus. The girl herself found the older, free man's attention rather thrilling, but she masked it by turning back to the villa's kitchen and the hares that needed to be prepared for the pot.

"Keep out of that travelling merchant's way," Senni warned. "He's a bad lot."

She couldn't help giggling as she returned indoors, pleased both by the peddler's obvious attraction towards her and her friend's jealousy about it. It felt like her feet hardly touched the ground as she made her way to the kitchen although, as she sat down and faced the half-skinned hare on the table before her a little shiver ran down her back. Sennianus very rarely had a bad word to say about anyone – even Sosthenes had escaped much cursing after the branded slave had beaten him – so for the lad to warn against the peddler, well…maybe Senni saw something she didn't?

Or perhaps it was simply jealousy after all.

Arethusa was nowhere to be seen, presumably called away for some other job. Lucia picked up the hare in the quiet kitchen and began her bloody work once more, picturing the bald man in her mind's eye and wondering what it would feel like to be held in his muscular arms.

"Girl! Get your arse to the baths, now."

Lucia huffed out a long sigh, then hastily shoved the last of her meagre afternoon meal into her mouth. After skinning the hares she'd washed vegetables which Sennianus and Merula had gathered in from the garden, then gone outside to water the flowers, just beginning to wilt after the recent sunny, dry spell.

She'd just sat down with a few of the other slaves in the kitchen to eat a little bread and cheese when Paltucca appeared, silently it seemed – wraith-like – and barked her latest order.

Her mealtime companions, Senni and Merula amongst them, made sorrowful, almost apologetic faces at her as she got up and followed the retreating manageress. She wondered what the manageress needed done at the baths, then remembered the mistress offering their use to the peddler and a thrill of anticipation ran through her.

Would he be there, in the water? Naked but for that charming, arrogant smile? She wouldn't be called upon to give to him a massage, that task would fall to one of the other girls. *Unfortunately*, she thought, grinning wickedly, then composed herself and walked into the atrium of the bath-house.

"Hello, Lucia," said the middle-aged, severe looking woman who sat behind the table where visitors paid to use the facilities.

"Good afternoon, Prima," Lucia replied pleasantly. Although the older woman looked perpetually grumpy she was actually quite nice, and good company too, often making ribald or dark jokes about slaves who'd crossed her in some way. "Am I just here to help clean up?"

"Aye, the usual," Prima nodded. "Just towel off the bathers and make sure their wine cups are kept filled. Good lass."

Lucia nodded then, preparing herself for whatever might greet her within the frigidarium or caldarium, she went inside, only realising Prima had used the plural to describe who was enjoying the baths that day.

Had some other visitor, beside the peddler, come to avail themselves of Villa Tempestatis's refreshing pools on this summer afternoon?

Hoping it wasn't Vibidius, that vile old lech who still hadn't died and insisted on undressing her with his eyes every time he visited, Lucia took up a position against the wall next to the wine cups and amphorae. She was astonished to see the peddler submerged in the warm water of the tepidarium, not with some visiting nobleman, but with the mistress, Dianna.

Only long years of experience kept her face impassive but, as she watched, her astonishment turned to shock and utter disbelief. Then, as reality hit her, so did a fury – a jealous rage the likes of which she'd never known before in all her life. And hatred, such hatred.

For the mistress wasn't merely enjoying the soothing waters of the tepidarium – she was pressed against the wall of the bath, beneath the waters but not enough to disguise what they were doing together. The peddler's arms rippled with muscle, holding himself propped up against the poolside as, below him, the *domina* bobbed up and down in time with the man's movements.

They were fucking!

For the first time – ever, as far as she could remember – Lucia had wanted, truly wanted, a man to make love to her, even if it were only a fantasy. Yet Dianna, who despised her now, had stolen the peddler from her. Was using him for her own pleasure while Lucia was forced to watch. And, when they were done, she would need to dry them both down and bring them cool wine and nice food and whatever else they demanded.

It took only moments before the man grunted like an animal and thrust upwards so hard that Dianna was lifted right out of the water, revealing her small breasts and an almost comical look of surprise on her face. Then he slumped down, apparently not caring whether he crushed his patrician partner beneath his now-sated body.

The peddler stood there for a while, half-submerged, sweat dripping from his toned back, and then he noticed Lucia watching and flashed the same cocky smile he'd bestowed upon her earlier. This time she didn't flush or feel a thrill of pleasure – now she just felt empty.

Another piece of her spirit had been crushed beneath their still-entwined, dripping bodies.

Sulis Minerva, what have I done to deserve this life?

"Is that it?"

The peddler looked a little surprised by the question, pushing himself back into the centre of the water and stretching luxuriously as he gazed, that arrogant half-smile still on his lips, at Dianna. "What d'you mean? Did you not enjoy that? I certainly did, and I haven't had many complaints from women in all my years, I must say."

The mistress looked angry now, and Lucia revelled in it. Dianna was regretting this shameful liaison already. *Good.*

"That's probably because you usually copulate with whores and slaves," the mistress spat, her face hard.

"True." The peddler's grin reappeared, and he dipped his bald head beneath the water, coming up again a moment later at the other end of the pool shaking droplets from him in a cloud. "I've never been with a rich noblewoman before – a tribune of Rome's wife too. It's quite a turn on for a man like me."

Dianna glared at him in disgust which Lucia knew was borne of much more than just sexual dissatisfaction, then the mistress turned to look at her. Lucia had been expecting it, and averted her eyes just in time.

"I'll leave you to enjoy the baths, peddler," Dianna said frostily, heading for the steps that led out of the water, and the slave-girl stepped forward, fresh towel rolled out and held up ready for the *domina* to step into and be dried.

"Thank you, Lucia." The mistress turned back one last time to stare at the peddler who seemed entirely unfazed by everything. "Do not touch the slave-girl, peddler, or I'll see you flogged bloody."

The man looked at Lucia and made a ridiculous, childish face, as if he was crying at Dianna's command. Then the mistress left, calling for her handmaiden to escort her back to her bedchamber, leaving Lucia alone with the peddler.

He relaxed in the water for a time, occasionally looking over at her with that now-hateful smile, apparently unable to read the loathing that emanated from her. Thankfully, before he could make any suggestion that she might join him in the pool, Regalis and Sosthenes walked into the steam-filled room, faces hard, eyes fixed on the peddler.

The mistress must have ordered them to make sure their guest left peacefully, without touching Lucia. Whether that was genuine concern for the slave-girl's wellbeing, or a desire for Lucia not to 'enjoy' the peddler's charms as well was impossible to say.

The peddler laughed at the sight of the two male slaves, his confidence and courage apparently unshakeable. Or perhaps he was just too dense to understand the possible consequences of his actions. If Dianna accused him of raping her Lucia would have to confirm that spurious version of events and the peddler would be punished terribly for his 'crime'. Castus might even have the man beaten to death – the master was a Roman tribune after all, he could do whatever he pleased, essentially.

"Ah well, I suppose I should be on my way," the peddler sighed, as if it pained him greatly to leave their company. "I've had a lovely time here, but my wares won't sell themselves, and a man has to make an honest living."

He stepped out of the water, completely naked, but Lucia had no interest whatsoever in him now. Regalis walked over and took the towel from her, tossing it to Vassinus who caught it and dried himself down before them unashamedly.

"I'll see you again, girl," the peddler said, looking at Lucia with hard eyes, bereft of the earlier playfulness, making the hairs stand up on the back of her neck as he was escorted from the caldarium by Sosthenes and the hulking Regalis. "Soon, I'll wager."

Sennianus had been right about the peddler, Lucia thought with a shiver. She was glad the man was gone but wondered what Dianna would do now that the slave-girl knew her sordid little secret.

If the *domina* hated her before this, and even stupidly feared her influence over Castus, today would surely make things much worse.

CHAPTER THREE

Two days passed but the mistress never called Lucia into her presence. The girl had expected to be quietly warned by Dianna not to say a word to anyone, especially Castus, about her dalliance with the peddler, but the call never came and life went on just as it always had. Perhaps the mistress simply expected the girl to keep her mouth shut, since the consequences of a loose tongue could be swift and brutal for a slave. Deadly even.

Lucia didn't tell anyone, even Sennianus, about what she'd witnessed – not through any misplaced loyalty to the mistress; she simply wanted to keep the secret to herself, suspecting it might come in useful one day, even if that day might be years away. Besides, it was good to know the despised rapist Publius Licinius Castus, glorious Tribune of Rome, had been cuckolded by his own wife.

It was a strange society, that of the Romans. Morally, they saw little wrong in a man sexually abusing his slaves, but a woman taking another lover? That was deeply frowned upon – a shameful act which, so people claimed, almost reduced the husband to the status of a slave himself! Lucia would never understand their twisted culture.

Once again, dawn broke with all the promise of a sunny, hot day, and Paltucca ordered many of the beds to be stripped and the bedding laundered. Lucia didn't like washing days – carrying soiled bedclothes to the laundry room was the easiest part. The women would soak the sheets in a tub of urine, using their feet to work the stale eye-watering liquid into the very fibres, before transferring them to baskets or carts to be rinsed off in the river.

It was an unpleasant job but at least it offered a chance to enjoy some time in the company of the other female slaves, gossiping and joking and fooling around. Lucia enjoyed those things as much as any young woman.

When the sheets had all been thoroughly scrubbed in piss the women headed for the river with their sopping loads. As they worked, clouds covered the summer sun and the temperature dropped a little.

"Think it'll rain?" Popillia asked, slapping a bed sheet down into the river.

Lucia shrugged. "Feels like it might. I'll be glad if it does though, it'll save us a job watering the plants and flowers in the garden."

"Only the ones outside," Popillia replied, slim arms working the sheet around in the water, rinsing off what she could of the urine the laundry had been soaking in. "All the ones under the walkways will still need doing."

"Suppose so," Lucia nodded. "It's not as if Paltucca would give us the day off anyway, whether it rains or not." She threw the sodden tunic she'd been rinsing into a basket. "She always has something for us to do."

"Don't you think you'd be bored if you were the mistress though?" Merula said thoughtfully. "I mean, she just sits around the place reading philosophy treatises and talking to guests. I don't think she even likes most of them."

"Bored?" Popillia burst out in disbelief. "You think it would be boring to live like Dianna?" She shook her head and turned back to beating the sheet beneath the water as if she was fighting off a giant attacking fish. "I'd take her life over mine any day."

"I didn't mean that," Merula mumbled, face flushing, clearly feeling foolish at her statement and its reception. "I just think it would be boring sitting about all day."

"I agree with you," Lucia said supportively, tossing another rinsed tunic into her basket. "If I was Dianna I'd find something to do with my time. Painting, or learning to play a musical instrument or something. Oh, yes, of course the stupid Romans look down on those who perform music, thinking it's beneath them, but they can jump in this river for all I care about their opinions. I'd love to play the lyre."

"You can play the lyre and I'll dance," Popillia grinned, jiggling around in the water which was almost up to her waist.

"We've all seen you dancing for the master's friends," Livinia the cook hooted. "Bits hanging out all over in the hopes of taking the fancy of one who might marry you."

Popillia stuck her tongue out good-naturedly but pointed at Livinia's own heaving bosom. "Bits hanging out? You're a fine one to talk, always flaunting those things whenever a wealthy visitor turns up to use the bath-house."

"Damn right," the cook laughed, pushing up her breasts and winking. "I don't want to be a slave all my days, and these won't stay firm for much longer."

"That's settled then," Lucia agreed with a smile, throwing the last of her wet garments into the basket ready to be hung up to dry. "Once I'm *domina* we'll just play music and dance around all day with our tits hanging out. Until then," she hoisted the basket up and started walking towards the house, "we'd best get this laundry into the drying room. No point in hanging them up outside if it's going to rain."

As she headed towards the villa something – a hint of movement – caught her eye down at the bottom of the hill near the entrance gate and she slowed her pace, trying to make out what it was. The terrible memory of the starving wolf was never far from her mind when she was outside but, whatever it was that she'd spotted, it was gone now.

She would have shrugged if her sopping load wasn't so heavy; it was probably just one of the other workers going about their business.

By the time she reached the drying room – essentially a barn with just an overhanging roof and open walls – Lucia's arms were sore and her throat dry, so without even hanging up the laundry, she walked to the kitchen for a drink of cool water. The room was empty but, through the un-shuttered window, she could see her companions wandering back with their own loads, still chattering and laughing together.

She poured a cup of water from an amphora in the larder and took a long pull, relishing the coolness which seemed to permeate every fibre of her being. A contented sigh escaped from her lips and she wiped sweat from her brow. It might be cloudy out, but it was still warm, and the slaves' physical labours would heat anyone, even in the depths of winter.

The sound of the returning washer-women's laughter carried all across the estate and Lucia couldn't help smiling, particularly at Popillia, whose giggle was utterly infectious, even at this distance.

The summer land all around the villa was glorious in various shades of green, with wild flowers of all colours drawing the eye, grey clouds overhead magnificent and brooding, and her friends an oasis of happiness in the middle of it all.

She was glad Castus was away to Rome and hoped he'd be gone for a long time so Merula – who was grinning with the rest of the approaching women – could enjoy the summer months without being molested for a time. Maybe they should share some of their food rations with her, Lucia mused, fatten the girl up so the master wouldn't find her attractive any more.

It was a silly idea – as if the other women would go hungry. They got little enough as it was, if you believed most of them, although Lucia couldn't complain about what she got to eat. It was enough to keep her fit and strong and that was all she needed.

She half-lifted her water cup to her lips then stopped, momentarily frozen as, again, she noticed movement in the fields where she wouldn't really expect anyone to be. She couldn't see any livestock in that part of the estate, so there would be no need for a sheep or cattle herder. And any of the men out hunting wouldn't be doing so in the open.

Her eye was drawn away to the road and she noticed a man walking towards the villa. When she looked back to the field, the figure or figures she'd thought had been there were gone, and she guessed her imagination was playing tricks on her. Glancing back to the road she saw the man was making good progress and would be there not long after the rest of the slave women came back with their wet laundry.

She rinsed her cup and put it back with the others before going into the drying room and hanging up her basket of wet sheets. It was a difficult task since the material was heavy with water but she was an expert by now and had everything neat and tidy by the time Popillia led the others in with their own laden baskets.

"I'm dying of thirst," Merula groaned. "The sun might have disappeared but it's so clammy out there."

"You finish your laundry," Lucia said kindly, touching the younger woman on the arm, "and I'll fetch you a cup of water. I know how you feel – it's terribly muggy today, might even be a thunderstorm later to clear the air. Does anyone else want a drink?"

"I'll take a mug of wine," Livinia grunted, muscles straining in her arms as she lifted a sodden blanket onto one of the thick drying ropes. "Not the cheap stuff mind – some of the Falernian from the master's own stocks."

"Ha!" Lucia waved over her shoulder at the cook and headed for the kitchen. "No problem. I'll even have Paltucca serve it to you in a silver cup while the *domina* feeds you grapes."

"Cheeky bitch," Livinia retorted loudly. "I'll just have some water then!"

Lucia was still smiling at the exchange as she reached the kitchen and found two cups. As she passed the window on her way to fill them she looked out at the road, wondering if the man she'd seen approaching was much nearer by now; he should be, unless it was a very old man, and his gait hadn't suggested that at all.

"Oh shit. What in Hades is *he* doing here again?"

A thrill of nervous disbelief ran through her and she stared out at the man who'd almost reached the house by now.

It was the peddler.

Merula and Livinia's refreshments were forgotten for the time being as she watched the visitor's long stride cover the ground between them. He moved confidently but without undue haste, as if taking a leisurely stroll to a friend's house, and today he hadn't brought his wagon of goods with him, suggesting he had business other than trading to attend to.

Lucia's first thought was that Dianna had invited him back, to continue their pleasures of a few days before. The mistress had been unsatisfied with Vassinus's selfish love-making after all – perhaps she now wanted him to properly finish what he'd started?

The slave-girl rejected the thought almost instantly. She might not know how the mistress, or any Roman noblewoman, thought, but it had been obvious how angry Dianna was when she'd left the peddler in the caldarium.

Another thought struck Lucia then: Regalis and Sosthenes had escorted the out-of-favour peddler from the grounds the other night. Surely the mistress would have given orders not to let him back onto the estate under any circumstances. Yet there he was, nonchalantly walking towards the house, having managed to pass the slave who watched the gate without any trouble.

Then Lucia remembered the figures she thought she'd seen in the fields and knew now that her mind hadn't been playing tricks on her.

She turned away from the window and sprinted as fast as she could back to the drying room, bursting in on the women in the middle of another good-natured and, no doubt lewd, joke.

"Get into the kitchen," she shouted. Her voice carried an unmistakable note of command that the other slave-women responded to instinctively, dropping what they were doing without even thinking and hastening towards the door where Lucia stood, drawing in deep breaths of air. "Go!"

"What's happening?" Livinia demanded, but she moved just as fast as any of the others.

"I don't know yet, but it's better to be safe than sorry. Barricade the door behind you and arm yourselves with knives and whatever else you can find."

Without waiting for a reply Lucia ran again, like the wind along the covered walkway towards the main house, praying to Sulis that she would be in time; that the peddler would continue to walk as nonchalantly as he'd been doing so far.

She arrived at Dianna's day-room and, without knocking, pushed the door open and burst inside. The mistress looked up at her from the wax tablet she'd been writing on, astonished by the unannounced intrusion.

"What is the meaning of this?" Dianna demanded, anger beginning to smoulder in her brown eyes. "How dare—"

"Vassinus – the peddler – is coming, *domina*," Lucia gasped. "And I don't think it's to sell more goods as he's not got the wagon with him."

Confusion replaced the rage in Dianna's face but before she could ask any more questions Lucia gestured.

"Come, *domina*. We must act. I'm certain he's here to do us some harm."

The mistress shook her head stubbornly. "What are you talking about? Find Regalis and have him throw the lout off the estate. Why are you disturbing me in this ridiculous fashion?"

"I will find Regalis, *domina*," Lucia agreed patiently. "But I fear the peddler has brought friends with him and…"

At last, comprehension flooded Dianna's face and she put down her tablet with a frightened sigh. "All right then, girl. What should we do?"

Lucia stared at her in surprise. Dianna was the mistress here, *she* should be taking charge, issuing orders and seeing to the safety of the estate. Yet the woman was looking to a slave for guidance. Lucia's opinion of the *domina*, already low, dropped even further and she had to turn away to hide the disgust from showing on her face.

"I don't know how many of them there are," Lucia said, leading the way out into the corridor, nervously glancing left and right for signs of intruders. "They might have the house surrounded so we should remain inside, find some hiding place."

"My *vestiaria*," Dianna suggested. "We have a secret vault there which Castus uses to store valuables and money. It has a metal door and can be locked from the inside."

This was the first time Lucia had ever heard of such a vault within the wardrobe room and, in spite of their peril, she wondered what was in there, and how much it was worth. As always, she filed the information away in the back of her mind for possible future use, although the curiosity must have shown on her face.

"You keep that knowledge to yourself girl, do you hear me?" the mistress said. "I don't want slaves trying to break in."

Lucia didn't bother replying and it was only moments before they reached Dianna's bedchamber. They went inside and the mistress headed straight for the adjoining wardrobe room with its chests of clothes and expensive dresses hanging on pegs on the walls. She lifted two of the dresses down, revealing a narrow door which Lucia had never noticed before, despite sweeping the floor of that room many times over the years. It had been designed to blend in with the wall and the builder had made an excellent job of it – only a keyhole betrayed its presence and Dianna pulled out the key from a necklace she was wearing.

The lock clicked open easily and the door opened silently. Lucia tried to peer in, to see what was hidden there, but it was too dim in the little chamber.

"Get in then," Dianna urged, but Lucia shook her head.

"No, *domina,* someone has to raise the alarm or the peddler and his friends will ransack the place unchecked."

Dianna pursed her lips and gazed at her. "You would put yourself in danger just to protect my husband's belongings?"

"Yes," Lucia nodded, glancing back at the doorway to the corridor, mindful of their danger. "My friends are the master's 'belongings' after all, and I will take the risk to make sure they're not harmed."

Dianna nodded, with something approaching respect in her expression. "Very well then, girl. Be careful, and know that you will be well rewarded for your courage should we all come out of this in one piece. Before you do anything else, though, run to the baths and send Elaine here. There's enough room for the two of us and I wouldn't want anything to happen to her, she is a very good handmaiden."

Lucia nodded assent, the door was closed and the lock turned from inside, safely enclosing the *domina*. The slave-girl quickly hung the two dresses back on their pegs, concealing the doorway again, and then she went back and peered out into the corridor. No-one was there, but she could hear men's voices – it was impossible to tell how many there were, but from their shouting back and forth she could tell they were inside the house already. That meant every moment counted.

Lucia glanced to the right, where the passage led to the nearby bathhouse and Elaine. The handmaiden's scowling, sneering face came to her and Lucia decided she would rather help her friends than a woman who had been nothing but hateful since the day they'd met.

Elaine would have to look after herself.

Sweat made Lucia's palms slick and she wiped them absently on her tunic before slipping out and, crouching low, ran for the western wing, the side of the house opposite from the raised voices. She knew there would be slaves in the east wing, working in the gardens, baths or guest bedchambers, and she prayed they wouldn't be hurt by the peddler and his companions.

Lucia wondered if Vassinus even was a peddler. He had looked strangely out of place at the head of the wagon, and his prices had been much lower than any of the slaves had expected – it had been a point of much happy conversation the previous evening – making her think the man might have stolen the wagon from some unfortunate merchant.

Selling the goods had put cash in Vassinus's purse, and his visit had allowed him to check out the villa and its layout. No doubt

Dianna had even told him, in the lead-up to their 'lovemaking', that her husband was out of the country on business.

The presence of Publius Licinius Castus, decorated soldier of Rome, might have made the villa seem a less inviting prospect to rob, but his absence made it a much easier target.

What else had Dianna unwittingly told the peddler? Had she innocently told him details of the daily routine on the estate? Lucia pushed open the door leading to the tower that rose over the house and listened intently, making sure none of the thieves were inside. Hearing nothing unexpected she climbed the stairs up to the top.

Was it mere coincidence that had brought the peddler's brigands here at this time of the day, when the men were mostly all away working in the fields, leaving just the women in the house? It had certainly been a stroke of good fortune for Vassinus.

Still, the bald peddler wouldn't have things all his own way.

The tower was used by Dianna and Castus sometimes in the summer, as a place where they could relax and enjoy wine and food, as it offered fantastic views of the surrounding land. It wasn't merely a lookout post though – this was also where the trumpet was stored should there ever be any need to raise the alarm, summoning aid from neighbours.

Lucia lifted it from its place in the corner and put it to her lips, pointing to the fields in the west. Made from copper, the trumpet was a long tube with a flaring end, clean and shiny as the slaves diligently kept it in good repair, and, as she filled her lungs and blew into it, a loud, clear, braying tone filled the air, carrying for miles across the fields.

The sound faded as she took another breath, then blew once more, this time to the north-east, a long blast even louder than the first. And then she put it back in its corner and ran down the stairs two at a time, knowing the robbers would converge instantly upon the tower in order to silence whoever had raised the alarm.

She could hear the sound of shoes slapping against the stone walkway leading to her position and raced towards the slaves' bath-house, hoping to hide in the hypocaust there. Surely the robbers wouldn't search for valuables in there? They would know that aid was on its way now and, with any luck, grab whatever they could before leaving the estate.

Skidding to a halt, she entered the baths which were located beside the male slaves' sleeping quarters. For once the chill in the room was welcome, as her exertions – and fear – were causing her to sweat profusely, and, without hesitating, she headed for the steps that led down to the hypocaust. Unlike the master's baths which were designed to look perfect in every way, here the architecture was crude and the entrance to the furnace wasn't hidden, meaning the whole room was blackened by soot that the slaves found impossible to clean away.

The door behind her slammed open, hitting the wall with a crash that made Lucia jump in fright as she descended the steps. Terror filled her as she realised the robber who'd been chasing her had seen her come into the bath-house and now there was nowhere for her to hide.

She looked back and a whimper escaped from her lips. Her pursuer was the peddler himself: Vassinus.

His charming smile was gone, replaced by a murderous glare as he chased after her. Reaching the bottom of the stairs she looked around for a weapon to defend herself, knowing as she did so that the sword he held so confidently in his hand would make short, bloody work of her.

It was gloomy in the room as the back door was shut, so although the furnace was burning gently, too little light escaped to reveal a shovel or poker that Lucia might use as a weapon.

She began to sob, cursing her stupidity at coming in here at all. Why did she think she might hide in the hypocaust when there was a good chance it would be in use? Why hadn't she simply run outside and headed for the fields to meet the returning workers summoned by the trumpet blasts?

"You little bitch, was that you that blew the trumpet? Well, you've ruined my plans, but I told you we'd meet again, didn't I?"

Lucia grabbed the only thing she could see that might offer some defence – a thin log from the pile of fuel for the hypocaust – and, breathing hard from fear and running, turned to face the peddler.

"Your alarm has cut short our raid," the man growled as he walked closer, "but I've got plenty of your master's trinkets here." He patted a sack that hung over his shoulder from a rope. "So I'd best be on my way before your scum friends return from the fields, eh? Does this door open?"

Lucia circled away as he sheathed his sword and, with a grunt of exertion, unbolted the door that led outside, never taking his eyes from her.

"It does. Good." He peered out, squinting against the daylight, apparently getting his bearings so he could make his escape, but, rather than running off, he turned once more towards Lucia and walked towards her.

"What are you doing?" she whispered, hating her voice for betraying her fear. "The men will be here any moment, and they'll not hesitate to kill you. Our master will reward them for it, in fact! You should escape now, if you value your life."

She brandished the log but, moving faster than her eye could follow, he darted forward and punched her, grasping the wood in his hand and tossing it with a clatter into the shadows.

"Oh, I value my life," he hissed, pushing her back, hand around her throat. "Especially now that I'm a wealthy man. But, before I take my leave, I'm going to put you to good use. I've thought about you a lot since my last visit, wishing I might have had you in that bath with me."

He pressed her head against the ash-blackened wall, making her gag, then she felt his other hand begin to lift her tunic. She went limp, fearing what was to come, and Vassinus bared his teeth, seeing the defeat in her eyes and relishing it.

Then the side of his head exploded in a spray of blood and bone, and Lucia recoiled as his weight fell away from her.

She screamed as hands grasped her, but it was Regalis who stood there, pulling her into a comforting embrace. She allowed herself to be gathered into his great arms, shaking with shock, eyes shut as tears squeezed past the lids, down her cheeks.

"Where did you come from?" Lucia finally asked, trying to pull herself together, knowing that their danger might not yet be past if the peddler's companions were still within the house. "How did you know I was here?"

"I've been here the whole time," Regalis replied, and his voice was calm and strong, which helped the girl regain some of her composure. "I heard you come in, but it was obvious something was wrong from the noises you were making, so I hid in the alcove there, where I store my tools, until I knew what in Hades was going on."

"Did you not hear my trumpet blasts?" Lucia asked, looking up at the tall furnace-master who shook his head in confusion.

"No, lass, I didn't. Don't really hear *anything* when I'm working in one of the hypocausts to be perfectly honest. The walls are so thick they mask outside noise, and that's when there's not even a fire burning, like it is just now." He frowned then, realising the import of her words and, undoubtedly, fearing for the safety of his wife and children. "Trumpet blasts? What in the name of Belenus was that peddler doing here in the villa again anyway?"

Lucia looked up at the black ceiling overhead and closed her eyes, breathing deeply the fresh air that blew in from the open door, pulling her tunic back down over her knees as she gathered her thoughts.

"He was robbing the house," she replied at last, letting go of his arms and stepping over the corpse of her assailant, trying not to look at the bloody mess Regalis's fire-iron had made of his skull. "But he wasn't alone. I don't know how many companions he had, but we should go and check on everyone else. Hopefully the men have all returned from the field and chased the robbers away by now."

Regalis nodded and bent down to retrieve the dead peddler's sword which he hefted in his right hand, as if testing the weight. Lucia wondered if the furnace-master had been a soldier himself at some time in the past.

"Here, you take this," he said, handing Lucia fire-iron he'd used to smash Vassinus's skull open. She shrank back from it, seeing the blood and gore still on its pointed tip and he wiped it clean on the peddler's clothes before holding it out to her again. She took it this time, glad to have a better weapon than a lump of wood, even if she didn't know how to wield it properly.

"Come on," Regalis commanded, leading the way back up the stairs to the corridor along the western wing of the house. "Stay behind me and don't get involved in any fighting unless you can hit one of the bastards from behind, like I did to the peddler, all right? Good, let's hurry. We should really check on the *domina* first but...Hades take her, I'm more worried about Antonia and the children!"

"Dianna should be safe anyway," Lucia said, staring along the corridor, straining to hear any sounds of conflict or destruction nearby. All was silent and she breathed a sigh of relief. "Forget the mistress for now, let's make sure our friends are safe."

They stepped outside, into the courtyard. It was damp as a light rain had started to fall, and Regalis ran towards the east wing of the house where his family's living quarters were located.

Greed had made the robbers careless and, as Regalis approached the open doorway two strangers appeared.

They stopped as they saw the massive furnace-master coming, and Regalis halted too, sizing them up. Lucia grasped her fire-iron in both hands and gritted her teeth, anger giving her strength and a willingness to fight these bastards to the death.

Emotions warred within her as she moved up behind Regalis and spread her feet wide in what she hoped was a good defensive stance. Fear, rage, shame, hatred, all those overcame the righteous pleasure she felt at Publius Licinius Castus – the master – having his possessions stolen.

The peddler might be dead, but what had his companions done to those slaves unfortunate enough not to be rescued by Regalis? Were Merula, Balbina, Popillia and the others still safely barricaded inside the kitchen, or had the room been breached by the invaders? Lucia imagined the carnage that might have ensued there, especially if her friends had tried to fight off the robbers.

And what about Sennianus? He wasn't out in the fields working, as his leg injury made it hard for him to travel even the relatively short distance there, so he spent most of his time in or around the house. He was strong in the upper body Lucia knew, picturing his muscular chest and arms, but he didn't have the agility, or combat training, to fight off a desperate robber. Especially if the peddler's companions were also old soldiers, like he obviously had been.

Another man came running around the corner of the house just then, and all eyes turned to see who it was, everyone hoping it would be another ally for them. It was Felix, the middle-aged, native, free-born Briton who did most of the more technical maintenance jobs about the place in return for wages.

Regalis nodded grimly, obviously happy to have someone on his side other than a slim, eighteen-year-old slave-girl. "Glad you're here, Felix," the furnace-master said, pointing the sword he'd taken from Vassinus at the two robbers. "I could use some help dealing with these bastards."

The intruders looked at one another then shifted apart a little, presumably so each could face their opponents one-on-one. They didn't appear particularly concerned at the prospect of battle, in fact, their faces were hard and composed, and they wielded their own weapons as if they were extensions of their bodies.

Lucia knew all this and so did Felix, as the maintenance man, apparently feeling no great sense of loyalty to Publius Licinius Castus or his slaves, turned back the way he'd come and, without a word, ran away.

CHAPTER FOUR

"Ha!" Both robbers burst out laughing and began walking towards Regalis, who uttered a curse at his would-be ally's cowardice. "Looks like you're on your own slave-boy," one growled, while the other moved out a little to flank their target. "Why don't you just step aside and let us be on our way, otherwise we'll have to slice you up and what for? You don't owe your master anything, do you? He's probably treated you like shit for years. You're no better than a dog to those Roman scum."

The second thief glanced back over his shoulder and cursed. "Let's do this quickly, Aesu," he urged. "I can hear more of the slaves coming; we need to get out of here."

Lucia, still astonished at Felix's capitulation, watched, open-mouthed, as Regalis suddenly lunged forward, sword outstretched. His target, the one called Aesu, jumped back, but the thief wasn't as fast as the slave, and a deep, red line appeared on the man's arm, very quickly turning the entire limb crimson.

The second robber launched his own attack on Regalis, but the slave threw up his blade, knocking his opponent's to the side, and then Regalis pushed himself forward, kneeing the man between the legs with eye-watering force.

As the unfortunate thief bent over, Regalis once again switched his attention in the blink of an eye, battering the oncoming Aesu's blade aside with a clatter that filled the courtyard, then aiming another cut of his own at the man, who dodged out of the way, snarling, and eyeing his slashed arm fearfully. He was losing so much blood Lucia could tell he wouldn't be able to fight very much longer.

Again, one of the robbers tried to speak, to reason with Regalis, but the furnace-master was lost in the battle-fever and, wordlessly, he feinted towards Aesu placing him on the defensive, but, before he completed his attack, Regalis spun the other way towards the man he'd kneed in the bollocks and tried to stab him in the face.

His thrust was parried, but Regalis continued moving forward, grasping the thief by the tunic and throwing him in the way of Aesu, so the robbers clattered together. The furnace-master hammered the edge of his blade into one who screamed in agony, then jumped back and faced off against his bloodied opponents again.

Lucia stared, stunned by her fellow slave's skill with a sword. She'd always known he was a hard, hard man, but to be taking on two muscular former soldiers like this, and winning? The whole thing had taken place in the blink of an eye, but the thieves were both bleeding heavily and as good as finished. Lucia hadn't even had a chance to *think* about joining the fight.

Her poker was forgotten in her hand as, at last, four male slaves came around the same corner Felix had appeared from. They carried the tools they'd been using to work in the fields: long-handled hoes and rakes, and they ran across to stand with Regalis, instantly taking in the scene in the courtyard and understanding what was happening.

"Lay down your weapons," the furnace-master commanded. "And we'll let you live."

"Live?" Aesu spat on the ground. "Your master will crucify us when he comes back from his trip abroad."

"Perhaps," Regalis shrugged, staring coldly at the thief. "But it's your only chance. Even if you and your friend manage to kill all five of us here, you'll both bleed out before you make it back to whatever hole you crawled out of. You need medical attention."

"He's right," the second thief muttered. "Bastard got me in the back good, Aesu. We need to surrender."

More slaves started to come into the courtyard – angry, frightened, confused faces looking at Lucia and Regalis, voices raised questioningly, men and women instinctively forming a circle around the hapless thieves. They were defeated, but even beaten men holding a sword could be dangerous, so there was a stand-off for a few heartbeats, as each side waited on the other to make a move.

It seemed as if time had stopped for Lucia until one of the slaves walked into the courtyard, bent with grief. It was Sulicena the stable-hand, a thirty-year-old, pretty woman who had been bought only a few years ago by Castus for her skill with horses.

"They killed Sosthenes! The bastards killed Sosthenes! He tried to stop them raping me and they—" She broke off, taking in the scene before her, then pointed a shaking finger at the wounded thieves, who had already looked frightened but now their eyes widened, knowing they were done for. "It was them. They did it!"

Regalis had heard enough. He moved forward, fast as lightning, thrusting the tip of his sword into one of the robbers' necks, pulling it out in a spray of red and spinning around behind the dying man to hit the second, remaining thief in the side. The furnace-master plunged his blade in three times to his target's torso, then kicked out, sending the man flying onto his back, blood pooling all around him from his various wounds.

Again there was silence, at Regalis's masterful display of violence as much as from the shock of the day's events. Even the birds and insects seemed stunned, the air taking on a stillness that appeared as out of place as everything else that had just happened. Lucia felt a knot in her stomach as she realised Sennianus wasn't one of the crowd. He'd have had no chance if the robbers had met him – they'd have made short work of him with his bad leg.

Paltucca stumbled out from one of the doors in the north wing just then, breaking the spell, her face bruised yellow and purple although her clothes were unruffled. The manageress looked at them all thoughtfully, then down at the dead robbers, and spat on the nearest one with a look of disgust on her face.

"Where is the mistress?" she demanded, as if no-one else mattered but Dianna. Someone muttered a barbed remark suggesting the *domina* was probably hiding somewhere to save her own skin. Lucia realised some of the slaves understood the woman's character better than she did.

She opened her mouth to tell Paltucca what had happened. To lead her to the mistress, safe – hopefully – in her locked room in the living quarters. Then she stopped herself. Why should she allow the manageress to be part of this? Lucia had been the one who'd raised the alarm, she'd been the one to take the mistress to safety, not Paltucca who'd only just appeared now, making demands and issuing orders as usual.

"No-one knows? Well, you men, go in pairs and search the house for any more of the bastards. Try to take them alive if you can – the master will want to see them pay for their work in Villa Tempestatis this day. Women – you also go in pairs with the men and help any of our survivors."

"Paltucca." Lucia called the manageress's attention. "I locked Livinia and some of the others in the kitchen, they should still be there. They will be needed to work the infirmary."

Paltucca raised an eyebrow and arched her back, as if she would upbraid Lucia for telling her how to do her job but seemed to think better of it. This was no normal day after all, and the girl's suggestion made sense.

"I'll do that," the manageress nodded. "Regalis, you come with me in case we meet more of *them*."

The furnace master nodded, took one last look at the men he'd killed, then moved after Paltucca. Lucia touched him on the arm and thanked him for what he'd done once again, and then she headed for the door Paltucca had just come out of in the north wing.

She ran towards the mistress's chamber, fire-iron still in her hand, and waited outside the room, listening. All was silent, so she went inside, eyes moving all around warily, and headed for the hidden door. Carefully, she lifted down the dresses, always mindful of damaging property, aware of the consequences for such an action. Again, she listened, just in case any remaining thieves were approaching, then, hearing nothing at all, not even from inside the vault, she knocked on the door.

"*Domina.* It's me, Lucia. You can come out now, I think the robbers are all dead or run off."

There was a pause, then a click, and the mistress's face peered out. There was no sign of her handmaiden. "Oh, well done, girl," Dianna smiled, nodding slowly and looking at Lucia as if she was a clever puppy.

She heard footsteps behind her and Lucia froze, but then recognised, to her relief, the familiar step-drag-step-drag of Sennianus's gait, and almost forgot to listen to the *domina*. He was safe!

"Thank you, Lucia," the mistress was saying. "Things might have gone very differently for me if you hadn't raised the alarm, not once but twice—"

The words seemed to crowd together in Lucia's exhausted, traumatised brain then, before she knew what was happening, the floor was rushing up to meet her, and her day was done.

CHAPTER FIVE

Castus returned from Rome just a few days after the peddler's raid. He didn't come back in triumph, as he'd expected when he made the outward journey – when he left he'd hoped for some reward for years of loyal service, a promotion to legate, or even a move out of the army into senatorial life. Lucia didn't know for sure what exactly the emperor had said to the master, but he didn't invite his friends and neighbours round straight away to celebrate his newfound status, so she knew it hadn't gone as well as expected.

His mood hadn't been improved by the discovery of his villa in disrepair after a bandit attack, some of his slaves traumatised, raped or even murdered, and his wife suffering the indignity of needing to hide away in a locked room. Her handmaiden, Elaine, was discovered drowned in the baths and that, of course, meant Castus would need to pay for a replacement.

Some of his property had been stolen too, as it was discovered at least one of the peddler's men had escaped with quite valuable silver cutlery amongst other things.

It also turned out that Vassinus had been no peddler – the body of the real travelling merchant was found, dumped beside the River Nene a few days later. It seemed the gang of thieves had murdered the unfortunate man and used his cart to get inside the villa where their brutal scheme had ultimately been thwarted.

The slaves couldn't be faulted for their part in events. They had done everything possible to stop the robbers and, crucially, the *domina* survived intact, and having suffered nothing worse than some time in a locked room. Regalis, Lucia and one other, Rogatus, a hugely built young black man who'd killed one of the robbers with his bare hands, were thanked personally by Castus. Even poor dead Sosthenes was awarded his freedom posthumously, in thanks for his bravery protecting the pretty stable-hand Sulicena.

A feast had been thrown that day in honour of the slaves' courage and they were all thoroughly enjoying the wine, beer and fine foods the master had laid on for them. Truly, this was the best fare most of them had ever tasted.

"Ah, there's the hero!"

Lucia turned from the conversation she was having with Sennianus and smiled somewhat self-consciously at Popillia who took the younger woman in a great embrace, grinning from ear to ear. Lucia's quick thinking had endeared her to everyone in Villa Tempestatis, particularly those, like Popillia, who'd been able to avoid the robbers' notice completely.

"You deserve everything the master gave you," Popillia said, holding her friend at arm's length and staring at her earnestly. "You saved many lives and much suffering. I always knew my teaching would lead you down the right path."

Lucia laughed at the suggestion Popillia had taught her much of great import, but felt slightly embarrassed by all the attention she was receiving. Especially since Elaine had been murdered – Lucia might not have liked the handmaiden, but she felt a little guilty over the woman's death, even if most of the other slaves were happy to see the back of her.

"Is it true you were offered your freedom?" Livinia demanded, with a quick glance over her shoulder to make sure Castus and Dianna weren't in earshot. Now approaching her fortieth year, Lucia knew the notion of finally being free preyed heavily on the cook's mind.

"No, not quite," she replied, still smiling. "The master did give me quite a lot of money though, which I can put towards buying my freedom sometime in the future. So…"

"That day is closer now then," Livinia said, nodding, her face deadly serious. "Good for you, girl. I wouldn't grudge you it." The middle-aged cook patted her once on the arm and then wandered off in search of another cup of wine.

"No-one would grudge you it," Sennianus agreed, sipping from his drink. He very rarely allowed wine to master him, hating his limp enough when he was sober, but he sometimes enjoyed a cup or two to relax. "You saved Dianna's life. Castus *should* have freed you."

Popillia added her agreement but Lucia simply shrugged. "Maybe if I was older he might have set me free. But I overheard them – the master and mistress I mean – talking over breakfast earlier and I think he's looking for us to replace the slaves murdered by the robbers." Her vow from years before, never to be set free until she'd had some measure of revenge on both Paltucca and Publius Licinius Castus was slowly being forgotten by Lucia, especially now, when the master was looking on her so favourably.

It was amazing how time healed old wounds – even those left by such a heinous crime as rape. She still hated Paltucca, but that day would come, the girl knew. A chance would come eventually to pay the manageress back for all the unnecessary hurt she'd caused not just to her, but to all the slaves in Villa Tempestatis over the years.

Popillia broke in on her thoughts, finally understanding the meaning of her last comment.

"Are you saying we'll be allowed to have more children?"

Lucia shrugged. "I assume that's what the master meant," she agreed. "Obviously, babies can't do the jobs Sosthenes and the others killed by the peddler's men did, but Castus thinks we need more workers here if the villa is to grow."

"So he'll buy a few more adult slaves," Sennianus muttered, staring into his cup thoughtfully. "And have you women provide him with a new generation of free workers to fill the gaps over the next twenty or thirty years."

It wasn't often Senni made a profound statement, but Lucia heard the sadness in his voice and shared his sorrow. Humans used as cattle, that's all they were to the likes of Castus and Dianna. It was...What? Sickening? Shameful?

No – it was natural here in this world they found themselves part of. It was The Way Of Things, and they just had to get on with it. Even the stoic Sennianus.

Popillia broke the maudlin silence in her usual light way.

"At least we'll have fun, eh?" she said, and nudged Senni suggestively. His face went red in a way Lucia found slightly irritating – he was a man now by the gods! – but they all laughed together in the easy way friends of years will do. His eyes took in Popillia's curves surreptitiously though, and Lucia, much to her annoyance, realised she was sticking out her own chest a little more.

She would never understand humans, even herself, who she was supposed to know better than anyone!

"We'll need a new engineer too," Sennianus said, complexion returning to its usual colour at last. "Since the master ran Felix off."

"Served the bastard right," Popillia said angrily. "He's known us for years, but couldn't stand beside Regalis to help fight the thieves off? Running away, leaving Lucia to stand there? He's lucky the master only punched him a few times before sending him away with his tail between his legs. If I was Castus I'd have taken my gladius and shoved it up Felix's arse."

Even Sennianus, usually so placid, was incensed by the engineer's behaviour.

"I might not be able to move very well, but I'd rather have died at their hands than run away from them like a frightened sheep," he proclaimed, and Lucia could tell the few drinks he'd allowed himself had gone to his head, giving him a bravado he might not have felt during the robbery. Where had Senni been during it? She didn't actually know, but she knew he'd not been as heroic as his words now suggested.

Lucia didn't say anything. She'd been hurt by the old engineer's abandonment but, on reflection, why should he put his life at risk for the sake of a few slaves? Lucia didn't know anything about his life outside the villa – was he a father? A husband? Maybe even a grandfather? Yet everyone, the master included, had expected him, a man probably untrained in physical combat, to stand against robbers who'd already raped and killed some of the slaves on the estate.

Lucia understood his cowardice and didn't blame him for it. Maybe she would have acted in the same way if the roles had been reversed, who could say? As she was slowly coming to realise, people were all different, and sometimes they acted in completely unexpected ways even against their own wishes.

More hours passed pleasantly, in eating, drinking and conversation, and it was only later, when the sun began to set, that Lucia realised the master and his wife were no longer around. Paltucca, too, had made herself scarce and some of the slaves were taking advantage of the lack of supervision.

Lucia saw couples pairing off and heading to dark outbuildings or secluded, tree-shadowed areas of the gardens. Popillia was kissing the big Nubian, Rogatus, despite her earlier flirting with Sennianus. For some reason, Lucia, despite being one of the more attractive of the female slaves, hadn't attracted much male attention and she wondered if Senni had warned the men off, claiming her for his own, despite the fact she'd never agreed to any such arrangement.

She had allowed herself to drink more wine than usual though, flushed with the master's approval of her actions during the raid and his generous monetary reward, and she wanted companionship that night.

It was offered by an unexpected suitor.

Lucia felt someone sit down, their warm body pressing against hers, and she turned to see Dentatus smiling at her. His toothless mouth looked quite hideous and it took an effort not to recoil from him.

"Hello," she said, and it was more of a question than a greeting.

"Hello," he repeated, moving along the wall they were sitting on when she tried surreptitiously to get away from him. "You look very nice today." His eyes moved down to her legs which were bare below the hem of the plain tunic she always wore and up, to her breasts, before he finally met her gaze again. He was very drunk, and leering unashamedly, as if his overt sexual attraction to her would somehow win her over.

"Thank you," she said, standing up and stepping away just a pace, trying not to be rude but unwilling to be so close to him. It wasn't just that he was unpleasant to look at, it was more the fact that he'd been rather unkind to her and Sennianus over the years. The man had a sadistic streak in him that unsettled Lucia. She certainly didn't see him as a sexual partner.

He stood up and walked over to her, again pressing his body against hers, this time leaning across to whisper into her ear. "Let's find somewhere quiet," was all he said but Lucia had heard enough and pulled away, this time making no effort to hide her disapproval.

"Get away from me," she said, trying not to be hurtful but with a hint of iron in her voice that would, hopefully, drive him off. "I'm not interested."

It worked. His face twisted, and he spat a thick globule of phlegm onto the ground before her, but his indignation was just as strong as her's and, without another word, he shuffled away to sit by the bonfire they'd all made at the start of the celebration with a cup of wine in his hand. Brooding.

Rather than waiting for him to become even more inebriated, Lucia hurried away to another part of the gardens, near the kitchen. She felt safer here as Balbina and some of the other, older women were sitting inside chatting and enjoying themselves.

She took a seat on the grass near the door where they could see her – the last thing she wanted was a blind drunk Dentatus trying to force himself upon her. She couldn't take that again – such a situation would not end well for the toothless little bastard.

The grass was soft and still warm from the day's sunshine, but, as the sounds of people having fun and enjoying themselves continued all around her, she wished someone would hold her close and help her forget Vassinus and his attempted defilement of her body.

So, when Sennianus appeared out of the darkness, took her hand and pulled her up, she didn't reject him. He was a good friend and the wolf hadn't damaged his handsome face, just his leg, so he might have taken his pick from any number of other slave-women. She was glad he'd chosen her.

They found a spot in one of the stables, passing Sulicena *and* Prima who were both in a stall with one of the young men who worked in the fields. Lucia had never thought the lad much to look at, but she had to admit he had an impressive body, and the trio appeared to be enjoying themselves greatly.

"That'll be two slave-children for the price of one," Senni muttered, shaking his head with a grin as, in the shadows behind them, Sulicena brought her young partner to climax only for Prima to demand he hurry up and do her next. "Lucky bastard."

"Oh, you'd rather have flat-chested Prima and Sulicena who's built like a man, than me?"

Senni pulled Lucia down into the hay in one of the other stalls at the other end of the stable and squeezed her buttocks.

"Of course not. He's lucky, but not as lucky as I am, being here with you, the most beautiful girl in all Britannia."

In contrast to the loud, rough, and at times quite ferocious activity taking place so near to them, Sennianus made love to Lucia as he always did when they were allowed the opportunity: softly, and gently, and with total respect for her. As usual, faithful Senni didn't allow himself to climax until he felt Lucia shuddering beneath him but at last they lay there, side-by-side in the flattened hay, breathing quickly, sweat coating their bodies.

The sounds of animal lust in the far stall continued long after they returned to the villa and their own beds in separate wings of the house.

The mezzanine over the kitchen was half-empty that night, as many of the women chose to sleep wherever they'd found to make love with their partners, even if that meant outside. It was a hot, muggy night and, as she waited for sleep to overtake her, Lucia thought of Sennianus's gentle hands, soft kisses and promises of eternal love, and wondered if she would *ever* be happy in this life.

The next day was a typical one, full of chores and hard work but again, as the sky turned orange with the setting sun, the slaves were allowed to congregate unsupervised in the gardens together, although with less wine allocated to them this time around. Still, that was no great barrier to couples – some the same as the previous night, some different – sneaking off to make love again.

Lucia didn't accept Sennianus's offer of a repeat performance that night though, or the next. Instead she sat in the kitchen working. Paltucca had ordered the women to begin making clothes for the babies which would undoubtedly be born in the spring and Lucia found it strangely pleasant to sit quietly with the few other slaves who didn't want to make love because they were too old or sickly or, like Merula, because they'd had their fill of male attention for a time.

Would Senni find another partner? Lucia felt a pang at the idea which, again, confused her – she was an adult now, why didn't she understand her feelings better? If she felt jealousy at the thought of Popillia or one of the other girls pleasuring Sennianus why wasn't she out there with him herself?

If life in the confines of Villa Tempestatis was so hard to fathom, how did the free people of the world manage?

Ultimately, she hoped Sennianus did enjoy himself with another woman – she loved him, certainly, and wanted him to be happy. If a night or two of rutting put a smile on his face, who was she to deny him?

And the babies that would be the result of all these unions the master had so generously allowed? Lucia loved children, but she never wanted one of her own. It was true Castus and Dianna were decent slave-owners, compared to some, but why would she want to bring a little boy or girl into the world when they'd be nothing more than a tool, to be used and abused and worked into the ground?

Then a thought struck her: she had never wanted to be freed, because she had made it her life's ambition to somehow gain revenge on Castus, and Paltucca too, for what they'd done to her. Lucia didn't want to simply kill them, she wanted something deeper, less visceral but ultimately more painful for her enemies.

Yet – while she still couldn't stand the sight of Paltucca – Castus had actually been quite gracious after she helped foil the peddler's robbery, and Lucia didn't quite feel the same old hatred for him burning inside.

Perhaps, as Sennianus always said, she should forget the past, and look to the future. With the reward money Castus had given her, she might buy her freedom before she was thirty – and that left plenty of time to have children before she was too old. Children who would be born free!

Yes, she would begin saving every denarius to put towards her future and one day, perhaps ten years from now, she might buy her freedom and become a mother.

CHAPTER SIX

It hadn't just been her part in stopping the peddler's men from ransacking the villa that made Lucia feel more confidence in herself these days – she came from parents who were leaders of their tribe, and it was only natural she should eventually grow in stature with the other slaves.

Castus, and particularly Dianna, showed her more favour, mainly just in small things such as saying "Good morning" to Lucia when they would ignore the others serving them breakfast, or letting her have choice scraps from the dinner table. And everyone noticed that even Paltucca spoke to her more respectfully, although it clearly pained the manageress to do so and must have been the result of orders from above.

"How are you today?" Balbina asked, breaking in on Lucia's thoughts as she sat at the kitchen table sewing together a pair of tiny socks. "Been sick again?"

The girl sighed and forced a smile. "Aye, but it's easing a bit now. I think the worst of it's passed."

Balbina looked at Lucia's swollen belly and nodded, a knowing look in her eye.

"That's often how things go," the midwife said, speaking from the experience of decades. "Some women suffer terribly with the morning sickness, but many, like you hopefully, get over it after a few months and things go easier for the rest of the pregnancy."

"Hopefully," Lucia echoed, and lifted the little socks to show the older woman her handiwork. They were just plain grey wool, but, to the expectant mother, they seemed the sweetest things she'd ever seen in her life and she could hardly wait to put them on her baby's feet. "What do you think?"

Balbina smiled warmly. "Wonderful, and they'll be needed, for it'll still be cold when the babe is born in March. He'll be grateful to have them."

"He?" Lucia asked, frowning. "How do you know it's a boy?"

Balbina shrugged enigmatically. "You get a feel for these things after you've seen as many pregnancies as I have," she said. "The way the bump sits is a good indicator, and you," she patted Lucia's bump gently, "show the signs of carrying a boy in my opinion."

Lucia took that in thoughtfully, not knowing whether a boy would please her more than a girl. It didn't really matter, she thought – either would be loved equally.

Of course, her original plan to remain childless until she was able to buy her freedom had been ruined by the fact that the night she'd spent in the stables with Sennianus had resulted in her becoming pregnant. Clearly, Sulis Minerva had thought their match a good one, for many of the slave-women who'd rutted like whores in an army camp at the same time hadn't fallen pregnant.

A few had though, and Castus was, as far as the rumours went, pleased at his crop of future workers who wouldn't cost him a penny to buy. It was much cheaper to let the slaves loose on one another with a few extra wine amphorae than to make a trip to the market at Durobrivae when the slavers were visiting.

Naturally, Castus had done that too, needing replacements for those – like Sosthenes – killed by the peddler's thieves, so there were a few new faces about Villa Tempestatis these days. Lucia was used to it by now though, after nine years living there. Slaves came and went for a variety of reasons including death, unruly ones being sold on, loyal ones being freed, or, very occasionally, a runaway who was never recaptured.

So, although life on the estate went on just as it always had for Lucia, the people she saw there changed over time. One of the newer ones was suffering at the hands of the old manageress right at that moment.

"You little shit, get that mess cleaned up immediately, and the next time it happens I'll see you beaten, d'you hear me?" Paltucca cuffed the little boy on the back of the head and he stumbled again, spilling more of the milk onto the floor from the bowl he was carrying.

Lucia looked up from her sewing and gritted her teeth. She had a soft spot for the boy, Aeneas, who was the son of one of the male field workers and a woman who'd died two years previously. Lucia couldn't even remember the woman's name now, never having much to do with her, but the boy had been spending more and more time performing chores around the house and Paltucca was, as always, harsh on him.

"Smacking him on the head is only going to spill more of the milk," Lucia muttered, shaking her head, and the manageress turned on her, face rigid.

"Don't start questioning my actions, girl." Paltucca's words were always hard, spat out like pips from cherries and, often, depending on their target, stung just as much when they hit home. "You think you're important around here now that the master's shown you some favour, don't you?" She strode across, Aeneas forgotten, and placed her hands on the table, glaring down at Lucia who looked up from hooded eyes, not willing to cower but not foolish enough to return the manageress's malevolent stare. "I'm still in charge of you slaves, and don't ever forget it."

Lucia sighed petulantly, feeling as small and impotent as Aeneas, but the sound irritated Paltucca and she grabbed hold of Lucia's hair which was tied back in a pony-tail. It was a favourite move of the older woman's when a female slave annoyed her and she was an expert in its execution. She pulled upwards, forcing Lucia's face down onto the table.

The girl had suffered this indignation many times over the past nine years, as had all of the other women, even those well into middle-age like Balbina who still found herself on the receiving end now and again.

This time, Lucia's temper flared, and she reached up, grasping Paltucca's wrist and twisting the skin so the manageress gasped at the burning sensation and let go of the pony-tail.

"How dare you treat me like that?" Lucia demanded getting to her feet, face livid, knowing she was making a huge mistake but past caring at that moment. Balbina, still seated at the table, reached out and tried to pull the girl back into her seat but it was no good.

Paltucca stared at her murderously, then hissed out a sentence like a snake eyeing its next victim: "I'll have you beaten and thrown in the basement, girl. You'll regret questioning my authority this day."

"No!" Balbina objected, but her voice wasn't filled with rage like Lucia's had been, it was pleading. Frightened. "She's pregnant. Beating her will damage the baby – even if you have her back whipped, the trauma will terrify the babe and we could lose it."

Paltucca stared at the midwife as if about to order she should be beaten too, but Balbina, noting the hesitation, took advantage of the silence to hammer home her point. "You know the master wants babies about the place. He'll not be happy at losing one, especially when it belongs to his favourite, Lucia, who did so much to stop that peddler and his friends."

There was an unspoken criticism in the words that visibly stung Paltucca: where were *you* when the place was being ransacked? the midwife's words seemed to imply. Why was it left to an eighteen-year-old girl to hide the women, and the *domina*, and raise the alarm?

For a moment the manageress stared at them, the vein in her temple pulsing like it might burst, and then she turned and stalked from the room. There was a palpable easing of tension once she was gone and Lucia sank back down into her chair as Aeneas found a rag to wipe up the spillt milk that had caused all the trouble. He smiled at her, and she returned his look somewhat shakily as he cleaned the mess up and then hurried off.

"That was stupid," Balbina scolded.

"I know, but she was hurting me and…I just couldn't take it any more. The thought of her spending the next decade making that little boy's life miserable really got to me." She looked fearfully at the midwife. "What do you think she'll do? Will she have me beaten?" Her hand fell instinctively, protectively, to her swollen belly and her eyes became moist.

Balbina reached over and grasped her arm reassuringly. "No, I don't think so. Even Paltucca isn't that vindictive." The words were meant to be comforting but the lack of conviction behind them made Lucia more nervous and, earlier courage and fury forgotten, she began to sob, panic-stricken at the realisation she'd put her unborn child at the mercy of the sour old manageress.

Their fears were only heightened when, a short time later, after Lucia had finally mastered her trembling hands enough to continue working on the tiny woollen socks, the kitchen door opened and ugly, toothless Dentatus wandered in. He had no business in the kitchen at that time of day – there could be only one reason for his presence.

Since Sosthenes had been murdered by the robbers Paltucca had taken to using Dentatus as the instrument of her punishments. He smirked at Lucia and stretched out his calloused palm, gesturing for the girl to stand up.

"Come on, you. Paltucca's decided you should have a few hours off from your work. Lucky you, eh? Lucky Lucia we should call you." He sniggered at his poor joke and the girl regretted the times when, as a youngster, she and Senni had laughed at the unpleasant, short man behind his back. He was certainly enjoying this moment of power over her, suggesting he'd known more about their mockery than they realised at the time.

"What's to happen to her?" Balbina demanded, looking at Dentatus as if he was a slug that had just crawled out of her sandal.

"None of your business you old hag," the man retorted, toothless mouth twisting unpleasantly. Then he seemed to think better of it, recognising another opportunity to show off his newfound status as the manageress's agent. "But if you must know, she's to spend the rest of the day, and all night, in the basement. Nice little rest for her, eh? While the rest of us have to stay up here in the fresh air working our arses off." He grinned again and grabbed Lucia's arm roughly. "Come on, hurry up, I want my midday meal – the sooner you're down in the hole the sooner I can get something to eat. Move it."

The girl walked towards her fate, frightened, as always, by the thought of the darkness with its hidden, crawling, slithering companions, but relieved by the fact Dentatus wasn't beating her before she was locked up. Lucia might have to spend a miserable, cold, hungry day and night in the bowels of the house, but the baby would be safe and that was all that mattered to her now.

She would learn a lesson from this experience, not to cross Paltucca again. At least until her child was safely born.

* * *

The fearful night in the basement was soon forgotten in the haze of the next few weeks, as Lucia's due date grew nearer and her bump expanded accordingly. Her back and feet ached, and the little one inside her kicked often and hard, waking her most nights and fascinating her whenever she saw the bulge a tiny fist or foot made in the stretched skin of her belly.

As the weeks went by it became clear the slave-women weren't the only ones Sulis Minerva had smiled upon, for the mistress began to develop her own baby-bump. The difference in their fortunes was rarely more pronounced.

Dianna would spend her days taking gentle walks in the gardens and lounging on sumptuous couches, being fed fruit and drinking imported watered-wine, while Lucia and the other pregnant slaves continued to work as hard as ever. Whether their place was in the fields, or the wash-house, or the kitchen, Lucia and the rest were expected to be as productive as ever, right up until they were too big to perform their duties. And, when Lucia found her tunic too tight to wear, she was simply given an old one that belonged to one of the heavier women. Some of the pregnant slaves even had to wear clothes belonging to men. In contrast, Dianna had wonderful new garments made to fit her, so she looked beautiful, and fashionable, and *comfortable,* even when her bump grew to its biggest.

And, unlike the *domina,* who had a surgeon visiting regularly to check that she and the babe were in good health, the slaves were treated much the same as they'd been before they fell pregnant. If anything went wrong there would be no surgeon to care for them.

It was all worth it though, Lucia thought. The excitement of being a mother had grown within her just as the babe had done, and now she simply couldn't wait until the child was born and she could dress it in the clothes she'd been lovingly making for months.

Winter had passed, fairly mildly this year for a change, and now, at the beginning of March, the daffodils were beginning to bloom, their bright yellow flowers chasing away the memory of long, dark, dreary days in Villa Tempestatis.

Some of the other slave women had already given birth and the cries of the infants disrupted everyone's sleep even though Paltucca, knowing so many babies would be born around the same time, had transformed a storeroom near the kitchen into a bedchamber for the newborns and their mothers. A squalling, hungry babe might be tiny, but they somehow had lungs powerful enough to fill the whole eastern wing of the house, and it was only amplified when one or two more woke up and joined the dissonant chorus.

In total, seven babies were due or had been born in the past few weeks, not including Dianna's. Of those, one had died during the birthing process, and one, born disfigured, had been exposed – abandoned outside to whatever fate the gods saw fit. Which, in this rural location, could only ever mean death. If the cold and hunger didn't see to it, wild animals certainly would.

Dianna and Castus's child was, of course, a perfect boy with a tiny thatch of blonde hair and as raucous a cry as any of the slave babies, while the *domina* herself seemed to return to her pre-baby size almost immediately.

Lucia was fearful of what was to come, naturally, but felt sure her child would be born strong and healthy and handsome. It came from good stock after all, and she often pictured it at different stages in its coming life – baby, toddler, boy, man. She had accepted Balbina's wise assertion that her babe would be male, not just because the midwife knew her business, but also from the strength of the kicks the little rascal battered her with all day.

At this late stage Lucia was still expected to work although she didn't have to do anything too heavy. Among other things she was able to tend the gardens in readiness for the summer's crop of vegetables and decorative flowers. That morning she was weeding the cauliflower patch and spreading chicken droppings about the soil to help the plants grow.

Dentatus was digging a nearby plot, turning the soil in readiness for planting something new.

The whole garden was a hive of activity – the sun was shining although it was still a little chilly, and Merula, Arethusa and Antonia were chatting away contentedly as they worked nearby. Lucia could see Sennianus up near the bath-house, giving the exterior wall a fresh coat of whitewash and she smiled fondly. He was infuriatingly easy-going, always ready to see the good in people and situations, and she could imagine him being quite content to live out his entire life here as a slave. They were opposites, and she hoped their child would take the best of their traits and be an even better person for it.

Senni himself had been overjoyed when given the news he was to be a father. He held none of the reservations Lucia had about the child being born a slave, but that was expected with Sennianus. He enjoyed taking care of the cats and dogs and other animals that were employed on the estate, and the chance to nurture a baby that he'd helped create himself was truly a gift from the gods for the young man. He was looking forward to becoming a parent almost as much as Lucia.

The women's gossiping suddenly dropped away and Paltucca appeared, striding towards Dentatus, who stuck his shovel into the soil he was turning and wiped sweat from his brow with a filthy sleeve. The manageress spoke to him, but they were too far away for Lucia to make out their words and she continued weeding without taking much notice of the unlikeable pair. She had an uneasy feeling of being watched though, and, turning her eyes surreptitiously back to them, realised Paltucca was staring directly at her, lip curled in wry amusement as Dentatus nodded and mumbled something.

Lucia refrained from shaking her head or cursing them, not wanting any more trouble with the manageress at this late stage in the pregnancy. She turned away, trying to ignore them, but the feel of their eyes boring into her was almost impossible to ignore and she threw herself into the task of weeding and sieving stones from the soil with some ferocity.

At last, the sound of Arethusa's giggle broke into her near-trance and she realised the women were chatting away again, signalling Paltucca's departure, and a little sigh of relief escaped her lips.

She peered at Dentatus but he was hard at work once more, digging with gusto, as if he was having a fine time. His lack of teeth meant he couldn't whistle a proper tune, but, irritatingly, that didn't stop him trying, and he was doing so now as he laboured, a near-monotone procession of high-pitched hisses punctuating his earth-turning.

Everything about him made Lucia uneasy and she wondered what he and Paltucca had been discussing. At least when Sosthenes had been the manageress's strong-arm man he had, deep down, been honourable and willing to help his fellow slaves, even if he had a sadistic streak in him.

Dentatus was simply loathsome.

Lucia turned back to weeding, digging out a dandelion with her little hand-shovel and shaking her head at her judgement of Dentatus. They were all shaped by their experiences in life and his had obviously been a hard one. Perhaps, like Sosthenes, there was a kernel of good inside the toothless man digging away so contentedly on the other side of the garden.

But then his eyes met hers and she shuddered at the look of malevolence on his face.

She soon forgot all about the toothless slave though, as a sharp pain in her abdomen made her gasp. A contraction. This wasn't the first she'd had by any means – they had been coming occasionally for a few days now, but this one was different. Perhaps it was just because she knew the baby's due date had passed the previous week, but, somehow, she knew this was it: the child was coming today.

"Are you all right?"

It was Antonia – she'd noticed Lucia's discomfort and recognised its source immediately. "Come on, let's get you inside to the birthing chamber. Arethusa! Run and tell Balbina to come immediately. We're about to have another little one keeping us all awake at night."

Regalis's wife smiled reassuringly at Lucia, grasping her arm in a strong, comforting grip that even her husband would have been proud of, and they made their way as quickly as possible into the eastern wing.

This was it!

Lucia was frightened – more frightened than she could remember being for a long time – but her excitement at the babe's imminent arrival, and relief that her body would belong to herself again after months of discomfort, made her return Antonia's grin until another contraction made her wince.

This would soon be over she told herself, as her friends led her along the covered walkway that ran the length of this wing of the villa and into the room they would use to bring her child into the world.

Sulis Minerva, protect my baby! she prayed silently, squeezing Antonia's hand as they helped her onto the bed and a pang of fear gripped her at what was to come.

And please, goddess – protect me too.

CHAPTER SEVEN

There had been quite a lot of celebrating recently, as the master allowed the slaves extra rations of beer and wine, ostensibly to give thanks to the gods for all the healthy children the villa had been blessed with in such a short period of time. Of course, everyone knew Castus's pleasure was purely selfish – he was understandably overjoyed with his own new son, which he'd named Maximus, but wasn't very interested in the slave children apart from the fact they would grow to be useful, valuable tools for working his estate.

Still, the slaves would take whatever cheer they could get and were making the most of the master's generosity this night as Lucia gave birth in the opposite wing of the house. Sennianus was frightened, a feeling that had threatened to overwhelm him all day, ever since he'd seen Lucia being taken to the birthing room by Popillia and the others. The knot in his stomach hadn't gone away and he knew it wouldn't until news came that his friend – he hesitated to call her his 'lover' knowing she would frown on such an epithet – and their child were both safe.

"Relax, Senni. What will be will be. The gods will look after them and you'll be a father before the night is done." Regalis grinned and clapped the younger man on the back but his words had little effect.

"Thanks," Sennianus muttered, sipping his beer half-heartedly, wary of drinking too much in case it made him vomit, given he was feeling sickly already with the stress of the day. He managed a smile though, as he looked around at the other slaves in the kitchen – mainly the men and older children, as most of the women were engaged in looking after the new babies or helping with Lucia – and saw the pleasure in their eyes and conversation.

Children are a blessing from the gods, Antonia had told him just the other day and Senni could only agree. He loved playing with the little ones and it was water off a duck's back when any of them teased him about his limp. Being a father was something he looked forward to immensely – they might be slaves, tied to this secluded part of Britannia for decades, but at least some of them could have families. Even many freedmen in the empire weren't afforded that luxury – indeed, some unfortunates had to sell their own children into slavery as they simply couldn't afford to feed the extra mouths. It was either that, or exposing them to the elements. In a busy city like Rome, that didn't automatically mean death for the babe, as many of them were rescued and brought up as slaves by families who didn't want to spend money buying labour from the market.

It was a horrible system, Senni thought, but it seemed to work for the Romans, who apparently saw nothing wrong with it.

"What are you thinking about now?" Regalis demanded, face flushed from beer and the heat in the packed kitchen. "You're away in another world from the looks of it."

Senni shook himself from his daydreaming and shrugged. "I'm just wondering how hard it must be for people to sell their own children, or to abandon them. My babe isn't even born yet and I already feel like I would do anything to protect it."

Regalis frowned, perhaps wishing he hadn't asked to hear Senni's thoughts given how serious they were, but he rallied and tried to impart the wisdom of his twenty-odd extra years on the planet to the young man.

"It's natural to love your children, and to be protective of them," the furnace-master said. "For most of us, it's not even a choice – it's just something that's inside. An instinct. Look at the jackdaw that swooped on you a couple of months ago, around April, because you strayed too close to its nest."

"That was an evil little shit," Sennianus muttered, shaking his head at the memory.

Regalis laughed. "Maybe," he said. "Crows do have a nasty streak in them at times. But it wasn't chasing you because it was 'evil' – it was protecting its babies. Despite the fact you're twenty times as big as that jackdaw, it was still ready to put its life on the line to take care of its young."

Senni nodded, focusing on the furnace-master's words in the hubbub of the room, glad of the distraction from worrying for a time.

"So, aye, parents want the best for their children. But we're not jackdaws, lad. We're men, and we know that sometimes we need to make terrible decisions that are, ultimately, for the best. Even birds understand this – a crow might have a few young in the nest, but if one or two are sickly, weak things, and food is scarce, the parents will only feed the stronger ones, wanting to give at least *some* of them a chance at life, rather than all of their brood starving."

"Really? I never knew any of that," Senni said, genuinely interested. He'd never given much thought to the habits of birds before.

"Really," Regalis affirmed. "It's a crow's equivalent of the Roman practice of exposure – abandoning children they can't look after."

A couple of the men had brought out dice and were starting a game which drew the furnace-master's attention. Standing up he moved to join the players, patting Senni reassuringly on the shoulder as he went.

"Don't be maudlin this night," he said, and it was almost a command. "Lucia is one of the strongest people I've ever met, she'll be fine, and so will your child. This is a night for celebration, lad, not worrying about what everything means. You'll only drive yourself mad if you travel down that path."

He moved away, and the dice players welcomed him into their group gladly. Sennianus – perhaps as a result of the beer working its way into his system, or maybe thanks to Regalis's words of wisdom – felt happier and more relaxed than he had all day.

Regalis was right – Lucia had an inner strength and force of will that put most of the men in Villa Tempestatis to shame. There was no reason to fear for her, all would be well.

He finished the beer in his cup and went for a refill, not even caring if drunkenness would make him fall over. He'd just sleep on the kitchen floor. He realised he must be quite inebriated already to think such a ludicrous thing – Paltucca would be in soon enough to shepherd the men back to their own sleeping quarters – but he just giggled. It wasn't very often he allowed himself to drink much beer, but if a man couldn't get roaring drunk on the night his child was born, when could he?

Grinning, he stood with his newly filled cup behind Regalis, watching the game of dice. It was good natured as although they were playing for money, it was only for small amounts. That was another rule of Paltucca's – gambling was allowed but never for much money as drunk men losing half their savings very often led to anger and, inevitably, violence.

Sennianus was in such a good mood now he was even seeing the manageress in an appreciative light, realising, for all her nastiness, she kept the villa running rather well. She was a sour-faced old hag, but she had her good points too.

He giggled to himself again, wondering what Lucia would say to such a thought, then he broke off as someone shoved him gently aside.

It was Popillia.

The woman bent down and spoke into Regalis's ear, and the furnace-master turned to face her with a look that Sennianus found impossible to read.

"Why?"

Popillia shrugged and pulled at the big man's arm until he stood up and, with a last look at Senni, allowed her to lead him out of the kitchen.

"Where are you going?" one of the dice players demanded. "We're in the middle of a damn game here, Popillia, what's happening?"

Neither Regalis or the slave-girl looked back and the men muttered irritably amongst themselves until they noticed the furnace-master had forgotten to lift his stake. The coins were quickly added to the prize pot which brought smiles back to the men's faces and the game resumed as enthusiastically as before.

Sennianus watched in silence as Regalis and Popillia disappeared through the door, wondering what was going on that required the big man's presence. Was Antonia unwell? Or one of their children?

He shook his head, knowing it was more than likely the master or mistress had simply decided on a whim to take an evening bath and that meant the hypocaust would need lit and fed by Regalis.

But even as he told himself that, Senni felt the knot of fear in his stomach return, heavier than ever.

Popillia hadn't met his gaze, but he'd noticed the tears in her eyes, and the tracks they'd left on her cheeks.

Something was wrong. What had happened?

It didn't take long for the news to reach them.

"Ho, Dentatus, where have you been all night? Fancy a game? We're down a player since Regalis left."

Sennianus looked round and saw the toothless slave come into the room and walk over to the table. He lifted a cup and filled it with beer, draining it in two long pulls before refilling it and turning to look at the gamers with an exaggerated, sad expression on his lined face.

"Bad news lads. My child's been born fit and well but the master's decided he doesn't need any more slaves right now and the little mite's to be exposed. That'll be why Regalis left. You know he's good at these things."

There was a hush in the room, and everyone looked confused.

"What are you talking about you fool?" the African named Rogatus demanded. He had no time for Dentatus, much like many of the other slaves. "Your child? What woman would lie with you, you ugly goat? Speak sense or get back out of here, by Hades. We were having a nice time until you came in."

Dentatus looked irritated but he turned to Sennianus and nodded.

"Who would lie with me? Lucia, that's who."

Senni stared at him, dumbfounded, and there was laughter from the others who shook their head and made to continue with their game, the stocky little man's tale boring them now with its absurdity.

"Aye, that's right," Dentatus went on, raising his voice over the babble. "The child she's been carrying is mine. You all thought it was Senni's but it's not – and the master just found out the truth."

Sennianus stood up and walked across to stand before the toothless slave, eyes narrowed, cup still in his hand.

"What are you mumbling about? Lucia wouldn't touch you. The child is mine, as we'll see when it's born and it's not an ugly little gnome like you."

"Ugly gnome?" Dentatus spat, his smile gone. "That may be true, but we'll never know. Paltucca told the master the truth: that I'm the father of Lucia's babe. Regalis is carrying it out into the grounds right now."

The man's words penetrated Sennianus's brain and started to make a twisted kind of sense. Paltucca had been furious at Lucia for weeks, ever since she stood up to the old manageress. But this?

Killing a child, simply to get back at someone? Even Paltucca wouldn't do something as truly wicked as that, would she?

Dentatus's smug face stared back at him and, for the first time Senni could remember, a murderous rage flooded through him and he lunged forward, bringing his beer cup round and smashing it against Dentatus's head.

"You bastard!" Senni screamed, bringing the broken cup back and hammering the remnants into his opponent's face once again as both of them fell to the ground. "You lying sack of shit, why would you do something like this?"

Dentatus tried to raise his hands to protect himself but he found it impossible to ward off Senni's powerful blows. The younger man might have had a disfigured leg, but his chest and arms were strong and Dentatus's face was bruised and bleeding by the time Rogatus and the other slaves managed to pull the men off the floor and away from one another.

"Say you're lying," Rogatus thundered, pinning the groggy Dentatus against the wall, as more slaves crowded around angrily. Lucia was a favourite among the men, despite her often melancholy nature which some took as aloofness, and Senni, who almost always had a smile on his face, was also well liked.

Dentatus was not, especially lately, when he'd been running so many errands, and doing so many little jobs for the hated manageress.

"Stay back, Senni," Rogatus shouted, holding out a long, muscular arm to keep the furious slave at bay. "You'll be punished for smashing the toothless shit, don't make it any worse than it's already going to be."

"Punished?" Senni cried, tears streaming down his face as he stared at Dentatus's ruined face. "What does it matter? If they've abandoned Lucia's – *my* – child I don't want to live anyway. They can crucify me for all I care!"

"I hope they do," Dentatus mumbled through bloody lips but Rogatus pressed his neck back against the wall again, silencing him.

"What are we going to do?" one of the other men asked. "How can we find out the truth?"

All eyes turned to Rogatus who seemed, in Regalis's absence, to be the natural leader. The tall black man shrugged and let Dentatus slump down onto his haunches. "We'll find out soon enough. Regalis will tell us what's happened when he returns. In the meantime, we better clean this place up. You can wash your face and get the blood off," he said, pointing at Dentatus, who sneered at him.

"I will not. Paltucca, and the master, will see what that bastard's done to me and punish him accordingly."

"No doubt," the black man nodded, then gestured into the corner where one of the younger boys sat, watching the action open-mouthed. "Bring me that bucket, Aeneas," he commanded, waiting as the lad hurried to comply. He took the full container from him as if it were no heavier than a cup of wine. "If you won't wash yourself, we'll do it for you, you horrible little prick. Come on, lads."

With that, the men grabbed Dentatus and forced his head into the bucket of water. He tried to get away from them but Senni's blows still made him groggy and the other slaves were much too strong for him to fend off. When they allowed him to resurface most of the blood was rinsed away, along with a layer of dirt.

"That's the cleanest I've ever seen you," Rogatus spat, shaking his head in disgust. "But your bruises and wounds won't heal overnight. I hope you're proud of yourself, Dentatus, you're now the most hated man in the whole estate."

The toothless, beaten slave glared around at them all, gasping for breath, water dripping from his face and hair onto the stone floor, and he shrugged. "I don't give a damn. Paltucca will make sure I'm alright."

"You better hope so," someone growled. "For you're a marked man now. If you've conspired with Paltucca to see Senni's baby killed, you'll pay for it, one way or another. By Jupiter, you *will* pay."

Dentatus was released and wandered off into a corner on his own, beer cup in hand, glaring at everyone in the room as they returned to their earlier positions although no-one felt much like celebrating or playing dice any more. Sennianus sat on a stool with his head in his hands, fretting, praying to the gods that Dentatus was lying and Lucia's child was safe in the eastern wing.

It was only a short time later when Regalis returned, although it felt like the longest wait of Sennianus's eighteen years. The furnace-master looked sorrowfully at Senni when he came in and muttered an apology which told everyone in the room all they needed to know.

Regalis poured himself a drink and then he noticed Dentatus skulking in the corner, battered and bruised, and the furnace-master shook his head, an expression of loathing on his face.

The only sound in the room was Sennianus's sobbing.

The next morning brought more unpleasant news for the inhabitants of Villa Tempestatis, as Lucia heard from the whispers of the women around her. She had been moved from the birthing chamber into the infirmary, which was a small room with only three sleeping pallets, used for slaves who were unwell. It was situated in the eastern wing, in between the kitchen and the room that was being used to house the newborn babies and their mothers. At that time, Lucia was the infirmary's only occupant but there was no door, only a curtain between the rooms, and she could hear everyone moving around, doing their daily tasks.

Taking care of their babies.

More tears formed in her eyes, but she had spent most of them by now, ever since she had understood what had happened the previous night. Now, she felt almost as if she was a different person, not Lucia any more, but someone else, cold and detached, observing the world around her dispassionately.

It was a mercy she knew Sulis Minerva would allow her for only a short time. The feeling would wear off soon enough and her pain would return with a vengeance. She wondered how her life could continue as it had before, now that her child—

"…the master's ordered the men to take weapons with them when they're going about their work," Popillia was saying to someone in the chamber on the other side of the curtain, and Lucia focused her attention somewhat drowsily on the familiar, pleasant voice. "Just in case they meet him."

"Meet who?" another voice demanded.

"One of the bastards that robbed us last year, remember? One of them escaped? Well, one that we know of, there might have been more since no-one has a clue how many of them were in the gang."

"What about them?"

Lucia recognised the new voice as Livinia, the cook, and wondered idly if it was time for the midday meal. Not that she was hungry – she doubted she would ever want to eat again.

"I just said," Popillia said irritably. "One of them has been seen in the grounds, watching the house. *This* house."

"What for?"

"By the gods, how should I know, Livinia? The master is worried the man is going to try and get revenge for what Regalis and Rogatus and the others did to his friends. Or maybe there's going to be another robbery. Who knows? But be vigilant, all right, and spread the word for everyone to keep an eye out."

There was the sound of a door opening and the familiar hushing of voices that heralded Paltucca's arrival. That brought a reaction to the previously apathetic Lucia: loathing. The purest hatred, and a burning desire to take the manageress's neck in her hands and squeeze until the woman expired – like her baby! – filled Lucia and she had to force herself to calm.

She would avenge her little boy one day, but it would have to wait.

Paltucca repeated, in a loud voice, what Popillia had just been saying, warning the women to keep their eyes open for strangers around the estate and to raise the alarm if they saw anyone suspicious.

"The master has sent to Durobrivae this morning for three more trumpets. They will be placed around the grounds so the alarm can be raised quicker than someone having to run to the tower in the north-west corner of the house."

Someone like me, Lucia thought grimly. *And my thanks for raising the alarm? The murder of my child!*

"If any of you don't know how to sound the trumpets, I will be showing everyone after dinner. Make sure you are at the tower once your meal is finished this evening – every person in this villa *must* be able to sound the alarm and I'll be checking periodically, master's orders. Anyone I find unable to blow the trumpet will be severely punished."

"Does that include children?" a small voice asked meekly and Lucia could imagine the sneer crossing Paltucca's round face.

"No, of course it doesn't, Merula you idiot. Children and those who don't have the strength to sound the trumpets are exempt. The rest of you better be able to do it or by Jupiter there'll be Hades to pay. So, if you've never learned how to do it, be at the tower after dinner."

With that, the door closed and the babble of conversation arose once again.

Lucia hoped the robbers *would* return, and this time they'd slowly flay the skin from Paltucca as she screamed in agony.

"Senni. Senni, come with us."

The young man looked up from the fence he was staining and squinted at the two figures framed by the morning sun. Regalis and Rogatus.

He turned away again and dipped his brush into the pot on the ground next to him. It was three days since his fight with Dentatus – three days since his son had been killed – and he didn't want to do anything other than lose himself in his work. Especially when the furnace-master had been the one who'd carried the baby out into the open and left it – him! – exposed.

"Come on, lad," Rogatus's deep rumbling voice was insistent and the black man reached down, grasping Sennianus's arm gently but firmly, drawing him up onto his feet.

"What do you want?" Senni demanded, glaring at them.

He had been lashed for beating Dentatus, and spent a night in the basement prison, but it had meant nothing to him and the pain in his back barely registered even now as the ache in his heart drowned out any other feeling. He had no interest in talking to Regalis or Rogatus – the only person he wished he could see was Lucia, but Paltucca had forbidden that of course. Part of his punishment for attacking Dentatus.

"Trust me," Rogatus growled, staring into Sennianus's eyes. "You will want to be part of this."

Senni glanced at Regalis who nodded and the young slave shrugged.

"Fine. Where are we going?"

"You'll see. Here, don't forget this, you might need it, and Paltucca will punish you again if she notices you don't have it."

Rogatus lifted the knife that Senni had been assigned as part of the villa's defensive measures since the robber had been spotted, and handed it to the limping man.

"What's happening?" Senni asked as they moved away from the house and down a slope that led towards a cave that he and Lucia used to play in when they were children. "Why are we coming down here? Has that robber been seen? You know I won't be much good in a fight."

"Don't worry about that," Regalis replied, and something in his voice made a shiver run down Sennianus's back. Despite the crushing sadness that filled him at losing his child, he began to feel apprehensive about this trip they were making. It was most unusual, and he began to wonder if he'd offended the two giant slaves somehow. Or perhaps Paltucca had ordered them to beat him and hide his body.

He glanced at them, noting the determined looks on their faces and thought he must be right – they were on some dark errand for sure – but then Rogatus met his gaze and nodded reassuringly and his fears slipped away.

The apprehension returned though, as they finally reached the bottom of the steep slope, moving slowly since Sennianus's limp made the descent much harder than it was for Rogatus or the furnace-master. The house was no longer visible from down here, and the main road to Durobrivae was hidden by trees and bushes and an old stone wall that predated Villa Tempestatis's construction.

A man was resting on the grass, axe embedded in one of the logs he'd been cutting, although the woodcutter had been taking a rest for some time, as they'd not heard any noise of chopping as they approached.

"Lazy bastard, sleeping as usual," Rogatus growled, and the woodcutter, startled, looked up at them, eyes wide with fear.

It was Dentatus.

Sennianus felt revulsion laced with a burning desire to avenge himself on the lying bastard who had caused – along with Paltucca – the death of his son. When he looked at Rogatus and Regalis on either side of him, he knew they felt the same and that was exactly why they'd brought him here.

"Let's get this over with," the furnace-master growled, looking over his shoulder and all around, making sure no-one was watching what they were about to do. "Take your tunic off, Senni, quickly."

"What? My tunic? Why?"

"Just do it, boy," Regalis commanded and the natural authority in his voice made the young man begin to pull off his clothing hurriedly.

Dentatus didn't need to see the naked blades in their hands to know why they had come down to the cave – the grim expressions on all three faces was enough. He was no coward, but there was little chance he could defeat the bigger slaves, even one-on-one, never mind outnumbered as he was here. He scrambled to his feet and ran.

Rogatus had expected the flight, though, and his powerful, long, black legs ate up the distance between them in moments. Sennianus looked on in horrified fascination as the muscular slave rammed the point of his knife into Dentatus's back.

The fleeing man fell forward with a howl of pain and fear, causing Rogatus to trip over him and the pair went down on the grass in a sprawling heap. Regalis ran up behind them and his sandalled foot flashed out, smashing into Dentatus's face with brutal force.

The fight was over already and Sennianus hadn't even moved, standing rooted to the spot, stunned. He didn't have the fighter's instincts of Rogatus and Regalis, who gestured him forward now impatiently.

"Hurry up, lad," the furnace-master commanded, landing another kick on the stunned Dentatus's head. "We need to get back to the house before someone sees us. Let's get this over with."

Sennianus walked forward, confused. What was he supposed to do?

"By the gods," Rogatus muttered, jumping back to his feet and putting his own, bloodied, knife into Senni's hand, pointing it towards the downed Dentatus. "Your child – and your woman – must be avenged for what he did. Now get on with it. If we're discovered out here all three of us will be executed!"

Sennianus stared down at the stunned, groggy man on the grass before him. Dentatus, a man who had never been kind to him or Lucia even when they were children. A man who had lied to the master about fathering Lucia's child. The man who had, essentially, taken the little tiny baby away from Lucia and had it dumped it like a piece of rubbish in the night.

Tears filled Senni's eyes and a lump came to his throat that almost choked him until he stooped down and plunged Rogatus's knife into Dentatus's belly. Then he pulled it out and did it again. And again, the vision of his innocent child overcame him completely.

Before he knew what had happened he was being led towards the cave, half-carried, by Regalis and Rogatus, his hand and wrist bloody, with specks of red all up his arm.

As expected, Dentatus had brought an amphora of water to drink – cutting wood was thirsty work – and Sennianus used it to clean the blood off himself as quickly as possible. When the crimson stains were all gone, and checked by Regalis to make sure nothing was left to incriminate them, Senni was handed his tunic and the three men made their way back to the house, leaving Dentatus where he lay.

"What will happen when his body's discovered?" Senni wondered, before the thought hit him. "People will know it was me that killed him. Everyone knows what he did and how much I despised him!"

"Calm down, my friend," Rogatus said, flashing his white teeth in a lupine grin. "There will be no problem."

"Why do you think we started the rumour of the robber hanging about the place?" Regalis said before Senni could say anything else. "Of course there was no robber – only a fool would come back here when his friends had already been killed and hanging on a cross would be his reward if captured."

Rogatus chuckled as if someone had told him a lewd joke. "When we get back to the house we'll raise the alarm. Everyone will assume the 'robber' killed Dentatus."

"The gods take the bastard, may he spend eternity in Hades for what he did to you," Regalis spat out. The villa came in sight and, seeing no-one around, they hurried into the kitchen and returned to their normal duties as if nothing had happened.

Sennianus went back to painting the fence outside the east wing, a knot of fear in his stomach. He found it hard to lift the brush as his hands began to shake almost uncontrollably at the realisation of what they – he – had done. Luckily, there were others going about their own work nearby but, uncomfortable and unsure what to say as a result of his recent evil fortune, no-one bothered him.

Eventually, the shaking in his hands subsided so he was able to continue painting, although the thoughts in his head were still churning.

He had killed a man! But he had deserved it, hadn't he? What would Lucia say when she found out? Would she be happy, or would she look on him in disappointment? Killing wasn't in his nature after all. But Dentatus had murdered their son by his actions – had told his lies knowing what the outcome would be.

Utterly lost in his own world, Sennianus painted the fence without even noticing he'd almost finished the job much faster than expected.

And then the *HARROOOOOOOO* of a trumpet broke his reverie and the villa became a maelstrom of frightened, frantic activity.

"Did any of you see a strange man, or men, lurking around today?" Publius Licinius Castus glared at the slaves gathered in the courtyard, his face a mask of rage. He stood, Dianna next to him, on the low steps leading up to one of the flowerbeds, and the extra height only made him seem more intimidating to Sennianus.

The young man hadn't really expected this; that the master himself might question the slaves in the aftermath of what they'd done to Dentatus. Of course, when the real robbers had mounted their – mostly failed – raid, Castus had been away in Rome, so the investigation of their crimes was carried out by, first, Paltucca, and then by one of the local government administrators from Durobrivae. And, of course, at that point Sennianus hadn't done anything wrong, so had nothing to fear.

He shook his head in answer to the master's question, feeling a chill run down his back as Castus's eyes swept over him, half-expecting the Roman to know instinctively that he was hiding something. But the stony gaze continued on without stopping and he almost allowed himself to relax. He knew others were watching him though – Regalis and Rogatus. He could sense their grim stares upon him, could almost hear their thoughts in his head: *don't crack or we're all dead.*

"None of you?" Castus demanded when none of the slaves came forward. He looked down at Paltucca who stood on the ground next to him. "What was this robber said to look like when he was seen hanging around previously?"

"Average height, master, with brown hair and medium build."

One of the men, a worker from the fields, raised his hand tentatively, looking from the manageress up to Castus then down to the ground as if half-hoping it would eat him and save him the anxiety of speaking to the two *de facto* rulers of his world.

"I saw someone that looked like that this morning," he attested. "Walking along the main road by the field I was ploughing."

His testimony seemed to give another man courage and he too raised his hand. "I saw him too, now that you describe him, Paltucca. Fitted that description perfectly."

Sennianus watched Castus face as it twisted unhappily, and he understood the master's exasperation. Average height, build and brown hair could describe probably half the men in Britannia. Yet it was all they had to go on.

Regalis and Rogatus had concocted their scheme very cleverly it seemed.

"Where was this man going?" Castus demanded, and the two slaves who'd seen the 'robber' looked at one another before the first replied, his voice as confident as could be expected.

"Towards Durobrivae," he said. "But he was looking up towards the house – you can just see it from that part of the road."

"Aye," the second witness agreed, nodding his head as if he'd never been more certain of anything in his life. "He had a dark look about him."

"In what way?"

"Well, *dominus*..." the slave stuttered to a halt before finishing lamely, "he just looked a bit nasty is all. Like he had mischief on his mind."

"Why didn't you raise the alarm then?" Castus shouted, and nearly every slave in the courtyard fell back a pace.

The unfortunate man who'd spoken drew in a breath and gulped before replying in a hoarse voice. "To be honest, master, and please, I mean no offence but..."

"Out with it you fool!"

"Well, lots of people walk past the villa and give it a black look. Locals I mean – Britons. I don't think they like a Roman living in such a nice house on their, well, what they see as their lands. Forgive me, *dominus,* I mean no disrespect."

"Oh, shut up you idiot. Get back in line." Castus sighed deeply. He had already lost one slave today, there was little point in punishing more of them when they seemed to have little reason for raising the alarm. "Why did he go after that particular slave..."

"Dentatus," Paltucca offered.

"Yes, Dentatus. Why go after him?" The master sat down on the stairs, staring into the middle-distance thoughtfully. "A slave chopping wood can't have seemed like a very attractive target for a thief."

"Didn't the toothless little fool rescue one of you women from being raped during the raid?" Dianna asked, looking towards Popillia and some of the other female slaves.

"Yes, me, *domina*," Sulicena said, stepping forward a pace and keeping her eyes on the ground that was compacted hard by the constant coming and going of delivery wagons.

"And what did your rapist look like?"

The slave-girl's face screwed up as she tried to recall her attacker's features before she gave the inevitable answer.

"About average height. Wiry. I think he had brown hair and needed a shave. His breath reeked of wine."

Dianna gave a self-satisfied nod, as if she'd just solved the entire mystery, and Sennianus was relieved to see Castus get back to his feet, also nodding as he brushed himself down.

"It makes sense then. The robber, or rapist, whatever, came back to get whatever meagre revenge he could on the inhabitants of Villa Tempestatis. Killing the slave who'd put an end to his fun with her," he jerked his head towards Sulicena as if she was one of the cattle in his fields, "must have brought him some measure of satisfaction." Again he sighed and this time he walked down the steps towards the main, northern wing of the house. "Dismiss them Paltucca, they can get back to work." He stopped before he left the courtyard though, whirling back round to glare at them all. "I suspect the murderer will flee the area now he's got this out of his system. But remain vigilant in case he comes back for more. Sound the trumpets if you see any more strangers with 'a black look' about them. It's bad enough luck I have to buy one replacement slave, without any more of you costing me money by getting killed."

He disappeared into the house with Dianna, and Sennianus let out the breath he'd been unconsciously holding in, sharing a look of relief with Regalis and Rogatus.

It was over. They'd got away with it, and not even Paltucca suspected a thing.

Sennianus headed back with the others to the tasks they'd been doing when the alarm sounded but as they walked, a solitary daffodil caught his eye, its bright petals beginning to turn brown and droop, and his elation turned to a deep, crushing sadness.

Dentatus was dead, but it hadn't brought his and Lucia's baby back to life.

BOOK THREE

CHAPTER ONE

Villa Tempestatis, AD 187, Spring

Lucia watched the handsome boy before her, eating the oiled bread and figs that she'd brought for his breakfast, and couldn't help feeling a small sense of pride as the morning sun came through the window of the dining room, framing him almost as if he were a demigod's son from a story. Since he was born ten years ago she had nursed him at her breast, wiped his backside, and scolded him when he'd been naughty, until now...

Maximus noticed her watching him and smiled before lifting his cup of water and taking a sip as he read the tablets on the table before him, occasionally making a mark in the wax or nodding his head at the information contained therein. He was a studious boy who enjoyed learning almost as much as getting into trouble.

Yes, she felt a sense of pride in the knowledge that he had turned out so well, but there was also an underlying bitterness for Lucia, a bitterness that would never leave, and would always bring her pain when she looked upon Max especially.

When Lucia's child was taken from her and exposed she had been bereft. When the mistress, Dianna, began to suspect Dentatus had lied about being the dead child's father she pitied Lucia and wanted to give the grieving young slave-girl something to cheer her up.

The *domina* had not enjoyed feeding her baby Maximus as he sucked too hard and left her nipples red and sore, so it seemed the perfect solution to have Lucia feed the child since the slave's breasts were filled with milk that wasn't being used.

To the mistress this was an honour and a privilege that any slave should embrace. Why wouldn't they? A lowly slave giving sustenance to Publius Licinius Castus's son? And later, as the baby grew into a toddler, to be allowed to look after him sometimes, to teach him the ways of Villa Tempestatis alongside his tutors?

Truly, Lucia should have felt like the gods had smiled on her.

Tears filled her eyes as she looked upon Maximus and cursed the fate the gods had given her.

That Dianna should think she was being kind to Lucia in allowing her to nurse baby Maximus was no longer the baffling shock it had been ten years ago. Like everything that happened in the villa, it was just *the way of things*.

Dianna didn't see Lucia as a person, not really. None of the slaves were truly human to the master and mistress.

So, as a young mother of only eighteen years old, grieving the abandonment and death of her much anticipated first child, it was almost impossible for Lucia to take when she was told to nurse Maximus because Dianna couldn't be bothered with the hassle. 'Why should the *domina* do it when a slave could do it just as well?' as Paltucca had noted at the time.

Oh yes, Lucia remembered that day with stunning clarity, as if it was yesterday. She recalled the manageress's smug face as she handed over little Maximus. Paltucca had known how much it would hurt Lucia, even if Dianna was oblivious.

And it had hurt terribly – to feed another little boy while her own lay dead outside, forgotten and unloved. It was too much to bear. Only one thing kept Lucia sane back then: the thought of vengeance one day. Vengeance on Paltucca, and the master and his entire family, even the babe she was forced to suckle in lieu of her own child.

A day never passed when Lucia didn't think of the boy, Alfwin, and wish he might have lived with them, even as a slave, here in the villa.

Senni had, of course, told her what had happened with Dentatus. The tale gave her a great sense of satisfaction and helped her deal with everything just a little better. To know the agent of their heart-breaking pain had suffered a violent death was some comfort at least – it satisfied the darkest part of Lucia's soul and she felt no shame for that. The bastard deserved worse and she only wished she might have been there with Senni when he'd been plunging the knife into the toothless liar, stealing his life as he'd stolen their son's.

All these events of Lucia's life had made her who she was today. She was very much a person of two sides.

Sometimes when she looked at Maximus she felt a little stab of loathing. What made him better than her son? But she never allowed her hatred to show on her face, or in her actions, and, most of the time, she liked the lad well enough. Every time she saw him though, it twisted a knife in her heart and took her back a decade, to the night when Regalis was ordered to take away her own son, Alfwin.

Or sometimes she recalled one of the many occasions when Maximus had struck her for daring to scold him.

Again, her thoughts spun away on a tangent and she relived in her head the morning seven-year-old Maximus spillt a cup of milk on the triclinium floor. It was no accident – the boy was tired, in a bad mood, and simply wanted to make someone else suffer. As usual in Villa Tempestatis that meant a slave, and, as a young serving girl had got on her knees to wipe away the white liquid from the mosaic cupid, Lucia admonished Maximus, telling him his behaviour was unacceptable in a civilised household.

His response had been to slap her hard across the face and remind her of her lowly status within that household. Castus and Dianna found out about it but took no action and that simply encouraged the boy to strike her any time he was in a petulant mood. Thankfully he'd grown out of it by now, but Lucia could still recall the pain in her cheeks, both from his blows and the humiliation of—

"Lucia!"

Maximus's youthful voice broke in on her thoughts and she blinked, realising someone else had come into the room.

Paltucca.

"Yes, master?" she said, ignoring the manageress and addressing Maximus who gestured at Paltucca. He knew very well how much Lucia hated the woman, it was hardly a secret.

"Come with me, girl," Paltucca commanded. Age had not dulled the severity of her expression or voice.

"Where to?"

"Don't question me, girl, just follow."

Girl. Lucia was twenty-eight now, yet Paltucca liked to address all the slaves as 'boy' or 'girl' rather than using their names. It was just another way of keeping them in their places.

As they walked, Lucia took in the older woman's figure and carriage. Still straight-backed and proud, the manageress's once plump body with full, if drooping, breasts, had begun to lose its firmness. The wide hips, jowls and flabby arms were replaced by a narrow waist, wiry limbs, and a gaunt face that made her look even more severe than she had in middle-age. Lucia thought, with a start, that Paltucca must be about sixty years, and looked even older.

The twisted hag couldn't have much time left in this life and still Lucia had never properly repaid the woman for her part in, well, so many things but especially the death of her baby. She had sworn vengeance on the manageress many times over the past two decades but an opportunity to truly pay back the evil bitch had never presented itself.

Time was running out though – if it came to it, Lucia would suffocate Paltucca in her sleep. It would be an unsatisfying vengeance but better than letting her die peacefully, without suffering any form of retribution.

Maybe Senni and Rogatus could do to the manageress the same as they'd done to Dentatus?

Regalis, of course, had passed away just last year, two days after his fifty-second birthday, a loss that all the slaves felt keenly.

Paltucca knocked on a door and, at a call from within, led the way into the master's office.

Publius Licinius Castus looked up from what he was doing at the heavy wooden desk which had probably cost more to buy than a healthy slave and smiled at them.

Neither of the women returned the expression, instead looking at the floor. Castus might not be as strict as some masters, but he still didn't expect his slaves to meet his eyes like an equal. Not even Paltucca who was the closest thing to a freedwoman in the estate since old Tiro had recently been allowed to leave Villa Tempestatis. The clerk had come down with an illness that made it hard for him to breathe, especially in the harsh winters of Britannia, and Castus had sent him away to live the rest of his days in the much more amenable climate of Corsica.

Another person whose loss was felt by the slaves, especially as they wondered who the master would enlist to perform Tiro's duties.

"Lucia, how are you?" Castus nodded dutifully at the woman's reply then went on, wasting no time in getting to the point. He might not be a soldier any more, but his duties still kept him busy, especially nowadays, since he'd been given a job as one of the imperial administrators of Durobrivae, a fact which he apparently saw as an upturn in his relationship with Rome. Marcus Aurelius was gone now, replaced as emperor by Septimius Severus and Castus fervently hoped his son Maximus would one day be accepted into the army as a tribune.

"You know that faithful Tiro has gone to live in Corsica on account of his health? Of course, we all miss him, especially me, as he was such a wonderful clerk. Before he left, though, he showed Paltucca here how to do his job."

Lucia was a little surprised by this – Paltucca a clerk? The manageress spending her time in an office, working on figures, balancing the books and whatever else a clerk might do? Instead of striding about the villa issuing commands to all and sundry and seeing that everything ran smoothly? Swapping a lifetime of dealing with people, for a job dealing with numbers?

That wasn't the biggest surprise of the meeting, and as Castus continued, his next statement left Lucia astonished.

"I want you to be the new manageress here in Villa Tempestatis."

If she hadn't spent a lifetime training herself not to show emotion, Lucia's mouth would have dropped open like a fish collecting plankton, for her thoughts were churning. Outwardly, her only reaction was to glance at Paltucca, who wasn't quite as successful at masking her feelings: the older woman looked outraged.

"*Dominus*," she said, then halted, unsure what to say. "I...I do not think this is advisable, *dominus*. The girl is a troublemaker and – "

Castus's eyebrows drew together and he raised a hand for silence. "Paltucca, I understand you do not particularly like Lucia, but the 'girl', as you call her, has done much for my family and I believe she will make a good manageress. Enough!" He slammed his hand down on the desk before him and Paltucca's face became stony as she closed her mouth again, thinking better of arguing any further.

"You *will* help her learn the role, Paltucca, I command it. Now," he looked once more at Lucia and nodded. "What do you say? Will you become the new manageress of Villa Tempestatis?"

The young woman glanced once at his face, still a little suspicious that this might all be some kind of joke, but the *dominus* gazed levelly back at her and she understood this was really happening.

Publius Licinius Castus was her master, and this was no offer – Lucia *would* be the new manageress whether she wanted the task or not. Did she want it? Well, why not by Sulis! It would mean more money in wages, not that she ever planned on using her savings to buy her freedom but…the manageress's position was a powerful one. The most powerful slave in the whole estate.

She looked again at Paltucca and wondered if this was her chance to get revenge on the old woman, the chance she'd waited all these years for. Lucia couldn't see how, at this point, but certainly being manageress would open lots of new doors for her, both metaphorically and literally. No room in the villa would be out of bounds for her.

It was a stunning opportunity. And it clearly infuriated Paltucca, which was always pleasing.

"Thank you, *dominus*," was all she replied. There was no need for any more, and that was all Castus wanted to hear anyway.

"Good, that's settled then," he nodded. "I always knew you would be a good investment, from the day I bought you in Germania, and you have proven me right time and again." He nodded again, his eyes appearing to mist over a little, as if he was lost in time, reliving his glory days as a young legionary officer. "Paltucca will begin explaining her duties immediately. Good luck, and if there is anything you ever need to discuss regarding the running of the household..." he gestured. "...my door is always open."

His gesture had been as much to illustrate his statement as to signal the end of the meeting and Paltucca once again led the way back out into the corridor, Lucia trailing in her wake.

They said not a word to one another all the way along the walkway, back out into the courtyard, then into the west wing of the house and into another office, this time Paltucca's. It was much smaller than the master's, and the manageress's desk was a simple affair someone like Regalis had probably knocked together some twenty years before. But when Paltucca sat down on the stool behind that desk, and said to her, "This will be your room from now on then," Lucia couldn't help but feel an almost overwhelming desire to cheer and spit in the older woman's bitter face.

CHAPTER TWO

It didn't take Lucia long to find her way as manageress. Her natural leadership qualities, and the fact Paltucca was always around to ask for advice – which she gave, if grudgingly – helped her settle into the role quickly. That the other slaves all liked, or at least respected, her, was also a boon.

The work was hard though, and any thoughts of engineering some as-yet amorphous revenge on Paltucca and Castus were soon forgotten. She had always known that some of the other slaves were, as she termed them, *lazy bastards,* but now that it was her job to get the maximum effort from them every day she started to sympathise, if reluctantly, with Paltucca.

Within a fortnight it had grown tedious: always telling someone like Pavo, the handyman who dealt with most of the villa's minor repairs, to get back to work instead of lounging around the place talking to the young women. Pavo was small and wiry, but he'd been a handsome young man when bought by the master seven years ago. Now his hair was falling out, as had some of his front teeth, but he still fancied himself as a ladies' man. He'd rather crack smutty jokes with Cornelia, the young cook with legs that every man on the estate eyed with appreciation, or Prisca, the large-chested, wide-mouthed young woman whose easy smile drew everyone, male and female, to her.

Eventually, in her third week as manageress, Lucia had become so fed-up with telling Pavo to leave the women alone and be about his duties that she'd ordered Rogatus to throw him in the basement prison for a night. It was her first real test as manageress, in terms of punishing her fellow slaves. She had always hated the way Paltucca could treat her peers so harshly, often for what seemed to Lucia like minor misdemeanours, yet she knew the slaves would see her as a soft touch if she didn't act firmly with Pavo. Besides, he was a good person to make an example of, as most of the men disliked him for his womanising ways and the older women were irritated by his laziness.

So Pavo spent a night in the basement, and his attitude towards her changed. Where he had once smiled at her and stood rather closer than he should have, he now looked at her from sullen, hooded eyes and kept his distance. Lucia had known such a reaction was inevitable, and, not having any particular affection for the man, his new dislike for her didn't matter much. The day would come, however, when someone she *did* care for – Popillia perhaps, or Merula, or even Sennianus – would have to be disciplined.

That was what it meant to wield power though, and there was little the new manageress could do about it. She would simply try to act firmly, but fairly with everyone, regardless of her personal feelings towards them. Hopefully the slaves would recognise she had a difficult job to do, and not look on her too harshly if she had to punish them for some transgression.

She vowed to never have the workers lashed or beaten with rods unless it was absolutely necessary, knowing that, from her own personal point of view, such physical violation was much harder to bear than a night or two in the prison. It wasn't the pain of the blows that Lucia had despised so much, but the feeling of helplessness, that she was powerless to stop someone hurting her, leaving her bloody and bruised, simply because she was a possession rather than a person.

Somehow, that kind of punishment was worse than being locked up alone in the dark without food for a night or two, and she knew from talking to the other slaves over the years that the majority of them felt the same.

So punishment beatings would only be used as a last resort, Lucia vowed.

And then a door handle fell off in her hand – a handle she had already asked Pavo to repair – and her irritation at the handyman grew. She walked along the corridor, out into the courtyard and gazed around, finally spotting Pavo lying on a low wall as Cornelia pulled weeds from one of the vegetable plots. It was a warm day and the slave-girl had tucked her tunic up to keep cool – it also revealed her long, shapely legs in a way that even Lucia admired.

Perhaps she should have a word with the girl? The new manageress shook her head as she strode across the courtyard towards her two charges – she could hardly tell Cornelia to cover herself on such a hot day simply because the young woman had an attractive figure.

Pavo saw her coming and a look of fear crossed his face before it was replaced with the now familiar disdain. He sat up, appeared to think about wandering off, then changed his mind and just glared as she approached. Cornelia, to her credit, was working hard, sweat coating her toned limbs and Lucia decided she really should have a word with her after all, before one of the men found the young woman too sexually alluring to resist.

"What are you doing, Pavo?" she demanded coolly, walking across and positioning herself with the sun at her back as she'd seen Paltucca do so many times. The handyman had to look up at her, and squint into the sunlight too, putting him at an immediate disadvantage. Lucia felt quite smug at her cleverness and mentally scolded herself for it.

"Just having a rest," Pavo grunted, looking away, blinking, his body set in a way that suggested he'd like to attack the manageress although Lucia knew he wasn't that stupid.

"A rest from what?"

By now, other slaves had begun to appear, acting as if they had some legitimate business within the courtyard, watching events surreptitiously. Their ludicrous attempts not to be too noticeable almost made Lucia laugh – she'd done the same thing many times over the years of course – but this was too serious a situation for her to appear weak in front of Pavo.

She was the manageress – Paltucca's replacement. She had to let the slaves know she wasn't one to cross.

"I've been in the hypocaust all day, replacing some broken tiles so the master and his guests don't suffocate from the fumes," Pavo said, meeting her eyes as if daring her to question the importance of his morning's work. "Are we not allowed a rest now that you're 'in charge'?"

Lucia was surprised to hear grumbles of agreement at that, and her bemusement was compounded when she looked around to see the same men she knew couldn't stand Pavo looking back at her. It seemed his comment had united them all, even though they knew she was, and always had been, one of them, while Pavo was a lazy bastard who was only using that last comment as an absurdly opaque way of gaining support.

She would need to learn fast as manageress.

"That door handle I asked you to fix last week in the east wing just fell off in my hand."

The handyman screwed up his face and shrugged. He even had the cheek to smirk at the onlooking slaves. "I've been too busy to get to it. Looking after the master's safety is more important than a fucking door handle, isn't that right lads?"

Lucia was astonished to hear the slaves behind her giggling at Pavo's impertinent comment. Not only that – their laughter *hurt*. Those men had always been on her side. Until now, it seemed. She tried to ignore her feelings, knowing she had to remain calm if she was to retain any measure of authority with the slaves.

"You've had all week to repair it," she said, trying to keep any emotion from her voice but Pavo was obviously encouraged by the other slaves' amused support.

"Sorry," he said, a huge grin on his face now as he lay back down on the wall, basking in the afternoon sun like a cat. "I'll sort it later, all right?"

Then he had the impertinence to use his fingers to make a walking motion, as if telling Lucia to go away. It took a monumental effort for her not to run across to him and kick him in the face, but she knew that would be the entirely wrong thing to do. Instead, she looked around and was relieved to see Rogatus watching from the back of the crowd. She waved him over then gestured for another massive slave, Vitus, a native of Britannia although one from the very far north of the island, with red hair and shoulders broader even than Regalis had boasted as a young man.

Pavo's attention was caught now, and he looked up at Lucia in alarm, mouth open as if ready to say something, but she didn't allow him the opportunity.

"Bare his back," she ordered Rogatus, who hesitated only for a moment before nodding and striding across to Pavo. The smaller man raised his hands, fear written plainly on his face.

At least the Nubian was still on her side, praise be to Sulis Minerva.

Vitus and Rogatus grabbed hold of Pavo who resisted only a little, knowing better than to fight, especially against the massive furnace-master. The two giant slaves pulled their captive's tunic down from the shoulders, revealing his pale skin, which was half-covered in dark hair and bright red pimples. Lucia could hardly have imagined a less attractive back but when she thought about what was coming, and how the man's body would look once it was done, she bit her lip and hid her face so the other slaves wouldn't see the anguish there.

This had to be done, or the others would see her as an easy target.

"You!" She pointed at one of the children, a boy of about eleven years, who gaped at her open mouthed. "Fetch me a birch wand. One as thick as your thumb. Hurry."

The laughing had stopped now but Lucia feared to look at the faces gathered around. She didn't want to see their distaste, or hate, or even disappointment in her. However she felt, she was no longer one of them. At least Sennianus wasn't there – he'd gone into Durobrivae with Nero, the foreman of the field workers, to buy essential supplies that morning and wouldn't be back until the evening. She thought of Senni as they all waited on the boy bringing the whip – as manageress she could have shared her bedchamber with whoever she liked.

But she slept alone.

And Sennianus never complained. He accepted it just as he'd accepted everything over the past twenty-one years in Villa Tempestatis. Lucia wished she could love him as he loved her, but—

"Here you are, mistress."

A birch wand as long as her arm was thrust into her hand and, jolted back to reality, she took it from the breathless boy with a smile that was more of a grimace, then, before she could change her mind and shrink away from this grim task, she walked over to Rogatus.

He looked at her and no words were needed. Taking the supple, grey branch from her, he stepped back from Pavo who was by now facing the wall of the east wing, looking back over his shoulder with a mixture of emotions on his face. Fear, anger, outrage. And hate.

Lucia could empathise with every one of those emotions, but she nodded to the giant Nubian and, raising his head to take in a deep breath through his wide nostrils, he stared at the sky, possibly offering a prayer to the gods of his own birthlands.

How many? She had seen Paltucca ordering as many as forty lashes at a time, leaving the unfortunate recipient a bloody, crying mess, but Pavo's 'crime' hardly merited that, did it?

She felt detached, as if someone else was in charge of her body. Yet she spoke, somehow.

"Twenty. Go."

There was a collective indrawing of breath from the gathered crowd, who could almost feel the agony Pavo would suffer even before Rogatus had landed the first blow. They understood Lucia was sending a message to them, and they would not forget it, even if their opinion of her had dropped.

That could hardly be avoided now.

The unmistakable sound of a thin branch whipping through the air filled the courtyard, then the slashing crack as it hit Pavo's skin, and the almost surprised, proud, nearly-repressed whimper of agony from the unfortunate victim.

Rogatus didn't hesitate, he continued to lash Pavo in a rhythmic, almost hypnotic, fashion. The victim, for his part, couldn't maintain his dignified attempt at silence – by the seventh lash he was shouting curses as each blow landed. By the fifteenth he was screaming in pain.

When the twentieth lash struck his tortured, bleeding back he was crying like a child.

Lucia wished she could do the same.

And she wondered how Paltucca could ever have stood, stony-faced, as double that number of lashes were landed on her fellow slaves. It was barbaric. Yet necessary?

Shit!

Lucia couldn't make sense of her emotions as she stood there, emulating Paltucca's hard face as Pavo lay on the ground before them, back a mess of red welts and blood, snot and saliva dribbling from his mouth and nose.

Did Paltucca feel the shame I feel now? she wondered, trying her best to keep her emotions from her face. *Did she hurt the way I'm hurting now? Or was she really the monster we always believed?*

Whatever the truth, when Pavo looked up from the ground and met her eyes, she knew he thought Lucia was as monstrous as Paltucca had ever been. She prayed silently that the rest of the slaves would take this as a message and there would be no more need for lashings.

"You did well today."

Lucia looked around, startled, as her chamber door opened without any knock of polite forewarning. Paltucca stood there and old manageress faced new. Lucia was glad her tears had dried by now.

"Thank you," she murmured, her eyes falling to the floor from long years of habit. Even when she remembered her new station as – ostensibly at least – Paltucca's equal, she didn't look up, in case her face was still puffy and red. She had no desire to ever show weakness to the old woman.

"May I sit?"

Now Lucia had no choice but to look up. "Sit? But…yes, yes of course you may."

She watched as Paltucca pulled over a small trunk from its place against the wall and sat down on the other side of the desk.

They faced one another, sizing each other up, but only for a moment so the atmosphere didn't become hostile or even unpleasant, then Paltucca nodded.

"Like I say – you did well having that lazy shit flogged. I'd have done it myself if he'd spoken to me the way he did to you."

Lucia wondered how the woman found out what had been said. She might have spies dotted all around the villa which meant Lucia would need to watch what she was doing. If she had harboured any thoughts of abusing her position, this realisation would have changed her mind, or at least made her tread very carefully. She had no desire to take unfair advantage of her place in the house for trivial things, but it was good to know how things stood.

"I don't like Pavo, but I hated seeing him being beaten." Lucia half expected the former manageress to smile nastily and brag about how much she enjoyed sadistically punishing the slaves beneath her, but instead the older woman wore an expression of understanding.

"You will get used to it."

Lucia's face must have betrayed her distaste and Paltucca's face soured again, falling into the same expression every slave in Villa

Tempestatis knew so well. "What? Do you not believe me? Do you think you are better than me? That you are oh, so compassionate and kind and will always feel like bursting into tears like a scolded child every time you have to deal out a beating?"

"I didn't—"

"You will grow to hate the slaves, Lucia," Paltucca broke in with a wave of her now-bony hand. "They are stupid, and wilful, and they'll make you wish you could drown them all in the river." She looked at the wall for a time, as if lost in thought. "Being manageress changes you," she finally muttered. "I am not the same woman I was when I was twenty, and neither will you be after a few months in charge."

The two women sat in silence for a long while until Paltucca said, as calmly as if reporting on the weather that day, "Like you, I have never known what it's like to be a mother, for I am barren. I have no maternal instincts and that is what made me such a good governess. Slaves do not need nurture like children – they need to be told what to do and disciplined with a rod when they do not perform as expected."

Paltucca had obviously come here to share a small part of herself with the new manageress, perhaps to win her over, perhaps just to let her know how hard her job was going to be. Whatever her motives were though, her words were merely hardening Lucia's hatred and years-old desire for revenge on the older woman. How dare she compare herself to Lucia? Lucia *was* a mother, she had carried her child and seen it alive in this world! Rage flared inside her but the older woman failed to notice, continuing her diatribe in a cold, flat voice.

"Once I was a bright-eyed, enthusiastic slave," Paltucca said unconvincingly. "Much like your friend Sennianus, in truth. But life does strange things to us all, eh? We all change eventually, and you will change too now that you're manageress. You can't be everyone's friend, or feel pity for them when they need punishing, or show favouritism."

"I should hate everyone equally?" Lucia growled bitterly.

Paltucca shrugged and shook her head. "I didn't order beatings because I hated a particular slave – I did it because it is absolutely vital to maintain discipline on an estate of this size, or people will take advantage. It's not about hate – although if you do develop an intense dislike for someone, you can make their life hell if you choose."

Like you did to me, you despicable, hateful bitch, Lucia thought, but kept silent, wishing the old hag would shut up and leave. It wasn't to be, not yet.

"Do not develop feelings for any of the slaves," Paltucca advised. "Or you won't be able to deliver punishments to them when required. And trust me – every one of them will need punishment at some point. Every single one. You can't let it get to you, or you'll be a broken shell of yourself within a year."

"I must be as hard as iron, as you are?"

"Yes. If the slaves like you, it's because they don't fear you enough. They will take advantage of that kind of weakness, believe me. And then the master will punish *you*. Is that fair? Should you be punished because someone like Pavo is a lazy little prick that only wants to empty his balls instead of getting on with his work?"

Lucia didn't answer but, when put like that, Paltucca's words made a strange kind of sense.

The former manageress stood up then, dusting herself down and eyeing Lucia grimly. "I need to be off and about my own business now. Tiro left things in good order, but he was a very clever man and found the clerk's job easier than I do."

Lucia also got to her feet and the two women faced one another, Lucia still struggling to hide her hatred while her predecessor appeared almost amiable now that she'd imparted her words of wisdom.

"If you ever need advice, you know where I am," Paltucca said. "Sometimes the job may become too much, and you will need someone with a firm hand to guide you."

With that, the former manageress left the room, closing the door at her back, leaving Lucia staring into the vacated space.

So Paltucca was offering her shoulder as some kind of mentor to the new manageress. It made little difference to Lucia. The old woman had been a sadistic bitch to the inhabitants of Villa Tempestatis for decades and was personally responsible for the death of Lucia's newborn child. Even if she was offering to be Lucia's best friend and confidante, it didn't matter – the woman would pay for her life's actions.

Lucia had always vowed as much, and now, as manageress, she felt the means to gain revenge were within reach if she could only figure out the best way to do it without being discovered.

CHAPTER THREE

Six months passed and Lucia learned how to be a manageress. She never had to order another punishment flogging in that time, but the slaves began to drop their eyes whenever she was around, just as they – as she! – had done over the years whenever Paltucca came into the room. It hurt Lucia to know her former peers, friends some of them, feared her so much now, but it was also pleasing because it meant she wouldn't need to punish them physically to exert her authority.

Looking back over the years now, she realised Paltucca had not really ordered beatings that often. Of course, when they did happen, it was a harrowing experience for everyone, not just the slave suffering the lashing. But, in all her twenty years in Villa Tempestatis, how many such beatings had Lucia seen? She couldn't be certain but, at the most, it only happened once or twice a year.

The marks such punishment left, both physical and mental, remained for so long though, that it seemed to the slaves as if someone was being brutalised almost perpetually. Which simply wasn't the case when looked at soberly. She herself had only been flogged a handful of times and never for long enough to leave her incapacitated for more than a day.

Still, Lucia remembered that terrible lashing Sennianus had suffered at the hands of Sosthenes so vividly, every cut of the whip stinging in her memory as if it had happened yesterday, that she desperately wanted not to have to deal out such a punishment any more than was absolutely necessary. She feared that, one day, an insolent underling would push her too far; she would order Rogatus or Aeneas to flog them as a result, and she would find herself enjoying the recipient's agony.

That day would, she prayed to Sulis, never come, no matter what Paltucca's words suggested.

One of her most important tasks was to check the financial incomings and outgoings of the estate. She would look over the books and make sure all appeared in order, before passing them to the clerk—Paltucca—to be signed off. Assuming all was in order, the master would never need to be troubled with anything. In fact, if Castus *did* ever need to be told about something it meant there was some problem Lucia and Paltucca couldn't deal with by themselves, and that would not look good for either of them.

Lucia prided herself on how well she'd managed to learn mathematics, having little prior experience of it before taking on the mantle of manageress. So she was confused one morning to look over the records handed in by Gallus, the master carpenter who was in charge of constructing any new buildings and repairing the existing ones. His figures didn't quite tally when Lucia looked back over his previous records – the amount of iron nails he'd been purchasing from the blacksmith in Durobrivae was much the same month on month, no matter whether he'd had a quiet period or, as had happened over the winter, the main barn and three storage sheds had needed major structural repairs.

Lucia knew from simply looking back over the numbers that Gallus was claiming extra expenses so he could line his own pockets.

The master would have him severely beaten when he found out, and probably sell him to be worked to death in the mines.

To compound her dilemma, Lucia actually liked Gallus. Yet what could she do?

With a heavy heart she ordered Nerva, the spindly-legged young errand boy and son of Regalis and Antonia, to bring Gallus to her. She fretted in the chamber, wondering how the man would react to being accused of such a terrible crime – stealing from one's owner was, of course, viewed as a particularly heinous act. It was pitiful, Lucia mused, staring at the wall as if in a daydream, that the theft of a little money was, in this twisted society, classed as worse than killing a slave's newborn babe.

There was a knock, then the door opened and the errand boy peered in. Lucia liked him and often rewarded him with extra rations. This was obvious favouritism, but she didn't care – Regalis, gods rest his soul, had been a friend to her, and what was the point in being manageress if she couldn't even spoil a child a little? He returned her nod and backed out into the corridor to go about his other chores as Gallus walked in.

The master-carpenter was about thirty years old, quite pleasant to look at, and tall, although not a giant like Rogatus. His main distinctive feature was his hair, which was completely grey despite his relative youth. It was most unusual and made Gallus appear rather older than he was.

"You wanted to see me, manageress?"

Lucia nodded. "Shut the door, Gallus. I have something to show you."

His eyebrows drew together in surprise – he plainly had no idea why he'd been called there – but he turned and closed the door before sitting on the stool Lucia gestured at. It was lower than the one she sat on so, despite his greater height, when they were both seated at the desk, Lucia was looking down on him.

"I won't waste any time, we both have work to be getting on with. Explain this to me."

She lifted four tablets listing the carpenter's expenses for recent months from a drawer beside her and placed them on the table, orienting them so he could read the figures scratched into the wax without any trouble. Lucia watched his face as he recognised what he was looking at, noting the fleeting panic that crossed his expression before he managed to compose himself. He peered up from the tablets to the manageress and shrugged as if in bemusement.

"Explain what, Lucia?" he asked, eyeing the figures again, apparently seeing nothing out of the ordinary there. As if all was perfectly in order.

His composure actually made Lucia wonder if she'd jumped to the wrong conclusion after all. She was no carpenter after all – maybe nails rusted away if unused, so stocks had to be maintained even when buildings weren't being repaired or erected. Would iron become brittle and unusable after such a short time? It didn't seem very likely.

She stared at him and he returned the gaze without looking insolent or arrogant. In fact, if he *was* stealing extra expenses, he looked strangely composed. Lucia genuinely had little time to waste on this, having other pressing tasks to complete before her evening meal was brought in. She could see no better way to proceed than to ask him straight out.

"You have bought a huge number of iron nails recently."

Gallus opened his mouth in an 'O', as if finally realising why he'd been called in to see the manageress but, before he could say anything, Lucia went on. "If we go to your store room will you be able to show me them? Or, if you've used them all, show me where, and why? Since nothing new has been built on the estate in the past few months I'm struggling to understand why you need so many nails."

He looked more concerned now, but still there seemed to be no trace of fear on his face. And now it appeared he saw no more reason to skirt around the issue than Lucia had.

"So I claim more money for nails than I should. Big deal."

The new manageress was so taken aback by this bold admission that she simply stared at him for a long moment. Gallus looked irritated and uncomfortable now but *still* he didn't seem to understand the trouble he was in.

Now it was his turn to speak without giving the other a chance to formulate a reply though, and he went on in a sullen voice. "Everyone does it. That's just how things work around here. One of the perks of being promoted to a better position. When I was just a labourer I took what I was given like the rest of them, but a master carpenter, or the chief cook, or, well, the manageress by the gods! We all take a little bit extra and why not? That's how it's always worked, not just here, but in every walk of life, in every—"

Lucia slammed her hand down on the desk angrily, bringing his diatribe to a halt.

"You said, 'the manageress'. What are you saying? I've never stolen anything from the master."

Gallus waved a hand dismissively. "Ach, you're new. You haven't learned the ropes yet, that's why you've pulled me in here when I should be at work. You'll be at it too, soon enough, just like Paltucca."

This revelation startled Lucia into another silence and the carpenter took advantage of it to continue his defence.

"Paltucca knew I – *we* – did it, and she did it herself. Like I say, that's how things work here in the villa. As long as we don't get greedy and take advantage of it, no-one bothers."

Lucia pondered his words, instinctively recognising the truth of them. Of course Paltucca must have known – the woman missed nothing. Yet, if the former manageress had been stealing...

This was information that might come in useful at some point.

"All right," she said, fixing the master-carpenter with her hardest stare. "I will check the other expenses for the past few months, from the cook and the furnace-master and so on and, if I find you're telling me the truth no more will be said about it."

He leaned back on the stool, relief replacing anger on his face and he ran a calloused hand through his grey hair.

"But from now on you rein it in, do you hear me? No arguments! I don't know if the master condones this, but I find it hard to believe he would be happy to find out the slaves are stealing so much from his coffers on a regular basis. For now, until I decide what to do about this going forward, you will halve the amount you are creaming off every month, and I will not tell him about our conversation."

He looked back at her angrily and seemed like he might argue but Lucia stood up and glared down at him sternly. "This is not a discussion, Gallus. You will do as I say, or I will go to the Publius Licinius Castus and tell him everything. I'm sure you can imagine the repercussions…"

He stood up, now towering over the manageress, but her expression of hard determination never wavered. "Make no threats, man, or things will not go well for you. Get out, and think yourself lucky that I'm allowing you to continue claiming a little extra at all."

He went, slamming the door behind him, and Lucia sank back down onto her stool, breathing out a sigh of relief that the meeting was over. For a moment she had feared Gallus might actually strike her, and his demeanour as he stormed from the room did not bode well – she would need to watch her back for a while, until he calmed down. If this kind of theft was as widespread as the carpenter claimed, word would get around that she was coming down on it and there would be a few unhappy slaves.

She laughed softly at that thought. *Unhappy slaves. As if there's any other kind!*

Well, apart from Sennianus of course.

She smiled at the thought of her friend and occasional lover, wishing he was there with her now, simply to offer some moral support and a face that wasn't twisted in a frown or worse. She seemed to draw a lot of black looks from her fellow slaves these days.

Yet this had been a very productive, enlightening day. She cared little for Gallus, or the cook. Their petty thefts were nothing to the overall turnover of Villa Tempestatis, which is why it had gone unchecked.

But the fact that Paltucca, as manageress, had been implicated in such behaviour suggested Lucia could do the same if she wanted. Yes, she nodded to herself. This knowledge could open up some very interesting opportunities…

She got up and stretched, arching her back to work out the stiffness from sitting so long. Tidying away her documents she decided to go for a walk. It would give her a chance to check everything was running smoothly about the place and do her good to get some fresh air.

Throwing her thickest cloak on, she walked along the corridor, breathing in the chill winter air. Outside a few of the slaves were busy mending damaged fences or sweeping leaves and Lucia wandered amongst them, nodding to those she felt were doing a good job and trying to ignore the slackers. Her presence would spur them on enough, without her having to upbraid them and bring yet more discontent to the villa.

At the edge of the gardens she stopped and looked out over the view. Even in winter it was a wonderful sight, with the wood smoke from works and homes curling into the air over Durobrivae in the middle-distance.

"Busy?"

Lucia's heart gave a lurch as she recognised the voice.

"*Domina*," she said, and she could feel her pale, cold face flushing red as she turned to look at Dianna. "I just came out for a walk to check the other slaves were busy—"

The mistress raised a hand and smiled, taking up a position next to Lucia and gazing out towards the nearby town herself. "You don't have to explain yourself. I know you work harder than anyone on the whole estate."

They looked around the countryside together in silence for a time, breaths clouding in the air, watching as a bird of prey – a sparrowhawk or falcon perhaps – hovered in the sky, hoping to spot a mouse rooting in the sparse foliage.

"It's a cold one today, isn't it?"

"Indeed, *domina*," Lucia agreed, pulling her cloak tighter about herself and shivering. "It's a day for thick clothes, even indoors."

Just then someone appeared from a grove of trees and Lucia could tell from the figure's confident gait that it was Paltucca. The clerk must have decided, like herself and Dianna, to take a walk in the crisp morning air.

"She's certainly wrapped up warm," the mistress noted. "Is that a new cloak she's wearing? New scarf too from the looks of it. Very handsome they are too."

Lucia couldn't quite make out what Paltucca was wearing and the sharpness of the *domina's* eyesight surprised her. Sure enough though, when the old clerk came a little closer Lucia could see the light blue scarf and dark woollen cloak Dianna had noted and they did appear to be new.

"Castus must be giving her too much money," the *domina* laughed. "Those are fine garments. I shall need to find out what my husband is paying her these days."

It was a simple joke, with no hidden undertones – just one woman making a remark on another's dress – but Lucia sensed an opening and, without thinking, shook her head.

"I know what the master pays Paltucca. It's not much. But she always seemed to have extra money for nice things. I've always wondered about it and so did the rest of the women."

They watched as Paltucca, pretending not to notice them, changed course so she didn't come past them, instead heading for the far side of the house, and then Dianna turned to Lucia with a frown on her face.

"What—"

"Lucia!" A cry came from behind them before Dianna could ask her question and the women both turned to see what was happening. Sennianus stood by the door leading to the kitchen, waving his arm. "Sorry Lucia, but we've got a problem with the evening meal, could you come and speak to the cook?"

"Oh, for Jupiter's sake," Dianna muttered, rolling her eyes. "Can those fools not do anything for themselves without asking someone to hold their hand?" She waved her hand in exasperation, dismissing Lucia. "Yes, you'd better go and see to it or we'll all be eating cold porridge this evening. Off you go, dear."

Lucia didn't need to be told twice and hurried away, thanking Sulis Minerva for the timely interruption that had stalled the *domina* questioning her about Paltucca's earnings. The remark would surely play on Dianna's mind, and she might even mention it to Castus.

In truth, Lucia had never once questioned Paltucca's income, and, to her knowledge, none of the other slaves had ever mentioned her having nicer things than would be expected of a woman in her position. The new scarf and cloak were, admittedly, rather nice, but nothing Paltucca couldn't afford on her allowance.

Dianna was not to know any of that though. She would wonder about it, and mention it to Castus, and he too would wonder about it.

And one day, perhaps, that little seed of doubt might be the hated Paltucca's undoing…

CHAPTER FOUR

The following months were relatively quiet and everyone who had been skimming extra expenses had either cut back on the amount they were taking or stopped completely, no doubt from fear of the consequences should their transgressions be brought to light by the meddlesome new manageress.

In the second week of a warm September the old lech, Vibidius, came to stay at the villa along with his wife. Now that she was manageress, Lucia knew why the elderly nobleman was visiting – he'd been a senator once, an old friend of the master's long-dead father, and apparently still wielded considerable power back in Rome. It had been his influence that helped Castus's family name rise again in prominence after the Emperor Marcus Aurelius had taken a dislike to him.

Publius Licinius Castus was very much in Vibidius's debt and so, naturally, the master commanded Lucia to make sure he and his wife were well looked after in every way. Castus didn't spell out exactly what he meant by that, but it was quite obvious.

Lucia had never forgotten the way Vibidius had touched her, and asked Castus to allow him to bed her when she was just a little girl. The memory made the bile rise in her throat to this day, and she vowed to make sure none of the youngest slaves, be they boys or girls, were used to serve the geriatric pervert. She knew from personal experience that the master did not allow his guests to violate the slave children, but, considering what Vibidius had done for him in the past few years, Castus might turn a blind eye to the man's tastes on this visit.

Better for everyone to avoid any problems by just having adults serve the senator and his wife, Lucia thought. Yet, although it was a good idea, it was much harder to execute in practice. Children did all sorts of tasks around Villa Tempestatis: milking the cows and goats, feeding the livestock, cleaning floors, weeding the gardens, carrying messages, and so on. It was impossible to keep the younger slaves out of Vibidius's presence completely, and it did, as the manageress had foreseen, cause problems within two days of his arrival.

The office door burst open without any knock and Popillia stormed into the room, glaring down at Lucia who was diligently checking the expenses everyone had been claiming. "You have to do something about that piece of filth, before someone else does."

The manageress hid her irritation at the uninvited visitor's bad manners and stared coolly up at her. Popillia had aged quite well, considering she'd given birth to seven children. Her breasts were still quite firm, her waist relatively slim, and her face creased but still very pretty. Lucia had liked her very much when they first met many years ago, and she still liked her now.

Yet a conversation such as this had to take place on the correct footing, and that meant making sure their roles were made very clear from the outset.

"It's customary to knock before you barge into the manageress's chamber."

The words, and the frosty tone they were delivered in, made Popillia start in surprise but the older woman rallied and nodded apologetically.

"Yes, mistress. Forgive me, I'm upset, I didn't mean any offence."

Lucia pursed her lips, not quite ready to show her forgiveness yet. Although she dearly wished to remain close to the likes of Popillia and Arethusa and the other women she'd called her friends for so long, there always now had to be an air of professional detachment, and respect bordering on fear from the slaves for their manageress.

It was hard to play mean with Popillia though, and Lucia waved a hand dismissively, inviting her to pull over the stool from its place in the corner and explain what the problem was.

"It's that filthy old deviant, Vibidius."

"What about him?" Lucia felt her heart sink at the man's name but it didn't show on her face.

"He's only been here a couple of days, yet he's been touching all the slaves and frightening them."

"You mean the children, I assume?"

"Aye. You know what the man is, I was there when he asked the master if he could spend the night with you all that time ago. He's only got worse with age it seems. He had little Aeneas, the errand boy, you know the lad? Of course you do, by Sulis I'm forgetting who I'm talking to I'm so angry. Anyway, he had him in tears this morning because he put his hands down the boy's tunic and kissed him on the mouth. Then, just now in the baths, he's pulled the clothes off the young girl bringing fresh towels and ordered her to join him in the water."

"Did she?"

"No! Prima shooed the girl outside and offered to deal with whatever needs the old bastard had herself."

"What did he say?"

"He said yes, and had her on the edge of the pool. Her back is skinned bloody and, well you know what Prima is like, she's trying to put a brave face on, trying to seem like it doesn't bother her, but she was sobbing when I saw her."

Lucia shook her head. Where did the man find the stamina? He must be nearly seventy, if not older than that.

"What can I do?" the manageress asked sadly. "Things like this are perfectly natural in many – most – households throughout the empire. It's just our good fortune that Castus tends to look after his younger slaves better than most. I can't go to the master and tell him to put a stop to Vibidius's behaviour, I don't have the authority. Prima has hopefully sated his lust for a while and there'll be no more…unwanted advances." She shrugged helplessly. "I'm sorry, Popillia, you know how I feel about this, but we're just slaves and Castus has ordered me to make sure Vibidius gets whatever he wants while he's here."

"Someone should cut the old bastard's cock off!" Popillia got to her feet, face flushed with impotent anger. "He'll rape one of the children before the week is out, mark my words Lucia."

"Like I say – we're just slaves. The master and his guests can do what they want to us. In many houses Vibidius wouldn't have to take no for an answer, he'd simply have molested Aeneas and the little towel girl. All we can do is hope his respect for Castus is enough to stop him crossing that line. He's only here until the end of the week anyway; we'll just need to deal with his depraved behaviour until then."

"But—"

"Get back to your duties Popillia. And don't let me hear you mention cutting the genitals off one of the master's guests ever again. By Sulis, you should know better than to talk about a free man, and a senator too, in that way. You'll get yourself into a lot of trouble."

"You'll do nothing then?" Popillia stood up and glared down at her as Lucia frowned back.

What did the woman expect her to do? Kill the old devil herself? Demand the master protect his slaves from the man who'd rescued his family honour? The notion was ludicrous, and she wondered at Popillia even coming here with this complaint.

"There's nothing I *can* do, Popillia, apart from ask you all to keep the younger slaves well away from Vibidius when possible. Now get back to work, we've spent enough time discussing this."

Popillia went away and Lucia sighed as the door slammed shut behind her. That was becoming something of a habit – it seemed everyone who visited left with a lower opinion of her than when they'd first come into the room. Any good will the other slaves might feel towards her was being slowly eroded away along with the battered doorframe.

* * *

At dinner that afternoon Lucia ordered the serving boys and girls – none younger than fifteen – to secretly water down Vibidius's wine even more than was usual. Of course, as manageress, Lucia wasn't expected to personally attend to the diners, but she could lurk around the kitchen, watching as each succulent dish was prepared and carried through to the triclinium for Castus, Dianna, Vibidius and his wife, Fausta, to enjoy.

Once, when one of the slaves went out a side door to bring in extra firewood from the store, Lucia noticed Paltucca outside and was surprised to see her talking to a dark-haired child. The little boy ran off and Paltucca turned towards the kitchen. The two women's eyes met momentarily before the door was closed again and Lucia turned her attention back to monitoring the meal.

Her ruse with the drinks didn't seem to have been noticed by the old senator and Lucia fervently hoped keeping him as sober as possible would allow the pervert to control his base desires. She was pleased to note the meal was a dignified affair, with lots of polite chatter – about politics and trade and the wars the legions were fighting that year between the men – although Vibidius spent much of his time looking out at the gardens.

Dianna, like Castus, spent much of her time in Britannia nowadays and so the *domina* always loved to hear about what the women were wearing back in the heart of the empire.

Rome sounded like an incredible place and even Lucia, who cared little for the goings on outside of Villa Tempestatis, drank in Fausta's words. The senator's wife was a small, thin woman, with white hair and long, delicate fingers which she used often to punctuate her words. The manageress rather liked her, and wondered if she knew about her husband's darkest vices.

Of course, she must – but women were like slaves in some ways. The men could do as they pleased, legally, while their wives had to put up with it. There were, no doubt, exceptions to that rule, but Fausta and Dianna were not them. Not openly at least.

Still, Fausta must have had some modicum of influence over Vibidius, as he always seemed to behave himself when she was around, just as Publius Licinius Castus only ever raped Lucia or Merula or whoever his favourite was at the time, when Dianna was out of the way.

Concealing their behaviour was, Lucia supposed, seen by the nobles as the fit and proper way to act like a beast. It allowed the Roman women, and the rest of polite society, to pretend it wasn't really happening, or at least didn't matter. Slaves were there to be used however their owners saw fit after all.

The manageress wondered how Castus would react if he found out he wasn't the only one who'd slept with someone else. Had Dianna ever told him about her sexual encounter with the peddler? Lucia seriously doubted it – he still drank to excess most days, and he was quite inebriated already even though it was only early evening. He'd probably kill his wife if he ever found out what she'd done and, being uncharitable, Lucia wondered if that was why the mistress had been nicer to her in the years since the whole thing with Vassinus and the robbery had happened.

A sudden thought struck her then, like a lightning bolt. She was dumbfounded, but, before she could follow the trail of it, Vibidius stood up, rubbing his eyes as if he was tired, and the manageress turned her attention back to the gap between the doors, watching to see what would happen next.

"It's very warm this evening, isn't it?" the old man was saying although, to be honest, Lucia didn't think it was all that hot – a light shower had cooled the air earlier in the afternoon and the leaves of the shrubs outside still glistened with the bright drops that hadn't dried even now. "I think I will retire to the flower garden for a little while to get some air, it looks so inviting. No, Fausta, you wait here my love, and enjoy the rest of your peacock eggs. I will return in a very short while; some time on my own will see me right."

He walked, rather faster than his supposed tiredness suggested, towards the side door of the dining room, which led directly outside. There was something in his manner, something in the way he'd been looking out the windows throughout the entire first two courses, that made Lucia feel uneasy.

"Thracius," she said, turning to the cook who was slicing freshly roasted meat. "I need to do something. Make sure the diners are not kept waiting too long for that boar, I'll be back soon."

She hurried out into the corridor, not noticing the black look Thracius threw her as she went, or the muttered, "Yes, empress, pfft, telling me how to run my own bloody kitchen, who does she think she is?" that followed her out the door.

Lucia sprinted towards the tower in the northwest corner of the house, knowing it would be remarked upon if anyone saw her in such a hurry but feeling impelled by some dark premonition. She went out the door there, quietly, into the garden, peering back towards the triclinium which stood out a little way from the rest of the wing, affording fine views of the gardens and surrounding lands for the diners.

Vibidius was walking, glancing back over his shoulder every so often, down the shallow hill towards one of the grain stores. What was he up to?

She hastened after him, taking care to remain out of sight behind the trees and bushes that dotted the grounds, fearing discovery not so much by Vibidius but from the master or mistress. As the house rose behind her, eventually dipping out of sight, she focused her full attention on the old senator and finally understood where he was going.

One of the children was playing a game amongst the low crab-apple trees that grew next to the grain store. Lucia recognised him now as Silvanus, the dark-haired, seven-year-old son of two field labourers.

The very child Paltucca had just been talking to. Undoubtedly the twisted old clerk had been telling Silvanus to play outside the triclinium, knowing Vibidius would see him there – perhaps the senator had specifically asked Paltucca to set things up just like this, so he could indulge himself without being caught.

The boy had a stick in his hand and was using it to slash at some long grass, occasionally jumping back or climbing halfway up a slim tree-trunk, as if he were the mighty hero in a fight against invisible enemies. It would have been a beautiful, innocent sight, the manageress thought, had Vibidius not been about to insert himself into the game.

What should she do?

She stopped walking, mind racing, desperately trying to think of some way to stop the senator from doing what he'd obviously been planning all throughout the dinner. Silvanus looked up, noticing Vibidius heading towards him, and the child's sweet smile faded, replaced with an expression of bemusement and fear. Rage flooded Lucia and she wished she could run down and smash the old pervert's head in with a rock before he harmed the boy, but that was out of the question. Especially when she spotted Paltucca hidden amongst a grove of trees, gazing back at her with a triumphant look on her face.

Never before in her whole life had Lucia felt so impotent and the desire to vomit, to cry, replaced her rage as she stood stock still, like one of the statues with their dead eyes that dotted the villa grounds. There was nothing she could do to help the boy, just as there had been nothing she could do to help her slaughtered parents, or Merula, or her own abandoned child.

Then Vibidius tripped on a shallow dip in the grass and fell over with a cry. Unfortunately, he wasn't injured, and got slowly back to his feet, smiling at Silvanus who hadn't moved since noticing the old man's appearance.

Lucia turned and ran as fast as she could back to the house, this time heading directly for the triclinium rather than the tower.

Castus, Dianna and Fausta were just digging into the freshly served roast boar in onion sauce when Lucia burst in through the door which Vibidius had closed behind him. All three nobles looked up in surprise at her breathless state and she cursed herself for not planning this better.

She hurried across to the master who was chewing his first mouthful of the main course and staring at her in consternation. Without thinking, Lucia bent down and whispered into his ear, using her hand to muffle the sound as much as possible so the women wouldn't hear.

"*Dominus*, Vibidius has tripped and, I believe, injured himself. I thought it best to tell you rather than having slaves go to him. I do not believe the senator would appreciate everyone seeing him in pain. We should hurry, I think he turned his ankle and may be in great pain."

Castus sat for a moment, as if trying to take in her words, and Lucia wondered if she should have watered his wine too as he was clearly very drunk. At last, though, he sat back with a jerk, staring at Dianna wordlessly, then got to his feet.

"What's wrong?" his wife asked, but he just shook his head and smiled at her in what he must have thought was a reassuring manner.

"Just a minor irritation, my dear," the master muttered. "Lucia needs me for a moment. You two women remain here and enjoy your food. I'll be back soon."

Dianna's eyes turned to Lucia and the old distrust and jealousy was there again, as it had been a decade ago when Castus was using Lucia as his plaything. The mistress's mouth tightened into a thin line and she stared at her husband, but she could hardly question him further without angering him.

"I see," was all she said, but her malevolent gaze bored into Lucia as if it might cut right through to her heart.

"Come," the master said, walking as fast as he could, if rather unsteadily, out through the door to the garden which Lucia had left open. She followed him but hurried ahead, leading him towards the senator's position impatiently, knowing every moment they wasted meant more suffering for little Silvanus. There was no sign of Paltucca amongst the trees now – the woman had probably panicked and hurried back to the house when she saw the master approaching.

"How did you know?" Castus slurred as they walked, far too slowly for Lucia's liking, down the slope towards the flower garden to the north of the house. "About Vibidius falling I mean?"

"I was in the tower," she lied, picking her way down the hill carefully. "Making sure the alarm trumpet was in good order. I'm always checking the thing nowadays, after what happened with those robbers ten years ago. From up there I saw the senator out for a walk, and then he tripped. I could hear his cry of pain even from up at the top of the tower, *dominus*, so I thought it best to fetch you to help in case he's broken something."

Castus almost fell over himself then, so unsteady was he, but he sniggered at his clumsiness and followed the manageress with a foolish smile on his face, which he tried to hide given the solemn purpose of their journey.

"Are we nearly there yet—"

They both stopped dead at the bottom of the short incline and stared at the scene in front of them.

Vibidius was there but showed no sign of any broken bones as he stood with his back to them. Lucia could tell immediately what was happening, but it took a moment for Castus to process what he was seeing, and then, frowning, he moved a little way to the side to get a better view, as if confirming he wasn't imagining things.

The beatific smile on the senator's face made Lucia shiver and once again a murderous rage filled her.

"What in the name of Mithras is the meaning of this?"

Castus might be drunk, but he barked the question as if he was back on the parade ground with a legion before him and Vibidius shrank back instantly, away from the boy on the ground who stared up at Lucia with a terrified, pleading look on his face that almost broke her heart all over again.

"Castus!" the senator muttered irritably, smiling through clenched teeth over his shoulder and pulling his tunic around in a pitiful attempt to cover his erect phallus. "I was just enjoying a walk in your gardens. How is dinner? Is it nearly finished? I hope you saved some dessert for me!"

The master glared down at the petrified slave-boy and jerked his head in the direction of the house. "Get back home," he commanded, and Silvanus didn't need to be told twice. He ran, sobbing, and Lucia wanted to go after him, to take him in her arms and hug him. To stroke his soft, dark hair and make things right.

But that was impossible now, she knew that all too well, and besides, she had to stay here until this was done.

Castus himself, drunk and befuddled, looked like he didn't really know what to say next. His anger was plain – that the senator should abuse his hospitality and trust like this…! Yet, the old man had supported him through hard times. Lucia watched as conflicting emotions warred across his red face, and then he spoke in clipped tones.

"The manageress said you fell over." He glanced at Lucia questioningly, as if he was beginning to understand her real motives for coming to fetch him. Indeed, she knew he'd have figured it out straight away if he wasn't so inebriated.

"What?" Vibidius had covered himself by now and turned to face Castus although his member was still bulging ludicrously beneath the skinny man's tunic. "Eh? Yes, oh, so I did, I tripped in a dip on the ground, that's right."

Both men stared at one another, unsure what to do or say next and the manageress knew this would be the end of it. Until the next time Vibidius wanted to empty his balls.

"Was the young boy helping you back to your feet, senator?"

Vibidius stared at Lucia, surprised at her temerity. "Of course he wasn't, you stupid bitch," he growled. "I think we all know what the lad was doing, don't we? Let's not play games."

That reply rekindled Castus's anger – Lucia had clearly given the man an excuse, as absurd as it was, for what he'd been up to with Silvanus, but the old fool was too arrogant to take it. Instead, he'd opted for the truth and admitted blatantly ignoring Castus's wishes not to abuse his younger slaves.

"You know how I feel about that, damn it, Vibidius," the master said, stepping forward and pushing his chest out as he did so.

Lucia watched the men face off, hoping they would come to blows and Vibidius would be thrown out, neatly ending any chance of future problems with him.

"After everything I've done for you, Castus, you ungrateful dog, I think I'm entitled to a bit of fun with one or two of your slaves. You're such a prude! You know you'd still be out of favour with Rome if it wasn't for my influence?"

"And I've done all I can to repay you for that, senator," the master growled. "Using children in such ways might be perfectly acceptable in other houses, but not in mine. You can do what you like with the older slaves – men and women – and even at that, none of my other friends or guests are allowed such freedom with the workers. You should think yourself lucky. I should—"

"You should what?" Vibidius cackled, eyeing Castus's raised fist in disgust. "Look at the state of you. In your cups as usual. You couldn't fight sleep, you useless sot."

Lucia couldn't believe what she was hearing – this was more entertaining than any musicians' performance or dancing girls, both of which were regular features at Villa Tempestatis when the master was in residence. This was the greatest show she'd seen in a long time.

It was about to get even better.

"Who do you think you're talking to?" Castus demanded, and he reached out as if to grab Vibidius around the throat, but the old man slapped his hand away and spat right in the master's face.

The transformation was instant. Lucia guessed it must have been Castus's old military training that took over then, as the drunk, babbling fool suddenly lashed out, landing a thunderous right hook on Vibidius's jaw. There was a loud click as the old senator's teeth came together and he flew backwards onto the grass.

Castus stared down at him, while Lucia watched, wide-eyed, wishing she could land a kick on the perverted old bastard herself although, looking at Vibidius, it seemed there was no need for any more blows.

The senator wasn't moving.

"By Mithras, what have I done?"

The master dropped to his knees beside the fallen senator and shook him, exhorting him to wake up, demanding to know if he was all right.

"I've killed him, by the gods." He turned to look up at Lucia, shock and terror on his face in equal measure. "What should I do? Vibidius is a friend of Emperor Commodus. I'll be beheaded for this!"

The inebriated master was close to hysteria and Lucia savoured the moment. Oh how she hated Publius Licinius Castus for all that he'd done to her. And now, here she would have her revenge, for she had engineered this whole situation and it had turned out beyond her wildest fantasies. The deviant Vibidius killed, and the master surely to suffer the same fate.

Lucia's mind was clear though, unlike Castus's, and she suddenly realised exactly what might happen when this crime was discovered. Commodus was a brutal, much-hated emperor who had recently executed a number of senators for plotting against him. He would not stop at beheading Castus – the entire family might very well be wiped out.

Including the slaves.

That wasn't the revenge Lucia wanted. And this day's work would give Lucia even more power within the household. She walked across to Castus and looked into his eyes, willing him to calm down for a moment.

"What are you talking about, *dominus*? The senator fell over and struck his head on that rock there." She pointed at a nearby stone and he glanced at it uncomprehendingly. "That's why I came to fetch you, remember?"

He stared at her, dumbfounded for a long moment and then, very slowly, he nodded as the light of understanding filled his eyes.

"Yes." The trauma of the events seemed to have sobered him up and his usual air of command began to return. "Yes, that's right. What a terrible accident. What should we do, Lucia?"

"You must pull yourself together, *dominus*, and break the bad news to the senator's wife. She will be upset and need comforting."

"Dianna will take care of her," he agreed, taking deep breaths but calmly now, no longer looking like he would lose control of himself. "What about the…body?"

"I will have the men carry him to the infirmary. I am sure the magistrate from Durobrivae will want to check it over before the funeral."

Castus paled at that, but the gears were turning in his mind and he knew Lucia's plan was essentially foolproof. The only person who might ruin things was the boy, Silvanus.

"The child Vibidius was with when we came here," Castus said. "He must be taken care of. If the magistrate questions him our scheme will fall apart and I will be doomed. We need to kill him."

"No!" Lucia was outraged. Castus had just murdered a powerful Roman nobleman after an argument over that boy, yet now was talking about killing him as casually as if discussing the weather? Truly these people were twisted. "It will look very suspicious if the only witness also dies suddenly, don't you think, *dominus*? Silvanus is a clever child – I will speak with him and make sure he knows exactly what happened here today. Trust me."

They faced one another in silence, each marshalling their thoughts, making plans, searching for possible difficulties in carrying off this deception. Then Castus nodded.

"Truly you have been the best of slaves, Lucia. You come to my family's rescue once again. I shall not forget it."

"Thank you, master," she replied, then gestured towards the house. "You had better go and break the terrible news to Fausta. I will take care of everything else."

She watched him walk back up the low hill, visibly pulling himself together as he went until, by the time he went over the summit his back was straight, shoulders set proudly. Commanding and in control of things as expected from a tribune of Rome.

Lucia might hate Castus, but she didn't wish the destruction of everyone in the house. She had other plans for revenge and the master's gratitude towards her for this day's work would come in very handy once she set them into motion.

She hurried back to the house and headed for the baths. Rogatus would be needed to help bring Vibidius's loathsome corpse back to the villa in preparation for burial, and a messenger must be sent to Durobrivae to report the terrible 'accident'.

As she walked she recalled the thought that had struck her earlier on in the triclinium – Maximus, the only child of Dianna and Castus, bore little resemblance to the master.

It was a decade now since the peddler Vassinus had visited Villa Tempestatis but Lucia could still vividly remember the man attempting to rape her before Regalis killed him. And, prior to that, the *domina,* naked in the baths with the charismatic visitor.

She knew now why Dianna had been kinder to her since that time: the *domina* had been terrified Lucia would tell the master his beloved son wasn't really his.

Maximus was the robber Vassinus's bastard son.

Lucia sent a prayer skywards, thanking Sulis Minerva for what had been a very productive, happy day.

* * *

The magistrate came and went. No-one doubted Castus and Lucia in the story they told. If Paltucca had been watching what had transpired, she never told a soul. Once, perhaps even now still in Rome, when something like this happened and slaves needed to be questioned it would be done routinely by torturing them. For some insane reason which Lucia couldn't even begin to comprehend, the Romans thought torturing people would make them tell the truth. Thankfully the practice had died out in Britannia – in this part of it at least. Young Silvanus told the story Lucia had given him and, since no-one suspected any foul play, the investigation was concluded quickly.

Vibidius's funeral followed, a lavish affair which cost a lot of money, with people the perverted old bastard had never even met wailing and crying as if he was their best friend. It made Lucia sick to her stomach to see the outpouring of 'grief' for such a despicable human, when her own baby had never been shown any respect by anyone.

No hired mourners, or feast, or earnest platitudes for him, no, but for Vibidius, no expense was spared. His widow, Fausta, had actually demanded they return his body to Rome so he could be buried near his beloved city, but the weather was so unseasonably hot that it was simply not feasible. So Vibidius had to make do with a plot alongside the best Durobrivae had to offer, in a cemetery outside the town walls.

Castus appeared genuinely sad to say farewell to his friend which probably helped allay any suspicion that might have fallen on him. Once the burial ceremony was over Fausta sailed home, and a week passed with no-one coming to accuse the master of Vibidius's murder. Castus seemed to relax and things around Villa Tempestatis went back to normal, much to everyone's relief.

Popillia gave Lucia a knowing glance whenever they met, a small smile, of respect and gratitude that let the manageress know

Vibidius's death wasn't regarded by the slaves as the unhappy accident it had been painted.

Lucia was very pleased indeed at the whole situation. The boy, Sulis, had been rescued from what would undoubtedly have developed into a longer and more brutal tribulation, while the slaves, and amusingly, Publius Licinius Castus too, viewed Lucia as some kind of saviour. Yes, everything had turned out well for the manageress, and it would surely allow her even more opportunities to put her carefully laid plans into place when the time came.

CHAPTER FIVE

"Have you heard the news?" Dianna asked Lucia at breakfast one morning. Very occasionally, the manageress would be invited to eat a meal with the master and his wife, so they could discuss anything important in an informal, relaxed setting. With business out of the way now, the mistress now steered the conversation in a new direction.

"What news, *domina*?"

"Castus is going to give Paltucca her freedom. Isn't that wonderful? The woman has been with us for so many years, it's time she was manumitted, don't you think?"

Dianna smiled but Lucia's stomach lurched at the suggestion her despised nemesis would escape any form of retribution for everything she'd done over the years.

Yet she kept her face impassive as the master nodded earnestly. "Paltucca might not be everyone's favourite person, but she has been a loyal servant to us, and she did an excellent job of taking care of the place before you took over her position Lucia. She deserves this, I believe."

"When will the rod ceremony be, *dominus*?"

"In a month, Lucia. Everything is being arranged by the magistrate, so if you could deal with the guests' invitations, food, drink, entertainers, and so on, it would be appreciated."

The manageress nodded. "Of course, *dominus*, I will see it's done."

He smiled at her. He'd been smiling at her a lot since they'd covered up Vibidius's murder together. Not in any sexual, or lover's way – it was more of a friendly expression, as if he finally saw her as something more than just one of his possessions. The master believed Lucia was utterly devoted to him of course – probably even suspected that she was in love with him, the blind, arrogant fool.

As she made her excuses and left the room to be about her duties, Lucia thought angrily of Paltucca's part in little Silvanus's violation and knew she could not allow the clerk to be manumitted.

It was time to move forward with the first stage of her vengeance.

* * *

Before she became manageress, Lucia had never left the estate since she'd been brought there as a child. Not once in all those years had she set foot outside Villa Tempestatis's extensive grounds. Some of the slaves were allowed to go to Durobrivae – Sennianus for example – but in general most of them weren't trusted. Slave owners, especially in a place like this, were always worried their workers would simply run off, never to be seen again. It didn't happen very often, but it did happen – Lucia remembered Sosthenes, who had been branded on the face to mark him as a captured runaway.

So, when Lucia was promoted she took the opportunity to travel into Durobrivae sometimes, to buy supplies and just to see a small part of the world outside the villa's enclosing walls. She'd also been visiting someone else during those trips, and she made her way there that morning, when Gallus stopped to unload the goods which they'd brought from home to pay their taxes. Wool and barley and oats and more, but Lucia left it all up to the master carpenter who knew this business very well. In fact, it was Gallus who had told her about the man in the dingy establishment situated a little way behind the main row of shops. She'd demanded to know where the carpenter kept the money he'd skimmed from his inflated expenses over the years, and he grudgingly told her about this other man.

The *argentarius,* or banker. The man who could be trusted to hold your money for you, so you didn't need to try and keep it safe within your own house. Most of the *argentarii* could be found in the forum of Durobrivae, but this fellow had a reputation for asking no questions while still being trustworthy enough; he had been serving those in the know from Villa Tempestatis for many years. Lucia had made quite a few deposits here recently herself, all of it stolen from the estate's profits.

She went through the sturdy iron-studded door into the low building which, for obvious reasons, was built from stone and had no windows. Two massively built men watched her every move, wooden cudgels tucked into their belts – Lucia had absolutely no doubt they would make short work of anyone trying to steal from the place.

"Today is the day," she said in a low voice, and the banker's eyes widened slightly before he smiled and hurried away into the back room, returning moments later with a ledger, which he placed on the counter between them. Together, they looked down at the meticulous records the little man had been keeping, with every coin noted along with the name, and signature, of the person who had deposited it and the date.

The column he had opened the page at showed a considerable figure, and Lucia nodded in satisfaction. This would be more than enough for her purposes.

Just then, the door was thrown open and all eyes turned to look at the newcomers.

It was Paltucca, who grinned in triumph as she locked gazes with Lucia.

"I told you, but you didn't want to believe me," the old woman crowed, addressing the man following at her back: Publius Licinius Castus.

The master stared at Lucia, disappointment and rage radiating from him like a physical force.

CHAPTER SIX

"I actually thought you'd make a good manageress," Paltucca said, moving further into the room, completely ignoring the two hulking guards who looked baffled by what was happening. "But you're just like all the rest of them at the villa. Greedy. You couldn't help yourself, could you?"

The old woman shook her head condescendingly and Lucia glanced at Castus who was glaring at her in the gloomy chamber, fists clenched, bloodless lips drawn together in a severe line. If there was one thing that the master hated, it was losing money, and there could be only one punishment if he found out someone had stolen a lot of his cash: crucifixion.

A shiver of fear ran down Lucia's back as she wondered just how well her plans had been laid, but there was nothing else for it now – she couldn't back out of this, it was too late.

"What are you doing here?" she asked Paltucca, as calmly as her tortured nerves would allow.

"You should have known I have eyes and ears all over Villa Tempestatis, Lucia. I'd heard you were taking extra wages every month," the woman replied. "And depositing them here with that little fool." She gestured towards the banker who raised an eyebrow but remained silent as her tirade continued. "A nice nest egg that you would come to collect once you were freed by the *dominus*. No doubt that ledger records everything," Paltucca smiled wickedly as she stepped across to place a gaunt hand on the banker's record book before he could remove it. "And signs your own death warrant, girl."

Lucia stared at her for a time, marshalling her thoughts, preparing herself mentally for what was to come. And then she turned to Castus and inclined her head.

"I think we should perhaps call the magistrate, *dominus*."

The Roman shook his head instantly and Lucia guessed why, having been privy to some of Villa Tempestatis's records herself: he was as crooked as any of the slaves, recording less profit than he should have been and, as a result, paying less tax into the imperial coffers. He wanted to do this as quietly, and unofficially, as possible.

"No, this is good enough," Castus grunted, gesturing towards the banker and the silent, staring guards. "I have enough witnesses to make a case, should it come to that. Tell me Paltucca is mistaken, Lucia. You haven't been stealing from me, have you? After everything we've been through together over the years?"

You mean like all those times you raped me? Lucia wanted to scream in his face. *Like the way you and your legion slaughtered my kinsfolk in Germania and stole me away to be your possession here in Britannia? Like the way you murdered my beautiful newborn son? Or the way I helped you cover up the death of Vibidius?*

She didn't say any of that; his time would come eventually. He would pay for what he'd done to her, but, today it was Paltucca's turn.

"All right then," Lucia said, turning to the old woman who still held her wrinkled hand on the banker's ledger. "Let's look at those figures and see what's been happening."

"This is a very serious business," said the banker, addressing Castus. "I will close the shop for the day so we won't be disturbed." At the tribune's nod of agreement, the banker looked towards one of the guards who silently walked to the door, threw across the three heavy iron bolts, and took up a position beside it. Now no-one could get in.

Or out.

"So," Paltucca demanded, taking control of the situation with the same confidence she'd always shown for as long as Lucia had known her. "Why are you here today? Gallus is taking the goods to the tax collectors, but you decided to come to see this banker, a man who works from a shop hidden behind the forum, unlike the respectable *argentarii*. A man with an unsavoury reputation."

"How do you know?" Lucia demanded in a voice as hard and cool as the older woman's. She couldn't afford to let Paltucca dictate things. "Never mind answering that," she went on, before Paltucca could reply, "let's just look at the ledger. That will clear everything up."

"Give it to me," Castus nodded, still glaring murderously at Lucia as Paltucca grabbed the record book from under the banker's hand and gave it to the master.

Lucia wished she could punch the old bitch in the face, wipe the insufferable, despised smirk away, but she held her temper in check, praying to Sulis to help her as the master began to check over the banker's figures.

Castus's eyebrows drew together as he read, then his tongue flicked up to clean something from one of his upper teeth and he looked thoughtfully at Paltucca, then to Lucia.

"What is the meaning of this?" he asked softly. "You remain silent, woman!" he thundered as Paltucca attempted to speak. Thanks to his years in the legions, his voice was still powerful enough to make everyone in the room shrink a little, even the burly guards. "I was speaking to her, not you."

Lucia stood up straighter and stared directly ahead at the bare stone wall of the shop. This was it, she couldn't slip up now.

"Paltucca has been claiming more expenses than she should have been, *dominus,*" she said. "It took me a few weeks to notice it, and I didn't want to report it to you until I could be absolutely certain. Today, I came to see the banker to confirm what I suspected." She nodded at the ledger Castus held in his hands. "I believe that says it all."

"What?" Paltucca shrieked, clenching her fists and taking a step towards Lucia, but the guard by the wall lifted a muscular arm and stopped her from charging towards the young manageress. "You're a damn liar! *You're* the one stealing from the master, not me. This is preposterous. Why would I—"

"Shut up, woman," Castus ordered, once again eyeing the banker's ledger with gritted teeth. "These records would seem to prove the veracity of the manageress's words. Or is this not your own signature?"

He walked across to stand next to Paltucca and showed her the writing on the tablet which was hard to see in the locked room with only a few guttering candles to illuminate the gloom. The old woman's face went pale and her mouth dropped open as she tried to stammer an explanation, but Castus again waved her to silence before he turned next to the banker himself.

"You are no doubt aware of who I am? Yes? I expect the truth from you then my good man, if honesty is possible for a fellow in your profession…The signatures in your book seem to be hers," he said, pointing at Paltucca.

"Indeed." The banker nodded agreement. "I know Paltucca."

"Did she deposit these amounts, and I'm only choosing the most recent here – ninety denarii, one hundred and seventy denarii, three hundred denarii – in person, and sign your ledger with her own hand?"

Paltucca looked disgusted with the whole situation now, and shook her head, clearly confident that the banker would tell Castus of her innocence and they could then move onto proving Lucia's guilt. She was to be disappointed.

"She did, tribune," the banker agreed quietly.

"You're lying," Paltucca suddenly screeched. "You must have been paid by that bitch to go along with this – she probably spread her legs for you, the slut!"

"Shut your mouth woman!" Castus roared, and he slapped the old woman across the face so hard that she fell back against the wall, slumping down onto the floor with tears of pain filling her eyes.

It was the first time in all her life that Lucia had seen someone strike Paltucca, and exultation coursed through the young manageress at the sight. How she had wanted to do that herself for oh, so long!

"She," Castus shouted at the banker, pointing again at the floored Paltucca. "Deposited these sums with you *in person*, and signed this book in her own hand? Yes? All right then." He turned again to Lucia. "Explain all this to me, before I lose my mind. I thought I was coming here today to catch *you* stealing from me. I am utterly confused."

"She has been stealing from you," Paltucca sobbed from her place on the floor. Lucia stared at her in shock; the old woman seemed broken – it was incredible. And wonderful. "I have been completely loyal to you for decades, *dominus*."

"Lucia has been more loyal to me than you could ever know," Castus growled, without even looking at the old woman. "Now that I think about it rationally, Lucia has no reason to steal from me. I owe her my wife's continued existence, and also my own. She might have asked for her freedom and a fortune in cash as a reward for what she's done for me and my family in the last year alone. Why would she seek to become rich in this ludicrous, roundabout way? Stealing a few denarii extra in expenses each month?"

"Why would *I*?" Paltucca asked softly, still crying, her ancient face soaked with tears. "When I'm about to be manumitted."

Castus's face clouded over at that – it was a good question. Lucia knew if she allowed the master to think about it he might become suspicious and her scheme would be turned back on itself. She stepped in close to Castus, cupped a hand to his ear and whispered: "She saw you killing Senator Vibidius. It was Paltucca who sent the boy into the garden to meet him, and she watched the whole thing."

Castus's eyes widened and he shivered as a thrill of fear ran down his spine. He looked down at the old woman on the floor and set his jaw. "After everything I've done for you," he grunted, lowering himself onto his haunches so he could stare directly into his former-manageress's eyes. "All you slaves are the same: scum. I should publicly crucify you."

Lucia bridled inwardly at his blanket insult but said, "We would need to involve the magistrate for a crucifixion."

Castus nodded slowly, taking in those words and their implication before he spoke again. "Now that I think about it, my wife told me a while ago that the slaves were gossiping about you, Paltucca. They had noticed you wearing expensive new clothes and wondered how you could afford them. I scoffed at her, but now it all makes perfect sense." He looked down at her once again, lip curling. "What should I do with you then?"

Unexpectedly, the banker spoke up again, gesturing towards the fallen, sobbing Paltucca. "She is still a slave? You have not freed her yet? Well, my boys here can take care of things for you, quietly and cheaply."

Castus seemed to think about his offer for a long time, gazing at the wizened old crone who had been his faithful servant for the majority of his years on earth, until now. Still, a message had to be sent to the rest of his slaves. No-one could be allowed to steal from him, especially someone who knew he was a murderer.

"Lucia will take care of your payment," he said, getting to his feet and shaking his head at Paltucca who looked up at him in disbelief, too shocked to even plead for his forgiveness or her own innocence. "I will see you back at the villa, Lucia."

Without another word he turned to the door and, at a nod from the banker, the guard threw back the heavy bolts. Sunlight flooded the dark room as the door was flung open and Castus walked out without turning back.

Paltucca saw her chance and, moving much faster than Lucia would have thought possible, jumped to her feet and ran, in a low crouch, for the exit, screaming, "Help! Help! Someone help!"

The guard was almost as surprised as Lucia at the old woman's nimbleness, but he was used to this kind of thing and, instinctively, without a hint of remorse, lashed out as she tried to pass him. His meaty fist caught her in the ear, landing with such force that even Lucia, who despised her, winced.

The door was locked again, the outside world shut out, and with it any hopes of rescue for the old woman. Lucia walked across and knelt down beside her.

"Twenty years," she said, to herself more than anything. "Twenty years I've waited for this moment, to see you broken, you evil witch."

Paltucca was conscious but only just. "Why?" she mumbled. "Why would you do this to me when I was finally to be freed after all my years as a slave?"

Lucia opened her mouth to lay two decades worth of charges at the old woman's feet. To explain to her in tiny detail how she had made Lucia's life a living hell. To remind her of Sennianus's ruined leg, and their baby killed by her twisted actions, and dark-haired Silvanus who would never forget what Vibidius had made him do.

It didn't matter. There was no need to explain herself to Paltucca – it was enough for Lucia to see her tormentor destroyed and broken on the floor before her.

"What will you do with her body?" she asked, standing up and turning to the banker who shook his head, a small smile on his lips.

"It's better if you don't know," he replied. "That way, if the magistrate comes asking questions you won't be able to give anything away. Suffice to say, she will never be found. My boys know their business, as do I. You can trust me, as I think you saw today."

Lucia nodded. That was certainly true. The man might have told Castus how she had come to him and asked him to conspire with her to frame Paltucca, but he hadn't. He had played his part perfectly.

"The money I deposited in her name," she said, gesturing towards the old woman who was trying unsuccessfully to raise herself to her knees. "That will be payment enough for this task?"

The banker nodded. It was more than enough for such a trivial matter, and Lucia had also paid him handsomely in advance for his testimony against Paltucca.

"I hope you will come back to see me again in the future," he smiled. "It's been a real pleasure to work with you, hasn't it lads?"

The giant guards grinned and Lucia, exultant at the success of her plan, returned the smiles with one of her own. She couldn't leave yet though; she had to make sure her revenge was complete.

The banker understood her hesitation to leave when the job wasn't completely finished but he shook his head. "You don't want to see this," he told her, gesturing to the rear of his shop, and Lucia knew he was right.

"I will wait out the back until it's done then."

A short time later, as she waited in the shadows, the corpse was dragged out of the back door, ready to be dumped by the now-breathless and sweating guards and Lucia was content. She had finally taken her revenge on Paltucca.

Now only Publius Licinius Castus remained, and this whole episode had given her an idea on how to deal with the master once and for all.

BOOK FOUR

CHAPTER ONE

Villa Tempestatis, AD 201, Spring

It was the fifth Nones of May – the birthday of Lucia and Sennianus's abandoned baby, Alfwin, and, as she had done for all the years since it had happened, the grieving mother came to a little dell hidden from view of the main house to commemorate the child's memory.

It had been over 20 years since the baby's birth, but Lucia, who was now forty-two years old, still sometimes felt the loss as keenly as if it was only a heartbeat ago. Yes, the pain had dulled so she could go about her life without constantly remembering, and wondering what might have been, but every so often the agony would strike her, and her hatred for Castus would flare into life once again. Paltucca had paid the price for her part in the child's unjust exposure, and one day the *dominus* would too. Soon, Lucia felt, for his health was at last beginning to fade now that he was growing old.

"Sulis Minerva," she intoned softly, eyes closed, breathing in the fumes from the little piece of frankincense that was burning on the makeshift altar before her. "Look after my little boy." She halted, her mind filling with images, not of a child, but of a grown man, gazing back at her with a smile on his handsome face. Of course, he would not remain a baby forever, would he? He would be a full-grown man now.

She wished so much that she could have been part of his upbringing.

"Sulis," she went on again, "tell my son I love him, and one day we will be together again, as we should have been. His father also sends his love. We both miss him terribly and think of him every single day." Tears spillt from her closed eyes and a sob shook her, but she remained standing, determined not to let sadness end the ceremony before it was finished.

Sometimes when she performed this ritual she was worried about being disturbed by some slave out walking in the grounds, but on other occasions she seemed to become completely lost in a trance and her connection between the worlds was so intense that time stood still. Today was one of those times, and she lowered herself down, sitting with her legs drawn up before her as she allowed herself to relax completely.

The smell of the frankincense, which had cost her a fair amount, filled the little shaded dell and she breathed it in deeply. There was a wine-skin next to her and she lifted it now without even opening her eyes and took a long pull. She sealed it again and set it back on the ground, then sat there, simply allowing her mind to quiet as the drink and pungent fumes did their work upon her.

The image of her newborn baby, just as he'd been when taken from her all those years ago, was clear in her mind. She could picture his tiny red face, and hear his cry as if it came from beside her here and now; but then the scene shifted and a little boy toddled across the vegetable garden towards her, falling onto his hands and knees and looking up at her, face twisted in pain, seeking her strong comforting embrace; then a taller lad, sharing a joke with the master's son, Maximus, as if they were friends; next, that same, tall figure of a young man that she'd imagined earlier, with a cheeky grin and the same slightly protruding ears of his father.

Lucia could feel his arms around her and she knew this was no dream or hallucination – her son was with her in the little dell and it made her so happy. He was safe, somewhere, and one day he would be ready to meet her when she took her own journey into the afterlife. They would be together then, and everything else would be forgotten.

There was a sound from nearby and, although she recognised it as simply a branch falling from the crack willow behind her, it broke her trance and her eyes opened slowly. She felt refreshed and relaxed, as if she'd enjoyed the best night's sleep of her life, and her whole being was infused with happiness as she breathed deeply once again the last traces of the burning incense.

It was hard to feel hatred for anyone – even Paltucca or the master – after such a wonderful experience. Especially nowadays, when Castus had converted to Christianity, which was one reason why Lucia had to commemorate Alfwin outside, hidden from prying eyes – no-one was allowed to worship 'false gods' any more, the slaves had been ordered to become Christian when the master had converted. Lucia didn't care for the new religion, and resented being told what she should believe in. It wasn't enough for Castus to chain them like dogs in life, but he had to control their spiritual beliefs as well.

She blew out the little fire on the raised altar she'd made on an old tree stump, and had to admit to herself that Castus had become a better master with his conversion to the new faith. Scattering the ashes of the now-spent Frankincense and gathering the bluebells which symbolised Alfwin for Lucia, she thought about her master. He no longer drank himself into oblivion and assaulted the female slaves, and genuinely seemed like a reformed character in his sixty-third year. There had been raised wages, larger rations, more frequent manumissions and generally better conditions all round for the slaves since Castus became a Christ-follower. In his old age Publius Licinius Castus had recognised the error of his ways and, following the tenets of his new religion, sought forgiveness from God. It was truly admirable.

The grass was soft under her feet as Lucia began the walk back to the house, looking around at the browns and greens of the spring landscape, dotted here and there with bluebells and clumps of daffodils and celandines, but despite the beauty of the estate, and her belief that she would be reunited with Alfwin forever one day, the manageress's mood soon turned dark again.

For whatever the improvements in his conduct, Castus had not freed his slaves. Despite the Christian religion's command to treat one another with love, and for its adherents to treat people as they'd like to be treated themselves, slavery was still the foundation of the entire Roman empire. Like any religion, its members merely followed the parts they liked, and ignored the rest.

It was ludicrous.

She walked into the house and stalked along the covered walkway towards her chamber, her earlier beatific mood now departed and replaced with the familiar grim determination and barely-concealed hatred.

No matter how much money Castus paid her, or how many prayers he offered up to his nailed God, the man had still brought her here to Villa Tempestatis against her will, raped her, and murdered her only child. Aye, the bastard thought his newfound faith would bring him an eternity of happiness in the afterlife he called 'heaven', but Lucia knew he would more likely end up in the fiery pit of hell. And she would see him off on his downward journey with parting gifts that had taken her three decades to gather.

Amen!

CHAPTER TWO

There was great joy in Villa Tempestatis that day, which even the threat of heavy spring rain showers couldn't dampen: two of the Gaulish slaves were being 'married'. Castus had agreed to allow the union which, although not legally binding, was just as significant to the participants who would, from now on, be allowed to have children and share a small chamber as a family unit rather than live in separate rooms.

Lucia had overseen the purchases of beer and wine along with extra food for the feast. There were even garlands of flowers draped around the courtyard where the celebrants would be formally joined – daffodils, bluebells, orchids, primroses and violets looked beautiful, contrasting with the grey walls and heavy clouds.

There would be none of the pomp and splendour of a wedding between two Roman citizens, but Castus was happy enough to provide a pleasant celebration for his workers, knowing it would lead to contentment, greater output and less trouble within their ranks. Lucia didn't even have to try and persuade him to allow this sort of thing – he'd always provided such feasts and his conversion to Christianity made him even more generous.

Lucia had wondered how his new religion would affect the wedding, since it called for a pagan master of ceremonies, the *auspex*, and an accompanying animal sacrifice whose entrails the *auspex* would interpret before the union could be formally pronounced. But, for some reason, the Christians didn't have any marriage rituals of their own, so, although Castus frowned on the old ways now, he allowed them to continue while there was no formalised alternative prescribed by the Church.

The pig was brought out by Haerviu, the *auspex*, a Briton from Durobrivae, hired for the ceremony by Lucia. The white-haired, white-moustached old man had been used often for such rituals in the villa over the years although, going forward, Castus told Lucia a Christian priest would take charge of all matters relating to his own family. She couldn't help wondering what the new religion's funerary rites were like and how much longer it would be before the master needed them. Hopefully not too soon, for she still had things to do while he was alive...

The *auspex* led the pig, an older beast with streaming nose and strangely intelligent-looking eyes, past the gathered slaves who smiled at the sight, knowing they would soon be enjoying its sweet roasted flesh. The betrothed couple stood next to one another nervously: the bride, Glaucia, with her hair tied up and a woollen girdle around her slim waist; Varius, the groom, smiling broadly, and no wonder, for his wife-to-be was one of the prettiest slave-girls Lucia had ever known.

All looked on as the pig was slaughtered, apparently not as clever as its eyes had suggested, since it didn't seem to sense its impending doom and died without fuss. The beast's entrails were then pulled out for Haerviu to interpret and he crouched low, eyeing them intently, looking up at the sky and watching as a jackdaw landed on the wall nearby, hoping to share in the bloody harvest.

The slaves stood in complete silence as the *auspex* seemed to take a long time before coming to his conclusion. "The omens are good!" he announced solemnly, and there were murmurs and sighs of relief as the bride and groom grinned at one another and the animal's carcass was removed to the kitchen to be butchered and roasted.

Lucia herself had never seen a proper Roman wedding, and she knew this was merely a truncated version of such a ceremony, but, even so, she found it powerful and strangely moving when Haerviu moved to stand between the bride and groom and Glaucia intoned softly her vow: "*Ubi tu Gaius, ego Gaia.*" Where you are Gaius, I am Gaia.

Varius licked his lips and replied in a hoarse voice: "*Ubi tu Gaia, ego Gaius.*"

The slaves all cheered then as Varius took his new wife's left hand and placed a very simple iron ring on the fourth finger. Lucia had always wondered why that particular finger was used for a wedding band, until old Tiro, the former clerk in Villa Tempestatis, told her about a book he had read by some Roman writer called Aulus Gellius: apparently when the human body was dissected by Egyptian embalmers a thread could be found leading from that finger on the left hand directly to the heart, so it made sense to put the marriage ring on that one.

Lucia smiled, remembering the old freedman fondly. It seemed like a very long time since he'd imparted that nugget of information to her – she was getting old herself now.

"They look really happy, don't they?"

She nodded and returned Sennianus's grin.

"When are you going to let me marry you then? Look how much pleasure it brings to the bride and groom, and," he gestured to the tables laden with food and drink, "it gives everyone a feast."

Lucia laughed and nudged him playfully with her elbow.

"I've told you hundreds of times, Senni, I'm not the type to marry."

"Why not?" he demanded, his voice still light but his eyes deadly serious as he gazed at her. "Is it just me? Am I not good enough for you?"

"Don't be silly," she said, not wanting to discuss the matter but knowing it was important not to hurt Senni, for whom she genuinely felt great affection. "You know I've never taken another man to my bed. At least," her voice grew hard and her eyes flickered back towards the house, "not by choice anyway."

"Then why can't we do as Varius and Glaucia are doing?"

Lucia sighed and wondered how to put her thoughts into words that would placate Sennianus without angering him and ruining the rest of the celebration for him. She thought about mentioning the fact he himself had taken various lovers from the slave-women over the years but, well, she couldn't blame him for that, when he so clearly wanted Lucia but she refused to commit to him. And his dalliances never lasted long anyway – either he grew bored with his partners, or, more often, they became irritated by his love for Lucia, which he found impossible to conceal.

"Maybe one day," she said, taking his hand and squeezing it. "When I've completed what I vowed to do when I was first brought here as a little girl against my will. You know how important that is to me. It wouldn't be fair to you, to…"

"'One Day'," Sennianus broke in, shaking his head. "That's what you always say. Your desire for revenge is twisting you inside. If you ever manage to get what you want – and I really don't see how it's going to be possible, even as manageress – you'll be too old to enjoy what's left of your life."

Lucia nodded sadly. He was probably right. She had ideas for ways to gain her ultimate, crushing revenge on Publius Licinius Castus, but she didn't have enough influence or power within the villa to put them into action. However, she had been working hard to set that right and, very soon, would approach the master about taking on even more duties. Maybe her life's work would be completed sooner than Sennianus thought.

"Come on," she smiled, pulling him by the hand towards the nearest wine amphora. "I do love you, and you know it. We'll talk of this another time – for now, let's just enjoy Castus's meat and drink." She took a full cup from the table and handed it to Senni, lifting another for herself and raising it in the air. "To us," she said, and, to her relief, he joined her in the toast, the anger gone from his face.

Not everyone looked as if they were happy to see Varius and Glaucia's marriage that day, though. Standing in the corner of the courtyard, a cup of wine in each hand, stood a red-haired slave who was almost as big as Rogatus and twenty years younger too. Argentokoxos, or just Argento for short. The master had bought him to work in the fields just a year ago and allowed him to keep his own name because, he told Lucia, he rather liked it. Argento was a native of this island, from the wild, unconquered tribes to the very far north, and, despite being allowed to retain his old name, he despised Castus, and the fact that he was now nothing more than a slave.

The master had been assured Argento was no warrior – he had been a simple labourer in his homelands, captured in a raid by a rival tribe who then sold him to the slavers, knowing his size would bring a fine price.

He may not have been a warrior, but Lucia had been forced to have him disciplined physically, and rather harshly, on more than one occasion as he quite simply refused to behave like the rest of the workers. She thought he was finally coming to accept his new position in recent weeks – his spirit broken just like all the other slaves had been, except her of course. Now though, looking at the hatred in his green eyes, Lucia wondered if she was mistaken.

Argento's was not the gaze of a broken man. She should really have a word with Castus about selling the troublemaker on.

Then one of the slave-women appeared next to him, grasping his arm in hers and smiling suggestively at him. Vita was another newly-bought native Briton, but, where Argento was tall, she was small and slim and very pretty. She noticed his hate-filled glare and turned her head to find the focus of his ire.

A shiver ran down Lucia's back as her eyes met Vita's and the Briton's lip curled in disdain. Argento was dangerous because of his size and his refusal to accept his life in Villa Tempestatis. But the manageress felt like she could control him well enough. Vita though, was another beast altogether. Small in stature, but sly and, Lucia suspected, her equal in intelligence, although the younger slave did well to hide it. Undoubtedly Vita harboured similar desires to overthrow her masters just as Lucia had done for the past thirty-odd years.

If the Britons were pairing up it would only mean trouble, and Lucia knew she would need to keep an eye on things very closely for the next few weeks.

Vita tugged on Argento's muscular arm and the man allowed himself to be led away, eyeing Lucia disdainfully as he went, to another part of the garden where Lucia could no longer see them.

"What are you watching?" Sennianus asked, finally realising his companion hadn't been listening to a word he'd said for a while. "Vita? She's trouble, you better watch yourself with that one."

"In what way?" Lucia said, turning her full attention back to him.

He shrugged awkwardly.

"Never mind trying to spare my feelings Senni, I know fine well I'm not the most popular person amongst the other slaves. Why should I watch myself?"

"'Not the most popular'," Sennianus repeated, nodding his head thoughtfully. "That's one way of putting it although, honestly, I don't think you really understand how people like Vita and Argento really see you."

"I'm not an idiot," Lucia began, but Sennianus broke in and what he said left her open-mouthed and shocked.

"They see you just as you saw Paltucca. You are their Paltucca."

For a long moment she didn't reply. She looked away from him, watching people eating and drinking and laughing and talking to one another and still she didn't say a word, because she couldn't quite believe his pronouncement.

At last she murmured, "All of them?"

Sennianus shrugged. "No, some recognise you are on their side and just trying to keep things running smoothly which benefits everyone, but...the likes of Vita and Argento hate you as much as you ever hated Paltucca, I think. They never knew you before, when you were one of them."

"It's not the same as it was when we were young, is it Senni?" Lucia said softly, staring into the middle-distance. That view, at least, hadn't changed, but much else in Villa Tempestatis had. "There was a camaraderie back then. Regalis, Antonia, Livinia. We cared for one another. Now..." She looked around at the slaves celebrating the wedding and sighed. "Maybe it's just me, but that bond doesn't seem to be there any more between the slaves."

Sennianus smiled fondly as he recalled those old, departed friends but he shrugged. "I seem to remember Balbina and Martina having a similar conversation with each other when I was about eleven or twelve. I think it's probably just us who have moved on, especially you, in your position as manageress. People become secretive around authority, and can you blame them? Vita and Argento have friends, certainly. Even Popillia seems to enjoy their company well enough."

Popillia. She had been a great friend to Lucia over the years but now even she was reticent around Lucia, their old bond no longer there. This pained the manageress sometimes but nothing could be done about it.

Lucia lingered at the feast for a little while longer, but her friend's words, and the strange looks from the two Briton slaves troubled her, and she soon made her way back to her chamber, planning to look at the coming week's work rota. Yet even in the quiet little room she found herself unable to concentrate, and eventually gave up trying, allowing her mind to take her back over the years once more, remembering the things Paltucca had done to her.

And, of course, what she had eventually done to Paltucca.

She had never cared to be popular, but it was strangely upsetting to think her fellow slaves saw her as the hateful, hated old manageress who had made Lucia's life so unnecessarily hard.

CHAPTER THREE

"Remember: no talking when we get inside. We can't afford to wake anyone or the whole thing will be undone."

The five figures moved quietly in the darkness, mere shadows in the dim moonlight as they skirted the villa walls. Although their blades had been coated in mud to avoid reflecting any light, their pointed shapes would be easily recognisable should anyone see them.

No-one was watching though; Vita was sure of that. This had been planned meticulously, over the course of the past twelve days. The rest of the slaves were safely locked away in their sleeping quarters – only these five stalking silhouettes were out and about, thanks to the skill of one of them as a locksmith. Otho had tampered with the mechanism on the door of the male slaves' chamber so that when Lucia locked up for the night, he was able to open it from the inside simply by thumping it hard. He, and his companions, Argento and two other Briton men, Blandus and Duilius, had then made their way in the darkness to the other wing and sprung the lock to free Vita.

"It's a shame we couldn't detour and get that bitch manageress too," Argento whispered, and even in the gloom Vita could see his features twist at the mere thought of Lucia.

"Well we can't. We have one room to visit, then we steal the horses, get out of here, and head for the north. Besides," she shrugged, "for some reason Lucia has actually been nice to me recently."

Argento grunted. "Me too. I wonder why."

"It's been since she saw us looking at her at the wedding feast," Vita said thoughtfully. "I think her lapdog Sennianus said something to her that changed her attitude towards us. She even allocated me an extra ration of salt for the month."

"Same here," Argento agreed and their companions grumbled that they hadn't been allowed anything extra.

"We must be her favourites," Vita laughed quietly. "Or maybe she's frightened of us."

"Whatever it is, it's too little too late," Argento said. "She's still a bitch and I'd like nothing more than to strangle her with my bare hands."

Their conversation came to an end as they reached the main entrance. Usually there would be a guard here, one of the retired legionaries from Durobrivae. Castus had hired four of them after Vassinus's men raided the villa twenty-odd years before, although recently there were only two who shared the watches throughout the night. While one slept, the other manned his post at the big entrance archway. Right now, it seemed no-one was on guard.

"Where are they?" Argento hissed, straining his eyes to make out the watchman in the darkness.

"Maybe they both went for a sleep," the locksmith suggested hopefully. He, like the rest of his companions, was no warrior and this night's work was making him nervous. "Must be a pretty boring job, just standing there night after night in the dark on your own with nothing to do. Nothing ever happens around here. They probably leave the place unguarded all the time and go for a kip. The master's none the wiser."

No one replied for a while, as all watched and listened for any sign of the guards, who were meant to be vigilant from dusk until dawn.

"I'll go and take a look," Argento said, and went ahead, knife gripped in his right hand. His companions watched him move silently around the entrance archway, and the conspirators gripped their own weapons anxiously, knowing discovery would mean a fight with the grizzled veteran soldiers and, ultimately, death for them all when the alarm was raised.

Argento gestured for his friends to wait, then he crept towards the eastern wall that surrounded the house. The guards used one of the storage sheds there as their sleeping quarters, and it was possible both of them were in that small wooden building.

"Shouldn't we follow him?" Otho whispered, trying to see Vita in the darkness. "If the guards are both in there playing dice they'll see him."

"If they're in there playing dice Argento will come back and tell us, and then we can decide what to do next," the woman growled. "Now be silent and stay alert."

The locksmith's fears were unfounded and the big northman soon rejoined them.

"There's no one around. What do you think that means, Vita?"

She thought it over but, not having much knowledge of the guards' regular habits, couldn't answer his question. Perhaps they'd been given the night off, or maybe they'd noticed something suspicious in the villa grounds and gone to investigate. It was pointless speculating.

"They're not here, that's all that matters," she said, knowing her soft voice would calm the men's fears. "I'd rather we'd been able to kill them now so we didn't have to worry about them later, but we'll go on with our plan and just be alert to their appearing again. Come on."

Vita led them towards a side door that opened into the north wing and nodded when it gave way at her touch. One of the master's personal slaves had been persuaded to join their cause and unlock the door from the inside, ready for their arrival.

Argento placed his hand on her arm, drawing her back so he could move inside the house first, ready for any trouble that might await them. The corridor, which ran halfway along the wing, was deserted.

He jerked his head for the rest to come in and again Vita took the lead, creeping slowly towards the master's bedchamber. None of these slaves had ever been in this part of the villa before, for it was Castus's personal quarters, but Vita had been drawn a plan of the layout by the same slave, Tullia, who had left the door unlocked for them. Vita knew exactly where to go, even in the near-total darkness.

They reached their destination in a matter of moments and took up positions around the door. Tullia had told them it wouldn't be possible for her to unlock the master's own chamber for them, but she assured Vita the latch wasn't particularly sturdy. It would be much quicker for Argento to smash the door open with a single kick than for Otho to pick the lock, possibly alerting the room's inhabitants and destroying the element of surprise.

Vita had found it hard to believe that the master, sufficiently worried about his own safety to employ veteran legionaries as nocturnal guards, would have such a weak barrier protecting his sleeping quarters. But Tullia had insisted it was true.

The five grim, anxious slaves stood in silence, holding their knives, hoping to hear snoring, evidence that the room's occupants were asleep. But there was nothing. It wasn't ideal, but on the surface at least, it seemed no-one was awake.

The time had come. Once she gave Argento the command to break open the door there would be no going back. Even if they managed to kill both Castus and Dianna without their raising the alarm, they would need to strip the room of all valuables and make their escape quickly. None of them had much experience in warfare and their makeshift weapons would be no match for the guards' swords and light armour, so Vita was relying on stealth and speed to bring them success. The road north was a long one, and pursuit would be relentless until they passed beyond the great wall of Antoninus and into the lands of their own kinsmen. A head-start was vital.

The only alternative was to return to their beds in the slave quarters and live the rest of their days as the possessions of Publius Licinius Castus, ordered around by the manageress Lucia and beaten like dogs whenever it suited her.

Vita looked into Argento's eyes. They seemed startlingly bright in the gloomy corridor and knew he was thinking the very same things as her. Both had come to the same conclusion and Vita set her jaw.

She would retake her freedom, or die fighting for it.

Argento saw her nod and took a step backwards. His fingers had found the position of the lock in the darkness and he drew himself up, taking a deep breath, preparing to put every fibre of his being into the kick he knew would be crucial to the success of their plan.

Castus may be elderly now, but he was once a decorated Roman soldier – if the door didn't go in on the first or second blow there might be a fight, and Argento would rather have full use of his arms if that was to happen.

"Ready?" he whispered.

"Do it," Vita growled, wiping a bead of sweat from her forehead. She watched Argento raise his right leg and it felt as if time had slowed.

The consequences of this raid flicked across her mind as the man braced himself to open the door. Failure would mean a painful death; that much was a given. But success would lead to dire punishments and possibly even death, for all the other slaves who lived on this estate. The Roman authorities would blame Lucia and Popillia and all the rest of them for not reporting Vita's conspirators. While she, Argento and the others were riding to freedom with Castus's stolen wealth in their sacks, the rest of Villa Tempestatis's workforce would in all likelihood be crucified.

But Vita was not responsible for them. They were their own people, they all had their own paths to follow and they had chosen to remain chained to their Roman master forever. The weak fools had made their own bed and they would have to lie in it.

A cruel smile touched her lips, and she was thinking how much she hoped Lucia would be the first in the line to be hung on a cross, when Argento's foot came up and reality returned.

There was a crash as the tall slave's kick hammered into the wooden barrier, then a curse as the door remained stubbornly shut.

"Hurry up!" Duilius cried, fear making his voice high and thin.

"Shut up you little prick," Argento retorted, bracing again for a second kick.

It never landed. From the corridor on either side there was a new sound, and Vita took a long moment to realise what it must be: the thump of shields coming together to form a wall.

"Vita?" Argento whispered urgently, but she knew her throat was too dry to reply in anything other than a nervous croak. She stayed silent, gazing into the darkness, fearing what flanked them on either side, preventing their escape.

"Vita!" Duilius shouted, panic overtaking him. "What's happening? What do we do?"

"Stay calm," she commanded although she felt anything but. "We knew all along that it might come to a fight, that's why we're armed. So ready yourselves. Argento, I want you at my side. Duilius! Calm! You, Otho and Blandus take the men on the east, all right? I said 'all right'? Good."

She was astonished to find her voice remained strong despite the fear now coursing through her at the prospect of a battle in the cramped confines of the corridor. She could hear and, just about see, despite the gloom, that they were outnumbered. Greatly so.

She felt Argento's muscular body pressing against her right shoulder and almost cried out with relief. If she was to die that night she wanted the big Pict at her side.

They prepared for battle as best they might, considering the darkness and confusion. But before a blow could be struck, Vita saw the cover on a bronze lamp removed and the western end of the corridor, the one which she and Argento faced, was lit up as if the sun had risen on a spring morning.

Budding daffodils didn't greet them though. Instead, the hard faces of six fully armoured legionaries stared back at Vita and, at their centre stood the master himself. Behind him were the two missing guardsmen. The smell from the olive oil burning in the lamp drifted her way, incongruously bringing to mind the memory of the meat cooking at the previous week's wedding feast. Unfortunately, this was not proving to be such a happy occasion.

Publius Licinius Castus had brought his old tribune's uniform out of retirement and, despite the advancing years, he still cut an imposing figure. His white tunic, bronze cuirass, greaves and helmet with horsehair plume were accented by a blood-red cloak, and his expression told Vita all she needed to know. Glancing back over her shoulder quickly she saw her three co-conspirators facing a similar number of soldiers. They were doomed. Even if the slaves had been seasoned warriors and armed with proper weapons, they would still have had little chance of surviving the coming fight, outnumbered and trapped on both sides as they were.

Her eyes, fully adjusted to the light cast by the oil lamp now, noticed one other slight form behind the master's row of legionaries: Lucia.

Vita thought of the manageress's recent change in attitude towards her, the extra rations, friendly smiles and lighter duties and, with a flash of insight, she knew Lucia was the one who had warned the master of the plot to kill him. She had no idea how the manageress had uncovered their plan, or how she expected the conspirators to strike tonight but Vita was certain her fellow slave was the architect of their doom here.

The two women locked gazes and, before the master could command his men to cut the rebels to pieces, Vita asked, "How? Why?"

Castus turned to look at his manageress and gave a small nod, allowing Lucia to explain herself should she choose to.

"How?" repeated the manageress. "That was easy enough. I gave you light duties in the bath-house with Tullia because I knew the two of you were close. You shared a hatred of our master that went beyond most other slaves', as well as a language. There is a tiny hidden chamber in the bath-house atrium which I used to spy on you while you worked. You're a very clever, sly woman, Vita, but, in a place like this, you should have realised the walls have eyes and ears."

Argento tried to spit on the floor but fear had made his mouth dry and the spittle merely dribbled down his chin. "Do we really need to listen to that bitch?" he demanded. "I'd rather get this over with than let her crow about the fools she's made of us."

"You're no better than me," Vita said to Lucia, ignoring her companion. "You're a slave like the rest of us, nothing more. And I've heard about the things they did to you in your time here – you must hate him," she pointed the tip of her short sword at Castus, "just as much as I do. More! You're just too spineless to do anything about it."

Lucia stared back at her without replying, but the master spoke up for the first time.

"You're wrong, scum," he said, and he used the voice of a legion commander rather than the long-domesticated villa owner he'd been for the past three decades or so. His words rang out along the corridor, confident and commanding, filling every corner. "Lucia has saved my life on more than one occasion over the years. She is like family to me, as are all my beloved, *loyal* slaves. I offered to free her from my service long ago, but she chooses to stay here in the villa because it is her home."

He spread his hands wide and Vita really noticed his gladius properly for the first time. It was exquisitely crafted and made the dull old blade in her hand feel cheap and worthless, but she knew her sword was just as deadly as his, especially if she could just get in close enough to the bastard to make it count.

Instead of ordering his legionaries to attack, Castus continued to speak, and Vita didn't know whether to be relieved or irritated by this further postponement of battle.

"Am I not a good master?" the Roman demanded, a genuine look of confusion on his face at the turncoat slaves' actions here. "I understand it can't be very nice being forced to work for someone like me when you've been used to a life of freedom, but!" He pointed his gladius at Argento's waist. "Have you gone hungry in my service? Not at all, judging from the size of you. Have I had you branded like some slave owners do? No, I have not. And what about you?" He turned his attention to Vita now and actually took a step forward, out of the line of legionaries that protected him. "Have you been raped? Not by me." He shook his head angrily. "Since becoming a Christian I've been kinder to you people than any other Roman of my station that I know. Yet this is how you repay me."

Vita was truly astonished at the sadness in his expression. He truly believed what he was saying! The Romans had become so used to being masters of the entire world that they expected some food, a bed to sleep in and a life without sexual abuse should be gratefully accepted. It was insane.

Yet his mention of being a convert to this new religion that was sweeping the empire gave her an idea.

"Your God preaches forgiveness," she said, lowering her outstretched dagger and staring at Castus as if they were equals. At last he nodded. "Then forgive us for what we planned tonight. Let us return to our quarters and continue to serve you as before. You have my word that we will not try something like this again. By Taranis, I swear it."

At her side Argento grunted in what she took as hopeful surprise, and she laid a hand on his arm and squeezed, bidding him be silent. The other three conspirators at her back made no sound at all but she knew they would happily go along with her suggestion since their deaths were otherwise guaranteed.

Unfortunately, Castus laughed. The sound was jarring in the stifling corridor, the obvious pleasure it conveyed making Vita angry. Only a Roman would laugh in such a situation she thought. The bastard was mocking them, playing with them, instead of just ending it.

"It is true," Castus said, "that we Christians believe in forgiveness. And you will be happy to hear that I *do* forgive you, all five of you."

Behind her, Vita sensed her three friends turning their head hopefully, to see if Castus was being serious.

"Oh, I am being completely truthful," he promised but the lupine grin on his face suggested more was going on in his head. "I forgive you for attempting to kill me and my wife Dianna, and for wishing to steal as much of my wealth as you could carry in those little sacks you carry with you. I even forgive you for caring nothing about the fate your fellow slaves would meet should your murderous plan have worked as you intended. Lucia may feel differently."

Vita looked back at the manageress but her face was as blank as the wall.

"Forgiving you does not mean letting you off without facing any sort of retribution for your acts," Castus went on, drawing Vita's gaze back to him. All amusement was gone from his face, replaced with a smouldering anger which the slave-woman knew could only be the precursor to violence. She gripped her dagger tighter and took up a defensive posture, choosing the legionary on the left of the formation facing them as her opening target. He was tall, but older than the rest, and she hoped her youthful speed might help her land a blow before he could react.

"Justice must be served, even if I do personally forgive your transgressions against me," Castus went on. "So, I give you a choice: surrender now and lay down your weapons, or else be cut apart like slabs of meat in the butcher's shop by my veterans here. It's up to you," he looked from Vita to Argento then back to the slave-woman. "I don't really care either way."

"You'll just kill us anyway if we give up our swords," Duilius shouted, his voice filled with fear. "Why should we surrender?"

"He's right," Vita said. "You said yourself you will punish us. I think it a much better option to fight and die like free men and women unless you have something else in mind for us."

Something crackled within the olive oil lamp Castus's man held – an errant moth being immolated perhaps – making the light flare momentarily, filling the corridor with flickering shadows and a sweet smell Vita didn't recognise.

"I despise killing slaves," Castus said. "As Lucia will testify – she's known me long enough after all. So, I propose to put out one eye in each of you." He held up a hand. "I will see it is done as painlessly as possible and you will be cared for to make sure infection doesn't set in, you can trust me on that. And then I will sell you all off, to different buyers. You may think it a poor bargain, but the alternative is violent death here and now, and if any of you survive I'll crucify you. So..." He shrugged. "I don't think you have much choice. Live, or die, what's it to be, Vita?"

For a moment Vita was too astonished to reply. *This* was Castus's bargain? She didn't even need to ask Argento's opinion and she couldn't care less what her other three companions thought of the offer.

"I'd rather die here and now, than live as a one-eyed slave for some other Roman piece of filth," she said, drawing herself up and setting her shoulders proudly. "Bring it on, old man, if you have the balls."

She could see Lucia nodding slightly to herself – the manageress, at least, knew what Vita's reply would be, but the rebel slave had no intention of letting Lucia slip back away from the inevitable fight without telling the bitch what she thought of her.

"The gods take you too, Lucia. May your flesh rot on your bones and your piss turn to black blood. You—"

Castus had heard enough and, at a signal from him, the legionaries began to close in. He took the oil lamp from the centurion and placed it in a sconce in the wall as the men filtered past him. He wanted no part of the fight himself and Vita cursed, knowing that, even if she managed to take down one, or even two of the Romans, she would never be able to get close enough to the master to kill him. The failure of their plot was a terrible blow, but knowing she would die while Publius Licinius Castus lived on enraged her.

The legionaries came forward as Castus and Lucia turned their backs and walked away along the corridor. The veteran soldiers' shields were locked in place just as Vita remembered from tales her countrymen told of battles fought against the Roman legions. She wasn't the only one driven mad with fury as they approached. At her side, Argento drew back his right arm, then, either forgetting or not caring that it would leave him unarmed, he threw his long knife.

The oncoming legionaries flinched out of the way behind their shields, but they weren't the slave's target: Castus was.

There was a scream of agony as Argento's knife slammed home in flesh, and then the battle was joined and Vita had no time to savour the death of their so-called 'master' as she was forced to parry an oncoming gladius.

"I love you," Argento roared at her, batting aside the blades of his own attackers' with his bare hands, and Vita could feel Otho and the others of her small conspiracy fighting for their lives at her back.

This was a battle the rebels could not win. Vita sensed her companions behind them fall one by one, and she saw Argento go down in a bloody heap as two, three, four gladius points found a home in his body as he cried out in pain and terror.

Tears streamed down Vita's face and she screamed one last curse before the tip of a Roman blade tore through the front of her chest and she dropped to her knees, mouth filling with blood.

As she died she could see Castus in the corridor and a final sob escaped her lips as she realised Argento's dagger had not hit the master after all—the tribune was completely unharmed. It was the manageress, Lucia, who'd been struck by the missile. She lay face-down on the stone floor, Argento's blade protruding from her lower back.

And then the Roman blades took their toll and Vita followed her companions into the afterlife.

CHAPTER FOUR

"I need a new villa manageress." Publius Licinius Castus said to Rogatus. "Or manager, of course." He smiled warmly at the giant slave. "Which is where you come in. I would like you to replace Lucia."

Rogatus raised his eyebrows in an apparently involuntary show of surprise and Sennianus, who was in the room as a server, remembered sadly how, long before, Lucia had taken the same promotion with similar disbelief. Poor Lucia...

"You are the ideal candidate," Castus continued, before Rogatus had a chance to respond. "The slaves respect you. They fear you even. And that is a good thing for a manager, as Lucia, and Paltucca before her, knew very well. It's perhaps a shame you weren't in charge these past few weeks – maybe your influence would have deterred Vita and her lapdogs from their cowardly plans and I wouldn't find myself needing to replace a fine manageress. But that's all immaterial now; you will have your own personal chamber from now on, Rogatus, an increase in your food rations, and a substantial pay rise."

The giant Nubian glanced at Sennianus, with a look that might have been embarrassment, but Senni's encouraging nod was enough to make Rogatus lift his head proudly and reply to Castus' request, which was essentially an order anyway.

"I will do it, master. Thank you for this great opportunity."

"Don't thank me just yet," Castus said, raising an eyebrow. "Your fellows will no longer be as friendly as they've been up to this point. Lucia realised that eventually, and greatly to her cost, isn't that right Sennianus?"

"Yes, master," Senni agreed, stepping forward and lifting the jug of wine he held to refill Castus's cup before moving back to his previous position against the wall of the dining room.

"But the rewards are worth it," the master went on. "And you're getting on a bit now. You could do with a rest from feeding the hypocaust after all these years, eh?"

Rogatus was only thirty-five but a decade as the legendary Regalis's replacement furnace-master had undeniably taken their toll on him. Senni thought it would do the big man good to spend more time out in the open air, inspecting the gardens and such, instead of being cooped up in the smoky, roasting-hot underground room that had been his domain for so long.

"It's a terrible shame what happened to Lucia," Castus said and Sennianus believed the sadness in his voice was genuine and heartfelt. "But life goes on and you, Rogatus, have been a loyal servant both to her, and to me. You will do well in your new position, I am certain. Now," he got to his feet and stretched up, working the kinks out of his neck. Castus was no youngster either these days Sennianus thought, although his life of relative leisure weighed rather less heavily on him than any of the slaves' years. "I am going for a walk with my wife in the gardens. Do you have any questions?"

Rogatus glanced again at Sennianus, a bemused look to his face.

"Questions? Yes, master. Where do I begin? I know nothing of running an estate such as this."

"Ha!" Castus barked, shaking his head. "My apologies, Rogatus," he said, looking at Sennianus and smiling as if they were all friends together, enjoying the same joke. "He will need someone to show him the ropes, of course. Well, who better to teach you than the person you're replacing? My new clerk, Lucia." He turned back to Rogatus, the smile still on his face. "You know your own way to her chamber I'm sure? Go to her then. And good luck in your new role!"

* * *

The surgeon had told Lucia she might never walk again. Argento's dagger had struck her in the back and everyone knew an injury to the spinal area could mean paralysis for life.

Her first thought was one of dismay: she would never get revenge on the master now, after all these years of work. It was a bitter blow to take, especially since she felt certain Argento's dagger was meant for Castus, not her. Had it struck its intended target, paralysing Castus instead of Lucia, it would have made her quest for payback easy – yet she was the one lying in bed, her back a mass of pain, legs unable to move at all, while the master wandered about the grounds of his estate as happy as a freshly-paid legionary in a brothel.

They had stopped the slaves' conspiracy and life went on as normal. Tullia, the slave who'd opened the door to the north wing for Vita and her friends had been arrested and taken to Durobrivae where she would no doubt be crucified for her part in the pitiful uprising. Thankfully, Lucia's intervention meant none of the other slaves would be punished – she managed to convince Castus that none except the conspirators knew anything about the murderous scheme and he accepted her word.

Her second thought on hearing she might be bed-ridden for the rest of her days was fear of being made destitute. "It will be impossible for you to monitor the slaves stuck in a bed or a chair," the master had told her, and, at first, her heart had sunk, thinking he was going to kick her out into the street. She should have known better of course – his new religion would never allow such barbaric treatment of a loyal servant, if it had even been in his nature. "Instead, I will promote Rogatus to the position of manager and you, Lucia, will become my new full-time clerk. You have earned it."

A spasm had run across her back just then, making her grimace in pain, which was fortunate, for she wouldn't have wanted Castus to see the fierce joy his words kindled in her. It would surely have raised his suspicions and, now that it had finally come after so many years, she fully intended to make the most of this incredible opportunity.

As manageress Lucia had been able to guide and manipulate many aspects of life within Villa Tempestatis, but ultimate control of the one thing she needed to fully realise her ambitions was held only by the clerk: money.

It was true everyone had to justify their expenses to Lucia as manageress, and she had responsibility for ordering supplies and so on, but that was only a small part of the estate's overall finances. It was the clerk who oversaw the vast income and expenditure of the entire villa, and that meant access to, and control of, huge sums of money.

Sums large enough to ruin Villa Tempestatis and its owner.

When Paltucca had been killed over a decade earlier, Castus had hired a local man to take her place as clerk. A small elderly fellow, with a shock of white hair and a squint from staring at ledgers all his life, Litegenus had been quite scrupulous; Lucia had been very careful never to let him catch her out skimming money. He was getting on now though, and taking longer to complete his duties. Castus had complained about him a number of times recently, but Lucia had never suspected she would be the one to replace the old clerk.

When Castus left her chamber that morning, Lucia had forgotten the continuous pain in her lower back and almost shouted out in happiness. The gods had smiled on her: this was the opportunity she needed to fulfil her life-long dream of destroying Castus and his entire line.

Was it enough?

She'd begun to grow very tired of life recently. Seeing other slaves marry and live in relative happiness over the decades, despite their lot, had taken its toll on Lucia. Years of rebuffing Sennianus's pleas of marriage, and his suggestion that they should ask Castus for their freedom, had tired her out.

It was a hard existence when all you had to sustain you was hatred and the burning desire for revenge. Things would be even harder now she couldn't even get out of bed!

Yet the gods had not forsaken her yet – promotion to clerk finally opened a way to fulfil her lofty ambitions. She didn't just want to ruin Publius Licinius Castus; she had much more planned than that.

There was a knock on the door and she sat up straight, composing herself and making sure she didn't look too pleased. "Come in," she said, and the smile returned to her face as the massive, reassuring figure of Rogatus filled the open doorway. "Come in," she repeated, gesturing to the chair beside her desk. "Take a seat, my friend."

To her surprise, Rogatus walked past the desk, right up to her bed, bent down practically onto his haunches and placed his arms around her. For a long moment he remained like that and, when he moved away both of them had tears in their eyes.

"I'm sorry to see you like this," the giant Nubian said softly, wiping his face unashamedly. "You should have told the rest of us about this crazy plan of Vita's. We would have stopped them before they got as far as they did."

Lucia simply shrugged. She had thought of that many times before opting to report the conspiracy to Castus. "I didn't want to put that responsibility on the slaves," she replied at last. "I knew I could always trust people like you and Popillia, but as Senni tells me, it's not the same any more – it's not like the old days. I feared some of the others might have been sucked into Vita's plans and who knows what might have happened then?" She sighed, then forced herself to brighten, not wanting to dampen what should be a happy day for Rogatus. "I hear you're to be my successor. Congratulations! You will make a fine manager I think."

A wry smile split the big man's dark face and Lucia was glad to see his tears had dried. He leaned in close, eyeing the door as if about to impart a great secret to her.

"I have no idea what being manager means," he whispered. "But the master promised I'd get more wages and meat and wine so..." He sat back, clapping his hands down on his heavily-muscled thighs. "I said I'd do it. It's got to be better than shovelling logs into that damn furnace every single day, right?"

Lucia laughed, although she wished she might get up from her bed and feed the hypocaust instead of being paralysed. "Aye, it's physically less demanding than your old job. But be prepared for your friends to desert you."

Rogatus shook his head dismissively. "Your friends never deserted you. Senni will be with you until the day you die, whether you like it or not, and those of us who have known you for years are still loyal. If only you'd asked." He waved one hand as if past mistakes no longer mattered and continued grimly. "You were fair with us, much more so than Paltucca ever was. I will do my best to act in a similar fashion. If anyone is too stupid to see that, well...to Hades with them."

They talked for a long time after that, Lucia outlining what the new manager's duties would be, placing particular emphasis on those which would be most pressing, such as the coming days' work rota.

"We will talk often," she promised once Rogatus stood up, protesting he'd already imposed on her time too much. "If you have any questions at all come and see me. Use Popillia for advice too – she knows how this place works better than anyone after all this time and she is a loyal friend. Senni will also keep you right, as you know."

The giant black slave nodded then held out his hand to her. They clasped arms like men about to head into battle, gazing into one another's eyes and liking what each saw mirrored there.

"You'll be a good manager," Lucia said confidently. "Just as you've been a good friend to me over these years and I will make sure you are well rewarded for it."

Rogatus frowned, confusion on his face. "You already have," he said. "The master told me it was your recommendation that made him offer me this promotion."

Lucia nodded before continuing very quietly. "It was. But – and keep this to yourself please – there may well be more changes in Villa Tempestatis soon, and I'll look to people like you to bring much-needed stability to the place. I trust you will be here for me again when the time comes?"

The puzzled look remained on the big man's face and his eyes narrowed thoughtfully but, after a moment he nodded.

"I will."

"Good. Get on with you then!" Lucia smiled, despite another stab of pain in her back. "You are the manager now, and that means you can allocate more food and drink to yourself. And finally …make Nona your wife and have a chamber of your own to start a family."

Rogatus stopped, his hand on the door latch, and turned back to her, a huge smile on his face as her words hit him. Once again tears came to his eyes and Lucia feared he might run back to her bedside and crush her in another embrace. But he simply smiled and left the room. From the sound of his footsteps hurrying away, he was doubtless on his way to tell Nona of their good fortune.

CHAPTER FIVE

Rogatus settled in well to his role as manager, although for the first two or three weeks he regularly visited Lucia in her chamber to seek advice. From setting up work rotas, to punishing slackness, and even how best to deal with the dark looks his former peers had started giving him recently, the big Nubian felt somewhat lost in those early days in his new position but, gradually his visits to Lucia became less and less frequent.

By the end of the first month, he had managed to figure things out and, after a stressful time of her own, learning how to maintain the books accurately and to a standard imperial law required, Lucia too felt more comfortable as clerk of Villa Tempestatis.

Sennianus, head gardener by now – a promotion bestowed on him some time ago by Castus himself, once he realised the lame slave had an affinity with plants and flowers – came often to Lucia's room to tend to her wounded back and also to help her pass the long hours she was forced to endure laid up in bed.

It was during one of these visits, on a dark, windy night in late October, when Senni brought her news of the mistress.

"Dianna has fallen ill," he said, sitting down in the chair by Lucia's bedside. He looked genuinely saddened by the news he brought.

"What's wrong with her?" Lucia asked, biting into the apple her friend had brought as a gift. It tasted sweet and the juice ran down her chin. Senni always brought her something when he visited and she particularly appreciated fruit, knowing it would help aid her recovery from Argento's knife wound. "I assume it's serious or you'd not have bothered mentioning it."

Sennianus nodded grimly. "Aye, it seems so. I haven't seen her – Popillia and her maid are tending her but they say Dianna is in a bad way. She had the runs after dinner last week, then spent the night vomiting. Ever since then she's been unable to keep any food down. Even watered wine comes back up more often than not." He shook his head as if fearing the worst for their mistress. "Popillia says she's wasting away and won't last much longer unless she can start keeping some food down."

"That explains why Castus hasn't visited me for the past few days," Lucia said. "I thought he'd just realised I was getting better at the new job and wanted to leave me to get on with it." She shrugged then and lowered her voice, as if fearful someone might overhear her next words. "Why do you care anyway? I thought you had no more love for Dianna than I do."

Sennianus looked at her thoughtfully for a long moment, eyes narrowed, before replying to her question. "I don't wish her any ill," he said. "She's never done me any great harm over the years, which is more than I can say for some people no longer with us. And I simply don't enjoy knowing someone in the villa is suffering so much from illness."

Now it was Lucia's turn to stare at him, wondering how he could be so forgiving. "She's never done you any great harm over the years? What about ordering our newborn child be exposed?" Her voice was low and hard, filled with anger. The same anger that had been with her all these long years and never abated.

"I don't blame her for that," Senni said quietly, refusing to become angry himself despite the accusation in Lucia's voice. "We're not the only couple to have our baby taken from us and dumped out in the open for..." He waved a hand and looked away, finally succumbing to the decades-old emotions he tried to suppress, mostly successfully, every day of his life. Leaning in close, he lowered his voice to a hard whisper. "We both know Paltucca engineered that whole situation, and we also know what happened to her and her conspirator, Dentatus. You've blamed Dianna and Castus all this time and carried that hate with you, like the chains the slaves at market are forced to wear. Yet never once did you think to seek revenge on Regalis, despite the fact he was the one who carried our babe out into the night and left him to..."

Tears filled his eyes but Lucia couldn't comfort him – instead, she felt outrage that he should seek to put any blame for what happened on the beloved old furnace master. "Regalis only did as he was told to do. If he hadn't done it, someone else would have. Dentatus perhaps. And that bastard would have enjoyed it too!"

"And like I say," Sennianus retorted, "dozens of other slaves have had their babies taken from them and exposed. Often by their own choice. That, as you should know by now Lucia, is life. Why should we be treated any differently to our companions? Besides, you know Castus and Dianna regretted their decision to expose our baby once they found out the truth, and they've given us their permission to start a family any time we want. It's been *your* choice not to do so."

Lucia glared at him, ready to repeat her reasons for never becoming pregnant again, but he sighed and his shoulders slumped and she bit her tongue. He wanted no more argument. As always, he accepted her decisions and was content to remain her lifelong companion no matter what, despite the fact most of the other slaves thought him a weak fool for not moving on and finding a mate from one of the other women living in Villa Tempestatis.

"You feel hard done by," he said, meeting her eyes once again and placing his hand on her leg, forgetting she couldn't feel it any more. "And I understand it. The master tore you from your family, just as he did to me, and then he raped you and dumped the child you'd carried as if it was a piece of rubbish. But you must be tired. Tired of carrying so much hatred around for so many years. What will you do if Dianna dies, and Castus follows soon after, his heart broken?"

Lucia thought about it then set her mouth in a hard line.

"Rejoice," was her answer.

They stared at one another then, silent, and Lucia feared she had finally pushed Sennianus away for good. Of course, she hadn't.

"What, before you've had a chance to exact the revenge you've wanted for your whole life? What exactly is it you have in store for him anyway?"

Lucia shook her head. She didn't want to implicate him in her plans. She had no fears he would betray her, but the less he knew what she was going to do the better. There could be no slip-ups, everything depended on the coming months.

"I had planned on challenging Castus to a sword fight," she said, laughing. "But that idea's not much use now that I'll never walk again."

Sennianus leaned in close to her again and they silently embraced, two scarred and disabled slaves united in a love as constricted as their own mobility.

* * *

The weeks passed and Lucia proved her surgeon's prognosis wrong: she was up and able to walk again after a little over a month, although she was weak and forced to take things slowly as she attempted to build up the atrophied muscles in her legs. Argento's dagger turned out to have missed her spine and, once the swelling from the injury went down, the feeling in her legs returned. Thank Sulis Minerva.

Similarly, Dianna's vomiting illness had not proved as serious as feared, passing with time and making Castus pray extra hard to his God in gratitude.

"Ah, good morning Lucia," the master said to her as he sat taking breakfast in the dining room on the ides of December. His tone was warm, in contrast to the blanket of deep snow that lay all across the estate, providing a stunning backdrop to the meal. The summer had been a long one this year, but winter threatened to last a similar length of time. Frost had settled on the land not long after the autumnal equinox and Sennianus, from years of experience in his gardens, predicted Nerva, Regalis's giant son and replacement furnace-master, would need every last twig of firewood that they'd gathered for the hypocaust before spring thawed the ground.

Lucia, eyes respectfully downcast as ever, couldn't help but look at the brand-new mosaic on the triclinium floor which had only recently been completed. Castus, on his conversion to Christianity, had torn out the previous colourful mosaic with its dolphin-riding Cupid and fantastic scenes from Roman legend and brought in an artisan from Corinium Dobunnorum to replace it at great expense. The central motif was a drably coloured image of the Christ, flanked by two pomegranates and some symbol, the significance of which Lucia did not understand, or care about. She simply felt the previous mosaic, which she'd known since her arrival in Villa Tempestatis, had been far more interesting and beautiful, and its removal had felt like another part of her own soul had been stolen away.

"How are you getting on?" Castus asked as Lucia hobbled across to stand beside his table. It was loaded with watered wine, honey-cakes, bread and butter and smoked ham, making her mouth water with the sight and smell of it all. "You seem to be moving a little easier today."

The clerk nodded and, resting one hand on the walking stick Sennianus had fashioned for her from a length of ash, placed the other on her back where the knife wound still ached. "The bruising seems to be healing at last, master, so the pain isn't as great any more. I just need to get into the habit of walking again."

"You're a strong one," Dianna said, wiping crumbs from her lips and looking up at the slave-woman with approval. "We should have known you'd prove the surgeon wrong."

"To be fair to old Sergius," Castus said reprovingly, "he did say there was a small chance the blade hadn't damaged Lucia's spine and the feeling might return to her legs eventually. It seems that's exactly what's happened, eh?"

This last to Lucia who nodded politely. "I think so master. And I thank you once again for paying to have the surgeon tend me. I know that, with wounds like the one I received, there's a good chance of infection setting in which…"

"I think that's enough of this sort of talk," Dianna said, distaste twisting her mouth. "I'm trying to enjoy my breakfast here."

"My apologies, *domina,*" Lucia replied, bowing her head and lifting a satchel from over her shoulder which she lowered onto the floor by Castus's feet before shuffling backwards on her stick. "I will be about my business. Those are the weekly accounts, master, if you could approve them before I submit them to the magistrates in Durobrivae..?"

"I will, Lucia, thank you."

The master and mistress returned to their meal in companionable silence, staring out at the snow which had begun to fall softly once more as the clerk, forgotten, passed through the doors, opened for her by one of the young slaves, and hobbled out into the corridor. When she was out of sight and alone again she leaned against the wall and breathed deeply.

It wasn't just the physical exertion that was making her feel breathless. She allowed herself a long moment to pull herself together before setting off towards the kitchen in the west wing.

For weeks now, she had suspected Castus no longer checked her accounts fastidiously, instead just glancing over them before signing his name in approval. She had seen him doing this herself one day and decided to make sure of herself today by making a deliberate mistake with the numbers.

It was only a small 'miscalculation' on her part, making it look like they had spent rather more on wine the previous week than they had in reality. If Castus was checking the figures thoroughly he should notice the discrepancy and order her to change it while being more careful in future.

If he did *not* notice her error, well…

She was too nervous to wait on the results of her experiment so made her way slowly to the kitchen. Paltucca never spent time working and living with the slaves beneath her and, for some reason, Lucia had simply followed her predecessor's lead. Thinking about it now, she didn't really understand *why* she'd taken the same path as Paltucca, considering how much she and everyone else hated the bitch, but recent events had made her re-evaluate things. As a result, Lucia decided to spend more time with the other workers, in the hope that the camaraderie of her earliest days in Villa Tempestatis might be brought back.

The kitchen was a hive of activity as women went about their daily tasks in a hubbub of gossip and laughter and advice on how to deal with everything in life from children to men, cooking to sewing, and any other of a seemingly limitless number of talking points.

The dozen or so slaves gathered in the room halted their conversations though, as Lucia opened the door, their faces registering, what? The clerk wasn't sure exactly what she saw on the women's expressions. Mistrust, irritation, fear, dislike, even scorn. She ignored it all and walked over to the big table which they used for everything. In a couple of hours it would be filled with the dinner dishes, but, for now, the slaves were using it to support the winter clothes they were crafting or repairing.

Merula was there, and she at least had a smile for the clerk, remembering the dark nights when Castus raped her and she had been by Lucia in the bed over the very kitchen they were in now.

Some things had changed around Villa Tempestatis, many people had come and gone over the years, but the buildings themselves remained as they always had been.

"Don't worry," Lucia said, smiling around at the hushed workers. "I'm not here to upbraid anyone – that's not my job any more anyway, it's Rogatus's! I'm just here to help with the work, so please, don't let me spoil the atmosphere." She walked slowly across to the table, sat down, and gestured for Merula to hand her a torn sock, needle and thread. Then, when she was suitably kitted out, she set to mending the thing.

She was shocked at how hard she found the task. The master made sure his high status slaves were always supplied with relatively new attire, so, as a result, Lucia had not needed to repair her clothes for years and it had never crossed her mind to sew or knit purely for pleasure. She had, at one time, enjoyed the therapeutic nature of such jobs, and the feeling of satisfaction when a fine new garment was completed but…her thoughts turned to her abandoned baby and the warm blanket she'd made especially for him.

"That's it, you're getting the hang of it again," Merula nodded encouragingly and Lucia snapped out of her reverie, smiling sheepishly at the younger woman.

"My fingers feel like an old woman's. They won't quite do what I want them to."

"Give it an hour and your old nimbleness will come back. Don't get disheartened."

Lucia mumbled in hopeful agreement and returned to the task while surreptitiously contemplating her old friend. Merula was almost as old as she was, face still pretty but quite heavily lined. She'd given birth to two children around a decade earlier, one of which was exposed as it was deemed to have a sinister look about it; the other, a boy, spent his time working outdoors with the chickens. Merula's figure, which had once been so attractive to Publius Licinius Castus, was now portly, rather like Paltucca's had been in middle-age.

Lucia doubted the woman cared about her appearance – it meant the master, and his often-lecherous visitors, left her alone these days. Sagging breasts were a small price to pay for a peaceful life.

Ah, the clerk sighed inwardly, thinking how hard life was for all the slaves here in Villa Tempestatis, not just her. Merula had shared similar hardships to Lucia, but every one of the slaves that had passed through its doors over the decades had been torn from their families and homes, forced to work like animals, often suffering beatings or worse.

They *all* deserved revenge on Castus and Dianna: their *owners*. Lucia only wished she had an army behind her that might put an end to the entire Roman culture once and for all.

But for now, socks and cloaks needed darning and patching and, with Merula chattering away amiably, the worn-out garments were soon perfectly useable once again. Indeed, the conversation, and friendly atmosphere that eventually returned to the cosy room after Lucia's entrance made the hours pass much quicker than the clerk had expected.

The table started to be cleared as the cook, Helena, a dumpy slave with a large mole on her face and a hairy upper lip who had been bought in from Rome itself, barked orders as she took charge of her domain. Despite her rather unattractive appearance, Lucia knew Castus valued Helena greatly and, having often tasted the leftovers from the master's feasts, she could tell why. Helena was a superb cook.

She was also an ogre in the kitchen and the clerk decided to retire to her chamber, out the way of the woman's hard voice and even harder stare as she demanded water be boiled, lamps lit, more wood brought in for the fire and a slab of butter brought in from the pantry.

"It was nice to spend time working alongside you again," Merula said, a look of genuine pleasure on her face as she took Lucia's arms in hers. "Like old times. Will you come back in a while and eat dinner with us?"

Lucia thought about the idea for a moment, tempted by the invitation and having greatly enjoyed the past hour or two in the company of the other slave-women but at last she shook her head. She didn't want to impose on them too much – today was a good start in rebuilding a closer working relationship with them. Better she leave them to eat dinner and relax on their own now, without the presence of an authority figure there to make them uneasy.

"Maybe another day," Lucia said. "But, for now I have work of my own to be getting on with and I'll eat in my own chamber as I always do. I've really enjoyed your company today though, thank you Merula."

They embraced warmly, and Lucia noticed the raised eyebrows from the other women bustling about. She bid them all a cheery good evening and, hobbling along on her walking stick, left the kitchen carrying one of the oil lamps stored in an alcove by the door.

The change in temperature between the kitchen and corridor made her shiver and wish she'd brought her white woollen shawl with her, but as she made her way slowly back to her own chamber in the north wing, stick tapping as she went, a strange feeling of rejuvenation settled upon her.

She truly had enjoyed being part of the group of workers today. Yes, it had felt like the good old days, which made her shake her head in bemusement. 'Good old days'? Those days had been the darkest of her life! It was funny how time made things seem different, and yet not everything about her existence in Villa Tempestatis was bleak.

Times spent working closely with her companions like Merula, Popillia, Livinia, Antonia and many others *had* been enjoyable, and today was a very pleasant reminder of that.

It was only when she reached her chamber, unlocked the door and noticed the small pile of wax tablets sitting in the gloom on her desk that she remembered the accounts, and her 'mistake'.

Heart pounding, she shuffled into the room and closed the door behind her. She looked at the tablets as if they might jump up and attack her, then pulled herself together, placed the oil lamp down on the table, and sat down herself.

This was a huge moment. Had Castus noticed her deliberate mistake? All her plans rested on his trusting her accounts to the extent he wouldn't even check them properly, never mind question her about them. If he'd spent the remainder of his breakfast going over Lucia's figures as he really should have done, her hopes would be dashed, possibly forever, given his advancing years.

She took a deep breath, looked upwards at the white plastered ceiling and offered a prayer to Sulis Minerva, then lifted the tablets. She dropped first one, then another back onto the desk finding the one she sought at the bottom of the pile. Her eyes scanned the characters – her own handwriting, pressed into the soft wax by the stylus Sennianus had bought her as a gift from Durobrivae not a month before – and found the line she sought.

It remained as she had written it. The mistake had not been corrected.

Now she looked down with rising excitement to the bottom of the document and almost shouted out a cheer of exultation as she saw the master's seal of approval pressed into the wax.

He hadn't checked her work.

He trusted her!

She sat back with a huge grin on her face, right fist clenched in triumph, breathing deeply to calm her beating heart, the scent of olive oil filling her nostrils just as it had when Vita and Argento had died.

This was just the beginning – now she could begin to put her plans into action.

After thirty-two years as his slave – his plaything, his beast of burden, his 'lover', and now his clerk – Lucia finally had the means to destroy Publius Licinius Castus.

CHAPTER SIX

The snows abated around the middle of December, during the period when even Christians such as Castus celebrated the winter solstice in the festival of Saturnalia. Despite the master's adoption of his new religion, this time was beloved by all peoples, even the native Britons, and usually meant a long and lavish celebration for everyone in Villa Tempestatis.

The winter solstice had always been celebrated of course – feasting and merriment were fine ways to brighten the long dark nights which, in a place like Britannia, sometimes never seemed to turn to day in December and January.

The estate had performed very well this year, with a fine harvest of grain and many new livestock born and sold at market. The stables, thanks to Sulicena's expert management, had produced not one but two champion racehorses, which earned the master a lot of money. As a result of this welcome upturn, Castus decided to celebrate Saturnalia even more ostentatiously than usual although the traditional role reversal aspect of the festival, in which slave became master was no longer such a prevalent part of festivities. It caused too much trouble, as the slaves often took things too far – like the time Sennianus had hit old Tiro in the face with that egg – and Lucia was glad when Rogatus informed the slaves there would be none of that kind of thing this year.

Lucia was, however, tasked with organising most things, since Rogatus had proved to be much better at managing the slaves themselves than dealing with logistics, ordering supplies and arranging feasts.

It was a different relationship between manager and clerk than Lucia had been used to with Litegenus, where the former clerk had only worked a few hours per week and that spent entirely on making sure the finances were all in order. Now Lucia and Rogatus worked together, almost as co-managers; it worked very well and Castus seemed happy enough. It also meant Lucia had total control over what monies came in and out of the estate, being accountable only to the master – and he no longer made any pretence of checking her figures.

Castus trusted her completely.

She had tested this again a number of times, just as she'd done before by making slight errors in her arithmetic. Not once had Castus noticed and it gave Lucia the confidence to begin putting her plans into place with little fear of discovery.

The Saturnalia celebrations which would take place between December the 17th and 23rd gave her ample opportunity to move towards her ultimate goal, especially since Maximus, the master's son who was visiting for the winter, insisted on making his own grand suggestions for ways to make their coming feasts more interesting.

Romans always had to show off their wealth – it seemed to be ingrained in them.

For her plans to be successful Lucia knew she would need money, and lots of it. So, when Maximus demanded a troop of musicians be hired for the period, Lucia doubled the price they asked for in her accounts, paid them their due and tucked the other half away with her back-street banker in Durobrivae. She did the same with everything: food orders; decorations for the gardens and house; gifts for family and guests invited to parties; even a stunning new mural depicting the birth of Christ painted on the dining room wall by a master artist.

Castus did enquire a couple of times as to how much things were costing, and Lucia told him quite frankly her own inflated figures. It was a measure of how much money the estate had earned during the year that he never questioned her or even suggested the celebrations should be cut back.

"By God, I almost wish Maximus hadn't decided to winter with us," was all Castus said to her on the matter. "He seems intent on spending all my money!" And off he went, shaking his head good naturedly.

Lucia watched him go, the wheels in her head spinning as ever, an idea already beginning to form on how to use that comment to her own advantage.

She had never thought of herself as sly or devious but, now that she'd committed everything to the matter of destroying Publius Licinius Castus it seemed she was constantly on the lookout for things to use in pursuit of her goal. Even an innocent throwaway remark became something that might be twisted to serve her machinations, if she could only figure out a way to use it…

As it drew nearer to Saturnalia Lucia found herself spending more time with Maximus. He would call her over to talk when he was having breakfast, or if he was walking in the gardens, and once or twice he even came to her chamber. It was always to talk about the coming celebrations.

The second time he came to her room she was working on the doctored accounts and, as was his way, he being one of the masters and she being a slave, he simply walked in through the door without knocking.

"Max. It's rude to walk into a lady's chamber unannounced," she scolded, covering her work as quickly as possible without making it seem too obvious she was hiding something. "I might have been getting dressed."

The young man simply looked at her as if she was mad. This was his father's house, and she a mere slave – he could walk into whatever damn room he liked, and if she was undressed, he could take full advantage of the fact however he pleased. All this passed across his face and Lucia gritted her teeth at the half-smile that tugged at the edge of his lips.

At least he didn't come right out and say any of it though.

"How can I help you, Max?"

He broke into a full smile now and took a seat on her bed. Some Romans would not appreciate slaves addressing them by their given name, especially a diminutive form of it, but Maximus had commanded Lucia not to call him 'master' any more once he reached manhood. She didn't know if it was some new fashion he'd picked up when visiting Rome, but he was quite insistent, reminding her to call him Max any time she forgot.

Lucia knew the other slaves appreciated his gesture – it made them feel just a little more human, to call one of the nobles by their name instead of some epithet that confirmed their own subservience, such as 'master' or *'dominus'* but as always Lucia differed from her peers. Yes, they might call him by his name, like equals it seemed, but when you were being *commanded* to do so, it merely hammered home the fact that you lived to carry out the hated Roman overlords' orders.

"I wanted to talk about the coming feast," the master's son said, unsurprisingly. "I thought we might have a cock fight after the first night's meal, what do you think?"

Lucia shrugged. "I expect your father and his guests would thoroughly enjoy that. Would you like me to hire someone to provide the birds?" She suspected the Christian clergy frowned on blood sports such as cock fighting, but then they seemed to disapprove of everything, and even the most devoted of the faith's adherents ignored many of their spiritual leaders' tenets when it suited them. Castus was no exception.

"Yes, that would be good," Maximus nodded, rubbing his hands in a way that reminded Lucia of him when he was a mere boy. The excitement in the gesture was quite innocent and, in a man of his age and station, perhaps a little strange.

"Forgive me, Max, but if you don't mind me saying, you seem rather more excited about Saturnalia this year than usual. I remember you were always a great fan of the feasts we celebrate during the year but never to this extent before."

Her words must have seemed like a rebuke for his face fell and, again, he reminded Lucia of his younger self after a scolding.

"You're right," he admitted at last. "You always were the sharpest of our slaves. No doubt that's why you're my father's clerk now." He looked at her and nodded. "I am to be married."

The statement surprised Lucia, as she'd heard no rumours of any engagement or betrothal, but it also confused her.

"I see. Congratulations then, Max, the lady is very lucky, but…What does that have to do with Saturnalia?"

He shrugged. "This will be my last winter as a free, unattached young man. It feels like the end of my childhood has come at last and, well…"

"You want to make the most of it before you're forced to settle down and be a dutiful husband?"

"Exactly!"

"You do realise, Max, that your bride-to-be probably enjoys festivals just as much as you? I doubt you will never be allowed to celebrate Saturnalia again."

He pursed his lips a little sadly. "I know that, but it won't be the same. I'll have to pay for it myself for one thing."

Lucia snorted with laughter. These Romans were quite ludicrous at times. Here was the boy – no, a man now, and not even a particularly young one – about to get married, and he was worrying about paying for his own entertainment at future

Saturnalias! What a life to lead, compared to those of the slaves he took for granted every single moment of his day.

She shook her head but managed to mask her distaste with a forced smile. "Well, your father's estate has performed excellently this year," she said.

"Undoubtedly thanks to your guiding hand," Max put in seriously.

"Perhaps, but mostly it's due to the performance of those two horses of his. They surprised everyone except Sulicena. She advised the master to bet rather more money on them than your father thought sensible in their first few competitive races. The odds were long and he made a killing."

"I know all that," the young man said. "But you downplay your own role in the estate's profitability." He gestured at the table she was sitting in front of, and the ledgers she'd hastily covered when he burst in. "You work much harder than anyone, even my father, expects, making sure everyone is doing their job as they should without creaming money off the top. Oh yes," he nodded at her wary look. "We know Paltucca allowed the slaves to claim more in expenses than they should. It became obvious when you took over as manageress and the claims dropped markedly." He stood up, the smile returning to his face as his thoughts turned once more to Saturnalia. "My father values your years of service greatly, Lucia. We all do. You will see to the cock fight preparations? Good."

With that he left the room, at least having the good grace to close the door behind him and, when he was gone, the clerk stared at the space where he'd been sitting, wondering just how much Castus knew about the erroneous expenses. Not just from years ago when Lucia had taken over from Paltucca, but, more importantly, now.

Did he have any inkling that she was skimming large sums from the accounts for herself? If he did she was finished. The thought made a chill run down her spine but she rolled her shoulders and straightened on the stool.

No, he had no idea what she was doing – he trusted her, thanks to all her years of service and the things she'd done for him proving, to his mind, her complete loyalty.

Still, she mused, turning back to open the ledgers again, the longer she took to carry out her final plan the more chance of her being discovered. She would have to move forward with more care, and more haste.

CHAPTER SEVEN

The snows continued to stay away in the run-up to the solstice, which meant the roads remained passable and guests were able to visit Villa Tempestatis for the festivities. Which was just as well, Lucia thought, imagining Maximus's childish disappointment had his parties not been well attended.

Dianna had taken charge of who to invite and on which days and, as expected, the first night's cock fight was a huge success with the guests. After a sumptuous meal of various dishes – thrushes in honey, boiled ham in bay leaves, pepper and almond cake, and assorted cheeses – the courtyard was cleared and, in the crisp afternoon air, the birds' handler set them to battle. The gathered nobles sipped mulled wine and ate sweetmeats carried around by the most attractive slaves, who were dressed in very little despite the temperature.

Lucia, with Rogatus beside her, watched from the shadows as guests of both sexes, drunk on wine and the excitement of cocks tearing one another to bloody bits, fondled the poor slaves as they passed by, sometimes quite roughly. Castus didn't seem to care; perhaps he'd decided to let his visitors do as they please. It was Saturnalia after all.

Lucia feared for the servers as the day wore on and more wine was consumed. She had no doubt slaves of both sexes would be raped this night and there was nothing she could do about it.

The master would take no part in the brutality of course, since his new religion prohibited such decadent abuse, but once he was nicely drunk he would retire to his chamber with Dianna and the debauchery would begin with no-one to check it. Even giant Rogatus could not step in if a noble guest wanted to use a slave.

Everyone cheered gleefully as one fight came to a gory conclusion, the bone-tipped prosthetic talons of the victor tearing feathers and chunks of flesh from its unfortunate victim. The laughing abated as more bets were made and winnings collected or reinvested in new wagers.

The slave Prisca suddenly gave a cry of pain as someone slipped a hand inside her tunic and grasped her roughly between the legs before she was able to move away. Lucia watched in disgust as the male guest, pale faced with eyes already shockingly red-rimmed, grinned at his friends and made some remark about what he would like to do to the slave-girl. To her credit, Prisca managed, somehow, to retain hold of the tray she carried without dropping so much as a single cup of wine and Lucia nodded approvingly.

Dianna, as she did with the guests, selected which of the slaves should be at the feast. Prisca was always chosen as a server because, although she was by now into her mid-thirties, she retained the fantastic breasts and shapely behind the gods had gifted her with in lieu of a pretty face. Male guests, and sometimes female too, loved the sight of Prisca wandering amongst them with very little on.

It would be a long, hard night for the poor woman but better her than one of the much younger, inexperienced girls. Their time would come soon enough to be subjected to this sort of behaviour, but not tonight.

Not ever, if Lucia could bring her scheme to a satisfactory conclusion.

"I don't think you need me here," she murmured to Rogatus, who looked down at her from bleak eyes. She sighed inwardly, one part of her glad that the big man had accepted his life as a slave, another wishing he still retained the fire of his younger days in the villa. But Vita and Argento showed what happened if a slave didn't learn to accept their fate. She wished she could share with him what her plans were but that would be folly. He would find out soon enough. Everyone would.

"I'll retire to bed for the night, my friend. Good luck with that shower of shit."

The Nubian nodded, then turned his attention back to the festivities and the guests Lucia had so eloquently described. He could not stop the slaves being molested, but he could step in if things became violent or overly vicious – Publius Licinius Castus would not stand for his servants being damaged physically.

Lucia half-hoped the little shit that had groped Prisca tried to harm her. The thought of Rogatus beating him to a pulp with those great black fists of his was a pleasant one.

Her bedchamber was far enough away from the cock fighting in the courtyard that she could barely hear it and she hoped to get a decent night's sleep. The master had provided extra rations of wine and meat for those slaves not on duty tonight to enjoy the first day of Saturnalia. Lucia did think about going along to the kitchen to join in but decided against it.

The presence of so many drunken people – slaves and guests – made her nervous. All it took was one bladdered buffoon to fall into a candle and the entire house would go up in flames. At least one person would be needed to take charge in such an emergency and Lucia knew that task would undoubtedly fall to her.

So she untied her hair, shaking it out gladly, enjoying the feeling as it settled about her shoulders, then stripped off her warm clothes, extinguished her lamp, and slipped beneath the blankets in just her knee-length winter tunic. The day had gone well, with the food being complimented by all, and the entertainment – the cock fighter – turning up early enough to have everything set up in time for the guests finishing their lavish dinner. Castus would be pleased with her. The master was probably making his way to bed now, or he would be soon, with Dianna helping him stumble along, grinning and muttering as he always did these days when drink got the better of him.

That was one vice Christians didn't have a problem with – in fact, they encouraged wine consumption in their most holy ceremony. Lucia shuddered at the bizarre practice before she rolled onto her side and began drifting off to sleep, praying that Sulis Minerva would protect Prisca and Silvanus and all the other slaves from the more depraved sexual habits of Castus's guests.

She woke up in the dark and instantly knew something was wrong. She wasn't alone in the room.

She lay without saying anything, listening, straining her senses to try and figure out who was in the chamber with her. Her eyes were adjusted to the gloom but all they could pick out was a tall black shape looming over the bed.

Soft breathing mingled with the sound of a breeze blowing through the bare trees somewhere nearby and Lucia wished she had a weapon to defend herself against the nocturnal visitor.

It was a man, but not Sennianus – the black figure was too tall. Why would a man sneak into her room in the pitch black? Fear flooded her and she felt like a sixteen-year-old again, the memories of Castus's sexual abuse bringing her close to uncontrollable panic. Was it the master, in his cups, having decided to visit his old favourite for old times' sake? The figure, black as it was, seemed about his size and build.

The man filled her vision as he stepped in close and, without a word, fumbled for the blanket. His clumsy fingers found what they sought and he lifted it up just enough so he could slide underneath, beside Lucia. She tried not to shrink away, still pretending to be asleep until she understood who the intruder was and what he wanted.

Perhaps it was nothing sinister at all – it wouldn't be the first time a drunken party-goer had become lost and ended up in the wrong bed. She'd even heard tales of revellers in Durobrivae going into the wrong *house* by mistake and climbing into bed with complete strangers. Frightening for the sober, unfortunate householders no doubt, but entirely innocent and, in the cold light of day, an amusing story to be recounted for wide-eyed, laughing friends.

Lucia could feel the man's warm breath on her face, sour with wine and the spiced food he'd eaten. Any hopes that his presence there was mere drunken accident were dashed when his right hand came up and touched her breast.

She squealed with outrage and jerked backwards, against the wall, her own hands coming up protectively to cover her chest.

"Who are you?" she whispered. "I think you've come to the wrong room, I'm Publius Licinius Castus's clerk."

The man laughed. "I know, Lucia. Do you think I'm so drunk that I might have stumbled into the wrong chamber in the house I grew up in?"

She froze, surprised and, as the reality hit her, shocked. "Maximus? What in the name of Sulis are you doing in my bed? Is this some kind of prank? You're too old to be scared of sleeping alone now."

Still, confusion clouded her mind and, later on, she berated herself for not understanding the situation much faster. His hands reached out again, this time touching the bare skin of her legs and moving up, beneath the tunic along her thighs then around to her backside as he pulled himself close in against her.

Why else would an inebriated man slip into a woman's bed in the dark of night?

Maximus groaned with pleasure and she felt his manhood pressing against her as he squeezed her buttocks.

"I've wanted to do this for years," he muttered, kissing her neck and taking one hand off her skin so he could fondle himself. "When I was young, just becoming a man, I used to pleasure myself all the time imagining what it would be like to come to your room and lie with you. In my mind, I've had you hundreds of times."

Tears ran down Lucia's cheeks but she couldn't speak and he carried on anyway, filling the silence with his husky mutterings.

"My father warned me not to touch you," he said. "He allowed me to sleep with the whores in Durobrivae but for some reason our own household slaves were off-limits. To me at least. I know he used to enjoy them himself – I used to sneak along to the room he used for the purpose and listen outside the door."

"He will be angry if he finds out about this," Lucia mumbled, hoping to frighten him enough to leave her alone. She should have known better – he was far too aroused to go away until he was satisfied.

"He'll never find out. I won't tell him and I'm sure you won't either – you wouldn't want me to get into trouble would you? He might cut my allowance and that wouldn't do, not when I'm about to leave home and get married."

He pushed her legs aside and clumsily tried to enter her but his penis slipped to the side and he cursed. He was certainly no expert rapist anyway, not like his father. Rather than trying again straight away he attempted to kiss her but, instinctively, she turned away in revulsion and his lips brushed her cheek instead.

He froze, and they lay in that awkward position for a long moment, Lucia's heart thumping hard in her chest as she waited for him to slap her and demand she perform her duty as a good slave should. Who was she to reject him anyway? She was his father's property after all, to do with as he liked.

"Are you crying?"

The question took her aback and she squinted into the darkness, trying to see his face. Some men liked it better when their victim sobbed and begged them to stop and the last thing she wanted to do was add fuel to Maximus's burning desire.

His hand came up and touched her face, feeling the damp from her tears.

"What's wrong?"

"What's wrong?" Lucia echoed, astonished. "What do you think is wrong? You're raping me, just like your father did so many times! I thought at my age I was safe from this kind of abuse."

"Abuse?" his voice was soft and he sounded even more confused by this turn of events than she was. "But I thought you liked me."

Lucia wanted to shout at him, to tell the pampered idiot that she hated him and Castus and Dianna and would like nothing more than to see all three of them dead, but she sensed from his tone that there was no need. No need to drive him away, for he was already going.

She felt the bed rise as his weight disappeared from it, then there came the sound of fumbling as he tried to pull his tunic back on without falling over in his rapidly-sobering state.

"I'm sorry," he muttered. "I only wanted to enjoy a night with you before I go out into the world on my own."

He lifted the latch and slipped out without another word, closing the door softly behind him. She lay on the bed, bemused and utterly relieved, listening as his quiet footsteps disappeared along the corridor.

And then her tears returned and she buried her face in the bed, crying until, at last, a long time later, she fell asleep once again.

CHAPTER EIGHT

Thankfully, Saturnalia was soon over and Lucia was kept busy for the next two days helping Rogatus organise the clean-up duties, storing whatever uneaten food could be kept for human or animal consumption during the rest of the winter and, of course, making sure all the celebration's associated bills were taken care of.

Maximus mostly kept out of her way and, on the few occasions their paths did cross he either refused to meet her eye or simply peered at her sheepishly, like a scolded child. He was, in truth, quite different to his father, but, strangely, that merely made Lucia view him with more disdain. Where young Castus had been arrogant, demanding and oblivious to the slaves' feelings, Maximus had grown into a softer individual than his father.

The old master was only human too, though, and just as the last of the guests were leaving in the morning, Publius Licinius Castus fell ill.

Dianna came looking for Lucia who was in her chamber, eating some bread and cheese.

"Lucia, Castus isn't well. Can you fetch Mauricus and have him attend?"

"In your bedchamber, *domina*?"

"Yes, I think the festivities have been too much for him. All the food and drink, plus the stress of making sure everything went well…it's taken a toll on him so he's resting now." She turned to go back to her husband then glanced back over her shoulder. Lucia was surprised to see a worried expression on Dianna's face, which was still quite unlined despite her fifty-plus years. "You might also send to the town for a proper *medicus*, if anyone is going there today. Just to be on the safe side."

Lucia nodded and promised to see it done, wondering to herself just what was wrong with the master. Dianna wasn't normally one to overreact to a simple hangover or bout of fever.

Suddenly the clerk felt a knot in her own stomach and a thrill of fear ran through her. Castus was quite old now – he was no longer the muscular, commanding legionary tribune that had ruled Villa Tempestatis for so much of Lucia's life. She'd noticed his limbs becoming thinner, almost spindly in the past year or so, the flesh around his jowls beginning to sag along with his once-proudly-erect posture. Perhaps he was dying?

Closing the ledgers, she stood up and hurriedly threw on her thick, hooded winter cloak then, locking the door at her back, walked briskly along the corridor to the door. The majority of the estate's workshops and storage sheds were located on this, the western side of the house, and it was to one of these Lucia made her way.

Frost coated the ground, making the mud, churned with many footsteps, uneven and hard to walk on, so she picked her way carefully despite her haste. Her injured back was much better these days but it occasionally flared up for no discernible reason and the last thing she wanted was a spasm causing her to lose her footing.

Her target was a wooden shed in good repair, from which the sound of hammering could be heard, accompanied by a jaunty, whistled tune.

The door was open to let in light, although the interior was still gloomy and Lucia's eyes, adjusted now to the weak morning sunshine, took a moment to make out the face of Mauricus, who stopped hammering and greeted the clerk.

"Lucia, what brings you out here?"

He was a man of average height, hook-nosed, not particularly handsome Lucia thought, but he had intelligent eyes and an air of competency about him that demanded respect. He was a slave brought over from Rome to work as a carpenter and had been in the act of repairing the leg on a wooden stool when Lucia disturbed him. He also doubled as a healer of sorts, having been trained as such by a previous owner.

"The master is unwell," she said. "I'm going to head into Durobrivae to fetch the *medicus* but the mistress wants you to attend him for now."

Mauricus put down his hammer and patted himself down, a cascade of dust and wood shavings falling onto the similarly adorned ground. "I'll go through the kitchen and rinse my hands and face on the way."

Lucia nodded, noting the sweat on his balding forehead and just imagining Dianna's irritation should the man wander into her bedchamber in such a tousled state. "Good idea, but be quick."

"What's wrong with him anyway?"

She followed him outside, but he moved much faster than her and she had to raise her voice to be heard. "I don't know, you're the healer."

He waved a hand in farewell and disappeared inside the house, leaving Lucia trailing, her mind spinning as she attempted to formulate a plan for how best to use her day.

Obviously, the most pressing task was to bring a competent *medicus* from the town, but a journey from Villa Tempestatis to Durobrivae during the winter wasn't as easy as during the rest of the year, when the roads were clear. Lucia wanted to make the most of the trip.

The cart would need to be readied, so changing course, she walked south, flanking the house, until she reached the stables which housed the horses of lesser breeding. Rather faster than oxen, the beasts weren't needed for ploughing at this time of year and were penned beneath the high roof with its hayloft in the rafters above. They watched her from staring brown eyes as she approached.

"Nepos! Where are you? Nepos!"

There was a grunt from overhead and Lucia looked up to see a man's face with an expression almost as vacant as the horses'. He held a long fork and was working with the hay.

"Nepos, come down and prepare the wagon for a trip into town please."

"Yes, mistress," the man replied, nodding deferentially before dropping his fork and hurrying down the steps, eyeing Lucia all the time as if she was the *domina* herself.

The man wasn't all there, Lucia knew, but he was a tireless worker who never questioned his orders and caused no trouble around the estate. She sometimes wished Castus would buy more slaves like Nepos, even if his perpetually fawning, half-frightened attitude could often be irritating.

"I'll just hitch one of the horses, if that's all right, mistress," he said as he walked past to gather the beast's harness. "If the sun melts the frost, the ground might get muddy, and the weight of the two of these big fellows," he patted one on the flank proudly, "will wreck the road and maybe even cause the cart to get stuck."

Lucia looked at him with surprise. It seemed a very astute observation for someone she'd thought incapable of such insight.

Then again, this was his domain, and even animals like those in his charge could learn from experience. She imagined poor Nepos, covered head-to-toe in mud, flailing his arms, shouting at the horses and trying to push a bogged-down wagon out of a quagmire. She had to turn away to hide her smile, not wanting to offend the farmhand.

"That's very clever of you," she said as he went about harnessing the chosen animal – a young black mare with a docile nature – and leading it out of its pen towards the wagon which sat by the side of the road a short distance away. "I need to collect some things from the house while you do that, Nepos. I won't be long."

Lucia went off, promising herself she'd reward him with an extra ration of oats today for his troubles.

Sennianus was tending plants in the corridor as she walked back to her chamber. Not much could survive the bitter cold months in Britannia, even inside away from the frost, but Dianna liked to see a spot of colour about the place. Sprigs of mistletoe, and holly with its vibrant red berries, adorned the walls, while Sennianus had somehow managed to cultivate a few primroses which were flowering already.

"I'm taking the wagon to Durobrivae," Lucia said, suddenly desiring companionship on her forthcoming journey, even if it was only a few miles. "Would you like to come? You can finish watering them later," she said, before he could protest. "The mistress won't notice – she has other things on her mind, trust me."

The thought of spending time alone with Lucia, on a crisp winter's day, brought a smile to his handsome face and he nodded. "Aye, that sounds good. If the *domina* asks, I'll tell her I wanted to get some weed ash from town to feed the plants. It's true." He limped away in the opposite direction to collect his own heavy cloak, promising to also collect a skin of wine and some bread from the kitchen to keep them company.

Lucia, wondering why weed ash would help plants grow and how Senni had discovered the fact, walked to the master's winter bedchamber in the northeast corner of the house. It adjoined the baths and shared the hypocaust so it was one of the warmest rooms in the whole house, offering a cosy place to rest no matter how thickly the snow gathered outside.

"Come." Dianna's voice called when Lucia knocked on the door and she went inside, taking in the scene before her. The mistress looked pale and anxious, while Mauricus was mixing some pungent smelling concoction in a cup, presumably a healing potion. Even the aroma of the herbs was not enough to mask the stench of vomit though.

Publius Licinius Castus coughed weakly, his face drawn and grey, and as he focused on her, he shivered and belched. It wasn't the type of belch a drunk or full man would do, it was the eruction of someone who'd emptied out the entire contents of their stomach so only wind and bile was left. Then he mewed pitifully and pulled his knees up to his chest beneath the blanket which looked damp with sweat.

It was a sorry sight.

"Have you sent someone for the *medicus*?" Dianna demanded, covering her mouth with her hand as if her husband's illness was making her feel queasy.

"Nepos is harnessing the wagon right now, *domina*," Lucia said. "I will go myself." She addressed Mauricus then. "Before I go I wanted to check, now that you've seen the master, if there is anything I can bring you from Durobrivae?"

The carpenter-cum-healer thought about it a moment as he continued stirring his potion then shook his head. "Just the *medicus*, I think."

"You might," Dianna said, as Lucia made to leave the room, "buy some honeysuckle if you can find any still flowering in town while you wait on the *medicus*." The mistress touched her nose. "It will freshen the air and help Castus recover quicker."

Lucia promised to do her best, given the time of year and the scarcity of flowering plants, then said farewell and went directly to her own room. She listened intently to make sure no-one was in the corridor outside the chamber, and then hastily gathered the scrolls hidden in a hole in the wall behind her desk. They were the most precious possessions she owned and she'd not wanted to use them just yet, in case their existence be discovered prematurely and her plans thwarted. Now though, with the fear of Castus's dying hovering over her like a black cloud, Lucia decided it was time to use them before it was too late.

The master did not look at all well. Of course, in her many years Lucia had seen much sickness. A malady like Castus was suffering from would usually pass in a few days – *if* the patient was young and strong. But when this kind of sickness overtook someone in their later years, when their fitness was in decline, it could mean the worst. Lucia had seen four or five slaves die from just such an affliction as this. It could take weeks before the emaciated victim succumbed, or it could happen within just a day or two.

Lucia could not afford to wait any longer. If she was to have the revenge she'd waited thirty years for, she would have to act now.

Don't let him die just yet, Sulis Minerva, let him suffer just a little longer!

* * *

The wagon was ready to go and Sennianus was already on board holding the reins when Lucia came back outside. Nepos waved them off unenthusiastically before turning back to his work in the hayloft.

True to his word, Sennianus had collected a sack of provisions from the kitchen using the clerk's name as authority, including a wine-skin, some cheese, a freshly baked loaf, and some smoked ham. Lucia looked forward to their moving picnic.

The sun was low in the sky but, thankfully, it wasn't in their eyes as the wagon covered the ground at a good, steady pace. For a time they just sat, listening to the creak of the harness and rumbling wheels on the hard ground. The horse's breath steamed in the sunshine and the travellers looked about them contentedly at the rolling landscape. Even at this time of year – when the trees stood bare and the only colours to be seen were drab greys and browns – the countryside was a beautiful sight.

"What happened between you and Maximus?"

Lucia stared at him in surprise. She hadn't told anyone what the master's son had done to her during Saturnalia, bottling her rage up inside as she always did, to deal with on her own.

"What d'you mean?"

"Come on, I'm not an idiot," he said. "It's obvious something happened – your manner towards him has been cold for days, and he looks away like a scolded child whenever he sees you."

She didn't reply for a while, feeling strangely content out there in the open, lowering clouds overhead and silence all around apart from the noises of their own wagon. Then she shrugged.

"All right, I'll tell you, and you'll see why I still hate that entire family as much as ever."

He sat quietly as Lucia recounted the events of that night and he didn't say anything for a long time after she finished.

"You see?" she prompted, grimacing as the wheel of the wagon bumped over a rock, sending a sharp jolt of pain through her injured back. "They never change. Even now, when I'm in my forties and risen to the highest position a slave can hold within Villa Tempestatis, they—"

"Wait." Sennianus broke in, shaking his head. "Let me get things straight in my head."

She raised her eyebrows, irritated at the fact he hadn't instantly condemned Maximus as she'd fully expected.

"He climbed into your bed and tried to have sex with you."

Lucia nodded and he went on, ignoring her black look.

"You told him you didn't want to, and he apologised and went away."

She was too surprised to say anything for a while, thinking over what he'd said, but finally, she grunted agreement.

"So, what's the problem? We're still slaves. He would have been perfectly within his legal rights to simply force you to open your legs for him, just as Castus used to do. Yet, he didn't. He left you alone, simply because you asked him to."

"That's not the point," Lucia protested, much angrier than logic told her she should be. "I was frightened, Senni, it brought back all the old memories that my mind had somehow buried away."

He smiled apologetically and reached out to squeeze her hand. "He's a silly, pampered boy, I don't think he intended to scare you. His lust got the better of him, that's all. And who can blame him, I feel the same every time I look at you."

She rolled her eyes in exasperation at his clumsy attempt at gallantry and turned away, trying to marshal the thoughts whirling about inside her head.

A jackdaw landed on a bush as they passed, sending a dusting of frost falling to the ground, its white eye fixing on her as if it suspected, somehow, that they had a sack of food in the wagon. Lucia knew better than to throw the bird a crust – if she did, a dozen of its companions would appear as if by magic and follow them all along the road. She glanced back as they rolled past and saw it wandering about the grass.

It might be hungry, Lucia mused, but at least it was free.

As she would be soon, and all the other slaves in Villa Tempestatis too.

"What are you planning?" Sennianus asked without preamble, breaking into her reverie with what he hoped was a welcome change of subject. "Is it you that made the master fall ill? Is that it? You're going to murder him in revenge for everything he's done?"

Lucia frowned and turned to him in surprise.

"Kill him? Me? Of course not. If I simply wanted him dead don't you think I'd have done it years ago? I've had enough chances after all. I've even *saved* his life!"

He grunted, nodding reluctantly and the look on his face told her he really had no idea what she had in store for Publius Licinius Castus. So, she told him.

It didn't take long for her to explain things since she didn't go into great detail. When she finished, Sennianus said nothing for a while, lost in thought, with a sorrowful expression on his face that seemed to Lucia to mirror the bleak land around them.

His voice was flat when he finally spoke and he turned to look into her eyes. "Please don't do this."

"Why not?" she asked, a little bemused. "Do you think I might be found out?"

"No, no, it's not that. I just think you've held onto this hatred for long enough. It's affected every aspect of your life. Of *our* lives. Even if you do manage to somehow pull off your mad scheme, what then? Have you really thought it through?"

Lucia shrugged and gestured at a deep pothole in the road ahead so Sennianus could guide the horse around it. "Not really," she admitted. "That part will take care of itself."

"Will it?" he shook his head irritably. "Seriously? Think about what you're taking on your shoulders. Castus's death will just be the beginning – what about all the people who'll be affected by what you're proposing."

"They'll be better off, I'll make sure of that." She pulled her cloak around her sulkily, half expecting Sennianus to try and hug her and make peace again, but he simply turned his attention back to the road. Durobrivae was in sight now, the stone bridge crossing the River Nene an imposing feature on the landscape.

As the horse's hooves ate up the yards Sennianus spoke once more, voice urgent and forceful.

"Please don't do this," he repeated. "When the master dies, well, you've seen his will, you told me so – he's going to free you and grant you a huge sum of money. I've saved enough for my own manumission. We can finally live our lives in freedom – together." He took one hand from the reins and placed it on Lucia's, his skin surprisingly warm despite the chill air. "You're still young enough to have another child. We can start a family, like we wanted so badly all those years ago."

The breath caught in her throat but she remained staring fixedly ahead as tears formed in her eyes.

Not another word passed between them as the wagon rumbled across the bridge and through the massive gates of Durobrivae.

CHAPTER NINE

The *medicus* was only too happy to attend Publius Licinius Castus. It was well known that the master of Villa Tempestatis paid well, and promptly, for the services of Durobrivae's best healers. So he followed Lucia to the wagon and climbed up behind Sennianus, who had already procured the plant food he wanted, along with smoked fish, some salt, wine amphorae and spices for cooking, all on Lucia's orders.

She herself had made a hasty visit to her banker and handed over the scrolls from her bedchamber. They would be safe with the little man, and she had already laid the groundwork for the rest of her scheme with the local lawyer named Salvius Pettius.

She thought back to the party to celebrate Martina's manumission over twenty years ago. Castus had slapped the dark-haired young lawyer and knocked him to the ground as everyone looked on, cheering and laughing. Salvius Pettius had never visited Villa Tempestatis after that humiliating day and Lucia knew his hatred, and the desire for vengeance, would have been festering inside him for all that time.

She was right, and the man, now a hugely respected lawyer, jumped at the chance to help her ruin the Roman he'd despised for more than two decades. He had barely even asked for a fee as he helped her prepare the necessary documents. Now he was just waiting for Lucia to give the word.

As they left, it was snowing softly again and the *medicus* had a broad smile on his face as they trundled along towards the villa, knowing he'd be allowed to spend the night there and enjoy Castus's hospitality without having to pay for it. Maybe even use the baths, which would be a wonderful treat – the public baths in Durobrivae were ghastly compared to the ones at Villa Tempestatis.

In contrast, at the front of the wagon, Sennianus and Lucia sat stony-faced and silent, their picnic untouched, neither seeming to even notice the white flakes that settled upon their cold, noses and hands. Lucia didn't even ask if Senni had managed to procure the supplies he wanted from the town.

"What did you say was wrong with Publius Licinius Castus again?"

Lucia glanced over her shoulder at the *medicus*, who was peering inside their sack of food with great interest. She barked at him to put it down, then said more mildly, "Vomiting, pale complexion, shivering. The usual type of thing."

"Fever too? Yes, well, that should be easy enough to treat then." He put his hands behind his head and rested it on the low wall of the wagon, looking for all the world as if he might fall asleep. "Some unwatered wine usually does the trick with this sort of illness. The drunker people get, the better they feel."

Lucia noted the man's face with its purple nose and puffy cheeks and guessed that if strong drink were the cure, then he rarely suffered from this kind of ailment.

"I doubt he'll be able to keep wine down," she said, glad to see the road branching towards home. "It doesn't seem to be a simple fever. I've not seen the master like this before; he's normally hale and hearty. So you'd better be good at your job if you want to be paid."

Her warning made his smile waver but the promise of a night in the sumptuous villa soon cheered him again. As the horse toiled up the hill, Lucia watched the house come closer. The snow was beginning to cover the ground and the wheels slipped several times, making the final stretch of the journey harder for the poor horse than it should have been. At last, they rolled into the courtyard and Sennianus brought them to a stop.

"You take him to the master," he said without even looking at Lucia. "I'll see the horse back to Nepos."

Part of her wanted to thank him for his help, but she was too stubborn and instead jumped down to the ground without a backward glance. She gestured imperiously for the *medicus* to follow her, and entering the villa led the way to the master's chamber.

"Where have you been?" Dianna demanded as they entered the room and Lucia was shocked at her tone, but one glance at Castus explained the *domina*'s anxiety. His condition appeared to have worsened in the time it had taken to go into town and back. He was no longer moaning and whining, but was instead very still and disquietingly pale.

He looked as if he were almost dead already.

The *medicus* had a good reputation, and he took charge of the room immediately, demanding to know what Mauricus, still hovering about, had given the master, and asking Dianna more politely to open the shutters in the room to let fresh air in.

"There's nothing more you can do here," the mistress said to Lucia as the *medicus* set about unloading his box of medicines, snow swirling into the room through the open window. "You should get back to your usual duties, make sure everything is running as it should."

"Yes *domina*, of course. Would you like me to have some food or drink brought to you? Have you eaten at all today? You should."

Dianna shook her head irritably, turning away to look back down on her stricken husband and Lucia left for the kitchens, intending to have the cook send at least some bread and cheese to the room. As she walked briskly along the corridor she wondered *why* she wanted to take care of Dianna. Didn't she hate the woman almost as much as she hated the master?

Her emotions, always a mystery to Lucia, seemed particularly unfathomable today. Why *did* she care if the mistress took a crust of bread and a cup of wine? And how could Sennianus even think about her marrying him and becoming pregnant again, after what had happened to them before? Did he believe having another child, one who would hopefully be allowed to live, would heal all the hurt of the past twenty-odd years?

With these thoughts assailing her, and knowing Sennianus would be in the kitchen eating his evening meal, she changed course and headed to her own bedchamber.

To Hell with Dianna. She could starve and die alongside her bastard of a husband!

* * *

The next day was fine and sunny and Lucia set many of the slaves to cleaning the grounds of debris that had fallen during the December storms. Trying to regain the strength in her injured back, she decided to join them, although her anxiety over Castus meant she didn't work with the other women and enjoy their usual gossip, but instead worked on her own collecting leaves and branches. Almost nothing was wasted in Villa Tempestatis: the dead branches would be used as fuel for the furnaces and cooking fires, while the leaves would be allowed to rot and used as fertilizer for the fields.

A delivery wagon visited, bringing things which the estate didn't produce itself – fish, flour, olive oil.

The wagon driver also brought a scroll, which he handed to Lucia when they were alone. Without opening it, she took it safely back to her own chamber.

It was from her banker in town, and confirmed that everything was in place and ready to go as soon as she confirmed it. She hid the letter under her bedding, just as a knock came on the door and one of the young slave-boys peered in at her from wide eyes beneath a mop of blonde curls.

"The mistress asks that you attend her immediately, Lucia," he said respectfully. Trying to ignore the knot in her stomach, Lucia forced a smile and nodded at the lad. "I will go at once, thank you, Crispus."

He ran off and Lucia got to her feet, stretching and trying to loosen her tense neck muscles. She smoothed down the crumples in her woollen tunic and took three deep breaths. It was time.

As she stepped out into the corridor she bumped into someone and jumped in alarm. But it was merely Sennianus.

"You seem nervous," he said with a knowing look. "Where are you going?"

"Dianna has sent for me," Lucia replied defensively, and her irritation at being accosted like this drove away her nervousness.

"Have you thought about what I said? Or are you still going to go through with your insane plan?"

"It only seems insane to you because you have no imagination, or desire to avenge yourself on those who destroyed your life," she said harshly, and began walking towards the north wing, hoping he wouldn't follow.

He didn't, but his words did, echoing along behind her. "Please don't, Lucia. Even he doesn't deserve what you're going to do."

She set her jaw and continued to walk without looking back. Publius Licinius Castus *did* deserve what was coming to him, and so did the rest of his family.

CHAPTER TEN

When Lucia reached the master's room, the door opened before she had a chance to knock and someone stumbled out, hand covering their face to mask their upset. The hair, still smooth and long despite her advancing years, told Lucia it was Dianna.

"*Domina*—"

Her words were cut off as Dianna, looking up and noticing the manageress standing there, took her hand away from her mouth and pulled Lucia into an embrace. The mistress sobbed into Lucia's shoulder for what seemed like a very long time until at last, embarrassment and the inappropriateness of hugging a slave made Dianna pull back, wiping her tears away with a finely manicured hand.

"What's happened, *domina*? Is he..."

Dianna shook her head. "No, he's still alive. In fact, he wants to talk to you, that's why I sent the boy." Their eyes met and a look Lucia had not seen for decades was on the mistress's face – it was the same expression of uncertainty, of a sense of being out of place, that Dianna had worn for the first few days she'd spent at Villa Tempestatis all those long years ago. "I don't think he will last the night, Lucia."

The woman had managed to pull herself together now and half-heartedly patted Lucia on the arm before brushing past her to go gods-knew-where. "Go in and see him. It may be the last time you ever will."

Steeling herself, Lucia went through the still-open door and looked around at the great bed which Castus lay upon. He seemed to have shrunk in the past few days of his illness, making him look almost childlike, but he somehow found the strength to smile when he saw the manageress standing beside him.

"Sit, please," he said faintly, gesturing weakly at the chair Dianna had occupied almost continuously for over a week now.

Lucia sat down and stared at Castus, hearing his rasping breath, as he laboured to stay alive another day, another hour, another few heartbeats. She thought about the contents of the scroll concealed beneath her clothes, and her fingers itched to pull it out and show it to Castus.

For many months Lucia had been syphoning off the profits from Villa Tempestatis, saving the money and using some to pay her banker and the lawyer, Salvius Pettius. With their help, and the fact she had access to the master's personal seal, she had crafted documents apparently written in Publius Licinius Castus's own hand, transferring ownership of the entire estate to her.

Everything would be hers.

Her eyes glowed as she imagined it. She would free the slaves, letting those leave who wanted to go home; and the rest she would retain as paid workers. Of course, there were laws against an owner freeing all of their slaves at once, but Lucia and her lawyer would find ways around that – no one in Villa Tempestatis would live and work there unless by choice.

No more slavery, no more beatings, no more hatred. At least, not in this small part of the world.

Dianna, the *domina* who had so perversely hated Lucia – she could do as she pleased. Without any money to her name she could work for Lucia in the villa, as a maid or washer-woman perhaps.

And Maximus, the pampered awkward son, no doubt his forthcoming marriage would be cancelled and he would have to find his own way in the world. Perhaps he would become a legionary, although without his father's tough character, Lucia expected he wouldn't last long as a soldier.

"I am dying," Castus said, intruding on her thoughts.

Lucia nodded. "So the mistress thinks."

"Yes. Dianna has been very strong during my illness," he wheezed, looking down sadly. "She's been a good wife to me, we've been happy."

Lucia clenched her fists but remained silent, letting him talk, knowing it would make her triumph all the sweeter, especially when she told him Maximus wasn't even his son. His talk moved from Dianna though, surprising Lucia with its new direction.

"I still remember that very first day I saw you," he said, drawing her eyes towards him. The expression on his face was unreadable. "You stumbled around the side of that house, face glowing in the firelight."

"From the houses of my people, which you and your soldiers had set fire to after killing my kinfolk."

It was the first time in her life that Lucia had ever spoken so forwardly to the master, but if he was shocked by it his face masked it well.

"Yes," came his soft reply, and Lucia put her hand inside her tunic and pulled out the scroll. Let the old bastard reminisce of his time as the great Roman Tribune, and his wonderful life as the wealthy owner of dozens – maybe hundreds? – of slaves, of how proud he was of the money his racehorses were making and what it meant to be able to leave such a great legacy to his wife and son.

She remembered his young muscular body pressing her down, as she wept and wished only for her mother and father. The feelings she'd had as she realised her own newborn child had been taken away from her forever, all on the word of the man lying before her. How she hated him!

The scroll came out and she began to unroll it, staring at Castus as he continued to ramble on.

Would the shock of what she had done kill him on the spot? It was very possible. She knew that, once she told him what she was going to do, there would be no way he could be allowed to live even one more hour, for he would tell Dianna about her scheme and that would be it. Lucia would be arrested and crucified.

So if Castus didn't die from the stress of what Lucia's scroll contained, there would be only one option left.

She would have to kill him herself.

* * *

"What's wrong? What's happened? You did it then, oh shit, gods preserve us…"

Sennianus must have been waiting for Lucia to return from the master's chamber but she didn't stop, simply kept walking quickly back to her own small room.

He followed but asked no more questions, not wanting to draw any attention to them. He might not agree with what she'd done, but he loved her, and would never do anything against her. The next few hours and days would be crucial to her plans Sennianus knew, and if anything went wrong, she would be dead.

They reached their destination and Lucia sat down on the mattress, head in her hands, shoulders shaking. Sennianus closed the door and jammed the stool against it so no-one could disturb them unannounced, then he sat down and placed an arm around Lucia, drawing her close as she cried.

It took a long time for her to calm down but, at last, she shook her head, wiped her face dry with her fingers and took a long, deep breath before turning to look at Sennianus.

"Should I be calling you *domina* now?" he asked, forcing a smile onto his face that never reached his eyes. "Please don't tell me you murdered him. Taking his entire estate away from his family would be enough, without adding that to your account."

Lucia sniffed and shook her head, drawing a sigh of relief from Sennianus.

"No, I didn't kill him. Didn't need to."

They sat for a time, Sennianus feeling strangely empty as he contemplated the death of the man who'd been his master for most of his life. If he thought about it, he did hate the old man for the way he'd abused Lucia so many times, but deep down Senni was a forgiving soul and it had to be said, Publius Licinius Castus *had* changed in recent years, ever since he found that new religion.

No, the man wasn't perfect, but the cruel unfeeling streak of his younger days had been tempered by the teachings of the Christ-followers.

To be told, on his death-bed, that his life's accumulated wealth was being stolen from him by a slave was a bad way for a Roman nobleman to go. No wonder Castus had died. It must have been a horrific shock to the system.

Sennianus closed his eyes and squeezed his forehead, feeling the beginnings of a headache coming on. What would all this mean now? Could he just stand by and watch as Lucia degraded Dianna and Maximus? Then what? With the fulfilment of her lifelong quest for vengeance, would she finally settle down. With Sennianus?

He could feel bile rising in his throat now that the initial shock of the situation was beginning to wear off and cold reality threatened to swamp him. Lucia might not have used her own hands, but she had essentially murdered an old, sickly man in his own bed and taken his estate from him.

It was monstrous. He realised only now that he'd never believed Lucia would succeed in this mad plan, it was simply too incredible.

And yet there in her hand now was the scroll that legally passed the dead man's entire estate over to the slave-woman.

Sennianus should never have doubted the depth of her hatred, or her intelligence.

"What?" Lucia had said something but, with the thoughts whirling around in his head he'd not heard her properly and so he asked again. "What?"

"I said: *he's not dead.*"

That took a moment to sink in, and then Sennianus jumped to his feet, the earlier shock turning instantly to panic. "That means he'll tell Dianna about everything then. You'll be arrested! We have to run away—"

"He's not dead, and I didn't tell him what I was going to do. Sit down, Senni. It's all right."

He did so, eyeing her in confusion, as if he didn't believe her. She shoved the scroll away beneath the mattress and took his hand in hers with a small smile.

"I don't understand."

"Oh, Senni, you never did, well, that's what I always believed but now...I think you have a better grasp of things than anyone else."

"What happened? Why did you come back here so upset?"

"I don't really know myself," she admitted. "Maybe I'm growing soft in my old age."

"Pah, we're not old yet," he grumbled. "I'm as fit as a fiddle and you've only got one or two grey hairs."

"Castus was babbling about Dianna and how wonderful a life he'd had, and I took the scroll out." She looked at Sennianus frankly. "At that point I was committed to telling him how, as soon as he died, the full estate would pass to me, leaving his wife and son – who isn't really his son – with nothing. I'd even accepted the fact that I might have to smother him to make sure he didn't ruin things."

"And...?"

"And he told me he was sorry for everything he'd done to me and...Do you know something? I could tell he meant it. Really *meant* it. He started crying and said he wished he could go back and undo the things he'd done to me – to all of us."

None of this greatly surprised Sennianus, who knew that lots of people, frightened by the reality of impending death, and tortured by the wrongs they'd done, repented on their death-beds and sought forgiveness. By all accounts, Christians suffered from this kind of thing more than others.

"He meant it, Senni," Lucia said. "And I started to think about what you'd said the other day in the wagon. About Maximus not forcing himself on me when he could have, and how I should let go of this hatred I've carried like a stone about my neck for my whole life." She squeezed his hand and smiled again. "And about trying to start a family of my – of *our* – own again."

This was all too much, too unexpected, for Sennianus.

"What are you saying?"

"You were right, Senni," she told him. "It took the sight of Castus's torment to make me realise: I don't want to come to the end of my days and look back wishing I'd done things differently. I hid the scroll back inside my tunic again. I want to live a life of happiness and love, Senni, not of vengeance and hate. I should have listened to you years ago!"

She grabbed his face in her hands and kissed him on the lips, hard, joyfully, then fell back on the bed laughing, dragging him down with her.

"What does it all mean then?" he said. "What now?"

"Obviously I'll need to sort out the finances," Lucia said. "Put all the money from my account back into the estate and so on. That shouldn't be an issue. Castus will free us both, and also gift us a large – very large – sum of money to begin a new life wherever we choose." She turned to look at him and the change in her was miraculous. She was smiling like an excited child, almost overcome with the promise of the future. "We can remain here if we like, doing our own jobs but as paid workers, not as slaves. Or we can start afresh somewhere new, it's up to us. We are going to be free, Senni, at long last. Free!"

THE END

Author's Note

Well…this book is rather different from anything I've ever written before. I hope, if you're one of my regular readers, you enjoyed it, despite the lack of battles or men rampaging about the wilds, sword in hand. I wanted to try writing a standalone novel, and, having just listened to the audio versions of *Rebecca, Jane Eyre,* and *Wuthering Heights,* the idea for *Lucia* came to me, practically fully-formed, in a weird moment of inspiration and I knew I had to start working on it straight away.

When I was researching the novel I wasn't really that surprised to find out just how abominably Romans treated their slaves. Books and movies, and the plight of more recent subjugated peoples, make humanity's seemingly inbuilt cruelty a sad fact that we all understand. Beatings, rapes, humiliation etc – it all still goes on, even in our supposedly enlightened time.

I *was* shocked however to learn about the number of babies, particularly girls, that were dumped like rubbish by the Romans – "exposed" as it's termed. One villa at Hambledon in Britain, when excavated by archaeologists, revealed nearly 100 buried newborn children. In a time when there was no reliable contraception, and scant food for many poor families, I understand that they saw this practice as necessary – a fact of life, to be dealt with and moved on from, until the next pregnancy.

Surely not *all* couples were so pragmatic though? Some of them, possibly even the silent majority (slaves have no historical voice after all, since no-one thought their opinion valuable enough to record it) were severely affected by it, as Lucia is in this book. It was, I thought, an important issue to look at and I'd be interested to hear from readers on whether they agree with my portrayal here or not. It was a very hard life back then after all – life was cheap and perhaps dumping a baby didn't seem that big a deal to the people of the time? Maybe they *had* to treat it as rather unimportant to avoid going crazy with grief…

I mentioned at the start of this note that the idea for the book came to me in an unexpected flash of inspiration, but that wasn't the only weird thing about *Lucia*. The week I finished the first draft I was at a shopping centre I rarely frequent, came back to my parked car and there, right beside my driver's door, was a bracelet someone had dropped. It was in poor condition but I could make out the name engraved on it very clearly: LUCIA. Now, bear in mind I live in Scotland and Lucia is not a common name here! Some might just see this as an amusing coincidence, but I tend to think of it as a sign that I was on the right track – that Lucia's tale needed to be told. I am very proud of it, mainly because it's not the type of thing I would normally write and, having tried to find another novel even remotely like it without success, I hope I've written something a little more original than readers expect.

Ultimately though, I just hope it's a good story and you enjoyed it.

One final note, before I go…Originally, *Lucia* had an epilogue, but it was left out of the Audible version which was published a year before these Kindle and paperback editions. It was an accident, but, when I looked at it, I realised the book was better without it. However, had I known in advance that there'd be no epilogue I might have written the last line differently as I know it jarred some listeners when they came to the end, but so fate decreed it should be. I may share that epilogue one day, if people are interested. As it is, I really like how the book ends now. It reminds me of John Fowles's *The Magus*, in that it leaves things open for the reader to use their own imagination and decide what happened next to the characters themselves. I know what *I* wish happened to Lucia and Senni – but you can decide for yourself.

Now, it's time for me to get back to Bellicus and my Warrior Druid of Britain series. Where's that sword?

Steven A. McKay
Old Kilpatrick,
November 25th 2018

Printed in Great Britain
by Amazon